# DANGEROUS SECRETS

## LEAH NASH MYSTERIES BOOK 4

## SUSAN HUNTER

Severn River
PUBLISHING

Severn River Publishing
www.SevernRiverPublishing.com

This is a work of fiction. Names, characters, businesses, places, events and incidents are either the products of the author's imagination or used in a fictitious manner. Any resemblance to actual persons, living or dead, or actual events is purely coincidental.

ISBN: 978-1-951249-69-4 (Paperback)

## ALSO BY SUSAN HUNTER

**Leah Nash Mysteries**

Dangerous Habits

Dangerous Mistakes

Dangerous Places

Dangerous Secrets

Dangerous Flaws

Dangerous Ground

Never miss a new release! Sign up to receive exclusive updates from author Susan Hunter.

**SusanHunterAuthor.com/Newsletter**

As a thank you for signing up, you'll receive a free copy of

*Dangerous Dreams: A Leah Nash Novella.*

*For my favorite brothers, Jim and Tim—*
*who both know how to tell a good story.*

# 1

The late-afternoon sun shone with a fierce light that set the autumn reds and yellows of the leaves on fire. I had passed the construction and congestion around Madison, and I was almost home on that almost perfect October day. I rolled down the car windows, turned up the music, and sang my heart out to Adele, Aretha, and yes, it's true, the Backstreet Boys. Don't judge.

I was eager to get back to my small-town home—Himmel, Wisconsin, after a pretty grueling two weeks in Michigan. I had been thrust into the role of primary caregiver for my Aunt Nancy, after she took a tumble from the stage during an energetic dance number in her local theater group's production of *Grease*. Normally, her husband, or my mother, or her daughter would have stepped in. But Uncle Jeff was on a fishing trip at some remote camp in Canada, and Aunt Nancy refused to ruin it for him. My mother was on a cruise, and my cousin Rowena was giving birth in Texas.

Enter me, Leah Nash, devoted niece, former reporter, current true crime writer, and unlikely home health care aide. I love my Aunt Nancy, but, sadly, I don't have a big reserve of tender-loving care to draw from. And Aunt Nancy, it turns out, doesn't have a big reserve of patience for forced immobility, cabin fever, and a steady diet of grilled cheese, Honey Nut Cheerios, and spaghetti. When I tried to vary the menu one night by making Cornish game hens, a favorite of Aunt Nancy's, it just underscored my domestic deficiencies. They were in the oven a little long—well, maybe, a lot long. After I served them, Aunt Nancy started calling me "Baby Jane," and asking me where her parakeet was.

When Uncle Jeff finally got home, both she and I were relieved. I flew out the door on a flurry of hugs, kisses, thanks, and don't-mention-its almost before he set his suitcase down. My tour of duty in the wilds of Michigan's Upper Peninsula was over. Himmel may not be a metropolis, but at least we don't have wolves in our backyard. And bears. I don't even want to talk about the bears.

The thought of sleeping in my own bed, in my own apartment, made me giddy as I neared home. If I had known it was the last time I'd feel unfettered joy for quite some time, I would've reveled in it more.

***

"Leah! When you get back?"

"Hi, Mrs. Schimelman, just now. I'm starving, so you're my first stop. What's good today?"

Clara Schimelman owns the Elite Café and Bakery just a short distance from my apartment. She's a friendly, gray-haired woman in her late sixties. Her large, comfortable frame is testament to the delicate pastries and delicious sandwiches she serves. The Elite, with its rickety old tables, squeaky wooden floor, and uncomfortable small chairs, is a Himmel favorite.

"Is all good," she said with justifiable complacency. "I make you *döner kebap*. Is a new menu item I bring back from Berlin.

Pita bread, roasted turkey, lettuce, tomatoes, onions, cabbage, chili flakes, garlic-yogurt sauce. It's the bomb." Mrs. Schimelman, a fixture in town for more than 30 years, still retains a strong German accent, but she loves her American slang—though she generally runs a few years behind.

"Sounds perfect," I said. "So, what's been going on?" I asked, as she turned to assemble the sandwich.

Over her shoulder she answered, "You haven't talked to no one?"

"No. Most of the time I couldn't get a signal on my phone, and my aunt's internet connection was so slow, I couldn't stand it. I texted a couple of times with Coop and Miguel, but that's about it. Why, did something happen?"

At that moment, the bell over the door tinkled and a frazzled looking mother with three rambunctious little boys came through the door.

"Coffee, just a really dark, really big cup of coffee, please, Mrs. Schimelman. Boys, one cookie choice. And don't forget please and thank you."

"Hey, Lanette, how are you?"

Lanette Howard is my mother's across-the-street neighbor.

"Leah, hi. Sorry, did we just barge in on your order? Dylan, don't lick the display case. Marcus, stop pinching Arlo." As she spoke, she deftly separated two of her children and swiped at the remains of Dylan's tongue print on the front of the case. "I'm so sorry, Mrs. Schimelman. If you have a cloth and some spray, I'll wipe that off. And please, go ahead, get Leah's order."

"No, that's OK, you go ahead. I'll just take a look at the paper and catch up." A copy of the *Himmel Times Weekly* sat on the counter, and I grabbed it and moved to a nearby table.

"Thank you. It's probably better for everyone if we get out as quick as possible. How's your aunt doing? And when's your mother due back?" The boys, having made their selections, were vibrating with anticipation as Mrs. Schimelman reached into the display case with practiced hand and scooped up their choices in thin, white bakery tissue paper. There was a moment of buyer's remorse while one changed his order, and the other wailed because his brother was "copying." Lanette sighed and said, "I know, sugar is a bad idea, but I had to have a coffee and I couldn't bring them into this divine bakery and not let them have a cookie."

"Hey, you'll get no argument from me. Aunt Nancy is doing pretty well. Mom will be back Tuesday or Wednesday. I can't remember which. Anything going on in the old neighborhood?"

She looked surprised for a second and said, "In the neighborhood? No, but—Marcus, that's it. Hand over the cookie. You *may* be able to get it after dinner, if you can ride home without picking at your little brother. I'm sorry, Leah, I have to get these monsters out of here." She managed to pay Mrs. Schimelman, grab her coffee, and wrangle her crew out the door without spilling, dropping, or losing anything—or anyone. I stand in awe of Lanette's multitasking skills.

I half-expected Mrs. Schimelman to share her views on parenting with me after they left. She's as generous with her opinions as she is with her portions, but she was busying herself slicing turkey and getting out condiments. I opened the paper and scanned the headlines. Trick or treat hours had been set by the city council; a car had fallen into a sinkhole on Maple Street; a potbellied pig was used to assault a man in a domestic dispute; and Mrs. Hanson's first grade class had participated in a trip to the zoo in Madison. A busy week, indeed.

I turned to the inside pages and checked the obituaries. It's an old habit I can't seem to break. My first assignment at my first newspaper, which happened to be the *Himmel Times Weekly*, was to write the obituaries. I'd envisioned covering police news, or at least a lively city council meeting—not dull, dead people stuff. When I had balked, my boss brought me up short.

"Every obituary is the story of a person's life. It's their final story. It's something their families keep, and reread, and pass on. It's a marker for their memories. It's not a throwaway job. You need to do it right, and you need to can the attitude. Understand?"

I did. Ever since then, I've never been able to put aside a newspaper without at least scanning the obituaries as a small way of paying respect to all those life stories. As I looked through them, one notice surprised me. I put the paper aside and saw that my sandwich was ready.

"Mrs. Schimelman, what happened to Duane Stanton? It says he died suddenly. Heart attack?"

"Oh, *ja*. Terrible that was. No heart attack. He fell from that bird-watching place. Watching birds. It's crazy." She shook her head.

"That's awful. He was a quirky guy, but I got a kick out of him. What do I owe you?"

"$4.50. And I give you pumpkin walnut cookie for free. Welcome home."

---

I pulled into the parking lot behind my apartment and was just hauling my suitcase out, when a familiar voice called to me.

"Leah, what are you doing here?"

"I live here, Courtnee, remember?"

"I thought you were fishing in Canada with your grandma."

It was typical of Courtnee Fensterman, a self-absorbed blonde who never really pays attention to anything that doesn't center on her, to mash half-heard information into her own particular version of fake news.

"I was in Michigan taking care of my aunt." I yanked the suitcase out and shut the door. Then I pulled the handle up, ready to head inside the back door to my loft.

"Aren't you even going to ask me what *I'm* doing here on a Saturday?" Her pretty but vapid face had taken on a frown, and her blue eyes held reproach. I noticed then that she had a cardboard box in her arms.

"OK, I'll bite. What are you doing here?"

"Well." She paused and shifted the box, then handed it to me. "Could you hold this for a minute? It's really heavy."

Reflexively, I grabbed it, looked down and saw that it appeared to contain the vast make-up collection Courtnee kept in her desk drawer, along with some framed photos, at least half of the pens owned by the *Himmel Times Weekly*, and several boxes of Junior Mints.

"What are you doing, moving out?"

"Duh. Yes. Keep up, Leah."

"Wait, what?" Courtnee leaving had long been my dream when I still worked at the *Times*. It seemed unfair that it should happen after I left.

"Rebecca is just so mean. I'm not, like, her personal slave. 'Courtnee, you're late! Courtnee, this message makes no sense. Courtnee, you can't close the office to get your hair highlighted. Courtnee, the conference room isn't your personal party place!' Like anything is ever a party around here. My mom said I shouldn't have to take that kind of thing. So, I finally quit."

I wasn't shocked that Mrs. Fensterman seemed to share Courtnee's view that slavery on the job consisted of performing duties in a timely, accurate and professional manner. She had to develop her skewed vision somewhere. But it did surprise me that her mother had encouraged her to leave a paying position. It's not like Courtnee's job skills would open the door to many careers.

"Wait, wait, wait. You quit your job? What are you going to do?"

She tilted her head and rolled her eyes the way she does when she thinks I've said something especially lame.

"I'm already doing it. I'm a secretary or something in the Public Safety department at Himmel Tech. My Uncle Lou got me the job. Rebecca didn't even give me a goodbye party or a gift or anything. And then she calls me today and says to come and get the rest of my stuff because the new girl needs the drawer space or something. Like, I've been busy, right? You'd think getting married might make her feel happy and be a little nice. But no. She's still a biatch."

I felt a fleeting frisson of sympathy for Himmel Technical College, but I was more interested in the last bit of information Courtnee had dropped in. I handed the box back to her, then leaned my face in close so she'd have to focus on me. I had to see if this was real news, or fake. "Courtnee, are you saying Rebecca is married? Who to?"

Rebecca Hartfield and I had clashed at our first meeting, and things had gone downhill from there. She was dispatched by A-H Media, the hedge fund that had bought the *Himmel Times* a year or so ago, to bring their latest purchase into line. Which, as far as I could see, meant squeezing every drop of profit out of the paper until A-H Media shut it down or sold its dried, dead husk. There's a reason I refer to it as Ass-Hat Media.

"Well, Coop, of course. They got married last week."

"Leah, you're pinching my arm!"

"Oh, sorry. Sorry." I released my grip. "Look, I have to go. Bye." I turned away and grabbed my suitcase, ignoring Courtnee's indignant assertion that she wasn't done telling me about herself.

Coop and Rebecca, married? I shook my head. She had to have it wrong. Coop has been my best friend since we were 12 years old. He's a lieutenant in the Himmel Police Department. He wouldn't get married without telling me—and definitely not to Rebecca.

When he had started seeing her, I had tried to warn him about her, but all that did was create a major rift in our friendship, and force me to listen to my mother sing "When a Man Loves a Woman" every time I mentioned it. So, I backed off. A couple of months ago, he found out for himself just how bad she was, and he dumped her. And now they were married? That just couldn't be right.

My apartment is on the third floor of a downtown building that houses the *Himmel Times* on the first floor. The rear doors for both the newspaper and my loft are in the same back entryway. Mine is on the right. The entrance to the *Times* is straight ahead as you walk in.

I could see Rebecca through the glass door. She was standing in the hall with her back to me. Her tall frame blocked my view of the person she was talking to, but judging by the amazing mane of red-gold hair that I could see, it appeared to be a woman. Their conversation looked pretty animated. Rebecca was shaking her head. I hesitated for a minute, then saw movement that seemed to indicate her visitor was leaving. I put my suitcase in front of my door. As I pushed through the entrance marked *Himmel Times,* the strawberry blonde was still there. I hung back to let them finish.

Rebecca said, "Kinmont isn't anything I want to remember."

"I'll never let you forget." The redhead laughed then, and walked down the hall without looking back. Rebecca continued to stand with her back to me.

When I heard the front door close, I said, "Rebecca!" my tone loud and curt.

She whirled around, a startled look in her eyes. I enjoyed the moment. It's not often Rebecca is taken unawares. Then she recognized me. She smiled coolly, her composure restored. When she spoke, it was in the patronizing tone she always affected with me—or anyone else she wanted to intimidate.

"Leah, you're back. I'm glad to see you. I wanted to talk to you, before you hear the news from someone else. David and I were married on Tuesday. I hope you'll be happy for us." She reached out with her long graceful fingers and touched me lightly on the arm.

When Courtnee had told me, it was a shock, but I held onto a faint hope that she'd gotten it wrong. Hearing the triumph in Rebecca's voice, I knew she hadn't. I stared at her, but for once I couldn't think of a single thing to say.

"Please, Leah," she said, still in that fake honeyed voice, as though she were reasoning with an irrational toddler. "I know we've had some run-ins, but at the end of the day, don't you think we should put all that behind us? For David's sake? I promised him I'd do my best to make us friends."

Rebecca is the only person outside of his mother who calls Coop by his given name: David Cooper. I hate it when she says it, because it feels like she's trying to make him someone he's not, trying to stake a claim on him that she doesn't have. Except now it appeared that she did.

"Rebecca, you and I both know that Mother Theresa and Nelson Mandela together couldn't make us be friends. 'Be happy' for you'? Uh-uh. You don't deserve him, and he sure doesn't deserve you."

I had succeeded in annoying her, and she dropped the faux warmth out of her voice. Her eyes glittered with anger as she answered.

"Time to give it up, Leah. I won. You lost. I told you I'd get him back, and I did. And there's nothing you can do about it. Now that we're married, don't expect him to be jumping every time you call. It won't happen." She fairly spat out the words, then took a breath.

In the pause I said, "Coop isn't a prize you won at the county fair, Rebecca. You don't own him, and I'm sure he'll make up his own mind about who he sees and when."

Her voice now was both condescending and smug. "Coop's his own man. That's why I love him. But a couple needs a lot of personal, private time to build a marriage, don't you agree? I don't think he'll have much left over for you. You'll have to get used to it." She tucked a strand of white blonde hair behind her ear and smiled again.

Usually, walking into my apartment gives me a little jolt of happiness. I love the hardwood floors, the exposed brick, the window seat that looks down on the street below. And after living for a while with my mother, I love that I've got my own space again. Don't get me wrong. My mom is great, but nothing says epic fail like hitting your thirties and moving back into your old bedroom. Which is where I had landed after an ill-considered career decision. Actually, it was more like a hissy fit than a decision. I really enjoyed being on my own again.

Right then, though, I wished I had a little company in the form of my mother there to talk me down from the mix of anger and hurt I was feeling at Coop's deception. He'd been really upset not long ago, after Rebecca had used her power as the publisher of the *Times* to force our local sheriff to resign. He'd finally seen her for what she was. I thought. He'd said that he was done with her. Obviously, he hadn't been.

Instead of unpacking, I poured a generous shot of Jameson whiskey, cued up a playlist of down and out blues on my speaker, plumped up the cushions on my window seat, then plunked myself down in the corner and stared out. I watched the traffic light change periodically, the cars start moving, the late afternoon descend into evening. I took an occasional sip from my glass as I contemplated life without my closest friend. Because I had no doubt that if Rebecca had succeeded in marrying him, destroying our friendship was next on her agenda. And clearly, she was good at this game.

My stomach started growling, and I remembered the *döner* sandwich Mrs. Schimelman had made for me. I wolfed it down. It lived up to her hype enough to take the edge off my anger. When I'd finished, my phone rang. It was Clinton, my agent.

"Leah, how's the writing coming? You must have escaped from—what did you call it? The Yoopie? That place where no one has cell phones."

Clinton lives in New York, and it amuses him to play the part of an East Coast elitist who never leaves the city. I happen to know he was born and raised in Ohio and visits his mother frequently.

"It's the U.P., Clinton, short for the Upper Peninsula. As you very well know. Yes, I'm back in Himmel. Just got in a little while ago."

"So, how is the book coming? Are you meeting your daily pages? You have a lot riding on this, you know."

"Sorry, were you my mother in another life? Don't worry so much. I'll make the deadline. It's months away."

"I'm just checking. I think this book is going to be bigger than the last one. And I'm still working on the movie rights. I can see it now. Emma Stone, no, wait, Jennifer Lawrence in the lead—"

"OK, OK, you can dial it back. Look what happened to the movie deal we thought we had for my first book."

"Hey, it's in turnaround. Have some faith in me. It could still be a nice Lifetime movie."

"Right. So, did you just call to nag me?"

"I resent that. I'm offering supportive encouragement, not nagging. And yes, that's all I called for. You've got a great outline, a *very* nice advance, now go out there and earn it. Clear eyes, full heart, can write."

"Thanks, Coach. Consider me inspired. Bye."

Clinton was the only agent who'd been willing to take a chance on me when I left the *Miami Star Register* under less than ideal circumstances. He wasn't able to sell my first manuscript, and I wasn't able to find another job until the place where I'd started, the *Himmel Times Weekly* took me back. But Clinton had stuck with me. When I wrote a book about some pretty evil goings-on at a residential school run by an order of nuns, he found a publisher for it.

In fact, his skill as an agent had secured for me the money that allowed me to leave newspaper reporting behind, move into my loft, and not worry about living paycheck to paycheck. He'd done even better with the advance for the book I was currently writing. Combined with the earnings from my first literary effort, I had enough to send my mother on the cruise she'd been dreaming of for years and to tuck away a comfortable sum. Now, I owed it to him, not to mention to my publisher, to actually produce the manuscript.

I carried my suitcase into the bedroom, unpacked, tossed some things into the washing machine, went to my office, sat down and opened my laptop. I felt quite virtuous. But before I got started, my eyes lit upon a picture of Miguel Santos and me that sat on the corner of my desk.

Miguel was a reporter at the *Himmel Times,* not long out of college, when I returned to the paper after a ten-year absence. His career was on the rise, while mine felt like it was sinking to the bottom. He was a big part of pulling me out of my dejection. I defy anyone to stay unhappy for long in Miguel's company.

The picture I was looking at had been taken earlier in the year, when for some reason Miguel had decided he wanted to learn how to fish. So, we took a day trip to a state park that offered a program for beginners.

I don't know what he'd expected, but it clearly hadn't involved hooks, bait, and squirming fish. I laughed so hard at his aghast face that I could barely help him get his catch off the hook. A bystander had captured a photo of us on his phone. Miguel had the picture printed and framed. It sat on my desk now, inscribed *Chica, always your amigo, hook, line and sinker.* Looking at his handsome, happy face, I couldn't help smiling.

On impulse, I punched in his speed dial number.

"*Chica! Cómo estás?* Are you back?"

"Yes, I got in late this afternoon. Hey, I've missed you. You want to come over and hang out? I could really use some talking time with you."

"Oh, I would love to, but I'm in Miami. I'm at a wedding. Remember, I told you? My friend Lori got married today."

I felt a sharp stab of disappointment.

"Yeah, of course. It went out of my head, I guess. I'm feeling a little unsettled right now. I just heard about Coop and Rebecca getting married. Then, I had a run-in with the ice queen herself. Hey, why didn't *you* tell me they were married? I had to find out from Courtnee, of all people."

He was quiet for a second, then in a rush he said, "*Chica, lo siento.* I wanted to, but I just found out the day I left for Miami. And then I didn't want to tell you in a text, and your phone connection at Aunt Nancy's was so bad, and ... " His voice trailed off.

"Never mind, it's OK. It isn't you that should have to tell me anyway. It's Coop."

That was definitely the truth. How long had they been back together? How could he not tell me they were back together? It was the same as lying to me. Every fissure in our friendship had happened since Rebecca came to town. It was like he was hypnotized by her. And no one else mattered. I felt my mood shifting from sad to mad.

"*Chica?*"

I'd gone silent as I'd given over to my anger.

"No worries, Miguel. I'm fine. I just figured out my priority list for tomorrow. Now, from the salsa music I hear in the background, I can tell you need to get back to partying." There was a loud burst of laughter and a voice shouted, "Miguel, come on, man!"

"*Sí*, I have to go. But, wait a minute. *Chica,* stay chill. I'll be back late tomorrow night. I'll come over Monday morning for breakfast. Don't say anything to Coop that will make things worse." His voice was a mix of anxiousness to get back to his friends, and anxiety about my state of mind.

I gave a short humorless laugh. "Worse? Coop is already married to Rebecca. It can't get any worse."

That, unfortunately, proved not to be true.

---

I woke up happy in my own bed, and stretched as luxuriously as a cat. Then, I remembered. Coop and Rebecca were married. Coop had lied to me. Rebecca had won. She proved that whatever hold she had, it trumped twenty years of friendship, loyalty, and trust.

As I brushed my teeth, and stood in the shower, and washed my hair, and let the hot water run way longer than was helpful either for my budget or the planet, I kept asking myself: What would make him marry a woman who had manipulated him, forced a good man out of his job, and, no small thing, treated his oldest friend—that would be me—like a pesky mosquito to be swatted away and finally crushed?

I pulled on jeans and a long-sleeved Henley t-shirt, and fooled around with my hair for a few minutes before giving it up. The asymmetrical cut a stylist had given my thick, straight, chestnut brown hair was intended to give me a more sophisticated, pulled-together look. I liked it, but I soon discovered that the uneven length made it awkward to put my hair into my favorite wash-and-wear style—yanked back into a ponytail or scooped up in a hair clip. And I didn't like the time it took to blow dry it into submission. So, I had decided to grow it out. In the interim stage, I was dealing with a raggedy mass of uneven strands of hair, each determined to go its own way. It wasn't pretty. I tucked what I could behind my ears and let it go.

I didn't bother to put on any make-up. Coop wouldn't be

impressed, and at the moment I didn't care much about what he thought anyway.

## 3

I strode into the Himmel Police Department, primed to march back to Coop's office and deliver my list of charges. *Isn't it true, lieutenant, that you willingly and with malice aforethought deceived your oldest friend? And didn't you violate the bonds of trust and friendship by not confiding in her the single biggest decision of your adult life? And isn't it true, Lieutenant David Cooper, that you have demonstrated your utter disregard for the loyalty, affection, and integrity which the injured party, Leah Marie Nash, has shown you for more than twenty years?*

I rapped on the counter when, as usual, the department secretary on the other side of it failed to acknowledge me standing there.

"Good morning, Melanie," I said. She looked up reluctantly from the computer screen that held her transfixed. Melanie is a sturdy, no-nonsense woman, given to long denim skirts and sensible shoes. However, her series of truly amazing hairstyles says there must be a secret font of whimsy beneath her stolid appearance. That morning her wiry hair was wrangled into a coiled bun on the top of her head, with a fringe of bangs grazing her eyebrows.

"New do?"

"Yeah." Melanie alternates between terse answers and outbursts of chattiness.

"Is Coop in?" He usually stopped by the office to catch up on paperwork on Sundays, and I often dropped in for a cup of coffee with him.

"No."

"Where is he?"

"Bemidji."

Time for a two-part question, or I was going to spend all day trying to coax information out of her.

"What's he doing there, and when's he coming back?"

"His grandma's 90th birthday. Late tonight. Be in tomorrow."

"Oh." I felt suddenly deflated. My one syllable response seemed to evoke an equal and opposite reaction in Melanie, who became very talkative on the subject of Coop.

"So, big news while you were gone. You probably already knew, right? But the lieutenant sure left the rest of us in the dark."

"Um, actually no, I just found out when I got back yesterday. You know, bad phone connections, not enough cell phone towers, I guess. And I left here in such a hurry. He really didn't have a chance to tell me. I mean, of course, he would have, if I'd been here. If I hadn't left so suddenly. If ... "

My face-saving excuses designed to protect both my wounded pride and my hurt feelings wound to a close.

Melanie had lost interest. Her gaze was drifting to her computer screen again. By way of dismissing me, she said, "Huh. That one's gonna lead him a merry dance, like my dad used to say." She gave an emphatic nod that caused her cinnamon bun of hair to slide down the side of her head. As she reached up expertly and rearranged some bobby pins to re-anchor it in place, I said goodbye and left.

"Why would he do that, Father? I would never do that to him. And now he's not even here, so I can tell him how furious I am. I mean, everybody but me knew. Now I can see why Mrs. Schimelman acted a little strange when I asked her what had happened while I was gone. And Lanette Howard, mom's neighbor, she couldn't get out of the Elite fast enough when I asked her what was new. Besides dumping all over our friendship, Coop made me look like the stupidest person in Himmel." I finished my sad little story and waited for Father Gregory Lindstrom to comfort me.

When I left the HPD, I'd taken a chance that the elderly priest of St. Stephen's parish would be at home after having finished eight o'clock Mass. I'm not much of a one for organized religion, but Father Lindstrom is my go-to guy. There are a few people in this life who are truly good. Not just nice, not just pleasant, but deep down, through and through good. Father Lindstrom is one of them.

"Is that what's upsetting you? That you feel stupid?" he asked, handing me a cup of tea, and then pouring some into his own favorite *X-Files* mug.

"No, of course not. Well, yes, partly, maybe. I just want the chance to talk to him face-to-face, have him admit that was a jerk move, and that he's an asshat. Sorry, Father."

He just sipped his tea and looked at me over the rim of his cup, his light blue eyes behind his glasses quizzical. When he spoke, his voice was mildly curious.

"What makes you feel more angry, the fact of Coop's marriage, or that he didn't forewarn you about it?"

"I'm mad because Coop treated me like our friendship doesn't matter. Like I don't matter."

He waited, and finally I continued.

"He's letting Rebecca get her way. He's letting her drive a wedge between us, and he isn't even trying to stop it. He's had girlfriends before. One was pretty serious, but that didn't mean he and I couldn't be friends. All of the sudden, with her, it's like there's no room in his life for me anymore."

"That's a feeling that must really hurt."

"You're doing it again."

"Doing what?"

"Trying to make me realize the error of my ways without telling me so. Trying to get me to think that my anger is really because I have abandonment issues, that the losses in my life make me vulnerable—all that counseling stuff."

"Well, what is it you'd like me to do?" His voice was gentle, and his eyes were kind, which made it worse. I wanted to feel the anger, not the pain.

"I want you to say 'Leah, Coop is behaving like a jerk. You're right to be angry and you deserve better than that.' Can't you just be on my side on this one?"

"I'm always on your side, Leah."

And I knew that was true. He'd come into my life when my sister Lacey was in a bad way, and mom and I didn't know what to do. He'd been a good friend then and ever since.

"Do you know the expression *tout comprendre c'est tout pardoner*?"

I nodded. "It means to understand all is to forgive all, right?"

"Yes."

"You mean there's more going on than I know, right? That if I talk to Coop, I could feel differently?"

He gave a little shrug, and smiled. "I think if you *listen*, Leah, that's possible."

I stopped by the store on the way home to pick up some milk and a box of Honey Nut Cheerios, because I couldn't decide if the fire in my belly was anger or hunger. But after I finished eating, I still didn't feel any better. The bright sunshine of the morning had departed, but I got my bike out for a ride anyway. I needed to burn off some of my irritation and then settle down to cranking out some chapters.

It was quiet as I rode down Main Street. People come downtown because they have to go to the city building, or the county courthouse, or the police department or the library, but it isn't a thriving commerce center anymore. Himmel residents complain about the decline of local businesses, but still we shop at the big box stores on the edge of town, or order online. The factories that once provided good paying jobs have been shuttered for years, and Himmel has shrunk from a community of 20,000 to a struggling town of 15,000 residents.

Even so, I'm not convinced my hometown is down for the count. Coop and I sometimes play *"What Would You Do If You Won the Lottery?"* We try to come up with ways we'd use it to make things better for the town. We've had some of our most heated discussions arguing over the right way to spend the millions we don't have. But there are people like Miller Caldwell, the attorney who owns the building where I live, who actually do have the money, the ideas and the willingness to invest in the community. I like him a lot, even if I did once accuse him of murder.

A light sprinkle of rain and the darkening clouds overhead made me cut my ride short. I had just finished tucking my bicycle under the stairwell in the street entrance to my apartment, when I heard a tentative tap on the door behind me. I turned and saw a short, roundish woman on the sidewalk, awkwardly balancing a cardboard box as she huddled beneath the awning to keep out of the rain. I opened the door.

"Hi! You're Mrs. Stanton, aren't you? I'm Leah Nash. Can I help you?" I recognized her from seeing her around town with her husband Duane, though we'd never met.

"Yes, thank you so much. I hate to bother you, but I'm going through some of Duane's things, and—" She shifted the box so that it rested on her hip. "I wondered if you might have just a few minutes?"

Puzzled but intrigued, I invited her in. Once upstairs I settled her on the couch, turned on the gas fireplace, made her a cup of tea, and then sat down with her.

"How can I help you, Mrs. Stanton?"

"Please, call me Phyllis. I feel like I know you after reading your articles in the paper for the last few years. And I really enjoyed your book. Duane did, too." She smiled sweetly. Her plump cheeks had begun to flush as the warmth from the fireplace suffused the room. She was a pretty woman of 70 or so, with soft gray hair. Her eyes held the sad, slightly confused look of the newly bereaved.

"That's nice to hear, Phyllis. I was sorry to learn about Duane's death."

"Thank you. Yes. He fell from the bird-watching platform we donated to the county. We had it built in memory of our daughter, Bonnie. She passed away four years ago. She was an avid bird watcher like Duane. Ironic, isn't it?" Her lower lip began to tremble.

"I'm so sorry," I repeated. I waited then, to give her a minute to compose herself. She sipped her tea before she spoke.

"You must think it's strange for me to just drop in. But I wasn't sure what else to do. My son says I should let him and my daughter-in-law take care of cleaning out Duane's things, because I get so emotional. But I can't. It hurts, but it makes me feel closer to him, too. Do you understand?"

"I think so."

"Well." She sighed, and again I waited. Then she reached down into the box at her feet and pulled out a desk pad calendar.

"Look at this."

I peered down obediently and saw a page full of scheduled appointments listed in handwriting so small and precise, it was hard to read.

"Wow. Duane really kept himself busy," I said. Was she trying to point out what an in-demand guy her husband had been?

She nodded and smiled. "Oh, yes. He was always on the go." She waited for me to respond.

I tried again. "He definitely didn't spend his retirement resting in his rocking chair, did he? Yes. He had a lot of appointments, all right." I still wasn't getting what she wanted from me.

"Yes. I used to tell him I felt like I had to get on his schedule just to get some time with him. It was just our little joke," she added. Then, tiring of my dull-wittedness, she leaned over and pointed to a notation on the side of the page set up for memoranda. "But I wanted you to see this note. It's why I'm here."

I followed her finger and read: *See Leah Nash, follow-up to September 30 meeting.* I looked up and she returned my gaze with an expectant one of her own. Did she think I'd talked with her husband before he died, maybe that I had some special message to impart?

"Mrs.—Phyllis, I didn't meet with Duane, if that's what you're hoping. In fact, I wasn't even in town. And I really didn't know him that well, just from city council meetings, that's all."

"Oh, I know, dear."

"Then?" I was really lost about what my part in this conversation was.

"Then why am I talking to you? Because Duane told me that

he was researching something he thought you'd be interested in."

I hoped my face didn't show it, but I highly doubted that. In his retirement years, Duane, a former accountant, had busied himself not only with bird-watching, but with ferreting out waste in city government. Nitpicky, pedantic, detailed—those were words that might be applied to Duane's research. But interesting? No.

While I was still at the paper, he was a frequent speaker from the floor at city council meetings, often accompanied by charts demonstrating the cost-savings to be found in managing pen inventories, double-sided copying, and re-using file folders. He was a hero to his coffee shop buddies, a group of men of a certain age who passed the time passing judgment on the failings of city hall. He was a thorn in the side of the city clerk charged with processing Open Information Act requests, which Duane never tired of filing.

To my knowledge, he had never uncovered anything more scandalous than the perceived overuse of manila envelopes in the treasurer's office. Still, he kept hunting for it, like Ahab for the white whale.

"The thing is, Phyllis, I'm right in the thick of writing my second book, and I'm pushing against a pretty firm deadline. If you think Duane was on to something, you might want to talk to Rebecca Hartfield at the newspaper. I'm not working as a reporter anymore."

"I understand. But the truth is, Duane was quite disappointed in his meeting with her. He didn't feel she took him seriously. I know you're very busy, but if you could just find a little time, just a few minutes, really, to look over this material from his desk? That's where he kept things he was working on at the moment. I'm not worried about things that were in his filing cabinet. I know those are what he completed.

"But it's bothering me that what he was busy with at the last, he didn't get to finish. Duane would hate that. Some people thought he was a fussbudget, and maybe he was. But he was an honest, kind man, too. And he really enjoyed his little puzzles, tracking down ways for the city to save money and be more efficient. I think it made him feel a little more important. After he retired, it was hard for him to feel useful.

"Duane always took such good care of me. He wouldn't have liked leaving something unfinished. Couldn't you, please, help me do this one last thing to take care of him? Couldn't you just take a look?" Her eyes filled with tears, and she fumbled in her pocket for a Kleenex.

"Of course, I can, Phyllis." The words were out before I could stop them.

The smile that broke through her tears was so happy that I felt an immediate need to manage expectations.

"It may be a little while before I can go through all of this, and you know, it could be that Duane—that what he may have found, well that it isn't, it doesn't …"

"Doesn't amount to a hill of beans? I know. Duane could get excited about things that other people didn't think were important. He just liked things to balance. That's why I want to balance, maybe just a little, all the love and caring he gave to me for more than 50 years. I don't mind if there isn't anything that matters in his file. I just want him to feel like it's tidied up the way he would have done it."

"OK, Phyllis. Leave this with me for a while, and I promise to follow up if there's anything that needs following up on. But it might take me a few weeks."

# 4

After Phyllis left, I carried her box into my office and tucked it in the corner. I went to the kitchen and made myself a large cup of coffee. Then, putting Coop and everything else out of my mind, I went to my office and started writing. I stopped long enough to throw a frozen dinner into the microwave and eat it, then I went back to work.

Hours later I had that good feeling that comes from pounding out a lot of copy that, for the most part, seems to hang together, move swiftly, and keeps the story going forward. I leaned back, lifted my arms over my head, stretched hard, yawned and looked at the clock. Wow. It was ten o'clock. My loft was in darkness except for the light on my desk. And, I realized, I was a little hungry.

I pulled on my pajamas and washed my face. I went to the kitchen and dug a half-full container of Ben & Jerry's Mint Chocolate Chunk ice cream out of the freezer. I ate it from the carton as I leaned against the island separating my kitchen from my living room.

I felt better than I had since I'd spoken to Courtnee yesterday. Coop and Rebecca were married. OK, we'd see where that went. Coop had lied by omission to me, but maybe there was a reason I hadn't thought of, and even if there weren't, maybe I could be a good enough friend to forgive him for it. Lord knew he'd had to forgive me for quite a few things over the years. And, finally, I was making real, true progress on my book. I licked the last bit of flavor off my spoon, ran water in the carton, tossed it in the recycling, brushed my teeth, and went to bed, eager to see Miguel in the morning and to reconnect with Coop.

---

BZZ. BZZ. BZZZZZZZZZZ. The noise of the buzzer to my apartment finally penetrated my coma sleep and woke me up. Had I overslept? My clock said one fifteen. I grabbed a robe and pushed the intercom.

"Miguel?"

"*Chica! Ay Dios mío!* It's terrible!"

"What is it? Come up!" I buzzed downstairs to let him in, then went to open my apartment door. As I did, Miguel all but fell inside.

"*Ay Dios mío!* It's terrible," he repeated.

"What? What is it?"

"*Horrible!* In my house, my living room. It was, she was—"

"Come in, come in. What happened?" I put an arm around him and led him over to a stool at the kitchen island.

"Miguel, please, what is it?"

"A woman. There's a dead woman in my living room!"

---

"What woman? What do you mean? Are you sure? Are you OK? Who is it? Did you call the police?"

My rapid-fire questions did nothing to calm him down. In fact, his teeth started chattering as we sat there.

"OK, it's all right," I said in a more soothing tone. I poured him a shot of Jameson and added ginger ale—Miguel's not one for straight liquor, but he needed something to brace him. I dumped a shot of the whiskey over ice for myself. Then I moved him from the kitchen to the couch, turned on the fireplace, covered him with an afghan, and urged him to take a drink. Only after he swallowed it down and let out a long sigh, did I start questioning him again.

"Now, let's try it again. A woman is dead in your house. Did you call the police?"

He nodded. "They came. I just finished talking to them, but I couldn't stay there and I—oh, *chica,* I know it's so late, I'm sorry, I —"

"No, stop that right now. Of course you came here, where else? Do you know the woman?"

"No. Yes. It's Holly Mason," he said, pulling the blanket closer around him.

"Who's Holly Mason?"

"I don't know." This wasn't good. Miguel's eyes, normally alight with fun, were wide and dark. His beautiful caramel-colored skin was clammy to the touch, and there was a slight shake in the hand holding his glass. I wrapped the blanket tighter around him. "Take another drink. A big one." He did as ordered, and when he finished I gave his hand a squeeze.

"All right. We'll take it slow. Can you tell me how you know the woman's name?"

He closed his eyes, then seemed to think better of it, as though the image of what he'd seen at his house had returned. Instead, he took another drink, then took a deep breath and let it out slowly before he began to speak.

"I rented my house out online, for the weekend, because I

was going away. *Mi amigo* Nathan does it all the time to make a little extra money. Holly Mason is the woman who rented it. But I never met her."

"You spoke to her, though?"

"No, just email and text. You just register your house with FVR—Fabulous Vacation Rentals—and then people contact you." His voice was getting steadier.

"When did you get home?"

"About eleven o'clock tonight. Our plane was late, and I was so happy to be home finally."

"Can you walk me through what happened after you got there?"

Despite the warmth radiating from the fireplace, he shivered again. "When I pulled in my driveway, I was surprised. The light was on in the living room. Then, I thought the renter must have forgotten to turn it off. But when I opened the garage door, a car was there. I was a little *irritado*, because she was supposed to leave by noon. But then I thought, well, maybe she got the date mixed up. I got my bags and went to the front door." He stopped again, hesitant to relive the scene.

"Miguel, what happened when you got to the door?"

"I knocked, because I didn't want to scare her. But she didn't answer. I tried the door, and it wasn't locked. When I walked in, I called, but it was so quiet. And then I went into the living room and, and—" He took a drink before going on.

"She was there, *chica*, lying on the floor by the fireplace. Her head, her hair, it was all over blood." He spoke a little faster. "There was blood on the floor and blood on her, and I just ran out. I called 911, and I waited outside. I couldn't go back in. It was, it was—" He stopped, unable to adequately describe the awfulness of the scene.

"Who came to investigate?"

"The new detective. Erin Harper."

"Miguel, how many people knew Holly Mason was staying at your house?"

He shrugged. "I don't know. I told Courtnee and Rebecca at work, my friend Nathan, my *Tío* Craig in case the renter had any trouble. I think I talked to some people at McClain's Bar about it, and Mrs. Schimelman at the Elite, Father Lindstrom. My neighbors. I was pretty excited. Such an easy way to make extra *dinero*—I thought."

Poor Detective Harper. Miguel's extreme extroversion meant she wasn't going to have an easy time narrowing the field of suspects, initially, anyway.

"So, you told the police all that."

"*Sí.* They kept asking me if I knew her friends, if I knew anyone in Himmel she wanted to see, if I knew why she chose my house. Her email just said she wanted a quiet weekend with the fall colors. I don't know anything else, *chica*, except I never want to see anything like that again in my life."

I reached over and gave him a hug.

"You know what? It's two o'clock. I'm going to get you a pillow and some blankets, and you can stretch out here and get some sleep. In the morning we'll eat, we'll talk some more, and when you're ready, you can put on your reporter's hat and follow up on this. It's an awful thing you walked into, Miguel. But it could also be an awfully good story, and you've got the inside track."

---

"So, I had breakfast with Miguel this morning, and he's doing a lot better. Amazing what a night's—or half a night's—sleep can do." I was perched a little uncomfortably on the visitor's chair in Coop's office at the Himmel Police Department. Coop sat across from me, behind his desk, a mug of the horrible sludgy brew he calls coffee in his hand. I had just given him a recap of the previous night's events.

"I haven't talked to Erin yet this morning, but I imagine she's pretty happy to be lead investigator on a murder her second week on the job. Does it seem funny that it's Miguel, not you, covering the story?" he asked.

"A little, I guess. But I've got my hands full with my book." Normally, I would have pumped Coop for whatever information he had on the murder. But this wasn't a normal conversation. So far, neither of us had even alluded to the fact that Coop was wearing a ring on the third finger of his left hand.

"Yeah, that's right. You've got that deadline hanging over your head. Well, I'm glad you were there when Miguel showed up at your place. Finding a dead body is a shock to anyone's system. And we know Miguel's an excitable boy." He fell silent then, as did I.

We were both equally reluctant to start the real conversation. The topic sat between us like an elephant-shaped wedding cake in the proverbial living room. Finally, I couldn't take it anymore.

"Speaking of shocks, that pretty much describes how I felt when Courtnee told me you and Rebecca got married." There. It was out.

He reddened slightly as though he were ashamed. Good. He had reason to be. He took off his HPD cap and ran his hand through his short, dark hair, a sure sign he's agitated. But when he spoke, it was in his usual measured tones.

"Leah, it all came together pretty fast. There wasn't time to talk to you. I tried to call you at your aunt's, but with the phone cutting out, and both of us asking 'Are you there? Are you there?' every other minute, it was ridiculous. Besides, I wanted to tell you face-to-face. I didn't want you to hear the news over a bad phone connection." He looked so pained, I felt a tiny bit sorry for him. Enough to keep from ripping into him, but not enough to hold back the snark.

"Oh, but you did want me to hear it from Courtnee? She was your chosen messenger for the biggest news in your life?"

"No, come on. I thought we'd be back before you got home. I'm sorry. I really am."

"But why, Coop? You dumped Rebecca. You said the way she treated Sheriff Dillingham was a deal breaker. You said—"

"I know what I said," he responded, with a touch of irritation that he quickly tried to cover. "I can't explain it exactly. It just sort of happened."

"But it must have been happening for a while. Why didn't you at least tell me that you were seeing her again?"

"Because it really wasn't any of your business."

I'd been leaning forward in my chair, but that set me back, literally and figuratively. I waited a second before I answered.

"OK, all right then, I've got it. Well, I think we've about covered everything." I stood up to go, but Coop stood, too, and came around his desk. He put his hands on my shoulders and gently pushed me back down. Then he sat on the edge of his desk, his hands resting on his knees.

My arms were crossed at my chest, and I sat all the way back in my chair. If ever body language said, "This had better be good," that did.

"Can we start over? I didn't tell you I was seeing Rebecca again, because I know how you feel and so does she. She wanted to prove to me that she could change, could be a better person. I thought she deserved the chance. You're right, she's done some pretty bad things in the past. But even so, there's something about her that's special."

"So special that it doesn't matter what she's done, or how she treats people?"

"That's not what I said. I know Rebecca hasn't exactly been

nice to you. And I know she can come across as cold. Even tough. But she isn't. It's hard for her to let people in. She doesn't like being vulnerable. You're not the most trusting person, either, you know."

I started to speak, but thought better of it.

"She knows that she was way out of line to put pressure on Sheriff Dillingham like she did. She's really ashamed of doing that."

My poker face was not in place. He could see I wasn't convinced.

"If you could just give her another chance, it would mean a lot to me. She really wants a fresh start with you. You know, she envies you. She wants what you have—friends, family. She says she's ready to live a different kind of life. That she thinks she can be happy here."

*Mein Gott im himmel*, as Mrs. Schimelman would say. My God in heaven, Coop was buying all her BS. I saw with sudden clarity that there really wasn't anything I could do. He was sold on Rebecca, and he wasn't going to make a return, no matter what defects there were in the product. I forced myself to tune back in to what he was saying.

"Can't you just be happy for me? Rebecca is my wife, but you're my best friend. Doesn't everybody deserve a second chance? You've made mistakes, too, you know. If you could just try to see her the way I do. I've never met anyone like Rebecca. She's smart, she's beautiful, she's witty. I know she can be sharp sometimes—so can you. But she's got this warm, caring side, too."

OK, I'd had enough. I might need to accept it, but I didn't have to sit around and join in the delusion with him.

"You know what, Coop? I think you're probably right. This isn't any of my business. And I don't want to fight with you, especially about something I have no power to change. Best wishes, good luck, congrats, and all that jazz. But that's all I got."

This time as I stood to leave, he grabbed my arm and said, "Would you just wait a minute? I'm not finished. The reason I didn't tell you that we were getting married, is that we just decided the very night you left. That's when Rebecca told me. She's pregnant."

I sat back down with an audible thud.

"Pregnant? Rebecca? But how—never mind, I know how—but if you've only been together a few weeks—"

"That's not strictly true, I guess." He seemed a little abashed as he recounted one of the oldest stories in the books—break-up sex.

"A few nights after I told her I didn't think we should see each other anymore, she called and asked me to come over. She was really upset. When I got there, she couldn't stop crying. It was tough to see her like that, so defenseless, so, I don't know, scared, I guess. I couldn't help feeling sorry for her. I tried to get her to calm down and then, well—"

"Never mind. I get the picture. You had a magical night, and you started seeing her again. So, you've actually been back together with her for a couple of months."

"Yeah, I guess that's about it. The pregnancy wasn't anything either one of us planned."

I'd be willing to lay odds that one of them had.

"She was really nervous about how I'd take it."

"I'll bet."

"You know how she told me?"

I shook my head, just wanting this to be over. He got up and went to the other side of his desk and opened the middle drawer and pulled something out. Then he came around again and handed me a small, flat box with a pink and blue bow on it.

"Go on. Open it."

Inside was a plastic pregnancy test stick, with a + sign.

"Eww. Gross."

He was too caught up in sharing his happy news to be upset by my reaction.

"I was just blown away. I know, I know, it's not ideal timing. But I'm not sorry. I'm feeling really good about it, Leah. A baby. Just think. I'm going to be someone's dad."

I looked at him then, and instead of adult Coop, a serious, steady man with quiet gray eyes and a slow smile, I saw the boy I had first met years ago. The boy who always had time and patience for his younger sister. I saw him teaching her how to ride a bike, bandaging her cut knee, helping her make a project for school. I saw the boy who always looked out for the little kids in the neighborhood, who never teased or bullied, who actually enjoyed babysitting. And I sighed.

"You'll be a great dad, Coop. When is the baby due?"

"The end of May. I'm going with Rebecca to her next doctor's appointment. She's seeing someone in Madison. She's over thirty-five, so it's a little trickier. She wanted a specialist with a really good reputation, to make sure everything goes right."

"I'm sure it will. Not much goes wrong for Rebecca."

## 5

When I left Coop, I walked down the hall to see if Dale Darmody was in, just to say hi. Darmody's been with the department since I was a kid, but his rank is still patrolman. He's not the brightest cop on the beat, but I have reason to know first-hand that he really believes in "protect and serve."

"Leah!" A smile wreathed his pudgy face as I rapped on the doorframe before walking in. "I didn't know you was back."

"Got in Saturday. So, things were really jumping while I was gone."

"You mean the lady that threw the pot belly pig at her husband?"

I recalled the news brief I'd read at the Elite while waiting for my sandwich.

"No—though that must have been pretty traumatic for all concerned, including the pig."

"I'll say. See, the wife she never wanted it, and the husband—"

"Yeah, I did read the story in the *Times,* Darmody. But what I meant was Coop's surprise wedding. And the surprise body at Miguel's house."

"Oh, yeah, I still can't hardly believe it. The wedding, I mean. Ya know, if I was to bet on it, I'da bet you and Coop, way before I'd put money on Coop and that one."

"Still going for the long shot, aren't you, Darmody? That was never going to happen, but I sure wish he and she hadn't either." I didn't really want to hash it over with Darmody. I had just wanted to get the inevitable out of the way. So, I refocused him on the murder.

"What do you hear about the murder investigation?"

"Erin Harper, the new girl—woman—detective." Darmody struggled with the, to him, perplexing world of non-discriminatory language. "She's got the case. She's got her own team workin' on it, so I'm just hearin' this 'n' that."

"So, what's this Harper chick like? She did a lateral transfer from Green Bay, right?"

"HPD recruited her. Chief was tryin' to get that city council member off his back, I guess. You know, Marge Burns. She's sayin' we don't have enough female cops."

"Well, you don't, do you?"

"I guess. But I don't know about this bringin' in cops just because they're females."

"Isn't she qualified?"

"Well, yeah, I guess. She was workin' in Green Bay. She made detective already, so I guess she must be smart enough." He shrugged his beefy shoulders. "She's kinda know-it-all. But maybe I can train her up a little, let her see what it really takes on a force like ours. She might be OK. Maybe—" His eyes widened as he looked past me, and from the expression on his face, I was pretty sure that Detective Erin Harper was standing right behind me.

"That's all right, don't stop now. Always glad to get feedback from the troops."

I turned and saw an attractive woman around my age. She

was a little taller than me. Her honey-brown hair was pulled back tightly from her high forehead in a French braid. She wore a well-tailored tan blazer over a white blouse.

"Sorry, Detective. No offense intended," Darmody said.

"None taken. I'll cop to being a knows-a-lot, but I don't think I know it all." She smiled at him with a lopsided grin that reached her light brown eyes. Darmody visibly relaxed.

"Well, I been around longer than anybody else in the department, that's for sure. I could tell you a few stories, couldn't I, Leah?" He nodded at me, then looked back at his lieutenant. "Yep, I pretty much saved her life, isn't that right, Leah?"

"Yes, for sure, Darmody," I said, both because he actually had come to my rescue once, and because I wanted to show some solidarity.

Detective Harper turned to me then and said, "So, you're the famous Leah Nash. I'm Erin Harper." She reached out and shook my hand with a firm, quick grasp. "Read your book. It's not bad. I happen to think police work should be left strictly to the professionals, but for a civilian amateur, you did all right."

She didn't seem quite so likable anymore.

"Thanks. I guess. Welcome to Himmel. Darmody was telling me you're investigating the Holly Mason murder. Anything you can say about it yet? Off the record, I mean. I'm not reporting, just curious."

Her eyes narrowed. "I'm curious, too. How do you know the victim's name? We haven't released it yet."

"The owner of the house where she was found is a friend of mine. Miguel Santos."

"Ah, right. Well, no, Leah, sorry. I can't give you anything, not even off the record. I like to keep information pretty locked down at this stage. Fewer problems that way. I like my team to move in quickly, stay focused and keep their insights in-house.

That's how you close a case. You probably don't know it, most people don't, but most homicides are solved in the first forty-eight hours."

"Forty-eight hours? I love that show. Maybe we can watch it together sometime." She didn't find my remark amusing.

"Murder is serious business, Leah. I don't pass out information like candy to a trick-or-treater. I've got nothing against reporters—or true crime writers, for that matter. But I've never seen one of you turn up anything useful, and I've seen a lot of you get in the way. When I've got the case wrapped, I'll be glad to give you an interview. Meantime, the best thing you can do is let us get on with our job. You stay out of my way, and I'll fill you in when the case is closed. Everyone has a part to play, but during an investigation, it's not your turn to be on stage. I'm sure you can understand that."

The condescension in her tone was designed to irritate—or so it seemed to me. Darmody shot me a pleading look, hoping I wouldn't say or do something that would make him look guilty by association with a civilian amateur like me. I ignored him.

"Yeah, I think I get the picture. But just so *you* do, don't count on freezing me out of things. I usually find out what I want to know." Then I turned and waved at Darmody. "See you later." I nodded at Erin Harper, but I didn't say goodbye.

It was close to ten, and the thought of a cup of coffee and another one of Mrs. Schimelman's pumpkin walnut cookies proved too much for me to resist.

The Elite was crowded. I'd hit break time for employees from the city building and the county courthouse, and it was also the hour when retirees gathered for their regular morning kibitzing. And, unusual for this time of day, there was a line-up of high school kids at the bakery case. After I paid for my coffee and cookie, I looked around for an empty table. Then I heard a shout from the corner.

"Hey! Nash! Over here."

Charlie Ross, a detective with the Grantland County Sheriff's Office, had once been my nemesis, but somehow had evolved into a sort of frenemy, with an increasing emphasis on the friend part—though he didn't like to admit it.

"Ross, what are you doing here in the middle of a work day?" As I put down my refreshments and pulled up a chair, I noticed he had a teenage girl with him. Was he delivering someone to juvenile detention, or a foster home? No, that was below his pay grade, and besides, even if he were, he'd hardly be taking her for a treat at the Elite. He'd made no move to introduce us, so I reached out my hand and said, "Hi, I'm Leah Nash."

She looked up from her phone, surprised, then shook my hand a little awkwardly, the way kids usually do, because they're not used to the grown-up gesture yet.

"I'm Allie Ross." As she said the name, I knew what I should have recognized immediately. This was the teenage daughter who lived with Ross's ex-wife.

She bore a striking resemblance to him, although in her, the features had somehow morphed into an unconventional but very attractive face. She had her father's rather small eyes, but hers were a brilliant blue with thick dark lashes that made them arresting. Her hair was dark brown, like Ross's, but where his had retreated to a semicircle bordering his bald head, her curls cascaded exuberantly down from a side part to her shoulders.

"Allie's goin' to Himmel High this year. Brought her over from Waukesha this weekend. Just got her all set up. Kids are off for teacher in-service today, so she starts tomorrow. I finally convinced her mother it's my turn to have her for a while."

"It's OK, Dad. You can say it." She turned to me. "My mother got bored with me. She decided it would be more fun to move to Arizona with her boyfriend. But she left me a note, so that's cool, right?" Her voice was flippant, but she couldn't quite cover the hurt.

"Hey, Al, I've been wantin' you here for a long time. I'm glad to get the chance. I think it's gonna be real good. You're gonna love it here. You already know the Chapman kid—what's her name? Kelly?"

"Kira."

"And, uh—" He struggled for a minute, doubtless looking for ways to put a positive spin on the fact that a 15-year-old girl had been abandoned by her mother, then uprooted from her school, her friends, her life. His glance darted around as though he'd find the answer lurking in a corner of the cafe. The surprising smile that he broke into seemed to say he had.

"Hey—there's the Frasers. They got their son Gus with them. I'm gonna call them over. You can meet him, make a new friend."

"No, Dad, don't." Allie's hissed words were to no avail. Ross was going to get his daughter a friend, by gosh.

"What? You'll like him. He's a heckuva basketball player." He half-stood and shouted across the room, "Will! Gretchen, over here!"

Will, the Himmel city manager, and his wife Gretchen, a nurse at Himmel Hospital, made their way to the table, with a teenage boy, presumably their son, in tow. Will is a pretty laid-back guy with light brown eyes, blond hair and an easy smile. I like him.

"Hey, Charlie. Leah. What's up?"

"I want ya to meet my daughter, Allie. She's gonna start Himmel High tomorrow. I thought maybe Gus here could tell her the score." The Frasers' son was well over six feet tall, with

Will's quick smile and white, even teeth. The height must have come from his mother. Gretchen is nearly six feet herself, a good three inches taller than her husband.

If there had been room, Allie would doubtless have slithered under the table. As it was, she settled for squirming uncomfortably on her chair, and after a small "Hi," began to pay ferocious attention to her cell phone. Gus, who seemed to be a friendly sort, was not deterred.

"Hey, Allie. Some kids I know are at that table by the door. Come on, I'll introduce you." With a slightly desperate backward glance at me, the shy Allie reluctantly followed the Frasers' son.

"Pull up a chair, why don't you? Let the kids get to know each other a little," Ross said to Will.

But it was Gretchen who answered, a little brusquely, "No, we can't stay, Charlie. Will has to get back to the office, and I have an appointment. We just stopped by for lattes to go and to drop Gus off."

I thought Will looked a little surprised, but he's not in the habit of contradicting Gretchen. No one is. Intense, uptight, and dedicated, she's the driving force on many a Himmel committee. Some say her patients get better because they're afraid not to. I can't exactly say that I like her, but I appreciate her.

Still, I couldn't resist messing with her just a little, so I introduced a topic it would be hard for them to resist despite Gretchen's desire to stay on schedule. "So, what do you guys think about the big news?"

"Coop and Rebecca getting married? Not much of a surprise to me. I thought they were headed that way," Gretchen said, a touch impatient at my attempt to keep her from her appointed rounds.

"Coop and Rebecca got married?" Ross asked, his voice sounding shocked. And well he might be, given that Rebecca was the reason Ross's boss was forced out. As a result, Ross was stuck working for the interim sheriff, Art Lamey. To paraphrase a favorite James Thurber quote of my mother's, while Art isn't dumber than an ox, he isn't any smarter either.

"No, not that," I said. "I'll catch you up later. I'm talking about the murder."

Will's eyes widened and lost their sleepy look. Gretchen appeared stunned.

"Murder? Where? When?"

"Here. In Himmel. At Miguel Santos' house. No, it wasn't him," I quickly added as I saw an alarmed glance pass between them. "His house is right behind yours, though, isn't it? Maybe you better get your alibis ready."

"That's not funny, Leah," Gretchen said. Her carefully tweezed eyebrows drew together, and her precisely outlined red lips pursed. She's pretty enough. I can see why Will was attracted, but she's so carefully assembled that it's hard to imagine her letting her blonde-streaked hair down—either literally or figuratively.

"You're right. Sorry. Stupid jokes are my default setting. But for real, you guys had to see a bunch of cop cars there this morning. Didn't you wonder about the commotion?"

"No, we didn't see anything. The three of us left together at six, and it was still dark. We had an appointment with Gus's surgeon in Madison, to make sure his knee was good enough to play ball again," Will said.

"That doesn't matter, Will," Gretchen said. "Let Leah tell us what happened."

"I don't have many details. Miguel rented his house out for the weekend through one of those online vacation rental sites. When he got home late last night, the renter was still there. Dead."

"Then that means someone was murdered, right behind us

practically! I'm glad I bought that gun for self-protection. Do you think there's someone breaking into houses in the neighborhood? Who was Miguel's renter?" Gretchen had turned to Ross for the information, despite the fact that I was the one who made the announcement.

"Don't look at me. Seems like Lois Lane here has more of the story than I do."

"Her name is Holly Mason. That's really all I know."

"But Miguel knows her?"

"No, that's the thing. They just emailed and texted. He knows she's from Chicago and that's about it."

"Man, that is one tough homecoming," Will said.

"Poor Miguel," Gretchen said. "What a shock to come home and find a stranger lying dead in your living room. Do the police have any suspects?"

"Not that I've heard. But this seems like a pretty tough one. Who in Himmel would want to kill her, and how would anyone know she was in Miguel's house?"

"Unless it was Miguel," Gretchen said.

I stared at her.

"I'm not saying it was, him, of course not. But I wouldn't want to be in his shoes. That's where police will look first, right? I mean, he found the body. And they only have his word that he got home when he said he did."

"Geez, Gretch." Will turned to us. "Pay no attention to her. She watches too many police dramas."

"I wasn't accusing Miguel," Gretchen said. "I was just making an observation."

Will stood up then, and Gretchen did too, saying "Well, we have to be going."

After they left, I looked at Ross.

"Gretchen was just being ridiculous, right? No one would think Miguel had anything to do with this."

"Nobody that knows him would take it too serious, but I hear the new detective at HPD caught the case. So, she may waste a little time diggin' in with your partner in crime, but I wouldn't worry about it."

"I guess you're probably right." But Gretchen wasn't the only one who spent too much time watching crime shows. A faint tremor of unease ran through me.

## 6

I had best intentions to march straight up to my apartment and start working on my book as soon as I got back home. But when I pulled in the back parking lot, I noticed Rebecca's car wasn't there. I decided to pop into the *Himmel Times* first to see how Miguel was doing.

I peeked in the newsroom, but he wasn't at his desk. Then I heard voices and laughter coming from the reception area, so I went up to the front of the office. A woman with her back to me sat in front of the computer at the reception desk. She must be Courtnee's replacement. Miguel leaned over her shoulder, pointing something out on her screen. They didn't notice me watching them from the hall at first.

"*Bueno*, April! I told you, you can do it!"

Though I couldn't see her face, her pride in her accomplishment was evident in her voice. "Thank you, Miguel, for being so patient. I'm a little nervous."

"With Rebecca as your boss, no wonder you're nervous," I said.

Both of them turned. "Hey, Miguel. Hi," I said to the new

receptionist, leaning over the counter and holding my hand out to shake hers. "I'm Leah Nash."

Her handshake was a bit damp.

"I already know you, Leah. I'm April Nelson. I'll bet you don't remember me." As she finished speaking, she ducked her head shyly.

Oh-oh. I sure didn't. I ransacked my memory. Wait a minute. That thin fine hair, cut short and lying flat against her scalp, the bright brown eyes magnified by the lenses of her glasses, the round cheeks that gave her the look of an eager chipmunk.

"April! April Nelson. Of course, I remember you. Tenth grade gym class—we hung out in the outfield hoping the ball wouldn't come anywhere near us."

The smile she gave me radiated happiness. "You do remember! I didn't think you would, because you know, it's a long time ago, and I wasn't exactly one of the popular kids in high school." An image of April, round-shouldered and perpetually pushing her glasses up on the bridge of her nose, always overlooked, always sitting by herself in a corner in the cafeteria, flashed through my mind.

"High school!" I gave an exaggerated shudder. "Who'd want to go back there? Definitely not me. But you haven't been in Himmel all along, have you? I feel like we would've at least run into each other at the grocery store since I've been back."

She shook her head. "I just moved back. My fiancé passed away last year." Her lower lip trembled, but she soldiered on. "I live with my older sister June, now. She has a pet boarding business. *Whiskers and Tails*? Maybe you know it?"

Ah, that explained the cat hair on her cardigan. "No, but then I don't have any pets. I'm not really mature enough to take care of myself, let alone a dog or cat."

She laughed as though I'd finished an Amy Schumer-style stand-up set. I was beginning to really like this girl.

"April."

Rebecca unexpectedly walked through the front door. She paused in front of the counter and stood with one arm wrapped around her narrow waist, the elbow of the other resting on it as she fingered the silver chain she wore. The warm atmosphere in the room was flash frozen in an instant.

"I see you've already met our former employee, Leah. I fired her, but she still keeps coming back." She smiled then, as though she were kidding, though I knew she wasn't. April looked at her uncertainly.

"Don't worry," Rebecca said. "We're all friends now. Is she telling you stories about her glory days reporting the news? Once you get to know her, you'll learn that Leah loves to tell stories. She's not keeping you from your work, is she?" Again, that smile that was really just a stretching of her lips.

"Actually, I already know Leah. We both went to Himmel High at the same time and..." April had fallen into the novice's trap of thinking that Rebecca actually cared what you had to say when she asked a question. She had already turned her attention to me, ignoring April's response as it trailed off.

"Leah, David said he told you our news. He's going to be an amazing father, don't you think?"

Before I could answer, Miguel exclaimed, "You and Coop are having a baby? That's *fantástico*! *Los bébes*, I love them!"

"That's very exciting news," April offered, then blushed at her temerity.

"Leah? What do you think?"

"I think Coop will be a great father. And you'll be the world's worst mother."

I left by the side door leading to my front stairs. Before I closed it, I looked over my shoulder and saw Miguel and April staring open-mouthed at me. Rebecca had a small victory smile on her lips.

I spent the next two days holed up in my apartment writing. Obviously, I didn't have a handle on this brave new world with Coop and Rebecca as a married couple in it. Withdrawal for a while seemed the best option. It also allowed me to report with truth and great virtue when Clinton called that I was totally focused on my work.

But when my mother phoned late Wednesday afternoon to let me know she was home from her Mediterranean cruise, I was more than ready to take a break. I volunteered to pick up a pizza at Bonucci's, the pizza place owned by Miguel's uncle, Craig Kowalski. He kept the original owner's name when he bought it, he said, because Kowalski's Pizza just didn't have the right ring to it.

As I pulled into the driveway of my ancestral home, a fairly nondescript one-story house, I knew that inside was a warm and welcoming place, created by my mother despite the chaos and losses our family had endured.

"Leah, why did you say that to Rebecca? Coop did ask you to at least try to give her a chance." Warm my mother may be, but she's also very direct. I had just given her the rundown on Himmel's happiest couple and my most recent dealings with the new bride. Actually, I had led off the evening update with the murder at Miguel's, but Mom had zeroed in on the personal first.

"Because, Mom, she is a smug, self-serving, cold-hearted, manipulative predator who will not only ruin Coop's life and our friendship, but probably damage for life the unfortunate baby she's having."

"Well, if you want my opinion—"

"You mean all these years and you never told me it was optional? Because I—"

"Don't be such a smart ass. I'm telling you, Coop is all in, and you need to get over it. There's a child in the picture now. You need to accept that it changes things. I agree with you. I don't think he's made a great choice, but it's his choice to make. I think it's a big mistake to keep harping on how much you don't like Rebecca and how wrong he is. You could damage your relationship beyond repair."

Irritated, partially because I knew she was right, I lashed out.

"Well, you'd know about big mistakes, wouldn't you?" Immediately I regretted it. We were in the process of mending a pretty big tear in our relationship that had followed a pretty big betrayal of trust. My outburst was a reminder that we weren't quite there yet. "I'm sorry, I didn't mean that."

"No, you're right. I screwed up royally, and I almost lost my own daughter. I'm not the best person to be giving relationship advice," she said, her voice a shadowy echo of her normal breezy confidence.

"No, Mom, you didn't almost lose me. I was hurt, and I was angry. But I didn't stop loving you, or wanting you in my life. I shouldn't have snapped at you. What happened between us then is done."

"You shouldn't let me off so easy. I hid things from you. No, worse than that, I lied to you. My motives were good, but I was still wrong. Instead of protecting you, I hurt you. I just don't want you to make the same kind of mistakes. What you're doing with Coop—well, I know you want to keep him from being hurt, but you can't. You need to stay out of this."

"I hear you. But let's just not talk about it anymore, OK? I appreciate your advice, but I can handle things with Coop."

My mother has spent a lifetime trying to organize, protect, direct, shelter, and empower me—objectives that are often in conflict. And I've spent a lifetime arguing, rebelling, supporting, respecting, and loving her—also sometimes conflicting objectives. She's working on stepping away. But her go-to response is always going to be: *You know what you should do ...* And mine is always going to be: *Don't worry, I've got this.* Even when I don't.

"All right," she said. "Let's talk about Miguel's murder. How long before he'll be able to go home? Do you think he'll even want to?"

"I think so, yeah. I mean, finding the body was a horrible thing. But he didn't know this Holly Mason woman. Even though Rebecca is acting like he and she were best friends."

"What do you mean?"

"She took him off the story. Said he was too close to it. He might not be able to be objective. I think she just did it to be mean because when she walked in on Monday, Miguel and the new receptionist and I were having fun together."

"Oh, come on."

"No, I'm serious. She's that petty. But, anyway, I haven't really talked to him since Monday night when he texted me. He said his house won't be ready to move back into until Saturday. I invited him to stay with me, but he said his Uncle Craig and Aunt Lydia have more room."

"I'm sure Nick will be happier with that arrangement. I don't see him warming up to Miguel sleeping on your couch. For someone with a wandering eye, he doesn't seem to like it if your attention is anywhere but on him. Doesn't he usually come down on Tuesdays?"

I shrugged. Nick Gallagher is my ex-husband. We had a not very amicable divorce after a brief marriage in my twenties. I discovered that he was sleeping with one of his graduate students. We didn't speak for years, but he sought me out when he took a tenure-track position at a small private college not far away. He's worked pretty hard to convince me he's changed, and so far, so good. But my mother does not approve.

"He'd be fine with it, I'm sure. He likes Miguel, but he's not coming down until Friday. He's at a conference in New York this week."

"Did he drive up to see you while you were at Nancy's?"

"Mom, it's a six-hour drive. No, he didn't. Besides, I was pretty busy. Aunt Nancy isn't the world's best patient."

"Well, it just seems like the new and improved Nick you keep talking about would care enough to give you a hand, or at least go and see how you were doing. Paul would have."

Paul is my mother's beau. He's a good enough guy, but to my mother, he's the gold standard for men. The lie she'd told to protect me had come between her and Paul as well, but he never lost faith in her. He forgave her when the truth came out, and he never looked back. Come to think of it, maybe he *is* the gold standard.

"Mom, remember that whole you-can't-make-decisions-for-other-people thing we were just talking about?"

"OK, fine. Do you want to hear my new doorbell ring?" If you're losing, change the subject is my mother's strategy.

I nodded. Carol Nash loves music, all genres. Ever since she figured out how to program ring tones into her doorbell from her digital tunes library, she's been unstoppable. A visitor who pushes the buzzer might be greeted by "Respect," or "String of Pearls," or "This Girl Is on Fire," depending on whether the day feels like Aretha, Glen Miller, or Alicia Keys to her.

But before she could reach the door to demonstrate her latest ditty, the opening notes of "We Are Family" pealed through the house. She danced her way to the entrance. She's still got the moves. She flung the door open, saw Miguel standing there, and grabbed his hand to execute a dance step with her. She stopped immediately as she saw the sober expression on his face.

"Miguel, sweetheart, what's wrong?"

"The police just arrested my Uncle Craig. They say he killed Holly Mason."

## 7

"Miguel, what are you talking about? Why would the police arrest Craig?" My mother had hustled Miguel into the living room. I sat next to him on the couch, while she took the seat in the rocking chair.

"Because of Sophia. The website, the leaky toilet, everything. *Que desastre!*" he spilled out, almost faster than I could follow. Sophia is Miguel's cousin, his Uncle Craig and Aunt Lydia's daughter. I couldn't think what she had to do with her dad's arrest, let alone how a leaky toilet and a website fit into Holly Mason's murder.

"I don't get it. You need to back up a mile or two."

He looked at our bewildered faces and saw that we needed more context.

"OK. *Escúchame.* The police think Uncle Craig killed Holly Mason, because she has the dating site for sugar daddies. SweetMeets."

"Your Uncle Craig was using a sugar daddies website? I don't believe it." Craig's wife Lydia is not only drop-dead gorgeous— that Santos family has some seriously good-looking genes—but she's also sweet, loving, smart. No way would her husband be trolling the internet for a sugar baby.

"What's a sugar daddy site?" my mother asked.

"There are sites on the web where older men with disposable income, sugar daddies, and younger women with financial needs, sugar babies, go to meet up."

"You mean like call girls and their johns." My mother said knowledgeably, revealing that I'm not the only one in the Nash family who watches too many cop shows.

"No, it's not quite as straightforward as that. Lots of the sugar babies are college kids, and they connect with men who can help them with tuition, rent, other expenses. And the sugar daddies are—well, I'm sure they have a variety of motives."

"But how would Craig fit in?"

I shrugged, and we both looked back at Miguel.

"It's not Uncle Craig. It's Sophia. She is, well, she was, on the site Holly Mason owns. SweetMeets. She was a sugar baby."

"Little Sophia? She can't be more than fifteen."

"No, Mom. She's nineteen, and she's at Northwestern."

"But why would she do that?"

Miguel sighed and looked sad. "She told me a few weeks ago. She said when Uncle Craig, he was so sick, she couldn't focus on school. Then her boyfriend broke up with her. She was *devastada*. She couldn't eat, couldn't sleep, her grades they got so bad, she lost her scholarships. She couldn't tell her parents. They were so proud of her, always. And they had so much on their minds."

"But Craig and Lydia, they would've understood," my mother said.

"I know, I told her so. But she was too ashamed to tell them. She felt like she had let them down. Then, when *Tío* Craig got the new kidney, the bills—*Dios mío*, there were so many, and so much worry. She couldn't tell them she didn't have the money for her tuition."

"Are you saying Sophia found a sugar daddy to pay for college?"

He nodded. "Her roommate told her about the SweetMeets site. She said her sugar daddy was paying her tuition and her rent."

"Lots of girls do it, Mom. There was a big story on it in the *New York Times* a month or so ago."

"But that's exploitation. That's taking advantage of those young women. It's like prostitution."

"Well, some people think that's not so bad, as long as the pay is fair and there's no coercion involved." She gave me a sidelong glance and shook her head, but then turned back to Miguel.

"But what does this have to do with the murder?"

"And the leaky toilet?" I added.

"When Sophia told me what she was doing, I said '*Niñita*, you have to tell your *mami* and *papi*. You can't hide it anymore.' So, then, last Saturday afternoon, she decided to do it. She came home, and she told them." He shook his head. "It didn't go well. Uncle Craig you know he has a quick temper—" Here he paused to jump up and fling his hands in the air in a volcanic gesture.

"He lost it. Lots of yelling and crying, and Sophia, she is *temperamento caliente,* too. He said she ruined her life, she shamed herself and the family, and she wasn't welcome in his house. Sophia said he was cold-hearted and controlling, and she was leaving and not to expect her back. Ever."

"Oh, no," my mother said.

"Oh, yes. Sophia ran out of the house and drove away. Uncle Craig, he felt so bad. But Sophia, she wouldn't answer his phone calls. Finally, she called her *mamá* and said she was at a friend's in Milwaukee and Aunt Lydia could come, but not Uncle Craig.

She never wanted to see him again. It was big family drama, and I wasn't even here." He added the last with a slight smile and a hint of wistfulness, despite the circumstances. Miguel does enjoy a big emotional display.

"So how does this relate to Craig allegedly killing Holly Mason?"

He sobered quickly. "I gave the renter Uncle Craig's number to call if anything went wrong in the house. On Saturday night she called him, because the toilet in the small bathroom was leaking onto the floor."

"Did he know she owned the website that 'ruined' his little girl?"

"No, I didn't even know. I mean, I knew her name, but I didn't know she was the one who owned the SweetMeets sugar daddy site. I didn't know anything about her. She was just my weekend renter."

"Then how did Craig find out?"

"He went over. He fixed the toilet. She tried to give him a tip. He said, no. Then she said OK, but she handed him her business card. And she said if he was ever in the market, she'd give him a discount on membership."

"Ohhh. He saw her name as owner or CEO or whatever of SweetMeets," I said.

"*Exactamente*. The site he thinks ruined the life of his little *bebé*."

"What did he do?"

"He didn't hit her in the head with a poker," Miguel said quickly, with a hint of anger so unlike him, it revealed how much strain he was under.

"Of course not, I just meant what happened next."

Immediately contrite, he said, "I know, *chica, lo siento*. I'm just so upset and so sad, and I feel so helpless. The police, they are so sure."

"I can't believe Coop would go after Craig like that. He knows him."

"It isn't Coop's case, Mom. It's Erin Harper's. The new detective—Ms. *48 Hours*. I wonder if she was running a stop watch on this one? But, Miguel, go back. What did Craig say happened with Holly after he figured out who she was?"

"He was really angry. He told her that she had corrupted Sophia; he said she was no better than a madam. He said she was a viper who destroyed his little girl and their family."

"How did she respond?"

"She just laughed. She said he didn't even know his daughter. But that he should be proud she was smart enough to use her assets so well."

"Oh, boy."

"*Sí.* He knew he better leave and calm down, so he did."

"And then?"

"And then, nothing. He went home. He had a glass of wine. He got out old family photos. He cried about his beautiful baby girl. He thought how much he loved her, and he felt like he had failed her. That if he hadn't got so sick, he could've taken care of her the way a father should. He felt sorry for himself, and about what he said to her, and he cried a little more, and he went to bed."

"But when you discovered the body, didn't he tell you he'd been at the house on Saturday night?"

"No! He didn't say anything to me. I just found out everything two hours ago, when Aunt Lydia called me."

"The police couldn't have just pulled his name out of a hat. How did they even know to question him?" my mother asked.

"They would've pulled Holly's phone records," I said. "If she called Craig the night she was murdered, that would have been a big red flag. Did he even tell your Aunt Lydia beforehand?" I asked Miguel.

"Only when the police came to question him. He had to, then. But they decided not to tell me."

"Why?"

"Uncle Craig said he didn't want Sophia to know anything about it, and he was afraid I'd tell her. And I would have. There are too many secrets in this family. He didn't know the police already found Sophia and talked to her. That's how they knew about the fight. He and Aunt Lydia thought if they didn't say anything, and because Uncle Craig didn't do anything, it would all go away. Only it didn't. The police got a warrant. They found Holly Mason's business card under his car seat."

"That doesn't seem like enough to arrest him."

"I don't know what else. Aunt Lydia was crying so hard, I couldn't get everything. She asked me to meet her at Miller Caldwell's office tonight. In half an hour."

"Miller? But he's not a criminal lawyer."

"I know, but he's a friend of theirs. *Chica*, will you come with me? I could use a friend."

Though I fleetingly wondered what good I would be, and whether I even belonged in this highly charged and frightening family situation, one look at Miguel's worried face made up my mind.

"Absolutely I will."

"Miguel!" Lydia Kowalski, her face tear-stained and tired, sprang from her seat at the conference table in Miller Caldwell's office as we walked in. Miguel wrapped her in a hug. As they spoke quietly for a moment, I turned to Miller, who looked fairly weary himself. Lately, I'd noticed that his bright blue eyes and the increasing ratio of silver to brown in his thick hair were starting to give him an Anderson Cooper vibe. Right then, with his eyes strained and the lines in his tanned face etched deeper through worry, he looked more exhausted than anything else.

"Miguel asked me to come," I said, by way of explanation, though my appearance didn't seem to surprise or concern him. "How's Craig doing?"

"He's all right, considering the circumstances."

"What do they have on him? Miguel told me he was at the house to fix a toilet, and when he found out that Holly Mason owned the SweetMeets site, he went after her pretty hard verbally. But, surely that's understandable. Craig's got no history of violence. He says he went home and stayed there, and Holly was alive when he left."

"The district attorney is pretty confident about the case. So confident, that he gave me a preview. They've got a neighbor who says Craig's car was at the house twice that night. So, they're going to argue it was a premeditated murder. That Craig fought with Holly Mason, left, then came back to kill her. He didn't come forward when her body was found. The first time they questioned him, he said he had no idea who Holly was. Then they found his daughter's connection to SweetMeets."

"How did they do that?"

"Cliff Timmins is so full of himself with the fast resolution to the case that he shared more than I would have if I were him. Craig was their favorite suspect from the beginning. Once it was established that Holly Mason owned SweetMeets, they checked to see if Craig was a client. He wasn't on the list, but another Kowalski was. Sophia. "

"Oh," I said, and nodded. "They did a classic good cop/bad cop with her, and got her to spill everything without realizing what the implications were."

"Exactly. She was frightened, and she talked too much. She told them about the fight and how upset Craig was. The police combined her story with the phone call from Holly to Craig, and the fact that someone saw Craig's car in Miguel's driveway late at night. It was enough to get a search warrant for Craig's car and house. They found Holly Mason's business card under the front seat. So, they knew Craig had lied when he said he didn't know who she was. That doesn't look good. Then they found a man's shirt stuffed in the bottom of a garbage bag in the garage. There were faint stains on the front. Their tests didn't detect blood—"

"Well, see then? It doesn't mean anything. It was just an old shirt he threw away. Big deal."

"The big deal is, it wasn't an old shirt. It was new. They're making the case that Craig wore the shirt when he killed Holly, and later he washed it in oxidizing bleach—unlike chlorine bleach, oxidizing bleach destroys blood evidence. Then, he got rid of it. When they found it, he said he'd spilled red wine on it, and when the stain didn't all come out, he threw it away. The police think the story is a little too convenient. Especially because he didn't mention drinking wine that night until after they found the shirt."

"Still, that isn't proof of anything. And he couldn't tell them about knowing who Holly Mason was and about the business card without telling everything about Sophia and SweetMeets. He was just trying to protect his daughter."

"It gets worse. The murder weapon is an old-fashioned fireplace poker. It's unusual. The handle is shaped like a top hat. Under its metal brim is a nice, clear thumbprint. Craig's thumb."

"But he didn't do it!" Lydia had obviously been listening. She looked ready to burst into fresh tears. Her long dark hair, which usually framed her oval face like a sleek and shiny curtain—the perfect advertisement for her *Making Waves* salon—hung lank and limp. Her brown eyes were red and puffy.

"I know, Lydia. I know. Please, sit down, please, all of you."

When we were settled, Miller said, "The police have a good case. Cliff is no fool. He wouldn't have had Craig arrested if they didn't. They've got a strong motive, clear opportunity, and physical evidence that includes the murder weapon with Craig's print on it. And Craig lied. No, just a minute—" he said, as Lydia started to interrupt.

"I've talked to Craig. He told me the same thing he told the police—that he washed his shirt because he spilled red wine on it. He said that he just grabbed some bleach off the laundry room shelf. He didn't realize that the kind of bleach he used destroys any evidence of blood. When it didn't get the wine stain out completely, he threw the shirt away. He said that his fingerprint was on the weapon because when he first got there, Holly asked him to help her get the fire going."

"There, you see?" Lydia said. But Miller shook his head.

"That's Craig's story, Lydia, it's not evidence. It's not proof that what Craig *says* happened, really did."

"Leah can find out what really happened. She can figure it out," Lydia said with certainty.

"Wait, what?" My sudden elevation to miracle worker was alarming. "I came for moral support, Lydia. I can't—"

"Yes, you can. You did it for your sister, you did it for your friend, you can do it for Craig. Please, Leah. If you work with Miller, I know together you can get Craig free."

Now it was Miller's turn to be the buzz kill. "Lydia, I'm not a trial lawyer. I explained that to Craig tonight. I know corporate law, but that's very different from what Craig needs now."

"I don't care about that. You know Craig. He needs someone who cares about him. Who believes in him."

He reached across the table and rested his large hand gently on hers. "The evidence against Craig is very damaging. I'm just not experienced enough for the case. We need someone stellar, someone who really knows the ins and outs of criminal law."

I liked how Miller used "we," instead of you. It's one of those things he does that makes you feel like you're not alone. Although I wasn't sure that I was ready for a spot on the team, one glance at Miguel's puppy dog eyes and I stopped protesting.

"Who are you thinking of?" I asked. I mentally ran through the lawyers in town, most of whom survived on court-appointed cases and dragged out divorces. I couldn't come up with one to whom the adjective 'stellar' applied.

"Gabriel Hoffman."

Miguel, Lydia, and I looked at each other. None of us recognized the name.

"Gabe is the nephew of an old friend of mine. He's been

working as a prosecutor out East for a while. He wants to make some changes in his life. I talked him into starting over in Himmel. He's going to join my firm. In fact, he'll be here Friday. He's already signed a lease on an apartment."

His answer surprised me. At one time, Miller had been president of the bank his great-grandfather had founded. He had also been a rising political star. Until a story I was working on uncovered a secret he'd been keeping for years. The collateral damage of my investigation had been unintentional, but tremendous. It had cost him a state senate race, a marriage, and for a while, estrangement from his teenage children.

He had rebuilt his life in a different way, with a focus on civic engagement and business law. But a sudden venture into the rough and tumble of criminal defense seemed impulsive and at odds with what I knew about him.

"Criminal law isn't exactly your line, Miller. And why would an East coast lawyer want to take up residence in Himmel, Wisconsin?"

"I've had some doors close on me in the last few years. I've gotten pretty good at opening new ones. I happen to think that Himmel could use a competent criminal defense attorney. And I'm ready to expand my practice. You know," he added, "I could ask you why a big city reporter would return to small town life. But that worked out pretty well, didn't it?" He gave me a wry smile.

"Touché," I said, but I hoped that for Craig Kowalski's sake, Gabriel Hoffman was coming to town with a lot less baggage than I had carried.

---

On Thursday morning, the paper carried a surprisingly small article for an event as major as murder. Rebecca had said

Miguel was too close to the story to do it justice. However, it looked to me like Rebecca was too distant. Her report was as bland and disinterested as though the killing had occurred three towns away. It said that Holly Mason had died, and a suspect had been arrested, but withheld Craig's name pending his initial appearance in court. No photos, no interviews with the neighbors. It read as though it were an ordinary police brief, the kind we wrote up for minor infractions. Proving once again, to my mind, that Rebecca had no news judgment.

Still there were enough people plugged into the Himmel underground communication network that when I stopped at the Elite, everyone was buzzing about Craig Kowalski killing Holly Mason. Miguel was scheduled to meet me for coffee with an update on his uncle.

I snagged a table in the corner and set up my laptop. Although I enjoy working in my office, or on my window seat, sometimes the hum of people around me, the overheard snippets of conversation, and the heady smells emanating from Mrs. Schimelman's kitchen are just what I need to get motivated. I was pretty deep into a tricky chapter when a familiar voice said, "Did you see my headphones? I must have left them at the paper, because I can't find them anywhere."

I looked up, but didn't say anything. Never a problem for Courtnee. "What are you doing? Did you hear about Miguel's uncle? Why are you just staring at me?"

"Because, Courtnee, I'm trying a new way to make you spontaneously combust with my mind powers. It takes concentration." I closed my laptop and moved it out of harm's way as she plunked down in the chair next to me with a very full pumpkin spice latte. "And no, I haven't seen your headphones. I'm not a regular in the newspaper offices anymore, remember? Shouldn't you be at work?"

"I am. My boss sent me to get coffee and pastries for a meeting or something."

I looked pointedly at her one cup of coffee and single rugelach. "And so, you're going to do a little loaves and fishes magic?"

"Is that a joke? Because I never know with you."

"No, not really. I'm not in a joking mood."

"Oh. Because of Miguel's uncle, right? I told my mom that Craig's really nice. I don't think he'd like, kill somebody. But she said, 'no smoke without fire.'"

"She and a disturbing number of other Himmelites, judging by the bits of conversation I've been overhearing."

"*Chica*! Courtnee, *muy bonita*, as always!" Miguel folded his lean frame gracefully onto one of the Elite's wobbly chairs. As he did, I noticed April hovering shyly behind him.

"April, hi!" I said, trying to keep the surprise out of my voice. What had originally been scheduled as a one-on-one meeting with Miguel had suddenly become a mini-party. He can't help himself. The boy has to social, even in the midst of crisis.

"I'm sorry to barge in. Miguel said it would be all right." She ducked her head, but not before I saw that her eyes were red and her cheeks blotchy.

Immediately, Miguel jumped up and put a hand lightly on her arm to lead her to a seat next to Courtnee, who looked decidedly displeased that she would not be the sole focus of his attention.

"April, this is Courtnee. She used to have your job at the paper. She works at the technical college now. Courtnee, April is learning about the front desk. She's having a *muy mal* day." He made no complaint about his own string of bad days that weren't going to be over until Craig was exonerated.

"Oh, Courtnee, it's nice to meet you. I think Rebecca is sorry that you ever left. There are so many parts to this job. I don't think I'm ever going to get it. I don't know how you could've kept everything straight. I'm afraid I'll never be able to do the job like you did."

*Let's hope not*, I thought, but in the interest of politeness, I refrained from saying it.

"I just can't seem to make Rebecca happy. She got so angry at me this morning. I think she might fire me." April's face flushed at the memory of her chewing out.

Cast in the role of wiser and more competent role model, Courtnee preened and bestowed a patronizing smile on her successor.

"It is pretty hard. And Rebecca can be a real biatch. People are always calling to complain their newspaper is wet, or it didn't get delivered, or somebody stole it. Like, who would steal the *Himmel Times*? But the thing is, just act like you care. All you have to do is say 'uh-huh' and 'oh, I see,' and then when they're done talking, just tell them you'll send a newspaper over right away. It's pretty easy, really, because then you just give it to Circulation to take care of. But then there's Rebecca. She always wants you to *do* things, like change her appointments or take her messages or whatever. Like you don't have your own things to do, right? Just pretend you're on the phone when she comes in, and fake like you're writing stuff down. The company phone, I mean, not your cell phone. She hates when you even like, look at a text on your own phone."

April appeared somewhat bewildered by Courtnee's passive resistance advice. "No, it's not that. I like to help, and the paper is so interesting. But today I thought I was doing something good, and it turned out all wrong."

"What happened?" I asked, shoving a napkin over to her as her eyes welled with tears at the memory.

"Well, you know she wrote the story about the murder, and —" Here she faltered, casting a glance at Miguel, but he was nodding sympathetically. "The news about the arrest came in so late, she just had time to squeeze in a couple of paragraphs. She had to change the layout and everything." I nodded. The situation wasn't all that unusual, and I still didn't see how that had set Rebecca off.

"Well, this morning I was working on the online edition, publishing some of the community news like Miguel showed me. And then I thought it might be good to post a picture of the woman who died. Not a picture of her body or anything," she added hastily. "Just a photo of what she looked like in real life. So, I Googled her and found a nice picture, and I grabbed it and posted it on the paper's website. I thought Rebecca would be happy. I was just trying to make her story better."

"That sounds like initiative to me. Maybe it just startled Rebecca. She's not used to it from the front desk." I looked at Courtnee, but the dig went over her head. She was sipping her latte and looking to upgrade her table for more interesting companions, as far as I could tell.

"She didn't like it at all. She made me take it down. She said I wasn't paid to make decisions, and if I couldn't do something as simple as follow orders, I wouldn't make it past my probationary period." Her lip trembled, and at that moment Mrs. Schimelman, who has a kind of Doppler radar for dejection, appeared at her side bearing food gifts.

"Here. You need some *apfelkuchen*. My apple cake make everything better. Ask Leah."

I nodded. "It's true."

"What's you name?"

"April."

"OK, April. You eat up. What's the 411?"

"Um, my boss, Rebecca Hartfield, she got really angry at me."

"Oh, that one." She shook her head. "You chill."

Then Mrs. Schimelman turned to me.

"I don't see it. That one and Coop. But what can you do? Love is strange, *ja*?"

"I guess," I said.

She leaned in confidentially, sweeping us all with her gaze. Nodding her head wisely, she said, "For Coop, it's like the *Bareback Mountain*. You know? He can't quit her." And with that she left.

Which is just as well, because despite April's emotional injuries from Rebecca's management style, and Miguel's ongoing worries, and Courtnee's unremitting self-absorption, and my disgust with Coop's choice, we looked at each other and couldn't stop laughing at Mrs. Schimelman's oddly appropriate misnaming of the movie *Brokeback Mountain*.

When we finished whooping it up, April reached for the napkins—this time to wipe tears of laughter from her eyes.

"Don't take Rebecca's criticism to heart," I said. "Obviously, you have much better news judgment than she does. I'd like to see a photo of Holly Mason and so would a lot of other people. In fact, I'm going to call one up now," I said, as I opened my laptop.

It didn't take long to find a photo of the owner of Sweet-Meets. In a shot that showed lots of leg and a cascade of red-gold hair, she smiled confidently at the camera. I turned the computer so the others could see. Courtnee looked up briefly from slurping down the last of her latte.

"Oh. Her. That's the woman Rebecca was talking to at the office on Saturday."

## 9

I glanced at Miguel and saw that he, too, had understood that we'd just heard the first tiny bit of information that might give us somewhere to go in Craig's case. But this was definitely not the venue to discuss it.

"Wow, look at the time! Courtnee you'd better go get those cookies and coffee, or your boss will send out a search party."

Courtnee remained unmoved, but my remark galvanized April into action. She sprang up from her chair.

"Oh my gosh! I have to get back to the office. Thank you, Leah, and you, too, Miguel. You made me laugh today, and I didn't think that was possible."

On impulse I said, "Miguel and I are doing dinner and a movie night at my place tomorrow. Why don't you come, too?"

The look on her face made me realize how lonely she must be. "Really? What time? Can I bring anything?"

"Around seven. Just yourself."

"OK, great! Thanks," April said, and she left smiling.

"What about me?" Courtnee's carefully arched eyebrows were drawn into a frown as she looked at me accusingly.

"What about you?" I asked, truly clueless. She had never

evinced even the slightest interest in any activity I was involved with off-hours, even though Miguel had invited her a time or two, over my protests. She never came.

"Well, maybe I'd like to be asked. Maybe people I used to like, work with every day, you'd think maybe they'd like to include me. Maybe they might miss me. You'd think. Maybe."

Hmm. She must be momentarily without a boyfriend, and maybe just a teensy bit jealous of Miguel's ready acceptance of April. Courtnee missed us—or at least some of us.

"OK. Fine. Whatever. Come if you want. But you'd better get going now."

"You're not the boss of me anymore, Leah."

"As if I ever was. Still, you'd better get."

Sensing that the only way we were going to be able to talk through the Rebecca-knew-Holly news flash sans Courtnee was to physically remove her, Miguel said, "Courtnee, I'll help you get your coffee and cookies and carry them to your car. You can tell me about where you got those *fabuloso* shoes. I love red *zapatos!*"

Smiling happily, her sense of importance restored, Courtnee tossed a "Bye, Leah," over her shoulder as she walked to the bakery counter. Miguel's phone buzzed with a text, and he glanced at it.

"*Chica*, I can't come over right away. Rebecca wants me to cover for her at the Rotary lunch, but I'll meet you at your place as soon as I'm done."

"That's OK. It'll give me a chance to do a little digging. See you when you get there."

———

I was so deep in thought considering the implications of Rebecca knowing Holly Mason that I didn't notice the car following me at a slow pace as I walked toward home. Until, that is, the driver rolled down his window and shouted at me.

"Hey! Nash! Where you goin?" It was Charlie Ross, in his own car, not his customary Sheriff's Department vehicle.

"Home."

"Get in, I'll give ya a ride."

"I'm less than two blocks from my place."

"I know. Get in." It was less an offer than a demand. I complied.

Once settled in the front seat, I asked, "What's up?"

"What makes you think somethin's up?"

"Let's see." I held up my hand and began ticking off items on my fingers. "One, you're tooling around town picking up girls instead of at the Sheriff's Department or out on an investigation. Two, you've never offered me a ride anywhere—though you've suggested I jump off a cliff several times. Three, you look like you did when Lamey took you off that overdose case."

"How's that?"

"Kind of like an angry bull terrier."

He was silent for a minute, and that was all it took for us to reach the parking lot behind my apartment. I waited. He switched off the engine and said, "Lamey put me on suspension this morning. I'm off the job until the disciplinary committee reviews my case."

"What? What for?"

"Insubordination. I told him he was a freakin' idiot. I said that if he didn't run the department into the ground before a real cop was named Sheriff it would be a miracle. And I mighta told him he'd be over his head in a two-inch puddle. I kinda lost track. I was pretty mad."

"Geez Louise, Ross."

I've been trying out some alternatives to my more "earthy" language, as my mother calls it. I'm kind of getting into some of the slang from the classic (and by that I'm talking black and white) movies that I love. I might just bring a few back—though I have to admit they don't always pack the punch I need.

"Yeah, I know. I just couldn't take any more of him and his dumbass decisions. He's only been on the job a couple of months and already he's let a judge's kid skate on a minor in possession, screwed up the chain of custody in a drug case, and promoted the only person dumber than him in the department."

No stranger to terrible bosses myself, I felt immediate empathy for him. At the same time, I knew the futility of fighting the situation with a smart mouth and bad temper.

"Ross," I began.

"No need to say it, Nash. I know. I screwed up. I'm mad at Lamey, but I'm really PO'd at myself. It's not gonna be easy for Allie, having kids think her dad got suspended 'cause he's some corrupt cop or something. And you know people. That's what they'll say. Or some of them, anyway. And if I get fired, which I probably will, I'm gonna have to find a new job, probably move, make Allie change schools again."

"Hey, whoa there, buddy. You're kind of getting ahead of yourself. Everybody knows what a moron Lamey is. He can't last much longer. He's going to explode with some monumentally stupid action, remark, or decision—or all three—that will blast him right out of his temporary office. Then, he won't be the one who decides if you go or stay."

"Maybe." Ross responded without conviction, looking so morose I couldn't just pop out of the car and forget about him.

"Look, it's almost noon. Come on up. I'll make us some sandwiches and you can cry in your beer. As long as you like Spotted Cow."

"So, they must pay you pretty good for typing, eh? Pretty nice place you got here."

"Thanks. I like it. You know, it's more traditionally known as writing when the 'typing' produces an actual book." My mild response caused him to look slightly embarrassed.

"Sorry, I—"

"I know, you just can't help yourself. That's all right, I can't either. I'm only cutting you slack because I don't kick a man when he's down. Usually." I handed him the cheese sandwich I'd made and got a bottle of beer out of the refrigerator for him. Then I grabbed my own sandwich and a glass of iced tea for myself.

"C'mon, you look as comfortable perched on that stool as a man on a flagpole. The window seat is nice. And roomy."

We carried our food over and sat companionably for a while, alternately chewing and drinking as we watched the traffic flow below. Finally, he said, "I read your book, you know."

"You did? You never told me that."

"I didn't want it to go to your head. It wasn't bad. You were a little rough on me, though. I'm a lot better lookin' than you described." He grinned. "Allie, she read it, too. She's been buggin' me to get you to autograph her copy. She wants to be a writer, too."

"She does? That's great. Have her give me a call. I'd be glad to talk to her."

"Yeah? Really?"

"Really. Is she settling in all right?"

He shrugged. "I guess. She stays in her room a lot. And she's always on her phone. She knows a few kids from spendin' time with me since the divorce, so that's good. She likes Kira Chapman. And I think she has a crush on the Fraser kid, Gus, but she gets mad if I ask her about him. It's kinda hard to know what you can say, what you can't. And what's

gonna make her run to her room cryin'. I don't want to screw
this up."

"I don't think you will. She's lucky to have a dad who cares
as much as you do."

He nodded his thanks, then just stared out the window. We
were done eating. I'd done my maximum daily outreach, but
Ross didn't show any sign of leaving. I wanted to get to my
laptop and do some thinking and checking on the Rebecca-
Holly connection. It felt a little heartless, but I needed to get
Ross out of there.

"Hey, you know what? Sit here, I've got something for you
before you go." I dashed off to my office, grabbed a copy of my
book and scribbled a short note to Ross's daughter. I figured I'd
hand it to him and walk and talk him to the door. As I turned to
leave, I banged my toe against something sticking out beside my
desk.

"Ow! What the—?" I bent down and saw that it was the box
Phyllis Stanton had left with me. I'd done absolutely nothing
with it. And now with Craig Kowalski's case looming, I wasn't
likely to any time soon. That's when inspiration struck.

I stumbled into the living room with the box and the book in
my arms.

"Ross, what are you going to do while you're off work?
Besides carpooling and side-stepping teenage drama, I mean?"

"Don't rub it in, Nash. I don't know. I never had this much
time off before."

"I've got something to take your mind off your troubles."

I put the box down on the window seat, and launched into
an explanation of Phyllis Stanton's request that Duane's last
"investigation" be completed.

"So, I couldn't say no, but now I need to help with Craig
Kowalski's case, and I won't have much time to spare."

"What do you mean, help? Coop's not heading that investigation up, and from what I hear, Erin Harper isn't someone that's gonna want you messing around in her case. She doesn't know you're a junior deputy, after all." He said the last with a small smile, referencing the many times he yelled at me to stay out of his business and to quit playing "junior deputy."

"Miguel wants me to help. And Miller is OK with it, and Lydia practically begged me. So, I think I'm on pretty solid ground. I'm a consultant for the defense," I said self-righteously —though no one had offered me that title.

"Well, good luck to ya. What I hear, it's not lookin' good for Craig."

"We'll see. But, anyway, what about Phyllis? Could you go through this box of Duane's stuff, and see if there's anything at all that might be worth pursuing?"

"Like the great paper clip robbery? Or the case of the missing manila envelopes? Come on, Nash. This nickel and dime stuff mighta floated Duane's boat, but you know as well as I do it doesn't amount to anything."

"I know, Ross. But it does to his wife. She loved that weird little guy, and I think it really matters to her to wrap up whatever big scandal he thought he had hold of. Sorting through that would give you something to do. You could chat with the city clerk or whoever's in charge of pencil stubs or whatever Duane was chasing, maybe write up a little report for Phyllis, and she'd be happy. And you'd be thinking about something besides Lamey and helicopter parenting. Please?"

He gave a mighty sigh and said, "I never thought I'd be takin' directions from you. But yeah, OK. I'll look into it and write somethin' up for the old lady."

And then, because he looked ready to settle back in, and I really couldn't be a drop-in center for depressed detectives, I thrust the box at him, and handed him a copy of my book as well.

"Here you go, then. And I had a copy of my book, so I autographed it for Allie. Tell her to call me if she ever wants to talk about writing. Thanks for coming over, and thanks for taking this off my hands." All the while I was talking, I had been closing in on Ross, adjusting the box in his arms, tucking the book inside it, and hustling him toward the door.

As we reached it, I said, "Call me if anything turns up. Thanks for coming by, Ross. Don't worry about Allie, I know she'll be fine. And, especially, don't worry about Lamey. I'm sure he'll be an ass, and get himself ousted before your review is done. I'll talk to you later."

And with a bright smile and a pat on the arm, I nudged him out the door.

There. Now I was free. And the first thing I did was zip over to my laptop, open it up, and Google Holly Mason. I was ready for a deep dive to see if I could figure out where and how she and Rebecca had first crossed paths. Because as I replayed in my mind the intensity level of the conversation I'd witnessed from a distance that day, I was sure that had not been a first-time meeting.

## 10

I decided to work back to front, because I was interested in Holly's origins first. I set the search parameters to cover everything up to the past year. After that I'd go back and see what she'd been up to in the last few months of her life.

I discovered pretty quickly that Holly Mason wasn't shy, and she wasn't a hypocrite. I found stories about her marriage to financier Ian Stoughton and their high-flying life in Chicago society, and then her tumble from the top when he was arrested for stock fraud. Most of those stories had an unpleasant undertone of schadenfreude. Then, she dropped out of site for a few years, only to resurface promoting her new web business, SweetMeets.

As the site began to take off, she was profiled in *Sassy Woman*, a local Chicago magazine, interviewed on *Entrepreneur Hour*, an early morning business show, and popped up as a guest on several podcasts. Taken all together, the sources pretty much laid out her backstory. Lower middle-class family that slipped into poverty when her father took off. Mother who was a religious fanatic, teenage Holly who rebelled. She left home when she went to Kinmont College in Los Angeles. She strug-

gled with the tuition until a customer at the upscale bar where
she worked told her about an easy way to make money. She
began working for an escort service, Sophisticated Ladies. Soon,
Holly was paying for college and had enough left over to help
her little sister. She eventually married a wealthy client, Ian
Stoughton. Quite the real-life *Pretty Woman* story.

The video clip from *Entrepreneur Hour* gave me the best
sense of who Holly Mason had been. In her figure-hugging
white dress, her thick, red-gold hair cascading down her shoulders, her bright blue eyes sparkling, she dominated the drab
studio set like a peacock in a desert landscape.

"So, Holly, you've been quoted as saying that your background gave you the foundations of success in your current
business. Can you tell us a little bit about that, and how it
helped you create your online dating site, SweetMeets?" The
host of the show was a type frequently seen on local chat shows
—not young, but not ready to surrender to middle age as his
overly white teeth and carefully styled hair demonstrated.

"Certainly, Jim. Years ago, I worked as an escort at a very
discreet, very successful agency. Sophisticated Ladies paid my
way through Kinmont College in Los Angeles. I left the business
when I married my husband—my ex-husband that is, but that
early experience came in handy when life threw a curveball
at me."

"I'll just tell our viewers, who might not know, that your ex-
husband is Ian Stoughton. He's currently serving a 25-year
sentence for a Ponzi scheme that duped investors out of millions
of dollars. How did his downfall, and the fact you were married
to "Mini-Madoff," as the press called him, affect you?" Jim
waited expectantly, perhaps hoping for a tear-filled recounting
of her emotional turmoil or a juicy sound-bite. Holly was
instead quite matter-of-fact.

"I put all my trust in Ian. I hosted his parties, attended his events, entertained his dinner guests. In return, he gave me a lifestyle I'd only dreamed of. But I had no idea what he was doing in his business. I was stunned when federal agents came to arrest him. Everything was confiscated—our home, our bank accounts, our cars—everything." Holly shrugged in the universal what-can-you-do gesture.

"Some people say there's no way you couldn't have known or at least suspected what he was doing. Some even say that you're sitting on hidden assets, waiting until your husband gets out of prison."

"To quote a friend of mine, I'm sitting on my best asset, and I've never hidden it." She grinned, giving him a chance to catch up with her joke. He smiled when he did.

"No, my husband Ian didn't leave any hidden treasure, Jim. In fact, I haven't spoken to him except through his lawyers since he was arrested. He simply refuses. The day the feds came, he kissed me on the cheek, said, 'We had a good run, darling. Take care of yourself.' And that was that. I lost everything, including the friends I thought I had. It wasn't the first time I've been left high and dry, but I decided it was going to be the last."

"And that's when you decided to set up SweetMeets?"

"Well, at first I didn't know what to do. I hadn't worked since college, and I had no skills. At least no conventional skills. I went back to my maiden name—Stoughton wasn't very popular in the Chicago area at the time. I connected with a discreet escort agency and started over. But it's a lot rougher in your thirties than it is at twenty-one. And I knew that the older I got, the tougher it was going to be.

"Then I read an article about an online dating service for sugar daddies and sugar babies. I've always believed in serendipity. I knew I could do that same thing. SweetMeets draws on something I know a lot about—what men and women want from each other. And the business gives me the control I believe all women should have over their own destinies."

"Can you tell our viewers something about how SweetMeets went from a gleam in your eye to an up and coming business? How did you launch it?"

"I had the basic parameters of how it would work laid out. Then we set a goal of getting five thousand subscribers before we formally launched the site. We recruited them through craigslist, banner ads, keywords on search engines. We hit that number within four weeks. The sugar babies get a basic membership for free, but they can upgrade for additional fees. The sugar daddies all pay the seventy-five-dollar monthly fee, but most of them opt for premium membership levels as well."

"You said 'we set' a goal. We? I thought SweetMeets was your company."

"It is, but I couldn't do it alone. I didn't have much capital to start with. My sister Suzanne is a social media marketer, and she really helped it take off. And, of course, I had to hire out the actual technology work. It would have been incredibly expensive, but an old friend agreed to do it for a share of the profits. It's worked out well for all of us."

"Did you have any idea it would take off as fast as it has?"

"I hoped, but I didn't know."

"One last question, Holly. How do you answer the criticism that what you're doing isn't really entrepreneurship? That it's actually prostitution, because you lure young women in to be exploited by older men?" He was clearly enjoying his attempt at hard-hitting journalism and waited with a "gotcha" expression on his face.

Holly leaned forward in an aggressive posture, forcing her questioner to lean back in his seat. "All the young women on our site are free to determine their own level of interaction and engagement, as well as the terms of their relationships. It gives women power. Some men, even some women, are afraid of that. I'm not. I won't allow you or anyone else to bully or intimidate me back to the nineteenth century, because I chose to control my own destiny." She wasn't smiling now.

It was fascinating to witness the way her surface cool confidence and good-natured bantering had dropped away in an instant. The interviewer's face looked as though the beautiful flower he had bent down to sniff had turned out to be a Venus flytrap.

Holly quickly realized she'd shown a side of herself that wasn't for public consumption. Without missing a beat, she resumed an attitude of bemused self-assurance. She smiled and touched the host lightly on his arm before sitting back in her chair and speaking again.

"Jim, forgive me if I was a little forceful. It's just that it's hard to keep answering a question that is really an attack on freedom of choice. Our sugar babies join SweetMeets because they want to. SweetMeets is all about their empowerment. Our site doesn't determine who they choose or why or when or how. We don't even receive any money from our sugar babies, unless they opt for a premium membership. I don't see our service as exploitation. I see it as a win-win for everyone."

The clip ended there. Public Holly was good. She came across as confident, frank, and much more sympathetic than I'd expected. But the angry response to the exploitation question, with its personal jab at the interviewer, gave me a glimpse into private Holly. It jibed with the harsh words she'd had for Craig as she taunted him about his daughter.

The video had given me a glimpse into who Holly Mason was. More than that, it gave me a clue into how she was connected to Rebecca. Holly had said that she'd graduated from Kinmont College in Los Angeles. Unless I was mistaken, and I didn't think I was, Rebecca had said that Kinmont wasn't anything she wanted to remember, and Holly had responded that she wasn't going to let her forget. Now, it seemed possible that Rebecca and Holly had attended the same college. There was one way to find out. A quick peek at Rebecca's resume.

## 11

I went down my front stairs and through the side door at the bottom that opens into the reception area of the *Times* to see if the coast was Rebecca clear.

"Hey, April, is Rebecca in?"

"Hi, Leah. No, she's at a hospital board meeting. Do you want to leave a message?" She was already reaching for a pink while-you-were-out pad, nearly knocking over a large Big Gulp sitting on the counter.

"Whoa there," I said, steadying the beverage as the ice sloshed around. "No, that's all right. I don't really need her, exactly. I need her office."

"Oh, well, I—"

"It's OK, I just think I may have lost an earring in there. It might have rolled under her desk or behind her file cabinet. I just need to take a quick look." April hesitated still, no doubt wary of incurring another Rebecca rampage.

"Seriously, it won't take a minute. I'll be in and out before she gets back. And if I'm caught or killed, like they say in the movies, you can disavow any knowledge of me." She grinned then, and I slipped quickly around the desk. "Thanks, April."

In the office, I made a beeline to the bottom right-hand drawer of her desk, where I knew Rebecca kept personnel files. I hoped that her own job-related files would be there as well. The drawer was locked, but the key was conveniently located in the middle drawer of her desk. Thank goodness Rebecca was unimaginative as well as orderly.

I unlocked the drawer, resisted the temptation to see what she had in my personnel file, and pulled out a folder marked "Career Moves." I leafed through and pulled her resume. A quick scan past her detailing of her fabulous qualifications, fantastic skill sets, amazing previous jobs, and I found what I was looking for. Bachelor of Science degree. Wait, this was weird. No mention of the school where she earned her degree. Why would she leave that off? I reached for my phone and took a photo of the resume. As I moved to slip the phone back in my pocket, my hand grazed the folder and knocked it off the desk.

"Drat!" Sheets of paper skittered across the floor, over and around the desk, and behind the file cabinet. I hurriedly picked them up and reassembled the folder. As I put it back in the drawer, I noticed a stray sheet under the far leg of the desk. I moved the chair and reached my arm as far as I could stretch, but I couldn't quite make it. I wriggled under the desk farther until the paper was within my grasp. As I did, I heard April's voice, about a hundred decibels above normal.

"HELLO, REBECCA. YOU'RE BACK. IT'S NICE TO SEE YOU."

Yikes.

"There's no need to shout, April, I'm standing right in front of you."

I scrambled from beneath the desk, banging my head loudly as I backed out. I gave an involuntary grunt of pain.

"What's that noise? Oh! Look what you did! How could you be so clumsy?" It was Rebecca this time who wasn't using her indoor voice. As she berated April, I put the paper in the folder, the folder in the drawer, locked the desk, and returned the key.

"Why would you have a bucket full of soda sitting on a work space? Do you know how many calories are in that disgusting thing?"

"I'm so sorry. You're right. I'm so, so sorry. I don't know how I knocked it over. Give me your jacket, please. I'll wash it. I'll get it cleaned, I—"

"Stop bleating! And stop swiping at my arm with that napkin. You're making it worse! You're leaving shreds of paper everywhere!" Her voice had returned to normal levels, which probably wasn't a good thing for April. Rebecca was always more deadly when she was calm.

I left her office and ran to the back door. I opened, then slammed it shut as loudly as I could. I sprinted to the front, rounding the corner so quickly I nearly ran into Rebecca. She had taken off her suede jacket to examine the damage. April stood to one side, her head down, like a puppy who had strayed from the paper.

"Rebecca! Oh, no. Your beautiful jacket. Oh, I'm so sorry."

"It wasn't you this time, Leah. It was April and her obesity-size soda."

"No, it was my fault. I was talking to her, and I left my drink on the counter when I ran out to get something from my car. If I hadn't, this never would have happened. Please, I know a cleaner in Madison that specializes in suede and leather. Let me take care of it for you." I took it out of her hands.

"Why would you do that? You didn't literally dump it all over me." She turned back to April. "For the sake of my wardrobe and your BMI, there will be no more drinking or eating at your desk. Understood?"

April nodded without looking up. I knew she'd sacrificed

herself to save me. Time to rescue her with a well-placed distraction.

"I'll get this back to you in a few days." I made as if to leave, then doubled back with an excellent *Columbo* move. "Oh, just one thing, Rebecca. I saw Courtnee at the Elite today. I was doing a little online research into the murder—I'm helping Miguel's family. Anyway, I pulled up a photo of Holly Mason while Courtnee was there, and the oddest thing happened."

"Well, Courtnee and odd go hand-in-hand, don't they? Nice seeing you, Leah—"

"Yeah. She recognized her. Courtnee said Holly Mason was the woman you were talking to in the office on Saturday afternoon."

"I doubt it. It sounds like another one of her faux celebrity sightings." Courtnee is convinced that Himmel is a mecca for famous people in disguise. To date she's "seen" Jimmy Fallon, Johnny Depp, and Jennifer Lawrence.

"Yeah, it kind of does. Except, I saw her, too. You were talking to her just before I came in. I saw you through the back door. I noticed her hair right away."

"What?" Her brow furrowed with surprise. "That's who that was? I can't believe it."

"You were talking to Holly Mason, but you didn't know who she was?"

"No. I didn't. I stopped by to pick up some paperwork, and as I unlocked the front door she literally followed me in. She might have given me her name, but I wasn't really listening. Started babbling about wanting a copy of the newspaper. She was one of those people who spew out a torrent of words without saying anything. So, that was Holly Mason. Incredible."

Yes, it was. The Holly Mason I'd seen online was not a babbler. And there are few people under the age of forty-five who actively seek out print newspapers. I'd really taken Rebecca by surprise if that weak sauce was the best she could come up with. I pressed my advantage. "You seemed pretty engaged in the conversation from what I could see."

"But you really couldn't see anything, could you?" Her eyes held a triumphant gleam.

"I can see farther than you think. For instance, I can see all the way to—"

I stopped mid-sentence as the front door opened and Coop walked in.

"David, what are you doing here? I thought you were at a meeting in Madison."

"I was. That's where I got this." He reached into the bag he carried and pulled out a soft, cuddly, teddy bear. "The woman at the toy store said this is the safest kind. The baby can't sleep with it at first, but she said they like to cuddle and it has these little silky ears. She said they like to rub them between their fingers when they go to sleep. But no buttons, nothing to be swallowed. Cute, isn't it?"

"Oh, yes," April said, shyly, adding, "Congratulations on the baby." She was rewarded with a broad grin from Coop.

He gave the bear to Rebecca so that he could shake April's hand.

"Good to see you again, April. It's been a long time since we were in Mrs. Byrd's history class." She beamed with pleasure.

And that's why Coop is a better person than I am. He remembered April, while I had to be prodded. And he made her feel like she mattered, while I'd basically just used her to get something I wanted.

"David, the bear is adorable. And you're adorable for buying it now. The baby isn't due for months," Rebecca said, anxious to focus Coop's attention on her again.

He smiled at her, and I felt something shift in me. He was so happy. He'd be such a good dad. And he was going to need all the friends he had to survive marriage to Rebecca.

"April, I'm sorry I got you in trouble with the boss. Rebecca, I'll have your jacket back to you in a few days. Maybe I can treat you to lunch to make up for the spill." Fake it 'til you make it. That was going to be my new creed. Although, really it was more like fake it, until you can fact-check it.

She looked at me with loathing, but in Coop's presence all she said was "I'll look forward to it." Though both of us knew it was never going to happen.

## 12

Coop's arrival had derailed my plan to put Rebecca on the spot about her link to Holly Mason through Kinmont College. Which, actually, I decided once back upstairs at my place, was a good thing. I needed more information before I confronted her. Sometimes the connections I see form a solid structure to build my theories on. But there are other times when my leaps go horribly awry. Then, I'm left with disconnected ideas that resemble a collapsed heap of blocks in a game of Jenga. I had to tread carefully, or Rebecca would go running straight to Coop.

Kinmont College, I learned online, is a liberal arts college founded in 1893. Its student population holds steady at around fifteen hundred. Alumni seemed mainly distributed in the business, law, medical, and academic areas, although there were a couple of recognizable names in the entertainment and government fields.

I did a search for yearbooks online that offered me a tantalizing peek at the *Kinmont Reflections* yearbook, but it wouldn't let me enlarge the pages enough to see the photos and captions up close. Not until I paid five dollars for a one-month pass to the site, which I did immediately. I could then zoom out the photos and even order reprints if I wanted to. Before I got started, my back doorbell rang. Miguel at last. I buzzed him through, but didn't look up as he walked in.

"There's iced tea or soda or a beer if you want it in the fridge. I'm just starting to dig into Holly Mason's, and I hope, Rebecca's past."

He didn't answer, and it hit me that the high energy buzz he brings into every room he enters wasn't there.

"What's going on?"

He pulled a stool up next to me at the counter, and I turned so I could see his face.

"I'm worried, *chica*. I've been thinking and thinking about all the evidence Miller said the police have. How can we fight that? Uncle Craig, he's like my *papá*. I love him so much. There's so much against him. We don't have anything *for* him."

"What? No way. Look, let's take a minute to recap here. One: your uncle did not kill Holly Mason, so that's a big plus for our side, right? Two: Gabriel Hoffman, Miller's big city defense attorney is coming to take on Cliff Timmins, and believe me, Timmins is no Jack McCoy. Three: the crack investigative team of Nash and Santos is on the case. Four: We already have a new person of interest, and it's Rebecca! How great is that?"

"Rebecca?" He said her name doubtfully.

"Yes," I said firmly. "Come on, Miguel, listen. Holly went to Kinmont College. That day she came to the office, I heard Rebecca say something like she wanted to forget Kinmont, and Holly said she'd never let her. They were talking about Kinmont College. It has to be. The question is, did Holly prearrange a meeting with her old pal Rebecca? Or was it a chance meeting? We don't know that yet. But does Rebecca tell anyone the dead woman is her old college chum, Holly Mason? Who she saw the very day she died? No, she does not. Now, don't you wonder why that is?"

"Well, yes, *chica*," he said, with less amazement at my powers of deduction than I expected. "But Rebecca as a suspect? Do you really think she could *kill* somebody?"

"You're seriously asking me that? Yes. Of course she could. And she's acting very suspiciously. Not only did she not tell the police that she knew Holly, she denied she had even talked to her when I confronted her. When that didn't work, she said she didn't know who Holly was when she spoke to her. If Coop hadn't walked in, she would have done a full Peter-in-the-garden and denied her three times. I was just about to spring their joint alma mater on her. I'm glad we got interrupted, though."

I filled him in on my act of espionage in Rebecca's office, and April's rescue mission. "April really stepped up for me. I hope Rebecca doesn't keep riding her so hard. And now I have to get the ice queen's suede jacket cleaned for her."

"I can drop it off for you. I have to take my leather coat in. Why are you glad you didn't ask Rebecca about Kinmont College?"

"Because, grasshopper, I don't want to tip her off about what we know. Or hope to know. She'll either try to sabotage our investigation, or have us assassinated. And you're young, you have your whole life in front of you. No, we're going to run this down and see. In fact, I don't want to say anything to your uncle or to Miller or the new attorney about it either. Let's just wait and see what we have. We don't want to raise false hopes."

He nodded. "Did you find out if Holly and Rebecca knew each other at school?"

"Just about to." I pulled up the Kinmont yearbook for 2000 and tilted the laptop so he could see the screen too. Then I zoomed to the senior class photos and found Holly Mason's right away. But when I flipped back to the page that should have had Rebecca Hartfield, she wasn't there. Miguel's face fell.

"No, wait. It could be they're not the exact same age. Holly might have been a year or two older. Maybe they were there at the same time, but not in the same graduating class. Let's flip through the pages and see if we can spot Rebecca anywhere."

Unlike a high school yearbook, this didn't have individual pictures for members of every year, only for the seniors. But there were candid shots of sorority and fraternity events, and sports and theater and debate groups.

"Remember, her hair will be a different style and maybe even a different color. I don't really think that white blonde can be natural, do you?"

We peered closely at the photos, going slowly, page by page. Miguel threw some serious shade at the hairstyles, male and female, but other than that we were silent. Dozens of photos of students cavorting about campus, playing sports and earnestly engaged in the classroom, but no Rebecca.

Then, on the next-to-last page, was a montage of photos from the Kinmont College Debate Society. There she was. Same white-blonde hair, same cool gaze, same confident stance. Except, instead of identifying her as Rebecca Hartfield, the cutline under the picture read, "Debate Society President, Natalie Dunckel."

———

"*Chica!* That's Rebecca. *Sin duda.* It's her—those eyes, that hair, that look. They have the wrong name in the cutline. We know that happens sometimes, right?"

"Yeah, it definitely happens. But I don't think it's very likely in a publication that gets vetted by as many eyes as a yearbook does. It's different at the paper. We're on a tighter deadline and have fewer people—especially nowadays. A yearbook has a lot longer for production, so, there's more time to get it right. And it's something people keep forever. It gets super-copy-edited. Getting someone's name wrong in a yearbook isn't a mistake likely to happen."

"But then—" His eyes widened, and I knew he'd reached the same conclusion I had.

"Exactly." I pulled the laptop over to me and quickly closed out of that yearbook and opened the one for the next year. I zipped through the senior pictures to the "Ds." There she was. Natalie Dunckel, aka Rebecca Hartfield. I shoved the computer toward Miguel, so he could see the photo.

"But why did she change her name? When did she do it?"

"C'mon. 'Natalie Dunckel' isn't exactly a power name, is it? It doesn't fit very well with Rebecca's persona. Let's take a ride on the Google machine and see what we find."

Some Dunckels and some Natalies but none that went together. "*Nada,*" I said to Miguel. "Let's try Rebecca's name."

The screen filled with dozens of hits from which it was possible to chart her rise through the ranks of the editorial side of reporting, her move to the business side, and right on through to her current job. The earliest mention was her byline on a story she wrote for the *Beacon-Banner,* a now defunct newspaper in Massachusetts.

"It looks like Natalie graduated from college, dropped off the face of the earth, and Rebecca was born. Let's see what Kinmont has to say about 'Rebecca Hartfield: The Dunckel Years.' "

Oddly, the answer was nothing. Colleges are allowed to release what's known as "directory information" about a student, which typically includes attendance dates, major, degree obtained, etc. However, a student can request in writing that even that information not be released. Which is what Natalie/Rebecca must have done, because it was a no-go with the registrar's office.

"But she'd have to let employers know. They'd want to verify her education," Miguel said.

"She could just tell the prospective employer that she'd changed her name after she graduated for family reasons or something. And then she could contact the school and give them permission to verify her graduation to a specific employer."

"Then we're at a dead-end."

"Maybe. Let me think a minute. In fact, you get the chips. I'll get the pretzels. And I think there's a bag of KitKat bars in the bottom drawer. Never underestimate the power of the three major food groups: crunchy, salty, and sweet."

We paused for refreshments, then I attacked the computer with renewed vigor. I went back to Natalie/Rebecca's graduation yearbook.

"What are you doing, *chica*? How is that going to help?"

"Oh, ye of little faith. See this guy?" I pointed to the photo of a pudgy, freckled, red-headed young man wearing glasses and a sweet smile. "I give you Merlin Duffy, our key to Natalie's past."

His doubtful expression didn't change.

"Merlin here is alphabetically linked to Natalie/Rebecca, and not just on the senior pictures page. How do schools organize groups of students? By last name. From the first freshman orientation through the last graduation rehearsal, Merlin and Natalie were seated or lined up next to each other. And, as an added bonus, he was also in the Debate Society photo. There's no way he won't remember her."

He jumped off his stool and pulled me off mine, smiling now. As he danced me around the room, he sang the last verse of Journey's "Don't Stop Believin'."

"*Chica*, I hate that song, but I love you. You are a genius. *Brillante*. We can do this for Uncle Craig, yes?"

"We absolutely can. And Rebecca is going to have a lot of

'splainin' to do. We are headed, my friend, for a karmic twofer. Which I think I'm about due for."

---

After Miguel left for his real job at the paper, I started poking around online. I found Merlin Duffy without any trouble. There were only two results, one for a seventy-five-year-old in Boca Raton, Florida, and the other for a thirty-eight-year-old in Good Fields, Oregon. Hooray for parents who bequeath unique names. Some additional surfing confirmed that he was our Merlin. The Kinmont College graduate was a veterinarian specializing in large farm animals, according to his website. The photo included with his bio showed that he hadn't changed much over the years.

Although it was nearly five o'clock in Wisconsin, it was only going on three in Oregon. I called Merlin's office number, but it went to voicemail. I left a somewhat ambiguous message. If Rebecca had been as nasty in college as she was in the office, he might not be that anxious to revisit the memories. I framed it by saying I was a writer doing research and I was hoping to talk to Kinmont College graduates from his class.

Then, because it was after five and it had been a very busy day, I poured myself a shot of Jameson over ice. It was getting dark, but I didn't turn the lights on. Instead, I went over to the window seat and watched as the street lights came on, slowly sipping my drink as I considered all the reasons why Natalie Dunckel might have decided to become Rebecca Hartfield.

## 13

"I can't believe I'm out." Miguel's uncle sat across from me at the conference table in Miller Caldwell's office. Miguel was on one side of Craig. Craig's wife, Lydia, was on the other. Miller was in the outer office talking to his secretary, Patty.

"And you're going to stay out," Lydia said, squeezing his hand. "Everybody knows you had nothing to do with this Holly Mason's murder."

That set off a fresh wave of tears on the part of Sophia, Lydia and Craig's daughter, seated next to me.

"I'm so sorry, *papi*. It's all my fault. How could I be so stupid?" Sophia's lips trembled and tears ran down her honey-toned cheeks. Even in despair she was lovely.

"*Niñita*, it's no one's fault, because your *papá* didn't do anything. Now stop!" Miguel said it sternly, but got up and came around the table to squat down beside Sophia's chair and put his arm around her shoulders.

"Miguel's right," Lydia said. "Your father didn't do anything wrong. Leah and Miguel are going to prove it. And they wouldn't have let him out of jail if they really thought he was guilty."

"Actually, that's not how it works."

The door to the conference room had opened without any of us noticing. A man with dark brown, slightly messy hair and a long, narrow face stepped into the room, closing the door behind him. He wore a white dress shirt with the sleeves rolled up. Though he sported a blue patterned tie and gray dress pants, no suit coat was in sight. "Gabe Hoffman," he said, extending his hand to Craig. "You must be Craig Kowalski. I'll be defending you."

Craig stood and shook Gabe's hand. "Miller says you're the best."

"He's right." His quick smile made him seem slightly less obnoxious. He shared introductions and handshakes with Lydia, Sophia, and Miguel, then turned to me.

"Leah Nash," I said, standing, so he didn't have the power position. His grip was firm, so I made mine a bit firmer, then released his hand quickly, before he could draw me into a handshake showdown. He gave me an amused look, affirming that he'd been aware of my small power play. Then he turned to Craig again.

"Sorry I missed your court appearance this morning. Unavoidable. Miller filled me in. You're lucky. Signature bond on a murder charge is hard to come by." His speech was quick with the intensity you often hear in East Coast natives, heightened by the gravelly quality of his voice.

"Then I guess it was worth replacing my St. Jude medal," Craig said with a wry smile.

"St. Jude?" Gabe didn't appear to be well-versed in Catholic saint traditions.

"He's the patron saint of impossible causes," Craig said. "Things have gone to hell since I lost my medal. Lydia got a replacement for me. Maybe that turned the tide in court today."

"Maybe we should all buy one. We need all the luck we can get," Gabe said.

"Craig doesn't need luck. He's innocent. He just needs you to convince the jury. You're supposed to be his lawyer. Isn't it your job to believe in him?" Lydia spoke with a flash of fire in her eye, and it was clear she wasn't very impressed with Gabriel Hoffman. First, he hadn't been there when Craig needed him. Second, he hadn't expressed sufficient support in Lydia's mind.

"*Tía*," Miguel said, putting his hand on her arm, "he didn't say he didn't believe in Uncle Craig. He just met him."

Gabe answered before Lydia could comment again.

"Actually, I don't have to believe in Craig, Mrs. Kowalski. I believe in the law. That's why I'll give your husband the best defense I can. And I'm a damn good attorney. Now, hold on." He held up his hand to hold-off Lydia, who was obviously not placated with the law's view of things.

"That said, I don't disbelieve Craig. I haven't even heard him tell his story yet."

"He's right, Lydia. But I'm going to say this once, so all of you hear me. I didn't kill Holly Mason. She was alive when I left at nine thirty that night, and I never saw her again." Every word Craig spoke was clear and carefully enunciated.

"Fine. Let's go with that. Now, Lydia, you and your daughter can take a break—go get something to eat, check on your business, whatever. I've got a lot of ground to cover with Craig. It will be easier without your input. Craig is my client, not the whole family."

"But—"

"Lydia, sweetheart, you're exhausted. Please, go home. Sophia can take you in her car, and I'll drive ours home when I'm done here. Don't look so worried. This is a good day, right? I'm out of jail, and I'll be home tonight. Let's be happy." He put his hand over Lydia's, and she gave him a small smile.

"OK, you win. But I'm not going to relax. I'm going to make you *arroz con pollo*. We're celebrating tonight."

Sophia didn't capitulate as easily.

"But, Dad, I should be here. This is my fault. If it wasn't for me, none of this would have happened. I want to help. I need to help."

Gabe spoke before Craig could. "Sophia, the best help you can give your dad is to let the two of us get to work. This is the first part of building his defense. I need him to focus on me and my questions, not on how you react to his answers. I understand that you feel bad. I would, too. But right now, you'll just be in the way."

"Sophie, please." The use of her childhood nickname seemed to break down Sophia's stubborn insistence.

"Oh, *papi*, I'm just so sorry, I—" Craig enveloped her in a hug, and when he released her, she wiped her eyes and said to Gabe, "All right. I'll go, but just so you know, I don't want to be left out of things. I'll do anything to help my dad."

"That's fine. Now, go, have a nice afternoon with your mother."

Lydia gave Craig a kiss on the cheek, then patted Miguel's arm. On the way out she turned back and said, "I'm counting on the three of you. But just to be sure, I'm going to make a novena to the Virgin Mary. For back up."

"I'm a big fan of back up." Gabe smiled, and after a second, Lydia smiled back.

Miguel and I had gathered our things to follow them out the door when Gabe stopped us.

"No. You two stay. I like my defense team to be in on things from the beginning."

"We're on the defense team?" Miguel asked, surprised as I was to have a formal designation.

"You bet you are. We've got to move fast. You need to be in

on what Craig and I talk about. If you're part of the defense team, then anything you hear falls under attorney-client privilege. And you never know when we might need to use that. I don't have time to check you out or look around for someone more seasoned. Miller says you're top-notch. I'm counting on that."

"Oh, we are," said Miguel. He stepped forward and draped one arm over Gabe's shoulder and the other over mine. "*Mira Tío*! Your new squad. And our squad goal is you, free."

Craig tried, but with Lydia and Sophia gone his shoulders had slumped a bit, and he only managed a weak smile in return. He started to speak, but Miller came in at that moment. Craig cleared his throat and started again.

"Thank you. All of you. The last week has been like a bad dream. What you're doing—especially you Miller, what you've already done. I'll never be able to pay you back."

Miller looked embarrassed and waved his hand in a deprecating gesture. Then he changed the subject.

"I sent Patty to the Elite to get some lunch for all of you. You've got a long afternoon ahead. Mrs. Schimelman's way with a sandwich will make you forget all about New York delis, Gabe. Right, Leah?"

"Absolutely."

"If you need anything else, just ask Patty. I've got a meeting in Madison that I'll be late for if I don't hurry. I'll catch up with you later, Gabe."

He clapped Craig on the shoulder and said, "You're in good hands."

**14**

---

We settled down with Mrs. Schimelman's sandwiches. Gabe took notes as Craig recounted his movements the night Holly was killed. After Craig had been through his story once, Gabe had him go over it again, only this time he interrupted him with questions.

"What kind of car did you drive that night?"

"My car. A Kia Forte5."

"What color?"

"Gray, I guess you'd call it."

"A neighbor says she saw you getting into your car as she got home around nine-thirty. Then, she saw your gray car back again around one a.m. How do you explain that?"

"I can't. I just know it wasn't my car, because I wasn't there."

"OK, we'll leave that for now. So, when you went over to Miguel's to fix the toilet, you had no idea who Holly Mason was?"

"None."

"And you were just being a helpful guy when you picked up a poker to stir the fire. That's how your fingerprint got there. Are you always so helpful, Craig?"

"I try to be."

"Whoever hit Holly Mason with that poker would've gotten considerable blood on himself." Gabe shifted gears suddenly. "Are you a helpful guy around the house, Craig?"

"Yeah, I try to help. We both work, so I do my share."

"Know your way around the kitchen, do a little laundry, that kind of thing?""

"Yeah, sure. But—"

"So, if you do the laundry, you'd know, wouldn't you, Craig, the difference between chlorine bleach and oxidizing bleach? You had both kinds in your laundry room."

"Yeah, we use one for whites and one for colors."

"What color was the shirt you were wearing that night, Craig?"

"It was white. A T-shirt. I was going over to work on a toilet for Pete's sake."

"Huh. OK, so let's go back to what you did when you got home after fixing the toilet—and having an argument with Holly Mason."

"I already told the police, and told Miller, and told you, when I got home I was pretty upset. I was angry at Holly Mason, but I was more angry at myself. I came down really hard on Sophia. I told her she had disgraced our family. I said some unforgivable things. But I knew that it was really my fault, my illness, my medical costs that made my little girl do what she did. Sophia is beautiful, brilliant, the light of my life. And because of me she degraded herself, and that woman made it easy for her to do."

"So, you were mad at yourself, but you were still pretty mad at Holly, then."

"You're damn right I was. She took advantage of my girl—of a lot of young girls, and she thought it was funny that I was upset."

"So, you'd already had one raging fight with your daughter that day. You were in a pretty bad temper when you went to fix the toilet, weren't you? And then when you realized who Holly Mason was, you got angry all over again. But you held it together, you went home. And then it started building again, didn't it, Craig? You sat looking at old family photos, thinking about your sweet little girl. You cried in your beer a little. Wait, no, it wasn't beer, it was wine, wasn't it? Your hand shook a little, you were so upset, and you spilled some on your shirt, right?"

"Yeah, that's what I said."

"Craig, do you drink a lot?"

"No. I never drink, not since I had a kidney transplant."

"But you drank that night, you say."

"I was in a bad way. My doctor told me I could have a drink once in a while. I felt like I needed one that night. Sophia and I had that horrible fight. Lydia was with her, trying to make peace. I worried that Sophia wouldn't forgive me. I said things to my daughter that I never should have. Nothing she could do would make me love her less or be less proud of her. I was just so stunned when she told me. Then to come face-to-face just hours later with that woman—"

"You blamed Holly Mason for Sophia's choices."

Craig repeated his story, trying to convince Gabe, who it seemed wasn't buying it.

"You're damn right I did. When I confronted her after I read her business card, she laughed, like it was really funny that she as good as turned my daughter into a prostitute. 'Get over it, Craig. I just put opportunities in front of smart girls.' She said sex is a commodity like wheat, or potatoes, or anything else you want to sell. For beautiful young women like Sophie, it's a seller's market. I wanted to shake her. I was so furious. But I didn't. I left then. When I got home, I was shaking. I needed that drink."

"OK. So, you had a drink. Maybe more than one? But it

didn't calm you down, did it? It fueled your anger at the woman who laughed at you, who made it possible, even inviting, for your daughter to make a terrible decision. And she'd get away with it. There was nothing you could do. You got more and more angry. You worked yourself into a towering rage, and then, finally, at one a.m. you what—decided to do the laundry?" His voice rose in mock incredulity on the last sentence. He stood and walked around the conference table until he loomed over Craig as he continued to badger him.

"You didn't do the laundry, did you, Craig? You got in your car and drove back to Holly's. You confronted her with all that rage that had been building for the last few hours. But she didn't care, did she? Your righteous anger had no effect on her at all. And the cooler she was, the hotter that anger burned inside you. Until finally, when she turned her back to show how little she cared, you couldn't take it anymore. You picked up the poker and you hit her, over and over, until she was dead!"

As Gabe spoke, Craig clenched his fists so hard the knuckles turned white. Gabe didn't seem to notice. Instead he leaned in, inches away from Craig's face as he continued.

"Then, you took her computer, her purse, and her phone, hoping police would be stupid enough to think it was a burglary gone bad. And you ran. You dumped Holly's things— maybe in a dumpster on the other side of town, maybe in the river, maybe at the bottom of one of those gravel pits I saw driving in. And when you got home, you did the laundry. And you used oxidizing, not chlorine, bleach on your white shirt, because you knew any trace of blood would be destroyed. The stains didn't all come out, but the evidence was gone. Then you threw the T-shirt away. You murdered Holly Mason and you tried to cover up your crime. Isn't that what really happened, Craig?"

Craig roared, "No!" and pounded the table. Gabe moved

aside quickly as Craig stood and pushed his chair back so hard it hit the wall. "That never happened!"

The commotion brought Patty scurrying in from the outer office.

"Everything all right?"

Craig was breathing heavily as Miguel put a hand on his shoulder, patting him, and gently pushed him back onto his chair.

Gabe walked over to Patty, who was hovering in the doorway.

"Yes, Patty. We're fine. Just going over some testimony," Gabe said.

She smiled uncertainly. "Well. All right then. Just let me know if you need anything." Clearly, she wasn't used to hearing thumps and shouting emanating from the conference room when Miller met with clients. As the door closed, Miguel turned on Gabe angrily.

"*Cabrón!* Why did you do that? You're supposed to be on his side!" I wasn't exactly sure what Miguel had called Gabe, but it was pretty clear it wasn't anything good.

Instead of answering Miguel, he turned to Craig. "The prosecutor is going to do that and a lot more. You have to be ready, Craig. He's going to try to get you to lose your temper, to show that you're the kind of guy who would lose control, pick up a poker, and whack a woman to death."

Miguel, in full protector mode, wasn't mollified by Gabe's explanation. "No! You didn't have to do that—push him like that. You're acting like he did it! Don't you believe him? He didn't do anything wrong! He—"

Craig spoke up then, sounding weary. "No, Miguel. He's right. I can't afford to give the prosecutor any more ammunition. Especially, when we don't have any of our own. I have to be ready for what he throws at me. And Gabe has to test me. My word is all we have."

"But it isn't!" Miguel said. Anxious to inject some hope into his uncle's dejection, he forgot that I'd asked him to keep the Rebecca stuff low key for the moment.

"We do have something. We—"

I caught his eye and frowned, and he faltered. I didn't want him spilling what we'd found out about Rebecca yet. It was too early and too amorphous. Also, I didn't know Gabe well enough to know how he'd respond. I didn't want to risk having him shut us down if he didn't think it was worth pursuing.

Miguel switched gears.

"We don't just have your word, Uncle Craig. We have your character—all the good things you are: honest, kind, the best uncle, the best father. When you say you didn't kill Holly, we know it's true. And we'll prove it."

"Craig's character is important, Miguel," Gabe said. "But it isn't going to be enough. Look, when I take a case, I'm all in. But I can't sugar coat it. This is going to be tough."

Miguel shrugged. "That's Leah's specialty. The tough ones." He turned to his uncle. "*No problema.* We'll prove you're innocent."

"The good thing is, we don't have to prove Craig is innocent," Gabe said. "The prosecution has to prove he's guilty. All the defense has to do is establish reasonable doubt. I need to develop an alternative theory of the crime—a plausible case that someone, or even better, several someones, also had motive, means, and opportunity to kill Holly Mason. I hope you're as good as Miguel thinks you are, Leah. I'm counting on you."

"She is," Miguel said firmly.

"*Chica*, why did you give me the stink eye when I started to tell Uncle Craig and Gabe about Rebecca?" Miguel and I were on the street outside Miller's office, about to part ways.

"I didn't give you 'the stink eye.' I just wanted you to remember that we agreed to hold back a little. I thought you were going to spill all our Rebecca ideas. We don't know Gabe yet, how he takes things. We need more information on Natalie/Rebecca before we share. All in good time, my pretty," I said, in my best *Wizard of Oz* wicked witch voice. "And you do look very pretty, Miguel."

Always sartorially splendid, even on casual Friday, Miguel was wearing a navy and green plaid shirt, untucked, dark jeans, an olive military jacket and khaki colored sneakers. Gosh, he's a handsome boy.

"*Gracias.* You know, you look *muy bonita* today. That green scarf with the burnt sienna shirt and the navy denim jacket, very nice," he said.

"You don't have to sound so surprised. I wasn't going to go to an important meeting in my Badger sweatshirt and jeans. And nothing's more important right now than helping Craig."

"It looks pretty bad for him, doesn't it? I was *furiosa* when Gabe kept questioning and questioning him, but I understand, now. I'm glad Sophia and Aunt Lydia weren't there. They're already so worried, and Sophia feels so guilty. I'm worried too, *chica*. Uncle Craig, he's always been there for me. You know, he's the first one I came out to, even before my *mamá*. He's not perfect, but he's a good, good man. I just want to help him so bad, but what if we can't?"

"Hey, hey, don't get down. Craig didn't do it. We know that. So, that means someone else did. We've only been on the case for a couple of days, and already we've got a lead. And once we dig deep into Holly Mason's past, that could turn up all kinds of people—and motives. Which reminds me, we should talk to her sister as soon as we can. The one who was in business with her.

"She could give us both a personal and professional take on Holly, and maybe on some of her friends—or enemies. Can you do some web searching and see if you can find any contact information for her? Her first name is Suzanne, but her last might not be Mason. She could be married or they could have different fathers. Look at SweetMeets first, the site and incorporation papers, she could be listed as an officer. You could try Spokeo, or Truthfinder or one of those other tracking sites.

"Sure, I'll see what I can find. But, you know, she might not want to talk to us. Especially me. My uncle is the one the police have told her killed her sister."

"Maybe. But sometimes people are so stunned and trying so hard to accept that a person they love is gone, that they have to talk. To anyone. We'll see what happens once we find her."

"OK. I have to shoot some pictures at the high school this afternoon, but I'll see you tonight. Can I bring anything for dinner?"

"Mom made too much vegetarian chili, so she dropped some off this morning, and some brownies, too."

"Oh, brownies! I love Carol's brownies."

"She knows you do. Don't think she'd bother to make them just for me. Anyway, if you want to pick up some bread at the Elite that would be great."

"Sure."

"Don't forget April and Courtnee are coming, too. We're watching *My Cousin Rachel*. The original with Olivia deHaviland. You'll love it. It's very dramatic, a lot of suspense. You don't really know if the villain is a villain or not—even at the end. I predict Courtnee will last about ten minutes after she realizes it's black and white."

## 15

"Your place is wonderful, Leah."

"Thanks, April." We had feasted on mom's vegetarian chili and a crusty loaf of bread, and then everyone helped with clean up. Except Courtnee, of course, who had taken a phone call which lasted just exactly as long as it took to clear the dishes, load the dishwasher, and wipe down the counter.

I moved the TV on its rolling cart into position in the living room and adjusted it so everyone could see. Miguel stretched out on the rug with a pillow. Courtnee and April sat on the L-shaped sofa. April looked happy. Courtnee was pouting. Something about her phone call must have upset her.

"I went with my sister June once to see *Citizen Kane* at a theater in Madison. I liked it, but I don't know much about old movies. Do you, Courtnee?" April asked shyly.

"I think old movies are stupid, and my boss is stupid, and my new job is stupid, and I hate it."

"*Chiquita,* why?" Miguel asked, instantly sympathetic.

"He's always telling me to do things, like type letters and make copies and schedule meetings. And I have to keep his calendar. Rebecca was bad, but at least she was gone a lot. He's always there. And he gets so mad if I get one little thing wrong. That was him on the phone."

Although Courtnee's job complaints aroused no sympathy in me, I knew we wouldn't be able to watch the movie in peace until she vented.

"What happened? Why did he call?"

"Why did they need a flyer anyway? Why couldn't they just put the notice about his talk on Facebook? But I didn't say that. I just did like he told me. I made his stupid flyer. I used spellcheck and everything. I had to go all over campus and put it up on bulletin boards and everything today. Now, he wants me to go take them all down."

That didn't make much sense. "Why would he ask you to do that?"

"Because I got one word wrong."

"That seems a little harsh. What was the word?"

She rolled her eyes and folded her arms, then finally said, "It was supposed to say: Anthony Griner, long-time director of public safety. I left out the 'l'. In public."

It took a second, but the three of us caught on all at the same time. And we started to laugh. We were laughing so hard even Courtnee had to join in, and we were so loud none of us heard the door to the loft open.

"You didn't tell me you were having a party tonight, Leah. I should've brought more wine."

Nick stood in the kitchen, a bouquet of red roses in one hand, a bottle of wine in the other.

"Nick!" Holy crap. I'd forgotten all about him. When we spoke on the phone earlier in the week, he'd said he'd be down Friday night to spend the weekend.

I leaped up and ran over to him. He thrust the flowers and the wine into my hands, and he didn't look happy.

"Nick, I'm so sorry. It's been such a crazy week. And with you at the conference in New York, we just haven't talked and I, well, I—"

"You forgot, is that the word you're searching for?" Nick is a very good-looking man with a charming smile and a pleasant, light voice. But he wasn't smiling at the moment, and his voice was more tight than light.

"No, no, that's not it at all. I just mixed up the date, I guess." That wasn't true. I had totally forgotten, but it didn't seem like a good idea to admit that at the moment.

"I'm so happy you're here. We were just going to watch a movie. Come on, sit down." I set the wine and the flowers down and took his hand to lead him to the couch.

"Oh, I should introduce you. You know Miguel of course, and Courtnee. This is April Nelson. She works at the paper now. We went to high school together. Oh, would you like a brownie? Mom made them, not me, so you're safe. You like brownies, right?" I was babbling now.

"Hello, April," he said, extending a hand to her and ignoring me. "Always a pleasure to meet Leah's friends. She has so many of them." April, unaware of the undercurrent, smiled happily.

Miguel is more sensitive to atmosphere, however, and I saw by his expression he knew trouble was brewing.

Turning back to me, Nick said, "Where's Coop? It's not a party without him, is it? Why don't you call the newlyweds? And your mother and Paul. And why not Father Lindstrom, too? Why don't we all celebrate our reunion together?"

OK, that was enough. It was a recurring argument between us. He felt I didn't value our time together as much as he did. It wasn't true. But my friends and family are important, too. I felt bad that I'd hurt his feelings. It really was just because so much was going on. But now his sarcasm was embarrassing the others and making me mad.

"You want to take this into my office, Nick? I don't think everyone else wants to hear you lay out your insecurities."

"Oh, really? Is that what this is? I'm insecure if I think that after being apart for weeks, you might want to spend some time just with me?"

Out of the corner of my eye, I could see that contrary to my assertion, Courtnee was very much wanting to hear everything in this relationship drama. But April had already grabbed her coat, and Miguel was taking Courtnee by the elbow as he said lightly, "Come on, *niños*. I think it's my turn to buy a round at McClain's. Let's go. It's not good for us to see *Mamá* and *Papá* fighting. We'll catch a movie another night." He touched his index finger to his forehead in a small salute to Nick, patted me on the arm, and shepherded his charges out the door.

---

"Are you happy now? You just embarrassed me, and my friends, by acting like an insecure jerk." I put the roses in water as I was talking, jabbing each stem down into the vase as though I were stabbing someone.

"No, I'm not happy. And I'm not an insecure jerk. I'm sorry if I was rude—"

" '*If*?' '*If* ?' you were rude? This is *my* house, even if you do have a key. Those are *my* friends. I invited them here. Courtnee and Miguel can take care of themselves, but April is very shy and doesn't need to be made to feel like she's unwelcome. Which is what you did. Nick, you acted like an ass. Ouch!" I jabbed my finger with a thorn and blood welled up. I turned to the sink, but Nick was already there running the water. He took my hand and ran my finger under the faucet. I was still mad, but I didn't pull away.

He turned off the water, then turned up my hand and kissed the injured finger.

"I'm sorry, Leah. I didn't mean to be an ass. I didn't mean to embarrass you or your friends. I was just disappointed. I've been looking forward to this weekend. Sometimes, I feel like you have more fun with your friends than you do with me."

"I have different fun, not more fun," I said, dropping my hand and folding my arms across my chest. "Having them here didn't make me any less glad to see you. I don't get all mad when you do stuff with your colleagues or your friends."

"But you don't just 'do stuff.' You're all in, all the time, and it feels like there's just not enough Leah to go around. And sometimes I wonder if you're still punishing me for that thing with Seraphina."

"Don't wonder. I'm not. And it wasn't 'that thing.' It was an affair."

"I know what I did. It was the biggest mistake of my life. But I'm different now. Losing you forced me to grow up. I've changed, and I've tried to prove it to you. I won't let you down again. I just want to know that I'm as important to you as you are to me." His wheat-colored hair flopped endearingly across his forehead. His green eyes, wide and earnest, brimmed with sincerity; his brow furrowed with concern. Lord, he was good looking.

I didn't answer at first. Nick was everything I'd ever wanted —when I was twenty-three. But I wasn't at all sure he was what I wanted now. I'd grown up, too. I no longer craved devotion. I didn't need outside affirmation of my worth—well, most of the time I didn't. But he still had a pull on my heart. And right then, I didn't have the energy for a soul-searching conversation with him. So, I opted for deflection.

"Nick, I'll be honest, I did forget you were coming. And if you'd done that to me, I would've felt hurt, too. But it wasn't because I didn't want to see you, or didn't have time for you. It's just been a pretty wild week. I texted you the bare bones, but it's a lot more than that. Do you want to hear?"

"I'll pour some wine. Then, we'll sit on the couch in front of the fire, and you can give me every detail."

And that's what I did. Nick is a good listener. I went through everything in detail: Rebecca's surprise pregnancy, Courtnee's firing, April's hiring, Holly Mason's murder, Craig's arrest, the case against him, Miller's new hotshot criminal defense lawyer, Gabe Hoffman, how I discovered Rebecca's lie about her name, and about knowing the dead woman, my agent Clinton's nagging about my book deadline. I even threw in the visit from Duane Stanton's widow asking me to go through a box full of Duane, which task I'd passed off to the suspended detective Charlie Ross. When I finished, I took a long gulp of wine.

"OK. You're forgiven. I guess you did have a lot on your plate this week."

"So? What do you think? It looks bad for Craig. But the fact that Rebecca is lying about knowing the murder victim, and that she's been living under an assumed name, that's pretty interesting, isn't it?"

"Yeah, it is. But she could have a lot of reasons for that. Maybe she's estranged from her family, and she didn't want them to find her. Maybe she changed it for professional reasons. Rebecca Hartfield sounds a lot more like an up and coming media magnate than Natalie Dunckel, you have to agree."

"I know, I know. But it's the only lead we have so far. I'm going after it full tilt."

"Sure, I understand. But does Coop know you're investigating his wife?"

"Not exactly. Not really. No. Not at all."

"How do you think he'll feel about that?"

"He might never know. If we don't turn up anything that

pertains to Craig's case, nothing need be said. Why are you looking at me like that?"

"Because I'm amazed at your unending capacity to deceive yourself. You know Rebecca is living under an assumed name, and you're not going to tell Coop?" He shook his head in disbelief.

"Leah, I know you. You won't be able to sit on that information, even if it turns out to have nothing to do with this murder. You detest Rebecca, and you want to protect Coop."

"Maybe. That doesn't mean that I'd deliberately try to hurt her—or him. I don't *want* her to be guilty of anything, but you have to admit, it sure looks like she could be."

"And pointing the finger at Rebecca would give his attorney —what's his name? Gabe?"

I nodded.

"It would give Gabe a chance to build his alternate theory of the crime, right? But throwing Rebecca under the bus isn't going to end well for anyone—Rebecca, Coop, or you."

"You forgot Craig. It's going to end very well for Craig if we can get him out from under a murder charge. And why do you care so much about my friendship with Coop? You're the one who doesn't want me to have any friends, remember?"

"No. I refuse to go back down that road. We're not going to fight." He took my wineglass out of my hand, and set it down on the coffee table. Then he pulled my head to his shoulder and began softly twirling a strand of my hair. The dark room, the fire, the wine. I felt myself relax and the irritation fall away.

"Mmm. You smell really good," I said.

"You do, too. And you look really good, and you feel really good. And I think I'd really, really like to kiss you."

His lips were soft and warm. Pretty soon I forgot about murders and investigations and Coop and Rebecca. And I didn't think about them again until Sunday morning.

"This is really good," I said around a mouthful of fried eggs, over easy. "I didn't know I had any eggs in the fridge."

"You didn't," Nick said, as he put more bread in the toaster. "I went to the store while you were still sleeping. All you had was an outdated carton of yogurt, three beers, wilted lettuce, and a Styrofoam container filled with an unidentifiable something."

"Ah, but you didn't look in the freezer, did you? That's where I keep my gourmet food stuffs: pizza rolls, fish sticks, and Ben&Jerry's."

"You need a keeper. I don't know how you subsist on the diet of a 12-year-old boy. I might have to move in just to keep you from starving." He smiled as he said it, but I felt my stomach clench. He'd dropped hints before about us sharing quarters. I ignored them, but they were getting more frequent. When I fell in love with Nick the first time, I was the one who wanted more, who wanted to talk about our future, who would have been thrilled to hear the undercurrent of longing in his voice. Now, however, it made me feel wary and ill-at-ease. I cared about him —maybe I even loved him—but I wasn't ready for the step he clearly wanted us to take.

"Not much danger of that," I answered lightly, ignoring the last part of his remark. "Not with the Elite just blocks away, and McClain's Bar&Grill within walking distance. And of course, Carol Nash's soup kitchen. So, you didn't finish telling me about your new research project. Who else is working on it?"

I knew he wouldn't be able to resist talking about his work. He told me in detail about the double-blind studies and control groups. He explained how he and his research partner were dividing up the work. He said he was optimistic about their chances for publication. And it made him really happy to talk about it.

Maybe instead I should have talked to him about where our relationship was, explained my ambivalent feelings, explored my reluctance to commit, listened to his perception of things. But I didn't want to risk our lovely weekend ending as it had begun, with an argument and hurt feelings. So, I listened, and I smiled, and I returned his goodbye kiss with as much fervor as he gave it. And I meant it. And yet...

## 16

"Leah, come in, come in," Father Lindstrom said, opening the door when I knocked later that Sunday afternoon. After a fire last year destroyed the rectory, he'd moved into a small apartment a block from St. Stephen's Church. It wasn't as convenient as his little house next to the church had been, but he never complained.

"Can I get you a cup of tea? I'm having one," he said, indicating the *X-Files* mug that sat on the coffee table. His living room had been decorated with cast-offs and donations—a swank leather sofa from Miller Caldwell, an oversized plaid recliner from the football coach's wife, a Tiffany floor lamp, an early American style rocker. As a result, it looked more like the furniture section of a thrift shop than a living room, but Father Lindstrom has the ability to make wherever he is seem cozy.

"I shouldn't. Mom called and asked me to pick up some photos for the church website. She said she didn't want to keep Mike Chapman waiting, because he's doing the site for practically nothing."

"I didn't realize she had left the photos here. I would've

taken them over myself if she'd called. You didn't need to make a special trip."

"Oh, but I did. Mom is cooking dinner for Paul, but she wanted to share the dessert she made with you." I pulled a tin of Mom's molasses spice cookies out of the bag I was carrying and opened it. "These will go good with your tea."

His light blue eyes lit up as he saw them. "Your mother is a treasure, Leah. A true treasure," he said, taking the tin from me.

"Mmm. So she tells me."

"Sit down for just a minute, have a cookie with me."

"You talked me into it." I took a cookie from the container he proffered and sat down in the rocking chair. He took one and returned to his seat in the plaid chair that was so large, his feet barely touched the floor.

"Don't tell Mom," I said between bites. "These are supposed to be for you."

"Well, it won't hurt me to forego one or two," he said, patting the slight paunch in his middle. "Now, tell me, how did things work out with you and Coop? I've been praying for you. Did you come to an understanding about his marriage?"

"Maybe. Not really. It's kind of complicated now. You know Rebecca's pregnant, right?"

He nodded, which confirmed my suspicion that he'd been holding back when I had talked to him the week before.

"Coop's pretty excited, and I was going to try and just shut up and be supportive, but I'm finding out some things I think maybe he should know. Things about Rebecca," I said. I hadn't intended to bring the fake identity up at all, but Father Lindstrom has a way of drawing things out of people, without doing anything but looking at you with the kindest expression on his face. All of a sudden, I was spilling everything I'd found out about Rebecca.

He didn't say anything. He rarely does unless he's asked. I continued.

"I think it might be a way for Gabe—that's Craig's lawyer—to show that someone else had a motive for killing Holly. Plus, Rebecca had the opportunity, too. She stayed in town while Coop was at his grandmother's on the night Holly died."

"Aren't you putting the worst construction on it? She wasn't with Coop, but perhaps she spent the evening with a friend, or was busy doing something quite innocent."

"Yes," I agreed reluctantly. "It's possible. I haven't had time to really check it out. But I'm not so much trying to pin the murder on her, as to just help Gabe establish reasonable doubt. But even if that doesn't pan out, don't you think that I should tell Coop that Rebecca changed her name? And anything else I find out about why she did it?"

"You're assuming that he doesn't already know."

That brought me up short. I'd been so focused on Rebecca's deviousness that I hadn't considered that she may have already told Coop what she'd done and why.

"Maybe she did," I said, my voice filled with doubt. "But in my experience, Rebecca isn't one to show her hand."

"But Coop is her husband. Doesn't it seem likely that she wouldn't keep anything hidden from him?"

"You don't really know her, Father. She's very capable of lying, maybe *especially* to her husband."

"But if she has told Coop, and he's chosen to keep her secret, might he not be upset that you've uncovered it? And even if she hasn't told him, do you think he'd welcome that news from you?"

"But if she hasn't, isn't the truth important?"

"Of course it is. But it's not always our place to tell it. An elderly priest I once knew gave me three guidelines that I have found very helpful in life. Perhaps it's my turn, now that I'm an elderly priest myself, to share them with you."

"OK. What are they?"

"Ask yourself: *Is it true? Is it my truth to tell? Can I tell it with love?* If you can answer yes to all three, then act on it."

I sighed and stood, my cookies gone, as well as my thoughts of telling Coop anything.

"I don't know if it's true. It's probably not my truth to tell. And where Rebecca is concerned, I definitely can't tell it with love. I see your point, but I'm not sure it applies here. This is a pretty big deal. But I'll think about it, I promise. Now, I'd better get this stuff over to Mike's."

———

Mike Chapman is the IT guy for the city of Himmel. I knew him a little from covering city hall, and his wife had been my high school art teacher. I pulled into the driveway as the front door opened, and she came out.

"Hi, Mrs. Chapman," I said.

"Leah! It's OK to call me Noelle, you know," she said with a smile.

"Right, sure, I know." It's funny, but even when they're not all that much older than me, I find it hard to call teachers I had in high school by their first names. I felt a little embarrassed at my ridiculousness and changed the subject quickly.

"That's quite a bumper sticker." I pointed to where bright yellow lettering, accompanied by a saxophone with musical notes drifting out said "I'm Saxy and I know it. Himmel Band Parent."

She rolled her eyes and laughed. "Kira is absolutely morti-fied. She plays in the band and Mike thought it was really funny to put that thing on his car. He's more of a kid than she is, I think."

I saw then that she had car keys in her hands and a purse over her shoulder.

"Oh, hey, I'm blocking you in. I just came to drop something off for Mike. I'll move—"

"No, no. You're fine. The van is parked in the street. I'm just waiting for my man, Brendan. There he is," she said, turning as the front door opened slowly. Noelle is a pretty woman with light brown hair and a wide smile that grew wider as a little boy, with big brown eyes and a blond crewcut, walked slowly toward us, favoring his left leg.

"Mom, Mom!" he said.

"Just a sec, Brendan, I'm talking to someone."

"Sorry, Mom."

His words were slow and very deliberate as he strived to enunciate clearly. Brendan Chapman was six years old. Three years earlier he and his mother had been in a serious car accident. Noelle had only minor bruises and sprains, but Brendan had sustained a serious leg fracture as well as closed head injuries. He'd spent a long time in the hospital. He was still going through therapy for his leg and for a speech impairment caused by his brain injury.

"Hi, Brendan. I'm Leah, do you remember me?"

He peered out shyly from behind his mother and shook his head.

"That's OK. I remember you, though. I took your picture at the preschool picnic when you won the stuffed panda bear. It was almost as big as you."

He grinned then, and tugged at his mother's leg until she leaned down. He whispered in her ear. She smiled and said, "You can tell her yourself, honey."

I put down the box I was holding and squatted until I was on eye level with him.

"What's the story, Brendan?"

"I. I have myee, myy ba-er, my bear, on my bed. Clancy." I strained to understand him as he concentrated fiercely to get his sentence out. It almost broke my heart to see him struggle, but I knew from what my mother had told me that he'd made tremendous strides over the past year.

"Wow. Clancy is a great name for a bear. I bet you have some good times together."

He nodded vigorously, and I held up my hand for a high five. When he gave it, I made a production of falling over with the force of his hit, and he laughed loudly. What can I say? Kids love slapstick, and I can't resist the chance to get a laugh.

"Honey, you forgot your towel. Scoot back in and get it, or we'll be late for swim therapy," Noelle reminded him.

"OK, Mom." He ducked his head and looked up at me from under his lashes with a shy smile that would make the hardest heart melt. "Bye!" He walked back to the house with a measured step that showed it was an effort.

"He's really a cutie, Noelle. It looks like he's doing pretty well."

She nodded. "It's amazing how far he's come. And frightening how much it costs. Mike's always been great with money —not me, I'm afraid. But Mike, he just jumped right in, reorganized our budget, started taking on more outside work, still keeps up with his job with the city. In fact, he puts in so many hours, I worry about him. But he never complains. He says it's all worth it, and I can't argue when I look at Brendan."

"I haven't seen Kira in a long time. How's she handled all of this?"

"Well, last week I would've said perfectly." She grimaced. "This week, I have to say she's a teenager. She's always great with Brendan—he adores her. But she's been pretty touchy with us lately, Mike especially. But when we call her on it, she just shuts down and says nothing's wrong. I think she may be having boy troubles, but who knows?" she shrugged.

"That sounds like pretty normal teen girl behavior to me."

"I guess. It's been so long, who can remember? Well, I've got to get something out of the garage. Go right on in the house. Mike's office door is closed. It's on the left at the end of the hall. He does that so the kids know not to disturb him, but you can just knock and go in. It was nice seeing you again. Say hello to your mother for me."

"I will. Good seeing you, too."

## 17

"Come on in," a male voice answered in response to my tap.

"Hi, Mike. I come bearing photos. Mom said you were in the middle of things, and she didn't want to hold you up."

"Thanks, Leah." Mike is around forty-five or so, and good-looking in a dorky TV dad kind of way. His ash blond hair is receding a little, he has a tiny paunch starting, and faint worry lines in his forehead. But his eyes are a startlingly clear blue. He's on the quiet side, and he has a husky, warm voice.

"I just saw Noelle and Brendan. He's sure a cute little guy." He took the box from me and set it on the long part of an L-shaped desk that held his computer and monitor.

"He's a trooper," Mike said. "So's Noelle. It's amazing what she's helped him accomplish. And she never complains, never lets him get discouraged. She's been terrific."

"Well, according to her, you're pretty special, too."

He waved off the compliment. "Noelle had to give up her job, something she really loved. All I've had to do is up my output a little doing side jobs, and it's something I like. It takes effort, but it's not hard if you're working at something you enjoy. You must know that, right?"

"Yeah, I do. Investigating and writing are things I love to do."

"I thought your book was really fine work. When will the next one come out?"

"You sound like my agent." I smiled. "I'm workin' on it, but I've gotten a little sidetracked lately."

"I heard you're helping Craig Kowalski's lawyer. Some East Coast attorney Miller Caldwell brought in. Do you think Craig's got a chance? I don't pay much attention to gossip, but it's hard to avoid hearing some of the details. People are saying Craig's daughter got tangled up in that woman's sugar daddy website, and Craig went ballistic. I'm not sure I blame him, if it's true. If Kira was ever taken advantage of like that, I'd probably do the same thing."

"So, everyone's decided Craig is guilty?"

"No. I didn't mean that. Craig's a good guy. He and Lydia helped us out a lot after the accident. It's just, you know, talk going around. You're working for him, so I guess you don't think he did it?"

"No, I don't. He loves his daughter, and he's got a temper, but I don't believe he'd kill anyone. He almost died himself not very long ago, from kidney failure. I think he values life too much to take it away from anyone. Craig's done a lot of good things for the town. I hope people can give him the benefit of the doubt." My tone was disapproving, and Mike seemed to think I was coming down on him. Which maybe I was, a little.

"I don't think anyone wants to hurt Craig. Lots of people like him. But it's just that everybody's kind of curious. You can't blame them, right? Mystery woman comes to town, gets murdered, local girl part of online hook-up site. It's pretty big news. That's all." He looked like he wished he'd never said anything.

Still, he was right. Holly's murder and the circumstances surrounding it were, after all, perfect fodder for speculation.

And there's nothing a small town likes more than a good round of gossip and conjecture.

"Sorry, didn't mean to kill the messenger. People like to talk, I get it. I just feel bad for what Craig and his family are going through."

"You think you're going to be able to help him? Have you got anything to go on yet? Any other persons of interest—that's what they call them on TV, right?"

"Maybe, but nothing I want to talk about."

"Right. Right. Sure. Don't want to give the defense game away. Well, I wish you luck. Craig, too."

---

On the way out the door, I met Mike's daughter, Kira, and Charlie Ross's daughter, Allie, as they were coming in. I was surprised at how grown-up Kira looked. The last time I'd seen her, she was a tow-headed kid trailing after her mother. Now, she was a tall, cool, blonde who made a sharp contrast with Allie's dark intensity. Kira said hello, politely enough, but it was Allie who greeted me like a bestie.

"Leah! Thanks so much for the book. It's sooo good. And the autograph was really cool, too."

"You're welcome, Allie. I'm glad you like it. What are you guys up to?" I turned to include Kira in the conversation, but she was busy texting.

Allie answered. "We were just hanging out at Gus Fraser's house."

Maybe helicopter dad Charlie Ross had played it right. Even though Allie had writhed with embarrassment when her father linked her up with the Frasers' kid. Now it looked like she had at least two friends in Himmel.

"Sounds like fun. Nice to see you. You too, Kira," I said with a light tap on her arm which elicited a perfunctory smile and a nod before she went back to her screen. I took a few steps down the driveway before Allie called me back. "Leah? Could you wait just a sec?"

I turned, and as I rejoined them, she said. "Um, I was wondering ... " She looked down and started fidgeting with the button on her jacket. Without looking up, she went on.

"I totally understand why you wouldn't. My dad said you're working on that Holly Mason murder, and you're writing another book. So, like I get that you're super busy. If you totally don't want any part of this narrative, no worries—" She looked up then and switched from fiddling a button to twisting a strand of her exuberantly curly, dark hair.

"Allie, just ask me. Please. The suspense is killing me."

She took a deep breath, then let it out and said in a rush, "I have this English assignment to write about a favorite author, and I was thinking maybe I could interview you."

"Sure."

"I know. I shouldn't have asked. Maybe another time. I— wait. What did you say?"

"She said sure." Kira, on a break from texting, answered for me.

"Oh. My. God. Really? I have to text Gus." Because, of course, nothing is really real until it's texted to someone. While she tapped in her message, Kira spoke up.

"Is that true? Are you investigating the murder?"

I nodded warily. I didn't imagine Mike and Noelle would think murder was a great topic for me to discuss with their teenage daughter.

"Didn't the police already arrest Mr. Kowalski?"

"Yeah, they did. But I'm part of the defense team."

"You think the police got it wrong?"

"The police are good at their jobs, Kira, but they aren't infallible. And in this case, yes, I think they've got it wrong."

Allie joined the conversation. "I heard he did it because of his daughter. I overhead my dad talking about it. His daughter was hooked into that sugar daddy site the woman who was killed had."

Kira paid no attention to Allie's attempt to join the conversation. She kept her focus on me.

"But if Mr. Kowalski didn't do it, then who did? Do you know? Is it someone from here?" Kira asked.

"I'm not that far into it yet. I don't have any idea, actually. Anyway, we don't have to prove who did it, we just have to show that someone else *could* have done it. So that his attorney can argue that there's a reasonable doubt that Craig—Mr. Kowalski—killed Holly Mason."

"That is so cool, Leah."

"Your dad doesn't usually think so, Allie. In fact, he tells me all the time to stay out of his investigations. He's kidding ... mostly."

"Oh, my dad," she said, dismissing Ross's years of professional experience with a wrinkle of her short, straight nose. "He says—"

Here she did a passable impression of Ross's gruff voice, " 'Solvin' crimes is about payin' attention. You gotta get the details right. Put in the legwork. It's not glamorous.' He makes it sound super boring. Not like in your book."

"Your dad's right. Good detective work is pretty painstaking. You can't compare what I do to what the police do. I don't have to bag evidence, or provide a chain of custody, or write up reports, or show cause for a search warrant. And I don't have a boss hanging over my shoulder." *Now that I'm out from under Rebecca.*

"I have more freedom than your dad does. I can take

chances and make intuitive leaps that he can't. Don't underestimate him." My words were a little surprising to my own ears, given the many clashes Ross and I had had over our investigative techniques. But I'd come to respect his commitment, even if I thought his approach was a little rule-bound. Besides, daughters should look up to their fathers, not diss them.

She giggled then, changing her expression from adolescent disdain to indulgent affection. "I just had a vision of my dad leaping. Anywhere. Never gonna happen. But, yeah, he's OK, I guess." High praise, indeed.

Kira, who had been processing the reasonable doubt issue while Allie and I talked detecting, said, "So, you could get Mr. Kowalski off by showing he wasn't the only person who could have done it. But you might not know who the killer really was?"

"Exactly. We don't have to find the real killer in order to give Craig's lawyer a way to cast doubt on the evidence against him."

"How can you do that?"

"Well, we find some other people in Holly Mason's life who had a reason to want her dead. Then, we see if they had the opportunity to kill her. We'll be looking at alibis, motives, all kinds of things. I believe Craig is innocent, and I'm going to fight to give him every chance."

"Sophia and I were in band together. Mr. and Mrs. Kowalski had me stay with them right after the accident, when my mom and dad were at the hospital so much. I cried all the time, I had these really bad nightmares that my parents and my brother had all died, and I was all alone." She had wrapped her arms around herself, and she gave a small shudder at the memory.

"That's really intense, Kira," Allie said, but Kira didn't seem to notice her friend had spoken.

"When Mr. Kowalski came home from work one night, I was sitting alone in the dark. Mrs. Kowalski and Sophia were sleeping, but I'd had another bad dream. Mr. Kowalksi found me there crying. He was so nice to me. He's a good person." I caught a glint of tears in her eyes as she finished.

"My dad says, if good people didn't do bad things, he'd be out of a job. Wow, just think about that guy's daughter, your friend Sophia. Man, it would really suck to have your dad arrested for *murder*. I mean, I thought my life was messed up," Allie offered tactlessly, clearly not tuned in to Kira's distress.

"Your life *is* messed up. Your dad's suspended, and it must be pretty bad. Police don't get suspended for nothing." All traces of tenderness had vanished from Kira's expression as her words lashed out and hit like the crack of a whip.

Allie took a step back, and said, "I'm sorry. I was just—"

But Kira wasn't done. "Find your own way home! And don't expect me to pick you up for school tomorrow, either." She stormed into the house, slamming the door behind her.

Allie and I stood in stunned silence for a minute. Then I said, "Come on. I'll give you a ride."

---

Allie was quiet on the drive to her house. But when we got there, she burst out, "I didn't mean anything by it—talking about the murder. Everybody is. Kira's been pretty salty the last few days. I guess it's because she knows the Kowalskis. But she didn't tell me that. I'm always saying the wrong thing." Her thick lashes veiled the expression in her eyes, but from her downcast stare, I knew she felt guilty and upset.

"Allie, saying things I wish I hadn't is a way of life for me. I'm sure Kira will get over it."

"I guess," she said, without sounding convinced. "It's just that Kira and Gus and me, we've been hanging out and it's been fun. I was starting to feel like I might fit in. Now she's all mad and ..."

"Seriously, stop it. It'll work itself out. Look, why don't you come by after school tomorrow. We can do the interview for your English assignment, and I'll bet you'll tell me that everything is cool with Kira again."

"At your apartment? Really? Sure, yes. I can be there by 3:30. Is that OK?" Allie was smiling now, like she just won the lottery. I sure didn't remember being that mercurial when I was a teenager. I'd have to check it out with my mother. No, maybe I wouldn't.

"Yes, that's great. Just text me if your plans change." I gave her my number and added, "You know where I live, right? Downtown, in the same building as the *Himmel Times*, up on the third floor. Just come in the back and ring the doorbell, and I'll let you in.

Back home I started to pour an iced tea, then decided after all the teenage *sturm und drang* I'd had to witness, a Jameson over ice was more in order. I was just sitting down with it when the buzzer rang.

"*Chica*, big news. Is it safe to come up?"

I hadn't talked to Miguel since the hissy fit Nick had thrown Friday night.

"Sure, come on up."

As I opened the door, he made a show of stepping in, like a police officer entering a dangerous situation. He held his arms out straight in front of him, hands clasped together. He crouched low, then motioned with his head for me to step behind him, while he did a 360° around the room.

"Very funny," I said.

"A little funny, *sí*?"

And, like always, he made me laugh. "It is. I'm sorry Nick acted like such an idiot. He said he is, too. So, I hope you'll get an apology from him."

"I already did. So did April."

"Good. Was April very upset? It wasn't exactly the evening I invited her to."

"No. After we left, we helped Courtnee take down her "pubic" posters, and then we went to McClain's for a drink. I think April had fun. After all, she got a good meal, a front-row seat to romantic drama, a field mission, and a drink with friends. Then, I went to Milwaukee to see some of my squad, and we danced all night at the *Caliente Club*."

He got up then and demonstrated, before flopping down beside me on the couch.

"Ah, to be young," I said.

"Oh, *chica,* you're not old. Even if you did spend all weekend in bed." He gave me a wicked grin as my face flushed, and I changed the subject.

"What's your big news?"

"I found the sister. Holly's sister, Suzanne!"

"You did? That's great. Where is she, who is she? How did you find her?"

"Melanie called me."

I drew a blank for a second, then said in disbelief, "Melanie? Himmel Police Department Melanie? Why did she call you?"

"She likes me. I found the sister's name online. It's Mason, the same last name as Holly's. But I couldn't get a number. So, I called Melanie to see if she would find it from one of the reports. Then, she called me back."

"She gave you the sister's number?"

"Better. She told me that Suzanne Mason is coming to

Himmel tomorrow morning around nine-thirty to pick up Holly's things at the police station."

"Hmm. That's going to be a little tricky. I'm not sure I'll be able to talk my way into an interview with her on police property, despite my considerable personal charm. Not if Detective Harper knows I'm there."

"No need—though you are *muy* charming. No. After she gets Holly's things, Officer Darmody is driving her to the impoundment lot to pick up Holly's car, so she can drive it back to Chicago."

I took his face in both hands, squeezed his cheeks, and kissed him on the forehead.

"You are a beautiful boy."

"*Chica,* you're giving me fish lips."

"But I don't know how you cracked the Melanie code. She never helps anybody."

"You called it, *chica*. I'm a beautiful boy." He grinned then and said, "I used to be her shampoo boy when I was in high school. You know, when I worked at *Tía* Lydia's salon. Shampoo boys and their clients can become very close."

"I'll take your word for it. This is great, Miguel. The lot is right across the street from the Eat diner. I'll be there waiting when Darmody shows up with Suzanne. Then I'll try to persuade her to have a coffee and a chat with me."

## 18

I pulled up at the Busboom Towing Service lot, which also serves as the impoundment lot for the HPD. I slammed the brakes on and jumped out of the car. I'd planned to arrive early, to make sure I didn't miss Darmody and Suzanne Mason. But my route there had been blocked by a fender-bender, and I had outsmarted myself with the detour I chose around it. I had ended up at a street closed for sewer repair, and had to back up and take the long way around. Now, it was almost ten o'clock.

"Big Mac!" I rapped on the window to get the attention of the very large man in the very small guard house, whose job it was to stand vigil over impounded vehicles. Startled, he dropped the sausage biscuit he was eating. Big Mac got his nickname both from his size and his love of all things McDonald's.

Despite the fact that I'd caused his favorite snack to plummet to the floor, his heavy-featured face showed no irritation as he slid open the glass. Big Mac has a mane of shaggy red hair and a head that appears to be directly connected to his barrel-chested frame, without benefit of a neck. His menacing appearance is an advantage in dealing with unhappy and sometimes irate vehicle owners. But it belies his easy-going temperament.

"Hi, Leah," he began. "I haven't seen you—"

I cut him off. "Sorry, Mac, no time to chat. Has Darmody been here yet?"

He nodded.

"Damn it!"

"He said he's goin' back to the station. You could probably catch him there."

"It's not him I want. I need to talk to the woman he had with him. Suzanne Mason."

"Oh. Her. She's the one gettin' in her car in the back of the lot. That green one." I followed the direction his hand indicated and saw a slender young woman with strawberry blonde hair, cut in a sleek, chin-length bob, opening the driver's side door of the car.

"Thanks, Mac!" I said over my shoulder as I ran toward the car.

"Suzanne! Suzanne! Can I talk to you a minute?"

She glanced up, surprised. I stopped, panting, a few feet from her. She looked like an Impressionist painting of her older sister. Where Holly's features had been sharply chiseled, Suzanne's were softer and more delicate, but it was clear they shared the same genes.

"I'm sorry, do I know you? You're not the press, are you?" she asked, her eyes suddenly wary.

"No, I'm not. My name is Leah Nash. I'm working with Craig Kowalski's defense attorney. I'd like to talk to you for just a few minutes. There's a diner across the street. We could grab a cup of coffee."

"What? No. Why would I talk to you? That man murdered my sister." She opened the door wider and slid beneath the wheel, but I grabbed hold of the door before she could pull it shut.

"But what if he didn't? Please, Suzanne. If you'd just give me ten minutes, that's all I ask."

She stared at me for so long, I feared she was readying a withering reply and would zoom out of the lot, leaving nothing but exhaust fumes behind. Instead, she said. "All right. Ten minutes. Where is this place?"

"It's the Eat More Diner, kitty-corner from the lot. I'll meet you inside."

---

"Thanks, Jeff," I said to the lanky waiter with scraggly hair and a sweet smile, as he poured a cup of coffee for me. I almost never eat at the Eat More Diner, only bargain hunters with strong stomachs do, but the coffee is always good.

Suzanne poured creamer into her cup as Jeff moved on, leaving the check before he went.

"I don't know why I agreed to talk to you. I don't know anything about Holly's death except what the police told me. And I don't want anything to do with her killer."

"Maybe it's because you'd just like to talk to someone about the sister you loved. I know what it's like to lose a sister. I really do. I don't want to upset you. I'd like to hear about Holly from you, to know more about the kind of person she was."

I held my breath while she drank her coffee and looked steadily at me. I let it out when she began to speak.

"Holly was unique, that's the only way I can describe her. She did what she wanted, the way she wanted to, and she didn't care if other people didn't like it. She was ten years older than me, so I always looked up to her. Our parents divorced when I was three or four, and my father just dropped out of the picture.

Mom found religion. She joined a very strict church, and everything centered on that for her. There were so many rules, I don't know how anyone could avoid going to their version of hell. It never made sense to me, but I did what Mom wanted. Not Holly."

"She defied your mother, then?"

"It's sort of hard to explain. Yes, she wore the clothes she wanted, and had the friends she wanted, and never, ever went to church. But she didn't argue with Mom, or yell and scream at her. She'd listen, and then she'd do what she needed to do. She didn't fight with her. She was just stronger than Mom, I think. After Holly graduated, Mom cut her off. Said she'd raised her, and that was all the Lord required. Now, the devil could have his own back."

"How did Holly take that?"

She shrugged. "Fine, I think. She stayed in touch with me, though I didn't let Mom know. She went to Kinmont College in Los Angeles. She worked as a model for a while after she graduated, at least that's what she told me. Then, she married Ian and moved to Chicago. Not long after, Mom started losing weight and feeling so bad, she couldn't go in to work. Her minister told her if she had faith and prayed, God would heal her.

"I called Holly, and she came right home. She got Mom in to see a doctor, but by then it was too late. She died in just a few weeks. Cancer."

"I'm sorry, Suzanne. Did you go to live with Holly and Ian then?"

She nodded. "Yes. I was with them until I went to college in New York. Ian paid for everything—I didn't know he was using other people's money to do it. After I graduated, I took a job with a social media company there. Things were good. I was happy, Holly was happy. And then, bam! The bottom fell out. Ian was arrested, their money was gone, the people he'd cheated hated her, the friends she thought she had abandoned her.

"I think the worst thing for her was that she felt so stupid. Holly always had a plan, and she always had her life in control. After everything went to hell with Ian, I think it shook her confidence. It's the only time I ever saw her depressed. I begged her to come to New York and start over."

"But she wouldn't do it?"

"No. She said she wasn't going to run away. She had skills and she was going to use them. I asked her if it wouldn't be tough getting back into modeling. That's when she told me she hadn't been a model. She said that starting over meant being honest with me, even if I hated her for it. She told me about the escort work. I didn't care. Nothing could change what she'd done for me, what she was to me."

"Sure, I understand."

"I was glad when she got the idea for SweetMeets. She was so excited. She asked me to help. I owed her, and I wanted to support her, like she always had me. So, I moved back to Chicago."

"And it was just you and Holly?"

"Basically, yes. Except for Kibre Web Development. The guy that owned it was a friend of hers, she said. I think maybe he was an old client, but it wasn't any of my business. She reached out to him, because we had almost zero startup money. She talked him into doing the work upfront in exchange for a share of the profits. He left about a year ago, but he wasn't ever a partner. And we didn't really need him anymore, because the site was running so smoothly. We farm that stuff out and customer service and accounting services, so we don't have much in-house staff. It's really just Holly and me. We don't—didn't—need anyone else."

"Are you going to keep running the business now?"

"I'm not even sure there'll be a business. Holly *was* Sweet-Meets. She had a plan for getting over the blackmail thing, but I don't know if I can carry it off. I don't even know if I want to."

"What blackmail thing?" My antenna had flipped straight up on that one.

"One of the sugar babies was arrested for blackmailing a client last January. You didn't hear about it?"

"I'm more of a hard news junkie." Mentally, I was kicking myself. I should've discovered the blackmail story when I researched Holly. I'd started with deep background, intending to finish up with the more recent information available online. But then, I'd gotten so excited by the Rebecca/Natalie story that I'd forgotten to check Holly's recent past. A rookie reporter would've done better than that.

"What happened?"

"It didn't have anything to do with SweetMeets, except that the girl and her sugar daddy were clients who met there. We don't match up the clients or track who's with who. We just provide the venue. We tried to keep the story under the radar. But word still got out and clients got scared that the investigation would spread further, and they might get pulled into it somehow. We lost a lot of people.

"We were struggling, and then Holly came up with an idea. She was going to do another start-up with two new websites, one targeted to professional women over forty-five, the other to the LGBT community. But she couldn't get funding because of the bad PR, and we were hemorrhaging profits. She tried to get Kibre Web back with the same deal—nothing up front and a generous share of the profits. But her friend said no. He didn't want to take a chance that he'd be connected to us somehow, with everything that was in the media. He had a family, and he didn't want to risk his wife finding out, Holly said."

"So SweetMeets is in serious financial trouble?"

"You could say that. Who wants to be on a hook-up site that's crawling with blackmailers? Not that we are, but the rumors have been brutal. We thought we just might be able to squeak by, and then we got hit again a few weeks ago. The extortion arrest must have given another sugar baby a better idea. She landed a contract to write a tell-all book about her life as a sugar baby and the 'daddies' she's known. A new story spread that we'd had an *Ashley Madison*-style data leak. You know, that adultery site? Frankly, I didn't see how we'd ever recover. But Holly said she had a plan."

"You don't know what it was?"

Suzanne shook her head. "No, sometimes she still treated me like her kid sister instead of her partner. She didn't want me to worry, I think. And I trusted her. Holly always landed on her feet. Until now." She swallowed hard then as a fresh wave of grief washed over her.

"Do you think coming to Himmel was part of Holly's secret plan?"

"I don't know. I didn't even know she'd left town. Not until the police notified me that she was dead."

"Did she often go away without telling you?"

"Sometimes. I did, too. It wasn't a big deal. We worked together so much, we were careful to give each other space in our free time. I called her Monday morning to check if we were still on for dinner. It went to voicemail, but I figured she wasn't up yet. Holly was always a night owl. When the phone rang later that day, I expected it to be her. Only it wasn't. It was someone from the police, and they said that Holly was dead." She dabbed at her eyes with a napkin.

My mind was racing through the possibilities the blackmail angle had raised. Maybe the sugar baby's attempt had given Holly an idea for solving her own financial problems. She'd certainly have plenty of compromising information. Was it possible she'd come to town to put the squeeze on a current SweetMeets client? Or one from her earlier escort days? Or could it be that she came to town to hit up an old college buddy for money, maybe someone who had something to hide, like Rebecca?

"Do you think your sister was desperate enough to—" I paused. How to put this delicately? There wasn't any way. "Do you think Holly was desperate enough to try some blackmail of her own to get the financing she needed? She must have known a lot of secrets from her own escort days, or from owning SweetMeets."

"Holly and I were really close, but her life was a lot harder than mine was—thanks to her. She'd had to be more ... ruthless, I guess you could say, than me. She worked hard for everything she had, and she didn't want to lose it. Was that so wrong? If she had leverage that would save her business, she might have tried to use it."

"Suzanne, would you be willing to give me a list of your clients?"

"No. We have a confidentiality agreement with the clients. I can't release that."

"But if Holly had targeted someone for blackmail—"

"Your 'if' doesn't matter. Even if Holly had pressured someone with information she had, that's not who killed her. The police arrested her killer. He was a hateful monster who beat my sister to death, because he blamed her for the choices his adult daughter made."

"But you gave the client list to the police, didn't you? That's how they found Sophia Kowalski, Craig's daughter."

"I'm not going to go into what I gave to the police. They found her killer. I'm sorry you don't like that it's a friend of yours, but I don't really care about your feelings. Holly was the only person in the world who was always there for me. I'm all

SUSAN HUNTER

alone now. I don't want to talk anymore." She was obviously fighting back tears, as she crumpled her napkin and pushed aside her cup.

She was ready to go, and I hadn't even asked her about the Kinmont College connection.

I said quickly, "Suzanne, do the names Natalie Dunckel or Rebecca Hartfield mean anything to you? I think they might have been classmates of Holly's at Kinmont College."

She paused from sliding out of the booth. "No. I was a kid then. I never visited Holly at school."

"Let me get that," I said, as she started to reach for her wallet.

'Thank you," she said.

I laid five dollars down. Maybe she'd consider it bad manners to ignore the final question I had, after I'd just paid the check.

"One last thing. You said Kibre Web Development did your site, that the owner was a friend, and possibly a client of Holly's once. What's his name? If she was in contact recently to try and persuade him to develop the new sites, maybe he knows something that would help."

"No. He's a nice person who helped Holly get started. He turned her down because he didn't want to get caught up in any bad publicity and upset his family. I understand that. Family is important. You'll have to find him yourself. And you can leave me alone, too."

## 19

When I got home it was almost eleven, which would make it eight in Oregon. I hadn't heard back from Merlin Duffy, so I tried again. This time I got a person instead of an automated answer.

"Duffy Veterinary Practice. This is Donna Lynn. How may I help you?"

"Hi, Donna Lynn. This is Leah Nash. I left a message for Dr. Duffy last week. I'm a writer and I—"

There was an excited squeal on the end of the line before I could finish.

"You want to talk to Dr. Duffy?"

If a simple request to speak to him elicited such high-pitched amazement, either Merlin had a monumentally unsuccessful practice, or a monumentally excitable receptionist.

In case it was the latter, I responded slowly. "Yes. Yes, I would, if he has a minute now. Or, it's fine if he wants to call me back when he's free."

"Oh, he can't call you," she said. She continued without giving me a chance to ask why.

"You really are Leah Nash? The one who wrote *Unholy*

*Alliances*? I loved that book so much. I'm having book club at my house next month, and the host gets to choose the book. We're reading yours."

"That's great, Donna Lynn. I'm glad you liked the book. Right now, I'm working on a new project that I need to talk to Dr. Duffy about. Could you help me out?"

"You're doing a book on farm animals? How could there be anything interesting about that?" she asked. Her voice conveyed her disappointment in me. Clearly, working in a large animal veterinary clinic was not a labor of love for her.

"No, I'm doing some research that involves Kinmont College, and I know Dr. Duffy is an alumnus. When did you say he'd be in?" She hadn't of course, but I was trying to steer us back onto the reason I had called.

"He's on vacation. In Africa. He's on a safari. A photo safari, not the hunting kind. He won't be in until some time next week. He said maybe Tuesday, but probably more like Thursday or Friday. He wasn't sure."

"Oh. I left a voicemail for him, but I guess that's why he didn't call back. I wonder, could you help me out, then? When he gets back, could you make sure he calls me? You know, maybe bump my message to the front of the line?"

"Is Dr. Duffy going to be in your next book? That would be awesome."

"No," I said quickly. I didn't want her to scare him away by suggesting that he was going to be a featured player in a book that didn't even exist. "No," I repeated. "This isn't for a book. It's a different project. Think you can help me out?"

"Well, maybe. If you could help *me* out?"

"How's that?"

"It would be so great if you could be at my book club! I mean, not be there in person, but we could Skype, and everyone could ask you questions and things."

"Donna Lynn, if you get Dr. Duffy to call me as soon as he gets back, you can count me in."

"Oh, I will. And, if you could do something kind of different —you know, something sort of fun and zippy, that would be really nice. Especially because you won't be there in real life."

"I'll definitely think on that. I promise to be at my zippiest."

"If you need to call me—at home, I mean, because I won't be back in the office until Dr. Duffy is—my number is 458-555-0100."

"Thanks, Donna Lynn.

---

I was disappointed that Dr. Duffy was out of reach. After I ate a peanut butter sandwich for lunch, I sat down on the window seat with my legal pad to take stock of where we were so far.

- Rebecca Hartfield was actually Natalie Dunckel
- Holly had gone to college with Natalie/Rebecca
- Rebecca had lied about knowing Holly
- Holly had worked as an escort in college
- Holly's SweetMeets business was in financial trouble
- Holly had a client who had blackmailed a sugar daddy
- Holly had a sugar baby who was writing a tell-all book
- Holly *might* have tried blackmail herself, to raise capital
- Could Holly have been blackmailing Rebecca? Had she known why Rebecca changed her name? Was that why she was in Himmel?
- Did Holly have a former client who lived in or near Himmel, and was he her victim?
- Merlin Duffy was a classmate of Natalie/Rebecca who might know something

It didn't seem like much for all the running around Miguel and I had been doing. Without the SweetMeets client list, it would be hard to make any connections between the sugar daddy site and anyone in Himmel. Maybe some of the discovery materials had gone to Gabe already. I picked up the phone.

"Gabe? This is Leah. Have you gotten anything from Cliff Timmins' office yet?"

"Leah. Yeah. A package was just delivered."

"Is there anything in it we can use? What's there from Sweet-Meets? How about the phone records? List of witnesses? Autopsy report?"

"I said it just got here. Like two minutes ago."

"Where's that hard-driving East Coast vibe? I thought you guys were always hustling. Come on, we have to start building our case, don't we? We can't just sit around and do nothing!"

"Did I say that's what I thought we should do? I think all I said was the first wave of material just got here. Come to the office if you think I'm not moving fast enough on it."

"I'll be right there."

---

"I was hoping we'd get the SweetMeets client list. Don't they have to give us that?" I asked, after looking through the materials Gabe had put on the conference table.

He took off the tortoise shell reading glasses he'd put on as we went through the documents and rubbed the bridge of his nose before he answered.

"Leah. It's Monday. Craig just had his bond set Friday. This is what I'd call responding in a New York minute. And I'm a guy who knows New York minutes. I need some coffee," he finished abruptly. He stood up and went to the rolling cart that Patty had thoughtfully brought in, laden not just with coffee, water, and cups but also some kind of energy bars.

"Want some? Or a water? Nice shirt," he added, as he

noticed the vintage Bob Seger T-shirt I was wearing with my jeans.

I looked hard to see if he was being sarcastic, but the thumbs up he gave me seemed genuine, so I nodded my thanks. He was dressed as he'd been on Friday—white shirt with a tie, sleeves rolled up, and no suit coat in sight. His eyes looked tired, and I gave a fleeting thought to how hectic things had been for him—he arrived in town one minute, and was building a murder defense the next. In addition to unpacking and settling in a new place. But there was no time for empathy. We had a lot of ground to cover.

"OK, but it isn't everything. Don't they have to give us everything they're going to use?"

"Yes, they do. But there isn't a set time, and it doesn't have to be all at once."

"Can you call them and find out when they'll release the client list? And the autopsy report, and their witness list?"

"And people think I'm pushy." He shook his head but then he said, "Yes. I'll check and see how soon we can expect the rest of the files. Meanwhile, there's enough to start on here."

"Start on? Hey, Miguel and I are halfway to building your case for you."

"Oh, yeah? Let's hear it."

Maybe it was because of the T-shirt thing. I instinctively like anyone in my generation who has musical tastes broad enough to encompass bands popular before we were born. Or maybe it was because I liked being treated like a full-fledged member of his team, not a bothersome amateur. Either way, I decided then to stop withholding,

He pulled out a yellow legal pad identical to the one I had with me. I began running through the list of things I'd compiled on my window seat. Then I floated a couple of ideas.

"It's possible Holly came to blackmail an old client from her escort days, or from her SweetMeets clients. Or maybe she was going after Rebecca. After all, she knew her at Kinmont College when she was Natalie Dunckel. She could know what made Rebecca change her name. And it could be something pretty dark in Rebecca's past. That's my personal favorite, but I'm keeping an open mind."

"At this point, anything is possible, Leah. At least it gives us a direction to head in. That's good work. Very good work. And fast." He smiled then—a broad grin that reached his eyes and I noticed what a dark, warm brown they were. "I like the way you move."

Wait. What? Was he hitting on me? Or had he unintentionally chosen a phrase that could be taken two ways?

But he'd already returned to his notes. "OK, now, Rebecca Hartfield—she's married to a cop, right? And she runs the newspaper?"

"Yeah."

"So, we should be ready for local law enforcement, including the DA, to circle the wagons if they find out we're poking around there. I'll call the district attorney's office right away. Try to get everything they have now. Before they get pissed off at us."

"Great."

"And, you'll want to walk softly around this Rebecca. You know the saying, 'Never pick a fight—' "

" 'With people who buy ink by the barrel,' " I finished. "Yeah, I know it. There's something else you should probably know, too. A sort of extra wrinkle here. Rebecca was my boss when I worked at the paper. She fired me once. I quit once. We basically can't stand each other. And the cop she's married to? He's a really good friend of mine."

"That's a complication we don't need." He rubbed a hand across the back of his neck as though he had suddenly developed a kink there. "Small towns. I've heard about 'em, now I see what people mean. How's that going to affect your investigation? The best friend, I mean. Things could get a little tense."

"No kidding." I sighed heavily. "Usually, he helps me out when I'm chasing down a story. It doesn't hurt to have a friend in the police department. Sometimes, he can get a little upset when he thinks I'm messing around in 'his' investigation." Here I made air quotes to indicate that I never took such warnings too seriously.

"But this will be different. He's in looove," I said, drawing out the words in the manner of a five-year-old reciting the rhyme about sitting in a tree K-I-S-S-I-N-G. "I think the longer he doesn't know, the better."

"Fine with me. But if you start turning over rocks, it won't take long before you have a pile of them someone's going to notice. The defense is subject to discovery, just like the prosecution is. We'll have to supply our witness list, the evidence we plan to use—but we don't have to give them our work product. That means we don't have to share our defense strategy, our alternate theory of the crime beforehand. Can I trust that you won't tip it to your cop pal, even accidentally?"

"Give me some credit. This is one case Coop and I can't even talk about. But he's a smart guy, and he's connected. The closer we get to Rebecca, the more likely it is he'll get wind of what we're doing."

"Coop? That's his name? Isn't he the guy who's in the book you wrote about your sister? The one who pulled you out of the river?"

"You read my book?"

"Yeah. I leafed through it," he said and shrugged. Then he smiled again. "No. I read the whole thing this weekend. It was good. Well done—on both the book and the investigation."

I like it when people like what I do, but it also makes me feel a little embarrassed.

"Oh. OK. Great. Thanks. So, what's next? I'd like to talk to the same people the cops did on their door-to-door. Maybe someone will have remembered something. If you give it time, you can pick up a lot in a casual conversation."

"Sounds good."

"I'll take the printout of the phone records, too. Just give me the page with calls for the week Holly came to town and the day she died. If we have to dive much deeper than that, we're gonna need a bigger boat. That's a lot of data for me to check out."

"No, I think the calls the week she died are probably the ones that count the most. At least, if we go with your theory that she came to town for a meeting with a blackmail victim. And your theory is the best thing we have going at the moment."

"OK, then. I'll take this stuff and get started. And you're going to call the DA's office, and see when we can get the Sweet-Meets client list, right? But try not to let them know how much you want it. Timmins is enough of an ass that if you do, he'll slow walk it just to show he's got the power."

"Thanks, I think I can handle it. I've been a prosecutor myself, remember? I know my way around the law. But, I don't know my way around Himmel. Maybe you could help me out there? I need to get a better sense for this town, and fast."

"Sure. We can meet up at McClain's bar one night. It's as good a place as any to get that Himmel feeling. I've got to go. I have an interview at three thirty."

"You've got a witness scheduled already?"

"No, a devoted reader. Allie Ross, a high school kid I know, wants to interview me. Seems I'm a famous author." I grinned, then gathered my homework and took off.

## 20

"Would you like a soda? Or some water? Or iced tea? I have some Doritos, too. And I think there might be a box of Pop-Tarts in the cupboard."

Allie had made a beeline for the window seat as soon as she walked into my apartment and was now sitting cross-legged in the warmth of the afternoon sun.

"Soda and Doritos would be awesome. We don't have any fun food anymore. My dad watched some TV show about teenagers eating too much junk. Now, he's on a health kick—for me, anyway—and all we have to snack on are vegetables and hummus."

I felt a little guilty at undermining Ross's parental strictures. I was also bemused by the thought of the man who was a burger's best friend turning into a healthy eating advocate. The wonders of parenting never ceased to amaze me. With the rationalization that an occasional treat is good for the soul, I handed Allie a bowl of the salty chips and a can of Coke. I settled down in the corner opposite her with iced tea and my own supply of Doritos.

"OK, ask away."

She turned her phone's voice recorder on, and between bites of her illicit treats, she asked some surprisingly good questions about research, fact-checking, cultivating sources, and weaving a story together. Then she asked one that took me by surprise.

"Leah, why do you do what you do? I mean, I get why you did the story about your sister, but you talked about other times, at other papers. What makes you so determined on stories that don't have anything to do with you?"

"I guess because that's what the job is. People become reporters because they have a drive to know, to get to the bottom of things."

"But those other stories you told me about, the Mandy Cleveland case, for instance. Other reporters gave up after a while. You didn't. But you didn't know that girl, you didn't have any personal connection. What keeps you pushing when other people are over it?"

I hesitated, because I wanted to give her an honest answer, but I wasn't sure myself what drove me.

"It's not for altruistic reasons, not because I'm such a good person, or that I like to do good deeds. I just have this compulsion. I think it started when I was a kid. My dad left when I was pretty young, right after my sister Annie died in a fire. I felt like I was falling and falling and falling—there was no ground beneath me. It was terrifying. My mom worked hard to reassure me and make things as right as she could.

"But ever since then, I've never felt really, I don't know, at ease, is as good a description as any. For me, finding answers, hunting down the truth, not accepting what *seems*, but digging for what actually *is,* gives me the illusion, at least, of putting order back in the world. Of making it safer to trust, because I know what's true." I gave an embarrassed laugh. I wasn't sure where that answer had come from. And I certainly hadn't intended to burden Allie with the overflow of my needy unconscious.

"Sorry, I got a little incoherently neurotic there. Let's just say, I follow the George Malloy philosophy. He was a famous mountain climber, and when someone asked him why he wanted to climb Mt. Everest, he said, 'Because it's there.' I guess that's why I have to follow-up on stories. Because they're there."

Far from being confused by my rambling, Allie was nodding her head. She shut off the recorder and said in a voice far gentler than her usual one, "I didn't know you had two sisters who died." She reached over and touched my hand, causing tears to spring unbidden to my eyes.

Sympathy always makes me weepy. I'd much rather have someone tell me to suck it up then look at me with sad, puppy eyes. It's easier to stay in control that way.

"It's a tough old world, Allie. You know that. You've had some rough times too."

"Yeah, well, that's true. My mother abandoning me for her boyfriend wasn't the greatest thing that ever happened. And it's been hard making friends and getting settled in here. But, what are you going to do?" She shrugged and tilted her head with a half-smile, curls softly framing her face. Her resemblance to a pre-Raphaelite painting was marred only by the smudge of Cool Ranch Doritos that clung to the corner of her mouth. It made me laugh, and though she couldn't know what I'd been thinking, she joined in. The pensive mood of our conversation was broken. Much to my relief.

"You're friends with Kira and with Gus Fraser, though, so you must feel like you're settling in, don't you?" I asked.

"Yeah, I guess. But you saw Kira yesterday, right? She practically jumped down my throat. We were always friends when I used to visit Dad on weekends and vacations and stuff. But now, ever since I moved here, it seems like she's always ripping on someone. Gus noticed it too."

"Maybe she has boyfriend trouble? Are she and Gus a couple?"

Allie shook her head. "They used to be, but now they're just friends. Gus is pretty cool. They both are," she added hastily. Hmm. Maybe Ross had been right about Allie's romantic interests. I decided to stay the cool adult and leave it to him to make unwelcome inquiries.

"Yeah, he seems like a nice kid. His parents are sure different, aren't they? Laid-back Will and super-structured Gretchen. But I guess opposites attract, right?"

"Maybe they attract, but that doesn't mean they stay together. I mean, when I was little, my mom and dad and me, we were happy—I thought. But then, well, stuff happens. That's what I told Gus and Kira. I'm no expert, but not a lot of people stay together, it seems to me. Worrying about it doesn't do any good. Kids are just kind of bystanders, even though we're the ones who get hurt the most."

"Wait a minute. Are you saying that Gus and Kira think their parents are going to divorce? Both of them?" I could see that the intense Gretchen might push even the easy-going Will to the point of wanting to leave, but I didn't want to hear that about Mike and Noelle. After all they'd gone through. Although maybe that was the point, the stress of a traumatic accident like the one Brendan had suffered, and its aftermath, could push any relationship to the breaking point.

"I don't know about Kira, she doesn't talk about her family much. Her mom and dad seem pretty cool. Gus is the one who's freaking. His mom and dad got into it so bad one night it woke him up."

"Well, married people fight. It doesn't mean they're going to get divorced."

"That's what I told him. But he feels all guilty or something, because with his bad knee, he's not sure if he'll be able to play ball like he did before. And then he won't get the scholarship his mom is counting on to send him to some super expensive school. His dad lost some money on some investment, I guess, and his mom isn't very happy with him."

I was beginning to feel a little uncomfortable getting an insight into Gretchen and Will's life that I was sure they'd rather keep in-house.

"Well, that's not anything Gus did on purpose, and I'm sure his parents would feel terrible if they knew he was worried."

"He can't help it. He thinks if him going to college wasn't such a big expense for them, his mom wouldn't be mad at his dad all the time."

"I doubt that's it. Parents have a lot of issues that their kids know nothing about. And it should probably stay that way. Try not to worry about Gus and his family. It'll work out one way or another. Just be a good friend. That's all you can do."

Although I liked Will fine, I could see that his casual approach to life had the potential to drive a goal-oriented woman like Gretchen crazy. And Gretchen's steamroller ways might have flattened out whatever love Will had felt for her when they married. Still, it wasn't my business or, thankfully, my problem to sort out.

After Allie left, I got busy on the phone records I'd taken from Gabe's office.

I took a quick look at the calls made and received during the week Holly had died. There were surprisingly few and most had a Chicago area code—though with people able to "port" cell phone numbers from one carrier and location to another, the area code isn't always a reliable indicator of where a call came from.

I was most interested in who Holly had spoken to or texted with on Thursday, the day before she was due to arrive, and the two days she was in Himmel. I recognized one number as Miguel's. She had probably sent a text to verify arrangements. I'd check with him to be sure. She made a call on Thursday night to what looked like a cell number that lasted less than a minute. An hour later there was a return call from that number that lasted ten minutes.

On Friday, she had texted to the same number, in the early evening. She was in Himmel by then. On Saturday, there was just one call, to Craig's home phone, no doubt about the leaky toilet. It would have been perfect if there had been a text to Rebecca's number, or even a call to the *Himmel Times* office, but alas there was not.

I took all the numbers and plugged them into an online search service that uses the NPA/NXX database of area and local exchanges, combined with other information, to track down the owner of a phone number. If the number is a landline, you can almost always get a name. But if it's a cell phone, things get more complicated.

I was able to see that the numbers from Chicago were for the most part local businesses—a caterer, a cleaning service, a bank, a hair salon. It also gave me Holly's sister Suzanne's cell phone number—there had been multiple calls and texts between them during the week Holly died. I tucked the number away for future reference. Otherwise, nothing of much use in that batch.

I had saved the number I was most interested in for last, on the theory that good things come to she who waits. That did not prove true. The number Holly had called on Thursday, and had received a return call from, and had then texted on Friday, came up blank. Well, not totally blank. I could see that it was a cell phone, and the carrier was listed, but no owner name appeared. Which in all likelihood meant that it was a prepaid cell phone. Major dead-end.

As I had learned from sad experience, prepaid cell phone companies, like TracFone or Go Phone and others, lease service from Verizon or Sprint or Nextel or some other carrier, and buy blocks of phone numbers from them, too. If you try to get the records for one of those numbers from a carrier, they won't have it. Because the owner of the phone is a customer of the prepaid cell company, not the carrier.

And here's where it gets really frustrating. If the phone was bought with cash, the prepaid cell phone company won't know who its customer is either.

My stomach started growling then. I looked up and saw that it was almost seven o'clock. I hadn't had much for lunch, and my Dorito snack with Allie hadn't had any staying power. I stood and stretched, then reached for my phone. In quick succession, I texted Miguel and Coop to see if they wanted to meet up at McClain's. I even, bless my magnanimous heart, included Rebecca in the invite. Although that was as much because I wanted to observe her up close with my new knowledge that she was actually Natalie Dunckel, as it was to preserve good feelings as long as I could with Coop. Finally, I texted Gabe, told him all roads lead to McClain's, and he should be there in fifteen minutes, if he wanted to see a slice of Himmel life.

## 21

McClain's is not a bar for fans of chi-chi drinks and sophisticated atmosphere. But, if you like old, dark, watering holes with
plenty of locals and decent bar food, then you should check it
out. The wooden tables are scarred and unstable, and the vinyl
booths feature tears masked by duct tape, but pours are generous, and the staff is friendly. With the exception of my high
school nemesis, Sherry Young.

"Is anyone joining you?" she asked as I sat down at my
favorite table toward the back.

"If by 'anyone joining' me, you mean is Coop coming, yes.
With his wife."

Her face fell. Sherry had a major crush on Coop when she
was a cheerleader, and he was on the football team. She still
had it, even after two kids with, and a divorce from, Travis
Young, on whom *I'd* had a major crush.

"Figures. You know, I don't get it. OK, so she's not bad looking, she has all those clothes, and she's a big shot in her
company, but still, she's a nasty bitch. Why did Coop choose
her?"

I couldn't blame Sherry for harboring *Hallmark* movie-style hopes that Coop would one day realize she was his one true pairing. But despite her cute and curvy figure, her big brown eyes, and her softly curling hair, she lacked something Coop always looked for in his girlfriends: smarts. Sherry just wasn't very bright.

"You have to let the dream die, Sherry. Rebecca has him. And she's got an extra hook."

"You mean because she's pregnant?"

News does indeed travel fast in Himmel.

"Well, yeah. That's a pretty big draw for Coop."

She shook her head. "Getting knocked-up might draw a guy in, but it doesn't keep him. I ought to know. Two kids weren't enough to keep Travis home nights."

"But Coop's not that kind of guy. When he commits, it sticks."

"They're all that kind of guy."

"No, come on. That's not true. Hey, I heard Timber just got divorced. You should give him a call." Timber Wolfe, born Tim, but christened with the obvious nickname in grade school, owns the Bang Bang Bump Shop in Himmel.

"He's not my type." The finality with which she said it made me think she'd already knocked on that door, and it hadn't opened.

"What's with you giving dating advice? Your husband divorced you, Coop didn't want you, and now you're back at square one, working to get your ex back." As if embarrassed that she'd let me see her forlornness, she'd returned to her usual snarkiness with me.

"For the record, I divorced Nick. Coop and I are friends. Never had a romance, never wanted one. It *is* possible for a man and a woman to be friends. And Nick is the one who's working to get *me* back. Now, could you please bring me a Jameson on the rocks and a burger basket? And a glass of water? If, that is, you're working tonight, and not just harassing customers."

She smiled slyly. As I said, Sherry's not very bright. However, as she had just demonstrated, she's cunning enough to get under my skin.

Before she could answer, Miguel and April came up to the table. I hadn't thought to ask her, but I was glad Miguel had.

"*Chica!* April and I were both at work when you texted, so I brought her along, Hi, Sherry, *mi bonita*. What's making your brown eyes sparkle tonight?"

She batted her lashes and giggled. Her morose mood had been lifted as much by seeing Miguel as by getting a rise out of me. "*Moo-ee grass-e-ass*," she said, mangling Miguel's ancestral tongue, but delighting him with her effort.

"*De nada.* But are you learning Spanish now?"

"I'm doing day care two days a week for a teacher up at the technical college. Her husband's Mexican. I'm learning a little Spanish from them."

"*Bueno!* Good for you. It's a beautiful language for a beautiful woman."

Sherry's mention of the fact that, in addition to waitressing in a bar, she also had to babysit to make ends meet, made me reflect on the harsh reality of her hard-knock life. I probably shouldn't begrudge her the chance to snark at me once in a while, or to bask in the glow of Miguel. But the gulf between what I should do and what I do continues. When the chit-chat finished and April and Miguel took their seats, Sherry took their orders.

"I'd just like a diet Coke, please," said April.

"I'll have a Bellini," Miguel said.

"Miguel, you know this isn't a fancy drinks bar. Davey isn't going to have the ingredients. He won't even know what it is."

"But there's only three," Miguel said, ever hopeful in his

quest to bring trendy cocktails to McClain's. "Vodka, peach puree and champagne."

Sherry shook her head, but she laughed. "I'll try, but I wouldn't get too excited if I was you."

She had left to put the orders in just before I spotted Gabe in the doorway. I signaled energetically, pointing him to our table. As I did, I saw that Coop and Rebecca were right behind him. She was wearing a bright yellow hooded rain slicker, just like the one hanging over the back of my chair. Great. At least I wasn't wearing mine at the moment, so we wouldn't look like dress alike besties.

Coop returned my rather frantic wave with a salute, though his expression said he was puzzled by my over-effusive welcome. As the three converged on the table, I went to Gabe, took him by the elbow and positioned him so everyone could see him.

"Everyone, this is Gabe Hoffman. He's joined Miller's firm, and he's Craig Kowalski's attorney. Gabe, you already know Miguel, but this is Coop—David Cooper—and his wife, Rebecca Hartfield." I was proud of myself for not stumbling over the word "wife."

They exchanged greetings, and then I said, "And this is April Nelson, the new receptionist at the *Himmel Times*. And an old high school friend of mine and Coop's."

April blushed as Gabe reached out to shake her hand, and I noticed that Rebecca's face showed displeasure. She probably didn't think it was appropriate to socialize with the lowliest staff member at the *Times*. Too bad.

Sherry returned then with drinks for April and me, and bad news for Miguel.

"Sorry. Davey says he's damned if he's gonna stock peach puree and champagne even for you. He sent you a screwdriver instead."

Miguel grinned. "Tell Davey *gracias*. And someday I'll take him to the Opus Lounge in the city," he said, naming a swanky cocktail bar in Madison. "It will change his life."

While Sherry took Coop and Rebecca's orders, Gabe, who was sitting next to me, leaned in and said, "I didn't realize you were having a party."

"It's not a party. You said you wanted to learn more about Himmel. Well, here's part of it. And one part of that is our up and coming murder suspect, right?" I whispered back.

"Leah, don't you know it's not polite to keep your new friend to yourself?" Rebecca's cool voice carried well across the table. Her precision cut white-blond hair fell perfectly as she tilted her head toward Gabe, and her pale blue eyes glittered.

"I'm the one monopolizing Leah," Gabe said smoothly. "I always thought small towns were dull. But I find Himmel fascinating. How do you find it, Rebecca? You're not from here, are you?"

"Hardly. But I've found it—or at least some of the people in it—fascinating, as well," she said, squeezing Coop's hand.

I had to sit on my own hand to force myself not to make a gagging gesture. Perhaps sensing my urge to say something rude, April stepped bravely into the conversation, even though I knew her shyness made it hard for her to claim attention.

"I grew up here, Gabe," she said. "Coop and Leah and I were in high school together. I lived in a big city for a while, but I like small town life better. So does my cat. Miss Oprah. Of course, she's an exotic shorthair, and they're very adaptable. Miss Oprah—"

"Gabe, we should do a profile on you for the paper. A personality piece to introduce you to the community. What do you think?" Rebecca had interrupted April as though she weren't even speaking. I looked at Coop, but his head was turned, talking to someone at the next table, and he hadn't noticed.

April shrank back in her chair. I leaned forward to say something sharp to Rebecca, but Gabe touched me on the arm. I let him take the lead. He ignored Rebecca.

"April, I'd like to meet Miss Oprah. I had a tabby cat named Hobbes when I was a kid. He lived to be 19. I still miss that cat."

April's smile was wonderful to behold.

Rebecca said nothing, but I had a feeling that Gabe had just made an enemy. Coop had finished his sidebar conversation, oblivious to Gabe's routing of Rebecca. He started talking to him about sports, and Rebecca left the table, presumably for the restroom. Miguel was chatting with April, and my burger basket had finally come. I was the only one eating, so I gave myself over to blissful absorption in a well-done hamburger and fries with just the right amount of grease. I enjoyed my unhealthy meal right down to the last bite.

Then, suddenly, into one of those lulls that inexplicably occur in public places, a querulous but loud voice dropped like a hammer. "Them cops got it wrong. I seen who killed that woman the other night. And if ya stand me a drink, I'll tell ya."

## 22

Instinctively, my eyes searched for Rebecca. Would Harry recognize her? She was rounding the corner from the ladies room as the bartender said wearily, "Harry, I'll give you a shot if you'll shut up, and then get outta here. You're stinkin' up the place."

But Harry's bleary old eyes were focused on the bottle in the bartender's hand, and he didn't even glance her way. Although his declaration had sparked interest for a moment, the normal buzz of conversation had resumed swiftly. The bar's patrons had obviously considered the source and dismissed it.

Harry is a familiar figure around Himmel, weaving his way through the streets most evenings, sometimes singing loudly enough to get a warning or even a trip to the station from the cops, most times muttering to himself on the way to and from the seedy rooming house where he lives on the ragged edge of town.

"What did I miss?" Rebecca asked, sliding into the table.

"Harry Turnbull just told everyone that he knows who really killed Holly Mason," I said, watching her closely.

"Is that the old drunk who wanders the streets? Someone

should put him in care somewhere for his own good," she said, betraying no sign of nervousness at Harry's news.

"Maybe I'll go over and have a chat with him," Coop said.

"What could it hurt?" I asked.

Rebecca ignored me and said to Coop, "You don't take him seriously, do you? Besides, it's not even your case."

"I know," he said, pushing back his chair. "But I just want to talk to him, and maybe pass his name along to Erin Harper."

"She won't welcome you interfering in her job. I know I wouldn't," Rebecca said.

"Maybe not. But she should know if there's a lead she missed." He leaned over and squeezed her shoulder as he walked toward the bar.

I was torn. I badly wanted to know what he found out, right there and then. But with Rebecca on the scene, I wouldn't have an opportunity to talk to him one-on-one. There was a slight chance he'd let his guard down a little if we were alone. No chance, if Rebecca was in the vicinity. My burger basket was finished, my Jameson was gone, Gabe had had his first dive into Himmel society. And I'd had enough of Rebecca. It was a good time to leave.

"I should get going. Say goodbye to Coop for me, will you, Rebecca? I've got some work to do." Without waiting for her answer, I turned to Gabe and said, "Can I catch a ride with you? I walked over, but I want to update you on a couple of things."

"Sure," he said.

"I have to go, too," April said. "Miss Oprah is on medication for asthma, and she really doesn't let anyone but me give it to her. It was nice to meet you, Gabe. I'll see you—" here she nodded at Rebecca and Miguel, "tomorrow morning. 'Night."

Miguel said his goodbyes, too. When Coop returned to the table, he'd have no one but his lovely bride waiting. Just the way she liked it.

On the short drive to my place, I updated Gabe on my lack of success with the phone records. "And maybe the cell phone number isn't anything significant. The others weren't. But she did talk to whomever owns it three times within three days."

"I can subpoena the records for the number. Then, it'll take a couple of weeks for them to tell me they don't know who they belong to, because the customer paid cash."

"I know. We could try to find out who owns it by looking at the numbers it called, or received calls from, and then tracing those phones to see if whoever owns them had some connection we can prove to Holly. But that would take money and time we just don't have. Do you think the prosecution will have information on who it belongs to? They've got more resources than we do."

"I doubt they even tried. Why would they go after a long-shot lead like that, when they've got a prime suspect who fits the bill like Craig does?"

"Thanks, you're making me feel so much better."

"I'm not here to make things pretty. We've got a lousy hand to play so far."

"But you did talk to Timmins' office today, right? When are they going to send the rest of the discovery materials?"

"He wasn't in. I talked to the assistant DA. Another box of material is coming tomorrow. But not the client list."

"Why not? They used it to find Sophia Kowalski and from there to connect her to Craig. That's inculpatory evidence, isn't it?"

"Someone's been binging on *Law&Order*, hasn't she? Sorry, but no. They don't have the client list. Suzanne told you the truth. They didn't trust Craig's story, and they were anxious to find a motive. She wouldn't give them the records without a subpoena, either. But she agreed to check for Craig's name. She didn't come up with his, but Sophia's was there, and that's how they got to her."

"But they didn't check to see if anyone else in the Himmel area was a client of SweetMeets?"

"I guess they didn't think they needed to. Once they had a motive, everything fell into place. We'll get copies of Sophia's statement. She's on their witness list. But they don't have the client list to share."

"A pox on all their houses!"

He raised an eyebrow quizzically.

"I'm expanding my cursing vocabulary," I said by way of explanation. "OK, so they don't have it to give to us, but you can subpoena SweetMeets, right?"

"Already served. How long into this partnership are we going to go before you think I know what I'm doing? They have ten days to produce the records. Or they can move to quash the subpoena. Which they may do, based on confidentiality issues. Then we have to decide how bad we want it, because that's another long-drawn out fight on our hands."

"Maybe I can work on Suzanne a little more, see if she'll at least let us have records from this area."

He shook his head. "Won't happen. It sets a bad precedent. Clients won't want to sign up if they think their information could go public. From what she told you, they're already struggling to hold onto customers. She won't do anything to make that harder."

"But if we get the records, we're only going to care about a very small portion of them. And if SweetMeets doesn't tell the clients the records were subpoenaed, how would anyone know? Look at all those data breaches that happen and nobody finds out about them until years later."

"I like your tenacity, Leah. But put that thought on hold.

Let's see how they respond to the subpoenas. Stop by the office tomorrow and get the rest of the phone records we have for Holly. See if that mystery cell phone number shows up again."

"I will." I moved to get out of the car, but he stopped me by putting his hand on my arm.

"Hey, how about seeing another part of Himmel Friday night? Maybe a nice restaurant, with a table for two, not twenty?"

OK, no doubt now. He was hitting on me. I'm slow on the uptake at times, but this was pretty clear.

"Gabe, thanks. But, uh—"

"I'm a great guy, but you're seeing somebody. You hope we can be good friends. Is that the letdown line you're trying to spin?"

I nodded. "Pretty much. I'm sorry. I'm with my ex-husband now. It's complicated. He, we, well, it's complicated," I repeated. Then I moved to full-on babbling. "But, I know a lot of women. I'm sure I could hook you up with someone. Just give me your type, and I'll see what I can do. No need for Tinder, or Sweet-Meets," I finished in a lame attempt at humor.

"I like smart, funny, bossy women with slightly crooked noses and wide-open smiles. I'm partial to the name Leah, too. Do you have anyone in mind who matches that description?"

I felt a surge of guilty pleasure at his answer. I shouldn't be enjoying this so much when I was in an exclusive relationship with Nick.

He continued before I had to come up with a response.

"If things with your ex are so complicated, you should maybe think about simplifying your life. In my experience, do-overs don't work. Keep me in mind if it falls apart. Meanwhile, friends?" He smiled. I smiled back and nodded.

"Friends."

I had intended to put aside thoughts of Craig and his case for a while, and devote some time to the book I was supposed to be writing. But after I sat down with my laptop, my mind kept wandering.

I'd like to say that I was thinking about the ins and outs of the investigation and the next steps that needed to be taken to help Craig Kowalski. But in truth, I couldn't shake thoughts of my conversation with Gabe. I tried focusing on Nick.

Nick and I had a history. I loved his dark blond hair and the serious expression his face took on when he put on his glasses. He smelled good. He kissed good. He was tall and fit. He was smart. And he said that he was in love with me.

Gabe was abrupt and cocky, and he wasn't even that good looking. His eyes were nice, that's true. When he smiled or laughed or listened intently their dark brown warmth drew you in. When he was thinking, trying to work things out, they shone with intelligence. He was quick, and he was kind—look how he'd focused on April and made her feel worth listening to when Rebecca had been so nasty to her. But he really wasn't my type. He wasn't very tall, maybe only a few inches taller than me. He was more wiry than fit, and he was bossy.

I shook my head, then my whole body to throw off the ridiculous places my mind was going. To set myself firmly on task, I moved to the desk in my office. I opened my book file and worked diligently until one a.m., when I finally closed up shop and went to bed. And all that time, I hadn't given a thought to Nick or to Gabe. Or even to Craig Kowalski.

## 23

"Leah, I think you should reach out beyond Himmel, don't you? I think people in Omico and Merrivale—maybe even Madison? —would find it worth the drive. Especially with a director coming from New York to put it together."

"What? What time is it?"

My mother has a habit of calling whenever a pressing thought occurs to her, regardless of the hour. She also frequently starts a conversation in the middle, as though whoever she's talking to has been privy to the thoughts running through her mind.

"Time? It's six-thirty. Aren't you up yet? I'm sorry, hon. I just got back from the gym. I always come up with my best ideas when I'm working out. But you're awake, now, right?"

"Yeah. I'm awake. But I have no idea what you're talking about."

"The Fall Follies. You do remember that you promised to work on publicity, don't you?" she asked, sudden suspicion in her voice. And she was wise to be suspicious. My agreement to help with the major fundraiser for the Himmel Community Hospital, secured by my mother while I was under the influence of her triple chocolate brownies, had absolutely slipped my mind.

"Of course I remember. I've just been working on the plan."

"Right. Well, then I'm sure you remember that you and I are meeting with Gretchen Fraser tonight at her house to discuss publicity."

"Tonight? I don't think I can, Mom. Things aren't moving as fast as I'd like on Craig's case. I need to spend some time—"

"Leah, you promised. And if you think you're going to wriggle out of it, you're crazy. I'm not doing this without you."

"But—"

"I'll pick you up at seven." And she was off.

---

Miguel stopped by around eight, before he started work. I explained what I'd found the day before—and hadn't found—in the phone records, as well as the disappointing news that we weren't going to get the SweetMeets client list—at least not yet.

"I think we're going to have to go ahead and get the rest of the phone records from Gabe. I didn't want to go there because it's such tedious, time-consuming work, but we need a little luck and maybe we'll strike gold there. I have a conference call today with my agent and my editor, and I've got a lot to do to get ready for that. Plus, my mom reminded me—at six-thirty this morning —that I promised to help with PR for the hospital follies. I have to meet with her and Gretchen Fraser tonight. Things are really piling up." If I was expecting sympathy, I didn't get any.

"Same here, *chica.* I have *muy* many photos to shoot this morning, and I have to cover a special meeting for the county board of supervisors. You know how long that can go. And the new stringer—she's a nice lady, but with the camera?" He paused to shudder. "I have to reshoot everything she took."

"Right. So, here's what I'm thinking. We need to follow up on Harry's claim that the police got it wrong. But we also have to get to your neighbors, especially the ones who live closest to you, to hear firsthand what they saw that night. They may tell us something they didn't think was important enough to tell the police.

"But, we both have pretty full plates. So, why don't I buzz over and talk to your neighbors on either side around five. Then, you don't have to try and rush through your assignments. You can interview Harry when you're done for the day. I'll take care of everything else." I tried to make it sound like a generous offer, but Miguel was not having it.

"Oh, no-no-no, *chica*. You get nice neighbors with cookies, and I get Harry Turnbull? No. How about I take my neighbors, and you take Harry?"

"Hey, do I need to pull rank as the senior investigator in the Nash/Santos Agency? We both know that Harry will be burping last night's whiskey and smelling like a dumpster. That is clearly a job for a junior partner. Besides, you know him better than I do. He lives in your neighborhood. Kind of."

"He doesn't live in my neighborhood, *chica*. He only winds up there sometimes when he loses his way home. He fell asleep once this summer in the Rosenbaum's hedges. Too *borracho* to get all the way home."

He grimaced. Miguel is a compassionate soul. But his fastidious sensibilities can't help an instinctive recoil from the down and dirty side of life, and they don't get much downer or dirtier than Harry.

"Oh, all right. You win. I'll take Harry and you take the neighbors."

I pulled together what I needed for my conference call with Clinton and my editor and was making some notes when I got a text from Clinton: *Reprieve. Editor out with flu. Will reschedule conference later. Get writing!*

That was a welcome break. I ignored Clinton's exhortation and refocused on my side job as defense team consultant. I headed out to pick up the rest of the phone files from Gabe.

Miller's law office is ornate and old-fashioned. Located in the bottom floor of a two-story brick building that once housed a doctor's office and a tailor, it has high tin ceilings, oak wainscoting and thick carpets. It's very impressive, but no more so than his secretary Patty Delwyn.

She's a petite and precise woman with pixie-cut gray hair. Her small, full mouth is always perfectly lipsticked in a pale shade of pink. With her round blue eyes and wire-rimmed glasses, she reminds me a little of Mrs. Santa Claus. But her sweet exterior conceals a steely determination to ensure that Miller is well guarded from unnecessary intrusions. Despite her diminutive size, she's a commanding presence. Instead of being overwhelmed by the heavy wooden desk, the plush carpeting, and the opulent furnishings, she seems to rise above them. Literally. I suspect she has her chair adjusted to maximum height.

"I'm sorry, Leah, Gabe isn't in."

I had mentally rehearsed an easy breezy encounter with him that included no mention of our conversation in the car. But it wouldn't be necessary. I felt oddly let down. Disappointment must have shown on my face.

"Don't worry, he left the documents for you," she said, pulling a folder out from a desk drawer and handing it to me. "That is what you wanted, isn't it?" The question was innocuous, but her delivery made me wonder if she saw more than I was comfortable with.

"Yes. Sure. What else? Thanks, Patty," I said, and beat a hasty retreat.

———

From Miller's office, I zipped over to the Elite to get a chai tea before starting on the phone records. I'd hit the sweet spot of the morning, just after ten thirty. Coffee breakers and yoga moms were gone, lunch crowd hadn't started. It was so quiet, in fact, that I decided to snag a table in the corner and start working through the phone records there. The warm bakery smells and the generally cheery atmosphere lifted my mood. I had gone through half a dozen pages with no repeat of the prepaid cell phone number when two hands clamped down on either side of my neck and squeezed. I shivered involuntarily and shook them off.

"Coop, you know I hate that. It gives me the willies." I marked my place on the page and looked up as he slid onto the chair across from me and set his cup of coffee down.

"That's why I do it." He grinned. I shook my head and smiled back.

"You left pretty quick last night," he said.

"Yeah, well, I had some work to do."

He nodded. "Gabe seems like a nice guy. Think he can do the job for Craig?"

"I don't know. It's not going to be easy. Your new detective, Erin Harper, seems like she's got her case pretty well sewed up. Not much wiggle room."

He looked at me with his gray eyes slightly narrowed, as though he were deciding something. "You should talk to Harry."

"Why? Did he say something to you at the bar? Did you give his information to Erin Harper? Did he really see a woman going into Miguel's house the night Holly was killed?" I had leaned slightly forward with excitement, grazing my chai with my hand. The cup wavered precariously. Coop reached over and righted it before the contents ran all over my phone records.

"Take it easy. I'm just saying it could be worth it to talk to him. I don't have any breaking news, but you might learn something. I can't give you more than that."

"I'm planning on it, later today. But did you tell Detective Harper what he said? Wait, no, never mind. Of course you did. Is she going to follow-up?"

"It's not my case, Leah. And I'm not her boss. This isn't you and me going back and forth over some investigation we're both working on. I gave her the information. It's up to her if she thinks it's worth pursuing. But remember, it's Harry. He's not the most reliable witness. If Erin talks to him, she might not be too impressed."

"Well, she wouldn't be, would she? If she takes Harry seriously, she might have to reconsider stitching up Craig for murder."

"Hey, now. That's not fair. Erin's OK. She's a little eager to make her mark, but any good detective, including me, presented with the evidence against Craig would reach the same conclusion."

I was shaking my head before he finished, a trait I hate in other people but find myself doing quite frequently in my urge to make my points. "No, no you wouldn't. Or at least you wouldn't exclude any evidence that didn't fit with your theory."

"Are you saying that's what Erin did?"

"I'm saying that your cops didn't bother to look through the SweetMeets database to see if anyone from this area had a connection to it. I'm saying they didn't go very deep into Holly Mason's background either. And—" I stopped abruptly, suddenly remembering Gabe's warning about tipping our hand.

"And what?"

"And I can't give *you* more than that, either."

For a second he looked surprised, and maybe a little hurt. He was always the one I kicked my ideas around with, even though sometimes it seemed he was kicking them down more than around.

"No, you're right. It's different this time."

I wanted to say *Everything is different, because you had to marry Rebecca, and you don't even know who she is*. Instead, I searched for a safer topic. And what could be safer than babies?

"How are things in daddy land? Buy any more Teddy bears?"

"Great! We've been figuring out how we want to fix up that back bedroom as a nursery. And I'm thinking about fencing in the yard. You know, so when the baby goes out, he—or she—can run around and play without us having to worry about cars or anything."

"Hmm. I don't know a lot about babies, but won't it be awhile before he—or she—is ready to roam around the yard? Doesn't it take like a year before they can even walk?"

"Some babies, sure. But I'm sure ours is going to be exceptional." He said the words in a teasing tone, but I knew that underneath he meant every word. He was more excited about the baby than I'd ever seen him about anything.

"No doubt, Coop. No doubt." I smiled and shifted the conversation to goings on at city hall, Charlie Ross's suspension, and other non-fraught topics. But beneath our casual chit-chat, I couldn't stop thinking about what might happen when Coop found out that Rebecca had lied to him about who she really was. And what that would mean for his baby dreams.

## 24

I had spent the bulk of the afternoon trolling through Holly Mason's phone records without much to show for it. The prepaid cell phone number had shown up only once more, a month earlier. The only interesting thing about that was that Holly had made the call, and it had lasted forty-five minutes. Still, that wasn't much. By the time I finished, it was nearly five. I had just about enough time to try and talk to Harry, and then get home to shower and eat before my mother picked me up.

Though I knew all about Harry, as is the way in small towns, we'd never actually met. We didn't exactly run in the same circles, nor had he ever done anything noteworthy or scandalous enough to warrant newspaper coverage during my various stints at the *Himmel Times*. Though Miguel had disavowed neighbor status with him, Harry did live only a few blocks away. But the area was very different from Miguel's well-trimmed part of town.

It's a toss-up how Harry's neighborhood will break. It could go on an upswing, buoyed by young professionals and families looking for bargains on houses they're willing to fix up. Or it could slide into further decline as landlords scoop up the dilapidated structures and turn them into low-end rentals. The house Harry lived in fell into that category.

I rang the bell. A thin woman wearing a T-shirt, sweatpants, and a sour expression opened the door. The smell of cooked cabbage and stale cigarettes wafted out.

"What do you want?" She shoved a piece of oily brown hair off her forehead and stared at me with hard eyes.

"I'd like to speak to Harry Turnbull."

"I'm not the maid. I'm the manager. You want Harry, go on up and see if he's there. His room's at the end of the hall. The one with the blue door."

She stepped aside so I could enter. As I climbed the stairs, she turned and walked back toward what I assumed were her own living quarters. I heard the door slam as I reached the second-floor landing. The corridor was narrow and dark. An odor of unwashed bodies and unemptied wastebaskets hung in the air and caused my nose to wrinkle involuntarily.

As I walked toward the blue door, I could hear the noise of television coming from another room, and the sound of a toilet flushing and water running at the end of the hall in what was presumably the communal bathroom.

I tapped on Harry's door. When there was no answer, I knocked harder. I heard a sort of snuffling sound, followed by a cough, but nothing else. I pounded harder and this time a querulous voice said, "Go away."

"Harry? My name is Leah Nash. I'd like to talk to you for a minute."

"Go 'way, I said. I'm sleepin'. "

"Open the door, Harry! So's the rest of us can live in peace, fer cryin' out loud," shouted a woman's voice from across the hall. Still there was no movement. I began talking loudly through the door.

"Harry, I heard what you said in McClain's last night. About the woman who was murdered. I just want you to tell me what you saw."

Abruptly, the door opened. Harry Turnbull, eyes rheumy and bloodshot, face unshaven, gray hair plastered to his narrow skull, gestured for me to come in.

The shades were drawn, and the room was so stuffy it was hard to breathe. Harry stumbled across to a chest of drawers and turned on the lamp that rested on the top. The light from its naked bulb threw the room into stark relief. A graying blanket that had once been white was crumpled on a bare, stained mattress. Under the window, stuffing poked through an upholstered chair. A stack of library books, tilting at a crazy angle, sat next to it. A coat rack, holding a frayed winter jacket and two plaid shirts, stood in one corner. And that was it.

The only decorative thing in the room was a page torn from a magazine and taped to the wall above Harry's bed. The camera had caught a farm scene at sunset. Golden light spilled across the fields of wheat in the foreground. A little girl with pale blonde hair sat at the edge of the field, her face buried in the ruff of a collie's neck. In the distance was a white farm house and a red barn. It was the only lovely thing in that sad and tawdry space.

Harry saw me looking at it. "I took it off a magazine at the library. I shouldna, but the girl looks like Evie. My sister. Looks like our dog, too."

It startled me to think of this shambling old man as a little boy who'd once had a golden-haired sister named Evie, and a dog, and maybe even lived on an idyllic farm. Which was stupid of me, because of course he hadn't been born a destitute alcoholic. He'd had a life and hopes and dreams, none of which centered on a grubby rental in a rooming house on its last legs.

"What was your dog's name?"

"Laddie. He was a real good dog."

"Did you live on a farm, then?"

But he was done reminiscing.

"You got money?" he asked gruffly. Booze-soaked his brain might be, but he was canny enough to recognize that he had something I wanted.

"How much?"

"A hundred dollars."

"OK, come on now, Harry. You were willing to tell it to the bartender for the price of a drink last night. Do I look like a winning lottery ticket to you? I'll give you ten dollars."

It wasn't that I begrudged him the money, from the looks of things he needed it. But I knew that in the grip of his alcoholism, he wouldn't use it for a warm blanket or a pillow or anything that might make his life slightly less bleak. He'd head straight for the nearest seller of rotgut whiskey. And to a man in Harry's situation, even ten dollars looked like a win.

He nodded and gestured toward the chair. I was leery, but perched gingerly on it as he sat down on the corner of his bed.

"Last night at McClain's you said you knew who killed 'that floozy.' Who did you mean?"

"Her. The one on the TV. Haley somethin'. You know, the prostitute. The one that got herself murdered right up the street." He gestured in the general direction of Miguel's house, his hand shaking slightly.

"What did you mean, the police got it wrong?"

"Craig, he don't give me money. But if I'm real hungry, he gives me food sometimes." He fidgeted as he sat on the bed, first bouncing his leg up and down, then repeatedly running his hand over his thin, lank hair.

My heart sank. Was Harry's assertion based on Craig's kindness to him? There were plenty of people in Himmel willing to provide Craig with a character reference. A recommendation from an always-under-the-influence Harry would carry no weight.

"So, are you saying Craig is too nice a person to kill Holly Mason? That was her name, not Haley. Is that why you think the cops got it wrong?" But Harry had lost interest while I was speaking. Without answering, he dropped to one knee and began rooting around under his bed.

"Harry? Are you all right? Can I help?"

He emerged triumphant, holding a bottle of Old Crow with about a quarter of the golden liquid left.

"Still some left!" He held it to his lips with a quivering hand, and drained off the remainder. Then he let out a satisfied "Ahhh!" and wiped his mouth on his sleeve. I had to admit his eyes brightened a little after the shot. Maybe it would help him focus.

"Harry, you were saying Craig is a nice guy. Is that why you think he didn't kill Holly Mason?"

He began coughing, a rattling hack that shook his thin body. When he stopped, he used the all-purpose sleeve to wipe his eyes, which had teared up from the force of the coughing.

"Nah. I seen her. I seen her go in the house. And then I seen her go running out. She had hair like Evie's. That's what I thought when I seen her."

My heart rose as rapidly as it had plummeted seconds before. She. With pale blonde hair like his little sister's. Like Rebecca's.

"Harry, what did she look like? The woman you saw? Do you know who she is?"

He took another swig from his bottle, gulping it down this time like a kid with a forbidden soda. The amount he had swigged in the past few minutes would've had me under the table, but long years had given him a high tolerance.

Impatiently, I prodded him again.

"Harry? The woman, the one you saw. Do you know her name?"

"She was pretty. Yeah. Real pretty. Like Evie."

"Did you know her, Harry?" I asked again. I leaned in to try to catch his attention, and struggled not to flinch at his whiskey-soured breath. "The woman. What was her name?"

He shook his head. "Dunno. I dunno her name."

Harry needed a reset.

"You want that money, don't you, Harry? The ten dollars I promised you?"

He nodded.

"OK, then listen hard. Put down the bottle, and we're going to walk through what you did that night. I'm going to help you remember, all right?"

He nodded again.

"You were drinking that night, weren't you?" I knew that was a safe assumption because Harry drank every night. "Sometimes when you drink, you take a little nap under a tree or a hedge, don't you? Is that what happened? Did you fall asleep under a tree or a hedge in someone's yard?"

"It was cold. I was real cold," he said, his eyes widening. Some synapse had fired off in his brain.

"Yes, it was the first really cold night of fall. Did you walk home from the bar?" Again, another safe assumption. Harry didn't own a car. "Were you hungry? Did you go to Bonucci's to see if Craig would feed you?"

"Craig wasn't there. That kid that runs the kitchen, he told me to get lost." He laughed a little then, though it didn't seem funny to me.

"I did get lost. I got lost goin' home. Then I got tired. Real tired. I hadda rest. I laid down."

"Do you know what time it was?" If Harry had been capable of rolling his eyes at me at that point, he clearly would have.

Instead, he settled for sticking his skinny, scabbed arms out and saying, "You don't see no watch, do ya?"

"Right, OK. Do you remember where you laid down when you felt so tired?"

He frowned at me as though he found my comprehension skills lacking. "Under the bushes. Them bushes. I fell asleep. King woke me up."

"A king woke you up? What king?"

"The dog. King the dog."

"What kind of dog? Whose dog?"

"Dunno. Like a police dog. One of them German kind."

"Who called him King?"

"The man that had him. The dog woke me up. The guy said, 'Go home, you.' And then he left, I guess. I wanted to go home. I tried, but I was real tired." I knew there was no point asking him what time this had occurred ... if it had occurred at all, I reminded myself.

"Then what happened?"

He shrugged. "I fell asleep again. Then the shiverin' woke me up. That's when I seen the car lights, goin' into the driveway. I watched and she got out. The woman. I was still thinkin' about how to get up and go home, when I seen her come out again."

Maybe, just maybe this story would hang together after all.

"You left the bar, and you went to Bonnuci's, but Craig wasn't there, so you didn't get any food. You started to walk home, but you got so tired, you fell asleep under a bush. A man walking his dog saw you, and told you to go home. The man and his dog left, and you fell back asleep. But later it got colder, and it woke you up. That's when you saw the woman go into the house?"

"She drove in real fast. Yeah."

"Now, were you sleeping next to the house she went into, or across the street?"

"Across the street. She couldn't see me. I was under the bushes."

"You were still lying down?"

"I was tryin' to sit up. It was hard," he said, an aggrieved note in his voice, as though I didn't understand what it was like to be old and drunk and stiff from lying under a bush. Which, thankfully, I didn't.

"What did the woman look like?"

"Pretty."

"OK. Was she old, young? Fat, thin? Blonde hair, black hair?"

"It was like Evie's hair. Evie was real pretty."

"Could you see her face, Harry?"

"Not so good. I got good eyes still. Don't need glasses. No cataracts or nothin'. But—" Here he hesitated.

"But you were pretty drunk, and it was hard to focus, right?"

He looked down and said quietly, "Yeah. But she was there. I seen her go in, and she come runnin' out."

"What about her car? What color was the car?" Miguel's next-door neighbor Oralee had told the police she saw Craig's car there around one in the morning. But what if the mystery blonde's car was similar in color to Craig's? Rebecca had a silver car.

"I think it was gray? Yeah, mebbe gray-like."

"Are you sure? It wasn't silver?"

"Coulda been. I'm gettin' awful thirsty."

I knew then I'd made a mistake. Harry was eager to please now and collect his money. I shouldn't have suggested the car might have been silver. I wanted it to be Rebecca's car. But having planted the idea in Harry's mind, I couldn't be sure what he'd actually seen. It was possible, maybe even probable, that Harry wasn't any better at describing colors than most men. The car could've been silver, but he'd used the word gray to encompass shades ranging from cinder block to charcoal. And now I'd tainted his memory.

There was no point in asking Harry how long between the time the blonde woman had entered the house and when she left. In his alcoholic haze, time wouldn't have meant much. I could check at Bonucci's and see when he'd been turned away from the kitchen. And if we could find the dog-walker, that would help establish when Harry had been there. And maybe the neighbors would have something to add. If Miguel's chat with them turned up the information from the dog-walker, that would establish Harry had been there, and at about what time.

It was going to take more than Harry's hazy memory to prove anything, but it felt like we might have a building block for an alternate theory, even if it was a bit wobbly just now.

## 25

"So, let's go over what we discussed," Gretchen Fraser said. She, my mother, and I were sitting at her highly polished oak dining table in a house that was pretty highly polished everywhere you looked.

We'd just spent an excruciating two hours, at least for me, going over Gretchen's detailed plans—which she had described as "just a few ideas I jotted down"—for every aspect of the upcoming follies fundraiser.

"Oh, I don't think we need to do that," my mother intervened. "You're an excellent organizer, Gretchen, and I'm sure the notes you've taken are perfect. We'll be able to follow them easily. You can just email them to us, right Leah?

"Right, Mom," I said, trying hard to convey in the simple phrase how much she was going to suffer for roping me into the project.

"Really? All right then, that will save time. Now," Gretchen said, as she rose from the table and moved toward the kitchen, "I've made some Kalamata-garbanzo hummus. It's gluten-free. It's really delicious with quinoa crackers. You must have some. We can't be all business, right?"

I gave my mom some serious side eye. If there's one thing I like less than committee meetings, it's olives. She kicked me under the table, but nevertheless, I persisted.

"Sounds, great, Gretchen, but I shouldn't. I'm behind on a deadline, and I really need to get to work on my book."

Even I, desperate to make an escape, could see the disappointment on Gretchen's face as she came to the table in all her gluten-free glory.

"Oh, we can spare just a minute, Leah. This looks wonderful," my mother said.

Note to self: remember not to ride with your mother, so you can exit at will.

"Now that I see it, Gretchen, how can I say no?" I added.

I piled some quinoa chips on the small plate she handed me, and tried to work around the olives as I spooned some of the hummus on my plate. The quinoa chips were actually pretty good.

"You must give me the recipe for this," my mother said.

"It's very easy, really. You just—" But before she could answer, she was interrupted by the banging of the outside door that opened into the kitchen. "Mom? Mom!"

"Gus, I'm in the dining room. With guests. Please don't bellow like that! And shut the door so the cat doesn't get out, please."

The Frasers' son filled the room with his large presence, his head nearly touching the door frame. Knowing about Allie's crush on him, I looked a little more closely than I had when I first saw him with his parents at the Elite Café. I decided I approved. He wore his brown hair cut close on the sides and a bit longer on top. The style made his ears, which were a little large, stand out a bit, but I found that rather endearing. His eyes were steady and a clear light brown, like his dad's. I liked the way he leaned down and put his large hand on top of his mother's perfect hair, causing her to squeal. "Gus! Stop it!" Her words were stern, but her eyes softened when she looked up at her son. He removed his hand with a grin and turned to us.

"Hi, Mrs. Nash."

"Hello, Gus, how are you?"

"Good, thanks." To me he said, "You were at the Elite a couple of weeks ago, right? I'm Gus. I know you're Leah Nash. Allie talks about you a lot."

"She's a good kid," I said. "Nice to meet you, Gus."

"Gus, we're finishing up a meeting. There's some left-over spaghetti in the refrigerator. Why don't you heat some in the microwave and take it downstairs to the den?"

He was already rooting in the refrigerator. "That's OK, Mom. I'll eat it cold, right out of the container. I'm starving. Bye, Nashes, nice to see you," he called out as he clattered down the stairs to the basement.

"He's a very nice boy, Gretchen, you and Will must be proud," my mother said.

"Yes," she said. "I couldn't ask for a better son."

I noted that she didn't say *we couldn't*, which seemed like what one-half of a two-part parental unit would say.

"Where is Will tonight?" I asked. "I wanted to tell him that the new lamp posts downtown look really good."

"He's at a meeting," she said, in a tone that indicated she had nothing more to say on the subject. And to insure it was dropped, she changed the topic.

"Leah, I heard that Miller Caldwell has a new attorney working with him. I can't remember his name, but Mary Beth told me that you're helping him to defend Craig Kowalski. Is that true?"

"Yeah. His name's Gabe Hoffman. Miller brought him in so he could start taking on criminal defense cases. I'm doing a little research for him to help out."

"Well, I hope he can plead mitigating circumstances. Craig and Lydia are such nice people. But I can certainly understand why Craig would do it. You can call it what you like, but a website like SweetMeets is nothing more than online prostitution. For a young girl like Sophia to be entrapped in that—well, it's no wonder Craig would go crazy. It's justifiable homicide, if you ask me."

"Actually, I don't think he did go crazy. I don't believe he did it."

She looked confused. "Oh, but I thought, that is, someone at the hospital said that it's an open and shut case. Aren't there witnesses who saw him there? And Craig's fingerprints are on the weapon, isn't that right?"

It's not that there aren't secrets in a small town. Believe me, there are. But once you've got a relatively public spectacle like a murder investigation, there's no shortage of "insider" information.

"Who's spreading that? Angie, Dale Darmody's wife? She's still a volunteer at the hospital, right? You know, Gretchen, I can't talk about the particulars of the case, but I will say I wouldn't rely too much on alleged inside sources. Especially not if they come attached to Darmody."

"Oh? There's another suspect?"

"I'll just say that the defense has a few things up its sleeve. It's not as cut and dried as the DA might want it to be." I shouldn't have said that much, but I hated that the whole town was talking as though Craig's conviction was a done deal.

"Really? Can't you tell me just a little? I won't tell anyone, if that's what you're worried about."

"Won't tell anyone what?"

I looked toward the doorway and saw Will Fraser standing there. He came into the room and dropped a kiss on the top of Gretchen's head.

"Cleo got out again last night, Will. Chasing that cat all over the neighborhood because you can't remember to close the door is getting old."

A pained expression crossed his face, but he didn't give her the snarky remark I would have, if my wife had read me out in front of guests.

"Hello, Will," my mother said quickly to sidestep the awkward moment.

I chimed in as well.

"Hey, Will. Good to see you. I was telling Gretchen earlier that I think the new lamp posts downtown look great."

His face lit up, and it was easy to see where Gus got his smile. "Really? Thanks, Leah. I've been getting an earful from some of the residents who think it was a waste of city funds."

"They're probably just trying to keep Duane Stanton's memory alive. With him gone, who's going to be on pencil patrol to make sure you don't throw out stubs longer than three inches?"

"Leah, that's not very nice."

"I was just kidding, Mom. Duane was a character, that's all."

"Yes, he definitely was. Millie Gertzman, the city clerk, said the other day it felt odd not to have Duane standing at the counter to file an Open Records Act request every week. I know what she means."

"That's you, Will, just oozing empathy for everybody. Seriously, can you name one thing that he ever uncovered that made any difference at all?" Gretchen asked.

"When it comes down to it, nobody makes a difference like you, I guess, Gretchen." Will's voice was deceptively mild. The expression on his face was not pleasant. I was starting to feel like I had stumbled onto the set of *Who's Afraid of Virginia Woolf?* I glanced at my mother, and she nodded imperceptibly.

"She certainly does make a difference, Will," my mother said. We both stood, and as she slipped her arm into the sleeve of her jacket, she said, "Thanks again, Gretchen, for everything. Leah's got a deadline, and I've got an early morning start tomorrow. Good to see you both. We'll be in touch."

She hugged Gretchen and Will, and I waved at them as we swept out the door.

---

"Well, that was a little uncomfortable," I said as we buckled our seat belts. "Did you see the look on her face when Will kissed the top of her head? Like if we weren't there, she would have grabbed him in a hammer lock and thrown him on the table—and not in an amorous way."

"It got pretty fraught in there, especially toward the end, I agree. But don't be so hard on her. Everybody loves Will, but it's not that easy to live with a full-time charmer. What they get away with, you end up having to clean up." Empathy for Gretchen was evident in her voice. My father had been a pretty charming guy that everyone liked. It was my mother who had to do the hard work of keeping our family running. I could see that she felt a little solidarity with Gretchen.

"Yeah, I suppose. You know, Allie said that Gus was worried because his parents have been fighting lately."

"I'm sorry to hear that. It doesn't surprise me a lot, though. Will is getting to that age when men think that life might be passing them by. Gretchen might sense that, and it's making her hold on harder. The trouble is, if you hold on to a relationship too hard, you can squeeze the life out of it. I know she loves Will, and you can see that Gus means everything to her. I hope they figure things out."

"Yeah, he seems like a really nice kid."

"Speaking of figuring things out, what's going on with the Leah Nash/Miguel Santos Detective Agency? You haven't told me what you've been up to for days."

"Well, that's not my fault. I would've stopped by Sunday, but you were all, 'I'm making dinner for Paul. The amazing wonder boyfriend.' " I said it in a teasing sing-song voice, because I really do like Paul, and I'm glad he and Mom are together.

She made a face. "You could've come for dinner, and you know it. Now, what's been happening?"

As I ran down my meeting with Suzanne, figuring out Holly's connection to Rebecca, my temporary dead-end with their Kinmont classmate Merlin Duffy, the unsatisfactory phone records, and Harry Turnbull's surprising story, I realized we'd actually done quite lot.

"Sounds pretty good, doesn't it?"

"Yes. But why aren't you more excited? Especially because you've got Rebecca in your sights."

"And that is absolutely, swear on a bible, secret," I said.

"When have I ever betrayed a secret of yours? And you've been giving them to me for years."

It's true. Mom likes a good rumor round-up as well as anyone, but she's very careful with a confidence.

"True that. Mom, I think we're on to something that could really help Craig. This whole Rebecca knows Holly thing, and that she lies about it, it has to mean something. Gabe was impressed," I said.

"Oh? What's he like?"

"I don't know. He seems pretty smart. He treats me like a member of the team, not an annoyance. I think he knows what he's doing."

"Hmm."

"Hmm, what?"

"Nothing. Just hmm."

"Mom, why don't you just say whatever it is you want to say."

"All right, since you force me. And don't say you didn't ask for my opinion. I've got it on tape."

"I wouldn't be surprised. But OK, what?"

"How does Nick feel about you getting so involved in all of this? You've got a book to finish and a murder to investigate, that doesn't leave much time for him, does it? And as I recall, Nick doesn't do well when left to his own devices."

"He's fine with it. He told me so. In fact, he's so fine with me that he's been talking about us moving in together, if you must know."

It was sort of fun to watch the internal struggle play across her features. She had so much she wanted to say. She disliked Nick, but she knew he was important to me. She thought she had crucial wisdom to impart, but she didn't want me to get mad at her for interfering. I made a mental bet on which Carol Nash would win. I should've put real money on it.

"Hon, do you really think that's a good idea? You've just settled down in your own space. You and Nick might be doing fine now. But how much time do you really spend together? Romantic weekends are a lot different from day-to-day living in a space that's great for one, but could be pretty cramped for two. And you haven't even really had a chance to see if he is, as he insists and you seem determined to believe, 'a changed man.' Leah, I know you don't like to hear me say it, but I just—"

"Don't think Nick is the right man for me," I finished for her. "I know you don't, Mom. To be honest, I'm not sure that I think he is either. He's been great—for the most part. But sometimes he makes me feel, I don't know, a little boxed in, I guess."

I knew she must be feeling a little victory thrill, thinking that her anti-Nick campaign was working. Well, let her. I wasn't about to tell her that my unexpected attraction to a fast-talking, brash attorney who wasn't even my type was at the root of my uncertainty. That would open a whole other line of questioning I wasn't ready for.

Showing admirable restraint, all she said was, "Well. I think that's wise, Leah."

---

## 26

The next day I worked diligently on my book, but my mind kept drifting back to the investigation. I was anxious to connect with Miguel and see what he'd found out from his neighbors. I'd called to tell him Harry's story, so he could see if anyone could verify that he'd been passed out under the bushes. I wanted to believe that Harry had been there and that the golden-haired mystery woman he saw was Rebecca, but I had to be careful. Sometimes you want things so bad, you believe in things that aren't real. And Harry was nobody's idea of a reliable witness.

However, there was a chance that someone had seen Harry, but hadn't mentioned it to the police, because it wasn't odd enough. When questioned about that night, they would search their memories for something not normal to explain how an event as horrifying and abnormal as murder had happened in their neighborhood. Harry sleeping off a drunk might not have struck them as unusual enough to report.

Late in the afternoon, Miguel buzzed and I let him in. He didn't look like he had good news.

"*Chica,* my neighbors are all nice, and they all said how sad they are about Uncle Craig. But nobody saw Harry, or anything else," he said, flopping down on the couch next to me.

"Did you find the dog walker?"

"No. Maybe he doesn't live on my street. It could've been anybody. Or nobody," he added gloomily.

"Even Miss Marple didn't have anything to say?"

Miguel's next-door neighbor is a retired kindergarten teacher named Oralee Smith. I call her Miss Marple, though not to her face. She's soft and fluffy, is very interested in the comings and goings of her neighbors, and likes to tell long chatty stories—though she's never shown signs of being an ace detective, more's the pity.

"She wasn't home last night."

"Well, then, don't be so down. She still might be able to help."

"She's the one who told the police she saw my uncle's car in the driveway the second time. She's the reason the police think he lied about that night."

"So, do you think Oralee is lying?"

"No, she wouldn't do that. But *Tío* Craig isn't lying either."

"OK. So that means there has to be another way to interpret what she saw. Harry said he saw a gray car, which is what Craig's is. But there are many shades of gray—no pun intended. Maybe the car Harry and Oralee saw was the same kind as Craig's, but a different shade of gray. It would be hard to tell at night. The second car could belong to Harry's mystery woman, but Oralee assumed it was Craig's. If we go over her story with that in mind, Oralee might be able to help."

"Well, maybe," he said, his naturally optimistic temperament beginning to surface.

"Think of this. Super-duper Detective Harper is trying to meet her 'forty-eight hours' deadline. She's pressing hard, and Oralee is getting more and more scattered. Finally, they nail down that she saw Craig's car twice, once at nine-thirty when he was leaving, and once around one a.m., parked in the driveway. The detective doesn't ask if Oralee saw anything else, because she's sure the car is the main thing. Oralee is too rattled to mention Harry. She might have even forgotten, or thought it wasn't important."

"That could be true." He nodded.

"Not only that, if we can find the dog walker, that's more support for Harry's story. In fact, if we get the dog guy, he can confirm Harry was there, and give us a time. Who knows? Maybe King's owner even noticed a grayish car going down the street after he left Harry, driven by a blonde."

"But we don't even know if the dog walker was real, or a dream of Harry's."

"Not yet. But prepare to put on your walking shoes my friend. Tonight, we canvas all the houses within a six-block area of yours to find a man with a dog named King. And, we'll try Oralee again. She has to come home sometime."

———

After serving Miguel one of my dinner specialties, a delicious and nutritious bowl of Honey Nut Cheerios, we set off on our door-to-door. The plan was to go up one side of the street and down the other, starting and ending at Miguel's, searching for a man with a dog named King.

Because there were no lights on at Oralee Smith's house, I started on the opposite side of the street, hoping that by the time I'd made my way back along Miguel's side, I might find her home.

I hadn't done this much house-to-house work since I tried to win a trip to Disney World during a school candy-selling fundraiser. This time I had more doors shut in my face. People are definitely more suspicious nowadays—or maybe I'm just not as cute as I was in fifth grade. Of those willing to chat, only two recalled seeing a man walking his dog in the late evenings around the neighborhood. One was sure the dog was a terrier, and the other thought it was a boxer. Neither had any description for the man, other than that he was "older" and wore a hat. But maybe not.

I was pretty discouraged when I finally wound up back at Miguel's. But my spirits lifted when I saw a light on in Oralee's window. When I knocked on the door, she opened it wide and invited me in.

Outside, Oralee's house is a red brick ranch style. Inside, it's what I imagine the interior of a gingerbread house looks like. Wooden shelves with cut-out hearts, gingham curtains at the kitchen windows, rag rugs on polished wooden floors, furniture upholstered with flower-patterned fabric, and lots of knick-knacks give a slightly overstuffed feel to the whole place. On this night, there was even the smell of ginger and cinnamon in the air. As I sat down at the kitchen table, Oralee put the kettle on for tea.

"I made gingerbread today, would you like some?"

"Yes, please."

She handed me a slice on a paper plate, then put a mug of tea in front of me.

"You go ahead, dear. At my age, I can't have anything too heavy on my stomach after dinner."

I smiled, took a huge bite of the warm cake, and immediately felt as though my jaws were glued together. I tried to release the thick, glutinous mass of doughy cake from the roof of my mouth with my tongue, but had to resort to a gulp of hot tea. Oralee, with her soft white hair, plump pink cheeks, and sweet expression might look like someone's cute, homemaker grandma, but she sure didn't bake like one.

I put my fork down. "I haven't had gingerbread in a long time," I said, choosing that as the most truthful but inoffensive thing I could say. And it would be a long time before I had it again, I did not add.

"I don't really care for it much, but my father always liked it. So, sometimes I make it just so the house smells like it did when I was a girl. I usually end up giving it to my sister Alice. Those grandkids of hers could eat a house," she said. Which might have gone down easier than Oralee's gingerbread.

"So, Oralee, I wanted to talk to you, because I'm working with Craig Kowalski's attorney."

"Yes, I heard. But I'm not sure I should talk to you about it," she said. "I don't know if Detective Harper would like that."

"I don't think it's a problem. I've actually already read your interview with the police. I just wanted to hear it in your own words."

"Well, I guess that would be all right. I feel awfully bad, you know, testifying against Craig. I've known him since he was a boy. It's so hard to believe that he could have murdered anyone. But I did see his car there twice that night. Once, when I came home from going to the movies with my sister. He was just leaving then. I called out to him, but he didn't answer. Then later, when I was going to bed."

"What did you do after you saw Craig the first time?"

"I went inside and changed into my nightie and robe. I washed and dried some dishes, took a load of clothes out of the washing machine. Then I checked all the doors and windows, just to make sure Arthur and I were safe and sound, like I do every night." Arthur, I knew, wasn't her husband—Oralee is a widow—nor her boyfriend. Instead, he was her cat. I also knew that Oralee regularly used home safety as a pretext for peering out of all her windows to make sure she was up on all the comings and goings in the neighborhood. Just like she uses working in her garden, or opening all the curtains to let in the light, as a daytime excuse for checking out what everyone is up to.

"You didn't happen to see anyone then? I mean, when you were checking the locks and things."

"No, no one was out. Well, that's not really true. I did notice that poor soul Harry. He was across the street under the Rosenbaum's bushes."

That had definitely not been in her statement to the police. In my excitement, I knocked my gingerbread to the floor, though not entirely by accident. "I'm so sorry! Let me get that," I said, picking up the plate and putting the gingerbread in the wastebasket.

"You saw Harry Turnbull the night of the murder? He was right across the street from Miguel's, did I hear you right? What time was it?"

"Yes, dear, that's what I said. It was just about ten-thirty when I noticed him. My grandfather clock had just chimed the half hour. I have it set so it doesn't go off from eleven at night until six in the morning. My husband George liked it to chime all night, but I never did. The first thing I did after George passed away was reset the chime on that clock. I did quite a few other things, too, of course. I—"

To avoid a discourse on life after George, I tried to refocus Oralee. "Did you see Harry in the neighborhood often?"

"Oh, yes. We're on his way home, you know. He doesn't usually sleep under the bushes, but it has happened a little more frequently of late. I wonder if he isn't perhaps suffering from the early stages of dementia. George got very disoriented when it started for him. It's hard to tell with the drinking, though. Harry's, not George's. I thought about going out and putting a blanket on him. I do feel sorry for him. But then I decided if I did that, he might just settle in for the night. He always wakes up after a few hours and manages to get home. So, I didn't."

"And then what did you do?"

"Well, I went to the den to read. I always like to read awhile before going to sleep. Arthur and I had started a very exciting book. It's all about a woman who has amnesia, and she marries a very wealthy man, only then, a man who says he's her real husband comes to their mansion. She doesn't want to go with him, but he has a marriage license, and I think—" I cut her off before she gave me a line by line recap of *In a Stranger's Arms,* the thick paperback I could see peeking out of her knitting bag in the corner.

"How long were you reading?"

"Well, long past my bedtime. It was such an interesting story. Not very real, maybe, but you don't always want reality, do you? I must have fallen asleep though, because the motion sensor light on my back porch went off. My son insisted on putting it up for security, but all it does is go off and annoy me whenever some night creature goes by. I looked at my watch and saw it was eleven-thirty. Then I took a peek out back to see if a deer had set it off. I've been having a terrible problem with deer. They're absolutely overrunning the town. They went through five pounds of bird seed in one night! I'm thinking about getting out George's old shotgun to chase them away."

"So, you saw a deer, and then you?" I asked to bring her back on topic, but instead she went further afield.

"Oh, no. It wasn't a deer. Just Gretchen Fraser, chasing after her cat. They live right behind me, the Frasers, you know. That must happen twice a week, at least. She told me that her husband Will doesn't shut the door tightly. She said she's going to get an electric fence to keep the cat in, but she hasn't yet. I've wondered if I should tell her that I've noticed, just in passing you know, when I happen to be glancing out the window, that young Gus has taken to coming and going at night through the basement window. And that's probably how her cat is getting out."

I was not interested in the nocturnal adventures of Gus Fraser.

"Oralee, did you notice? Was Harry still under the bushes then?"

"Yes, he was. I decided to make myself a cup of cocoa with a little peppermint schnapps, so soothing, I think. On my way to the kitchen, I looked out and I could see Harry still stretched out under the Rosenbaum's bushes. He stirred a little bit, like he was having a dream.

"Arthur and I went back to the den. I drank my cocoa and read for a while, even though I was getting very sleepy. I wanted to see how Basil—that was Arianna's wealthy husband—was going to react when he found that the marriage license was a forgery, and—"

"Please, no spoilers, Oralee. So, you told the police that you went to bed about one o'clock, and on your way, you looked out the window and noticed that Craig's car was back again at Miguel's. Is that right?"

"Yes, I'm afraid it is."

"And did you also look to see if Harry was still there?"

"No, I didn't. I didn't come to the front of the house at all."

"And you didn't tell the police about Harry?"

She looked surprised.

"Well, why would I? They asked me if I saw anything unusual that night. So, of course, I told them about Craig's car being there twice, the second time so late at night. It was unusual, especially with Miguel away. But I didn't think of Harry in the bushes as being unusual. And Detective Harper was asking questions so fast, it was hard to think. I was trying to be very concise. I know I tend to wander a bit. But I'm afraid she got a little impatient with me, and I got a little flustered, and Harry went right out of my head. Was it important?"

"I don't know yet, Oralee. But it could be. Now, one last thing. How did you know it was Craig's car that you saw? A lot of cars look alike, don't you think?"

"Oh, yes. I agree. The other day at Woodman's parking lot, I got right into a white car that I could have sworn was mine. So embarrassing, especially because a gentleman was sitting in the passenger seat. And I'm afraid he said something that was quite rude!" Her cheeks flushed at the memory.

"So, how can you be sure that the car you saw that night was Craig's? Isn't it possible that it was another car that was similar, but it wasn't Craig's?"

"Oh, but I'm sure it was his. It must have been?" But she said the latter with the uptick of a question in her voice, and she looked a little uncertain. "I know when I looked at it, I immediately thought, *Craig is back again, I wonder why?* Now, just a minute, I had a thought ..." She paused and tapped her finger to her forehead as if to jar a memory loose.

"Yes, that's it!" she said triumphantly. "It was the bumper sticker on his car. Sophia put it there a few years ago when she was in the band. I think it's so good for children to be in band instead of doing all this Spacebooking and inter web nonsense. Look what that can lead to. That prostitution site that made Craig kill that woman."

"Thanks for your help, Oralee. I appreciate it. But just FYI, SweetMeets isn't a prostitution site. And I don't believe that Craig killed anyone."

She pursed her lips together disapprovingly before saying, "You're very loyal, Leah. But as my grandmother used to say, 'Never let your loyalty make a fool of you.' Not that I'm saying you're a fool, my dear. But I'm sure you get my point."

## 27

"I'm so happy, *chica*," Miguel said, as we sat down for a quick coffee and debriefing at the Elite the morning after our neighborhood canvassing. "I was worried because I couldn't find anything else on Harry's dog walker. But now, we don't need him!"

"Yes. Miss Marple came through. We know Harry's story is at least partly true. He was there that night. Now, we just have to find the pretty woman with light blonde hair that Harry saw going into your house. And if God loves me, and I hear He loves all His children, then the woman will be Rebecca!"

"I still don't know about Rebecca, *chica*. I—"

"Hey, let's keep us both in a happy mood this morning. Let me bask in the pleasure of thinking of Rebecca on the way to getting her just deserts—locked up for the rest of her mortal days. Did you turn up anything about Kibre Web yet? I'd still like to talk to the guy who used to be one of Holly's clients."

"He may not be so easy to find. Kibre Web Development isn't incorporated—at least, it's not on any of the databases I checked. But it could be just a DBA—you know, 'doing business as' name."

"True. That would help him keep some income under the table. You know he reports some of his money through the DBA, so everything looks OK, but a lot of it he doesn't. Kibre Web could be a pretty small operation, though he'd have to subcontract with other techy-types for big jobs like SweetMeets."

"I'll keep trying."

"OK. And I'm going to stick with the Rebecca trail. I think I'll call Merlin Duffy's receptionist and see if she'll give me his personal cell phone number. He might have built a few extra re-entry days into his vacation before he has to go back to work. He could be back already, even if he's not at the office."

"Anything else?"

"Not for you. But I think I'll talk to Gabe this morning. See if he's got anything on the SweetMeets client list yet."

Miguel grinned.

"What?"

"It's only been three days. He said it would be at least ten for them to answer the subpoena. What are you checking on, the list or the lawyer?"

"Well, I have to give him an update on what we're finding, don't I?"

I knew where his teasing was heading.

"Maybe not Coop, maybe not Nick. Maybe the new *abogado* is your OTP?"

"You are hopeless. No. Gabe is not my one true pairing."

"He seemed *muy* interested when we were at McClain's. I invited him to my Halloween party, you know. He asked me if you were coming."

"He did not. Did he? Anyway, I'm not even sure if I'm going. I don't have a costume, and every time I go to one of your parties, something bad happens to me."

He put on a faux hurt expression. "*Chica,* how can you say that? What happened at my Christmas party?"

"I wound up in the ER."

"Oh, that's so not fair. That happened *after* the party."

"Well, what about your *Cinco de Mayo* party? I had the worst hangover of my life, and the next day I got pushed off a cliff."

"Again, *chica*, my party wasn't the problem. I didn't tell you to drink a pitcher of margaritas."

"All right, fair enough. But how about Founders Day? I got tossed in the trunk of a car."

"Ah, *sí*, but that wasn't a party at my house. We were all just going to party together, after the fireworks. That doesn't count as *my* party. Especially because in the end, I didn't even go. I gave it up to find you. That's how much I love you, *chica*, because you know how much I love a party."

"You have to admit, even if your parties don't cause bad things to happen to good people like me, they definitely seem to go hand-in-hand with them. And like I said, I don't have a costume."

He shook his head. "That is some weak sauce. You don't have to wear a costume. Some people will, some won't. I, of course, have a fabulous costume."

"I can only imagine. OK, all right," I said grudgingly. "You know that I'm going to your Halloween soiree. Nick is, too. But don't," I added sternly, "do any of that stupid teasing about Gabe in front of Nick."

"Total silence. But if Gabe can't control his *pasión* for you, well what can I do?" He shrugged and smiled again broadly, showing me his perfect, white teeth.

"I give up. Why are you in such a happy mood today?"

Not that I minded. It was good to see Miguel's sunny disposition reassert itself.

"I don't know. I just woke up happy. Maybe because my new

kicks are so awesome," he said, holding out his feet so I could admire his shoes. "And my party is this Saturday, and *Tío* Craig is home, and Mrs. Schimelman even has my favorite pumpkin muffins today."

His face expressed his pure enjoyment in the moment. I wanted him to stay feeling that way, which was why I'd tried to put a positive spin on where we were in the investigation. Privately, I felt that although we had plenty of threads to follow, it could be tough to weave them together in a way that would show us who killed Holly Mason—or at least prove that Craig hadn't.

After Miguel left, I decided not to connect with Gabe until I had definite, business-related news to relay. His teasing had stung a little. It was time to start acting like a serious journalist, not a third grader. If I didn't get hold of myself, the next thing I knew I'd be giving Miguel a note to pass Gabe, asking him if he liked me. Not that Miguel wouldn't love to be in the middle of something like that.

I'd just pushed back my chair and made a move to leave when I saw Charlie Ross come through the front door.

"Nash! I was gonna call you. You goin'? Stick around a minute, I got some information for you."

I got another tea—and another cookie—while Ross ordered coffee and a piece of *apfelkuchen*. We headed to a table in the back and settled in.

"So, first off, thanks for bein' nice to Allie. Havin' her at your house and all. Now she thinks she wants to be a reporter like you." He shook his head. "I didn't have the heart to tell her what a pain in the butt you are."

"Thanks. I guess."

He nodded. "But what I was gonna call you about, you know that Duane Stanton stuff you gave me to follow up on for the widow? I think he was on to something."

I was so surprised, I stopped my tea halfway to my mouth. Duane was about the last thing on my mind, and I'd never seriously thought Ross would find anything at all. "You mean Duane had a line on some actual fraud?"

"It's startin' to look that way."

"What have you found?"

"So, I went through his box, see? And he's got these newspaper clippings about embezzlement stories in other towns, city halls, county governments, like that. No big deal, I mean that's what the guy was interested in, right? Fraud and waste and all that jazz. And then I look at his desk calendar. It's all nice and tidy. Appointments, notes, little reminders in this teeny little printing. I practically had to use a magnifying glass to read it."

"OK," I said, still waiting for something surprising.

"The week he dies is pretty much like all the weeks—he's got an appointment with Will Fraser, one with your old boss, Rebecca, a birdwatcher's meeting. All crossed off—that's what he did every time he finished something. There's notes, too—get flowers for his wife's birthday, tape some bird show on PBS, and one to make an appointment with you."

"Yeah, Phyllis showed that to me. But I didn't hear from him. So?"

"I'm tellin' ya, can you wait a minute? Like I said, everything is on there all neat and proper, just appointments, meetings, reminders. But then, there's this triangle thing. This little drawing he keeps repeatin' on the edge of the page. He's got it down there three, four times. That's not like Duane. He's not a doodler. There's nothin' like it on the other pages. So, it gets me wonderin'. Maybe it's a symbol of some club or the Masons or something like that. So, I go online to check it out."

"No." I grabbed his hand in mock horror. "Charlie Ross turned to the internet? Ross, did you actually, dare I say it, use 'the Google.'?"

"Can you just let me finish?"

"All right. Sorry."

"The triangle thing Duane was drawing, it's got a P on one side, and an O on the other, and an R along the base. Turns out it's called a fraud triangle. Financial auditors and forensic accounting guys use it to explain why a person commits fraud. The P stands for pressure, the O stands for opportunity, and the R stands for rationalizing." He took a huge bite of his apple cake, and I had to wait until he finished and washed it down with a slurp of his coffee before he went on.

"It's like this. Say you got a guy who's got credit card debt or high medical bills, and he can't see a way out. That's the P. He's under pressure. Then, say this guy has a job where he's got the know-how to game the system, and the controls in the business aren't that good. That's the O, for opportunity. Finally, this guy, who isn't a bad guy, maybe never did anything illegal in his life, he talks himself into how it's OK to embezzle, say, because he's underpaid, or he's going to pay it back, or he's in big financial trouble and there's no other way out. That's the R, the rationalization."

"And you think Duane saw a fraud triangle at city hall?"

"Hold on, hold on. I'm gettin' to it. There's some other stuff in the box, too. Some blank city Open Records Act request forms. That's not a big deal, he probably ordered them by the gross as often as he was asking for records. But it gets me thinkin'. Where's all the filled-in requests Duane was workin' on? He's the kinda guy would've kept copies of everything. Shouldn't they be in the box?"

"Maybe he'd finished everything and filed them away."

He was shaking his head. "I thought of that. His wife let me look through his filing cabinet. There were plenty of old forms and old files, but nothing for the past year. Now, there's no way Duane didn't get a bee in his bonnet about something the city was doing wrong in the past year. Just not possible."

"What about his computer?"

"He didn't have one. Phyllis said he didn't trust computers. Didn't like 'em. Can't say I blame him. When he was still working, his secretary did all that for him, so he never learned. Phyllis never got the hang of it either. She's got one of those iPads, but she just uses it to see her grandkids on Facebook, she said."

"Ross, I don't get where you're going."

"Aren't you seein' a pattern here yet, Nash? Let me spell it out for you. After I didn't find anything at Duane's, I went to see Millie Gertzman. She's the clerk that handles Open Records Act requests for the city. I asked her if I could see Duane's requests for the last year. She goes to her computer, clicks a few things, hits the side of her machine, tries again. Then, she tells me Duane's files aren't there. She says she put them in, she knows she did. Says just because she's old it doesn't mean she can't work a computer, but every time something gets screwed up, they blame her.

"She calls Mike Chapman, the IT guy, to come down. Reads him the riot act, says it's not her fault and goes on her break. Mike pokes around for a while, but he comes up dry. He tells me on the QT that he tried to Millie-proof the system, but she's always hitting clear or delete all or not saving things, and then she blames the software."

"So, you still have nothing?"

He shook his head at my failure to get his point.

"Think about it. Duane's files at home are gone. His requests for records at city hall are gone. There weren't any copies of requests he was working on in the box of stuff from his desk. That's a whole lot of nothing, but it adds up to a big something."

"What?"

"The fraud triangle, Nash. The fraud triangle. Who works at city hall and is under big time financial pressure? Who's got the IT skills to kill Duane's requests in the system? Who knows how the financial software works and what the processes are for the departments?"

I felt a knot in the pit of my stomach as I finally understood where he was going.

"Mike Chapman? No. He wouldn't embezzle money. He's—"

"What? A nice guy? Yeah, but he's a guy under pressure. Couple years ago, his wife and kid are in that accident. Medical bills, sky-high. The kid still has therapy and needs more surgery, I hear. That ain't cheap. So, there's your P for pressure. Mike's been at city hall a long time, writes programs, knows software, knows how the departments work. He could fiddle with the funds and hide it easy. That's your opportunity. And yeah, you're right. He's a good guy, loves his family, likes his job. But the way he sees it, he doesn't have a choice. He's got to do it for his kid. Maybe he plans to pay it back when he can. That's your R, your rationalization."

The knot was no longer in my stomach. A big sinking feeling had taken its place.

"I'm not sayin' Duane knew who was cookin' the books. I think he figured out something was funny, but he didn't know who was doing it. But Mike's no dummy. If one of the times Millie Gertzman asks him to recover some files she deleted from the database, and he sees what Duane's after, he knows the game is up. He coulda deleted all Duane's requests on file right then, to buy some time to figure out what to do. He knows the trail eventually leads to him. He's lookin' at jail, disgrace, losin' his family even. He's probably goin' out of his mind, tryin' to decide if he should just cut and run."

I knew a little something about cutting and running, because that's what my father had done when things started to fall apart for him. He had been a nice guy, too, one that everybody liked. Like Mike.

"But before he has to make a choice," Ross continued, "he hits the lottery and Duane dies."

"Geez, Ross, could you be any more insensitive? I don't believe Mike would feel like Duane's death was the equivalent of winning the lottery."

Ross refused to be abashed. "Hey, I would. Now, he can see a way out. With Duane dead and the files at city hall destroyed, he goes to Duane's house—they don't lock up, by the way. Phyllis wasn't home when I got out there, but she told me if she was late, to go on in." He paused to shake his head but stopped himself from going into a full-on diatribe about homeowner's lax security measures.

"Mike just has to go to the house while Phyllis isn't there, check for any files connected to his embezzlement, check the desk for anything incriminating and bing, bang, boom. He's home free."

## 28

On my walk home, I kept looking for holes in Ross's idea, but had trouble finding any. And it made me feel slightly ill. It wasn't hard to imagine the desperation Mike had felt as the bills piled up. Embezzlement must have seemed like the only solution. And I was sure that he would've intended to pay it back when he could. But then how frightened he must have been when he realized that Duane was on a hunt that would eventually lead to him.

I didn't agree with the idea that Mike had rejoiced like a lottery winner at Duane's death, but it was easy to understand why he'd been eager to take advantage of it. If Ross's theory panned out, a world of hurt was waiting for the Chapman family, and they'd had plenty of that already.

Ross and I had agreed not to tell Phyllis anything until he had nailed everything down. To do that, he'd have to talk to Will Fraser at city hall. This wasn't going to be very much fun for Will, either. Besides the fact that he was a friend of Mike's, an embezzling scheme carried out under his nose wouldn't look so good for the city manager.

I was so absorbed in my thinking that I didn't notice a raised piece of concrete sticking up from the sidewalk until it caught my foot. I only avoided a face-plant in front of God and everyone by grabbing hold of the bike rack at the *Purrrfect Kitty Boutique*. When I looked up, Davina Markham, a crazy cat lady if ever there was one, was smiling through her plate glass window and giving me a thumbs-up. On impulse, I walked into her store.

"Well done, Leah. I give you a 10 out of 10 for trip recovery. And I'll be making a call to city hall about that sidewalk."

"Thanks, Davina. I'm pretty proud of that one, myself."

Into a very small and narrow space, Davina had packed every conceivable toy, treat, and fashion accessory a pampered cat could desire. Her own fluffy white Persian, Sabrina, was draped across a glass-topped counter. She eyed me suspiciously and gave one long, lazy lift of her tail before resting her head back down between her paws.

"She just loves you, Leah. She never gets that excited for anyone else."

Davina gives credence to the theory that pet owners, over time, come to look like their pets. Her long, white, fluffy hair frames a face with big, round, blue eyes, a short nose, and full cheeks. Viewed from the right angle, she looks very like a Persian cat herself.

"Well, she's a beautiful girl," I said, as I always do. I learned a long time ago that nothing warms a cat person's heart like praise of her—or his—feline companion.

Davina's little cat mouth turned up in a smile. "Yes, she is, isn't she? You know, the animal shelter has a really sweet little tabby kitten I think you'd just love. Cats make great pets for busy single people."

"I'm sure. The problem is, I don't think I'd be such a great companion for a cat. But now that I'm here, how about finding me a cat gift? It's for a woman who loves her cat almost as much as you do."

"What's she like?"

"She's quiet, a little shy. Just started working at the *Himmel Times*."

"The cat, Leah, the cat."

"Oh! We haven't been introduced. But April, that's the friend, assures me that she's remarkable."

"They all are, sweetie. They all are. Now let me see, where did I put that?" Davina kept up a running commentary as she scanned the full-to-bursting racks and shelves of her tiny store looking for whatever it was she had in mind.

"I heard you're working with Craig Kowalski's attorney. The new one Miller brought to town. It doesn't sound too good, though, does it? I hope you can find some way to help him. I just love Lydia."

"Me, too."

"Did you know that I actually met the woman who was killed? The day she was killed? She was right here, right about where you're standing, on that very Saturday afternoon."

"Are you serious? Did you tell the police?"

She paused for a moment to rub the belly Sabrina had rolled over on the counter to present. "Well, no. Do you think I should have? It wasn't anything, really. I mean, she didn't say she was afraid for her life, or being followed by assassins, or anything like that. It was very casual."

"Davina, it could be important, anything could be important at this stage. Tell me exactly what happened, exactly what she said."

"All right, sure. Umm, let me think a second." She closed her eyes and pulled down her brows in a frown of concentration. Her small mouth pursed, and I'd swear her nose twitched with the effort of thinking. Then, her blue eyes flew open, and she started talking.

"Business was slow for a Saturday, and I was just organizing shelves and doing busy work. In fact, I was under the counter when the bell rang, and someone called hello. I popped up and saw this gorgeous woman with red-gold hair. She took off her sunglasses, and I knew who she was right away. Holly Mason.

"How did you know?"

"I saw her picture in a magazine a while ago. Some story about how she started her own business after her husband what's-his-name, you know the one with all that financial stuff, insider trading, whatever it was, went to jail. Normally, I wouldn't have glanced at it, but she was holding this beautiful Russian Blue. It was striking how their eyes—Holly's and the cat's—were the exact same shade of green. Russian Blues are wonderful cats. I read the article, but there wasn't anything about her cat, except her name. Anastasia."

Davina's voice was puzzled, as though it was incomprehensible that any opportunity to feature a cat had been ignored.

"She sounds lovely, but let's get back to Saturday. What did Holly say? What happened?"

"Well, nothing, really. She was very friendly, very nice. She made a fuss over Sabrina. I asked about her cat. She told me she'd left her at home in Chicago."

"Did you ask her why she was in Himmel?"

"She said she was here for the fall colors, she rented a house not far from here. I asked whose, and she told me Miguel's. She said she was out for a walk and noticed my shop. We just, you know, chit-chatted and looked at pictures of each other's cats. Oh, wait, there was one thing." She stopped and turned to the large photo on the wall behind the register. It was a picture taken last year of Davina receiving a Chamber of Commerce award for Downtown Business of the Year. The close-up showed

Rebecca handing her a decal denoting the honor to put in her store window.

"She asked who was handing me the prize. I told her it was Rebecca Hartfield, the president of the Chamber of Commerce. She started laughing then, and said that I should tell Rebecca she had a doppelgänger in California. She said Rebecca was the exact image of her college roommate. I said, 'You can tell her yourself. The newspaper office is right up the street.' "

"What happened then?"

"She left."

"She just walked out? In the middle of your conversation? She didn't say anything else?"

"Well, Gretchen Fraser came in about then, and you know how Gretchen is, she just sort of commands attention. She cut right in front of Holly, didn't even look at her or say excuse me. Holly just sort of smiled, gave me a little wave and left. I was very put out at Gretchen."

I was feeling the same, given that Holly might have said something helpful if Gretchen hadn't barged in.

"You're sure she didn't say anything else?"

"I'm sorry, no. See, I told you it wasn't really anything."

But it was something. It gave added weight to Courtnee's assertion that Holly was the woman Rebecca had been speaking to at the office on Saturday. Up to this point, she was the only one who could identify the woman Rebecca talked to, for sure. I'd never seen her face. It's always a good idea to find external corroboration for anything Courtnee says.

"She was quite rude when I told her who Holly was. She practically sneered when I said she was staying right in her neighborhood at Miguel's. She said Holly was only famous because she was a prostitute. And I said that's a little harsh. I don't think what she does—did—the SweetMeets, I mean, is so awful. I say live and let live. What do you think, Leah?

I'd only been half-listening until I heard my name. I refocused.

"Yes, well, you're Aquarius, right? Aquarians are known for their open minds, aren't they? " Davina's other love besides cats is astrology.

She preened a little and looked more cat-like than ever. "Yes, that's true. I was in the musical *Hair* in college. You know, Gretchen wants me to do charts as a fundraiser after the Follies is done. But I don't think I will, now. Especially because do you know what else she asked me?"

I zoned out again as I tried to decide if Holly had come to town specifically to see Rebecca for a spot of blackmail and had just been playing with Davina, getting some kind of perverse pleasure out of knowing Rebecca's real identity, when Davina obviously did not. Or, if she had come to see someone else entirely, and spotting the photo of Rebecca really was a surprise. Maybe she truly had dropped in at the paper just to say hello, and Rebecca, for reasons I could guess, had made up a story to keep her secret.

"Cat fences should be illegal in my view. I told Gretchen I don't believe in torturing an animal that's just doing what's in her nature. Don't you agree?"

Again, I'd only been half-listening. I needed to get home where I could think. "Yes. I'm totally against animal torture. You know, I really should get going, do you think you could find that cat toy you had in mind?"

"Oh, sorry. Now, just a minute. Wait, I know where it is." She moved quickly to the back of the store, and two minutes later, I walked out with a package of catnip mice that Davina assured me were Sabrina-approved.

I was anxious to take up my thinking spot on the window seat to go over what Davina had said about Holly, but first I popped into the *Times* office.

I had the happy surprise of seeing Coop chatting with April at the front desk.

"Hey, you guys. Where's Rebecca?" I tried to make the last part sound like a casual inquiry after a friend, not a like a sentry challenging the enemy. Coop turned at the sound of my voice and smiled, while April looked up and said, "She's at a Chamber luncheon. She won't be back until after one o'clock."

"I thought I'd take her to lunch, but I missed out. How about you? Want to grab some lunch?" Coop said.

"Geez, Coop, you really have a way with words. 'Hey, Leah, the person I *really* want to have lunch with isn't here. You want to come?' Some people might be insulted by that. Lucky for you, I have a very high insult threshold. Sure. But let's just go up to my place. I'll make you a cheese sandwich. I have something I want to kick around with you." I turned to April then.

"I got you something for Miss Oprah."

Her face lit up as I handed her the small bag. She reached in and pulled out the mice. "Leah, that's so nice. She'll love them. Thank you, so much."

"No worries. It's not a big deal. I just happened to be in the kitty boutique, and you know how it is. You go in one of those small places, and it just feels kind of rude if you don't get something."

"But it was a big deal. You don't have a cat. Why would you go into the kitty boutique, except specifically to get something for Miss Oprah? It was really thoughtful." She looked back and forth between Coop and me. "You both have been so friendly to me. I just—" she blushed and blinked rapidly as her eyes watered.

Hadn't anyone ever been nice to this woman in her life? I glanced at Coop, tossing the awkward conversation ball to him.

"We all survived Himmel High, right? That's an unbreakable bond," he said.

April smiled, and the phone rang and emotions settled back down

## 29

"Do you want chips, or would you like to carry the cheese theme through with some Cheetos?" I asked Coop as I put mustard on his sandwich.

"I'll take chips. And some Coke, if you've got it."

As we settled down at the bar I said, "OK, now that I've plied you with food and drink, I want you to listen and not say anything until I'm done."

"To what?" he said, then took an enormous bite of his sandwich.

"It might sound a little crazy, but hear me out before you say anything."

"Don't I always?"

"No."

"True. But that's because half of what you say isn't a little crazy, it's a lot crazy."

"Did I ever tell you how funny you are? Because if I did, I was lying. Cut it out, this is serious."

"All right. I'm listening. Seriously." His gray eyes looked out at me from under lowered eyebrows to indicate how gravely he was taking my request, but his expression only made me laugh.

"What?" he asked, his tone offended.

"You look like your dad did that time you 'borrowed' his car when we were fourteen and you backed it into Darmody's patrol car."

"Then you shouldn't be laughing, you should be quaking in your shoes. I got into some serious trouble that night, and it was *your* idea. In fact, I think we can trace most of the serious troubles we've faced to times when I listened to you. Like remember when—"

"OK, we can go down memory lane some other time," I said quickly, because in truth several of the times we had found ourselves on the wrong side of a good idea the fault did lie with me.

"Anyway, this isn't even my idea. It's Ross's." I proceeded to tell him what Ross had discovered about Duane's missing files, and his conviction that Mike Chapman was the most likely culprit.

When I finished, he whistled.

"If Charlie's right, that's one hell of a mess for Mike, for his family, for the city. It's going to be ugly."

"But do you think he *is* right? When Ross laid it out, he made it sound possible. But maybe he's just trying to find something to prove he's a great detective and Art Lamey isn't. You know, he could be getting ahead of himself, reading things into a situation that aren't there, couldn't he?"

Coop tilted his head to one side and tapped his ear with one hand. "I'm not sure I heard that right. You think Ross is jumping to conclusions?"

"Maybe," I said.

He shook his head. "I feel like I'm in one of those movies where the lead characters have switched bodies. Leah Nash is the voice of reason, and Charlie Ross is the one chasing down a crazy theory?"

"Don't be sarcastic. I genuinely want to know what you think. Look, I know Ross is an experienced investigator. And no one could accuse him of having a runaway imagination. But he's going to be stirring up a political hornet's nest. If he's right, it's kudos to him. If he's wrong, it could be the final nail in his professional coffin. And he's only digging into it because I asked him to do the job I told Phyllis Stanton that *I'd* do."

"Charlie's a big boy. If he didn't want to do this, he wouldn't. And he's a bloodhound. It's too late now. If he's got his nose on the scent, nothing you say will get him off it. That's something you two have in common."

"Ross and I have nothing in common," I said.

"Have it your way."

"But do you think Ross could be right?"

"Sure. I've seen people do some pretty desperate things when they get into a financial bind."

"Yeah, I guess."

"So, what are you going to do? Jump into the middle of this while you're already waist deep in Craig's case?"

I shook my head. "I can't. I'm drowning there, plus I've got a book deadline to meet. I just feel guilty tossing it Ross's way, when it could go down really bad."

"Or really good. If Charlie's right, and he proves it, that puts him in a pretty good position."

"Yeah, that's true. Nothing I can really do about it anyway. Ross is Ross, and he's going to do whatever he wants."

"Again, that sounds very familiar."

"OK. Fine. Charlie Ross and I are twins, separated at birth. We share one soul. Are you happy?"

He shrugged. "I'm just making an observation. You're a little better looking than Charlie, if that makes you feel better."

"Thanks. You want some Oreos?"

He shook his head and took his plate to the sink. "Did you ever go and see Harry?"

"I did."

"What happened? Did he tell you anything?"

"He told me a lot of things. Now, we just have to see if they were fact or fiction." I resisted the urge to go over my interviews with Harry and Oralee and what Davina had said today. That road was not safe to travel in the present circumstances.

"I can't really talk about it, Coop. Like we said before, this time it's different. And I wouldn't want to put you on the spot. If I told you something Erin Harper should know, you'd have to tell her, and I think we should let her make her own mistakes."

"Yeah, OK. But you think she's making a mistake?"

"Everybody makes mistakes, right?"

I joined him at the sink and ran our plates under water before putting them in the dishwasher. He stood watching me, his hands pressed down on the counter behind him. When I finished loading things in and wiped down the sink, he was still standing there, staring at me.

"You look like you have something to say."

He seemed uncharacteristically uncomfortable. Coop is a pretty quiet guy, but he's not shy, and it's a rare situation that renders him tongue-tied.

"More like something to ask."

"OK, so ask."

"Leah, would you consider being the baby's godmother?"

A flood of emotions rushed over me: surprise, happiness, confusion.

"The baby's godmother? Me?"

"I understand if you don't want to. I don't want to pressure you."

"It's not that I don't want to. I'm honored that you'd ask me.

But, Coop, I'm not religious. I wouldn't be a very good spiritual guide for the kid."

He smiled then. "Leah, I'm not asking you because you're such a good Catholic. I'm asking because you're such a good friend. The best friend I've ever had. There isn't anyone I can think of who I'd trust to look out for and love our baby more than you."

Tears pricked at the back of my eyes. I blinked quickly and opened the refrigerator for a soda I didn't want to buy some time to compose myself. I unscrewed the cap and took a swallow before I answered.

"Coop, that's hands down the nicest thing you've ever said to me. But what does Rebecca think about it?"

"We haven't really talked about it yet, but I figure I'll pick the godmother, and she can pick the godfather. She'll be all right with it. I know you'll never be close friends, but I like to think that two people I care about, who say they care about me, can figure out how to get along. Maybe the baby will help."

*And how will you feel when I tell you that your wife has been lying to you since you met her? That she isn't who you think she is— literally or figuratively? And that it could even be worse than that. She could be a murderer?* I didn't give voice to the thoughts running through my head. Instead, I said, "If Rebecca's OK with it, I'd love to be a godmother. But if she isn't, no worries. I'll understand."

"That's great. I'm really glad." Coop gave me quick hug. "Well, I'd better go. I'll talk to Rebecca tonight about it. She'll be fine with it."

"Don't be surprised if she picks Darmody to be the godfather, just to pay you back."

After Coop left, I paced around my apartment trying to shake the really bad feelings I had over deceiving him, withholding information from him, and being a bad friend in general. He had a right to know about Rebecca. But if I told him, he'd be hurt, angry, disbelieving even.

During the giddy excitement of discovering Rebecca's deception, I'd thought mostly about the impact on me. I'd be able to show her up for the fake she was. I'd be able to rescue Coop from her clutches. I'd be able to get her out of all of our lives and extract a little payback for all the nasty things she'd done to me, to Miguel, to April, to basically everyone who wasn't of immediate use to her. I hadn't really thought about the baby at all. Not until Coop asked me to be the godmother.

But that baby was real. And whatever happened to Rebecca would have a lifetime impact on her—or him. It had been fun, a sort of intellectual exercise imagining that Rebecca could be Holly's killer. I hadn't wanted to admit to myself the devastation that would result for Coop and his child if my suspicions proved true.

And maybe they wouldn't. Maybe I was wrong. We had a long way to go to figure out how and why Rebecca could have killed Holly Mason. I couldn't say anything to Coop, not only because I was part of Craig's defense, but because if I was wrong, he might never forgive me for what I had thought.

But in my heart, I didn't believe that I was wrong. And maybe that would be even worse.

## 30

"Boy, am I happy to see you," I said, grabbing Miguel's hand and pulling him through the door to my kitchen.

"*Gracias.* But you just saw me this morning. Why are you so happy now?"

"Because," I said, leading him over to the window seat and pushing down on his shoulders until he was sitting on the cushions. "I need you to help me think."

I told him about what Davina had said about Holly's visit to her shop.

"Miguel, it keeps coming back to Rebecca. I mean, it's still possible that Holly was here to put the squeeze on a Sweet-Meets client, but I just have a feeling that she came to see Rebecca."

"You 'have a feeling,' *chica,* or you just want Rebecca to be the evil one?"

Sometimes Miguel is quite insightful. It can be rather annoying.

"Maybe I do, but that doesn't mean she isn't."

"OK, if she came to see Rebecca, why did she pretend to Davina that she didn't know Rebecca?"

"I already thought of that. I think she just enjoyed telling a secret without telling it. Like a little game. She told Davina that Rebecca looked just like her roommate, when of course she actually was her roommate."

"So, Holly and Rebecca stayed in touch after college? Even though Rebecca changed her name and hid her college records and pretty much did everything she could to disappear?" His voice was skeptical.

"Yes, I know. Natalie Dunckel is dead, long live Rebecca Hartfield. But still, even a self-sufficient iceberg like Rebecca wouldn't want to feel totally unmoored in life. I'm not saying they were besties. But I think it's quite possible that she felt safer staying in occasional contact with someone she shared the same secret with. Though in Holly's case, she didn't keep it a secret."

"You really think—"

"That Rebecca was an escort like Holly? Yes. It makes sense. Holly was a beautiful girl who found the escort life a financially rewarding way to pay for college. Rebecca was also a beautiful girl. If they were roommates, she'd know what Holly was doing and either get recruited or ask to get in on the action."

"So, you think that because Holly's business is going under, she came to ask Rebecca for money? Would Rebecca even have enough money to help her? She's not rich."

"As far as we know. But then, what do we really know about Ms. Rebecca? She could be sitting on a big nest egg. Or I'm sure she has plenty of A-H Media stock she could convert to cash. Or maybe Holly was after her to cosign a loan, or connect her with financing. Maybe one of Rebecca's old clients is a financier. I don't know, I'm just trying out possibilities here."

"But would Rebecca *kill* Holly because she asked for money?"

"It's not about the money, Miguel. It's about the secret. Holly threatened to tell the world that Rebecca was a high-class hooker. And yes, the Rebecca I know would kill to keep that secret. She had a lot to lose if it came out."

"So, Rebecca went to my house to see Holly that night? And it was her car that Oralee saw, not *Tío* Craig's. Her car is silver, his is gray. But they could look alike in the dark," he said, working through the theory out loud.

"Yes. And remember that Harry Turnbull saw a woman with hair like his sister Evie's—light blonde. Like Rebecca's. She went into the house, and then she ran out, he said. But maybe it wasn't as fast as it seemed to Harry. He wouldn't be a good judge of time."

As Miguel saw the possibilities, he got more into the spirit of things. "So, Rebecca and Holly they talk. Holly says she is going to tell Rebecca's secret, if Rebecca doesn't help her. Rebecca tells Holly no, but Holly isn't bluffing. She says she will let everyone know. Rebecca, she sees that everything she worked for—lied for, even—Holly can take it away from her—her job, her husband, her reputation, maybe Coop would even take her *bebé*. She is *furioso*, she can't think."

I stepped in then and acted out the scene. "She grabs the poker. She hits Holly, then hits her again and again. Holly crumples to the floor. Rebecca realizes what she's done. Her instinct for self-preservation kicks in. She wipes her prints off the poker. She takes Holly's purse, her computer and her phone to make sure there's nothing there that connects the two of them. Maybe the police will think it was a robbery gone bad. Then, she runs out. That's when Harry sees her, but she doesn't see him. She gets in the car, she gets rid of the purse, the computer, and the phone. And then she waits."

Miguel picked up the narrative again. "After I find the body, she takes the story away from me, so she can keep it on the down low. It's all good for her when the police find a motive for

Uncle Craig, Sophia's connection to SweetMeets. So, Rebecca gets away with it. It could be true, *chica*," he said, caught up in the excitement of a way to free his uncle. But then his face fell.

"But what if you're wrong? What if Holly didn't know Rebecca was living here?"

"She can still stay on our suspect list. Listen, let's change it up, and say that Holly comes to Himmel to blackmail a Sweet-Meets client, not to see Rebecca. Rebecca hasn't talked to Holly in years, has no connection. Holly finds her by accident; the scene at Davina's was real. But she can't resist checking out this woman who is the image of her old friend Natalie. She shows up at the paper. Rebecca gets the shock of her life. Holly wants to reminisce, she starts talking about their working girl pasts, and Rebecca wants her to shut up and get out of there. She agrees to meet up with Holly later. But she's already thinking that Holly could blow her cover at any time. So, she realizes she has to kill Holly, and she does. See? She still works as a suspect."

"But how can we find out which is true? Or maybe that neither one is."

"Oh, ye of little faith. The phone, Miguel. The prepaid cell phone. The one Holly texted the night she got into town. We find out if it belongs to Rebecca."

"Rebecca? Why would she—"

"Lots of people have a second cell phone to keep business and personal stuff separate. And knowing Rebecca, it wouldn't surprise me if she had more than one secret that shouldn't see the light of day."

"But you'll never find the owner of a burner phone. *Es imposible*"

"Ah, but maybe we can. I downloaded an app that lets you text anonymously. I'm going to text the prepaid cell number and set up a meeting with whomever owns it, which I think will be Rebecca."

He shook his head doubtfully. "But why would she come? *Especialmente* if she doesn't know who is asking to meet her. I wouldn't."

"That's because you have a clear conscience. Here's what I'm sending." I flipped my phone around so he could see the text: *Be at Founders Park 11 tonight. Paul Bunyan statue. You know why.*

"What do you think? It's my version of *All is discovered. Flee at once.* I've always wanted to write a note like that."

"*Chica, y*ou're setting up a meeting for us with someone who could be a killer. That could go very wrong. I'm still young."

"I didn't say meet up with 'us'. You don't have to go."

"If you're in, I'm in. *Pero*, maybe neither one of us should be in?"

"We're not going to actually *meet* anyone. We're just going to watch and see who comes. We'll be in that stand of fir trees near the Paul Bunyan statue. We'll be, like, a hundred yards away."

He didn't respond, but the look he gave me said it all.

"All right, maybe closer to forty yards. But we'll be hidden. She won't. The full moon will give us enough light to see her— or whomever."

"Did you talk to Gabe? What did he say?"

"I got busy. I haven't talked to him today. And don't you talk to him, either. All we're trying to do is see who owns the phone. If we're right, then we'll see where we go from there."

"What if Rebecca doesn't show up tonight? What if someone else does? Or no one?"

"If she doesn't come, it doesn't prove she didn't do it. It just proves she has nerves of steel. If someone else shows up, it probably means the prepaid cell phone isn't Rebecca's, but again, it doesn't let her off the hook. In fact, that would give us two additional suspects besides Craig—the person who owns the prepaid cell, because he or she obviously has a secret connection to Holly, and Rebecca would still be on the list, too. Because even without the phone, she has all kinds of reasonable-doubt-making connections to Holly."

"OK. I'm in. Like always."

I sent the text into cyberspace without expecting to get a reply, and none came. I hoped that wouldn't be the case that night.

---

"Get comfortable," I whispered. "We don't want to be fidgeting around when she gets here."

It was only ten-fifteen, but Miguel and I had decided we would arrive early to make sure we were in position well before Rebecca—or whoever, but I knew it would be Rebecca—came. The statue of Paul Bunyan, a folklore favorite in Wisconsin, is an impressive ten-foot figure resting on a five-foot pedestal. It sits not far from the river's edge, where once real lumberjacks cut and sent white pine logs floating down the Himmel River to the sawmills.

Little kids gaze in awe at the mighty mythical man, bigger kids try to climb up and touch his cap, and generations of teenagers have found it hilarious to place inappropriate things around his neck, balance ridiculous bonnets on his head, and hang school spirit signs off his axe handle. The statue also serves as a gathering place for families whose various members spread out in the twenty-acre park to wander the trails, or fish off the dock, or buy an Icee at the refreshment stand. "Be at the Bunyan in one hour," is a familiar directive from parents to kids old enough to roam on their own.

I had selected a thick stand of pine trees for our stakeout spot. We knelt down, using the low hanging boughs of the trees for cover. Both of us wore dark jeans and hoodies. The moon was fairly bright, which would help augment the dim light streaming from a lamppost a few yards from the statue.

Forty-five minutes is a lot longer than you might think when you're waiting in late fall temperatures in a damp, dark place with poky branches and a reluctant partner.

"What if she doesn't come?"

"She'll come."

Minutes dragged by during which I didn't dare shift position for fear of shaking the branches at the exact moment Rebecca arrived.

"My foot is going to sleep."

"Deal with it."

I looked at my watch. Fifteen minutes to go. And that's saying she was on time. I sighed.

"It's freezing! I should have worn my military jacket over my hoodie. You know I saw an olive-green sweater at Old Navy that would be *perfecto* for you. I—"

"For Pete's sake, Miguel. We're on a stakeout, not *Project Runway*. C'mon, we only have a couple of minutes to wait!" I hissed in a fierce whisper.

I was wrong. We continued crouching in our cold, uncomfortable hidey hole as the minutes crawled by. I looked at my watch. It was ten minutes after eleven. Maybe she wasn't going to show. Maybe she hadn't received the text. Maybe—Miguel nudged me hard with his elbow and whispered excitedly, "Someone's coming!"

I nodded and pressed my finger to my lips. We listened intently to the sound of footsteps crunching on the gravel road that circles the park. A dark figure came into view. Tall and slender, she wore a jacket with a hood that shaded her face. Her back was to us as she glanced from side to side, her pace slower as she came within a few feet of the statue. Miguel moved slightly to get a better look. A branch scraped along his cheek and released a sudden whiff of pine. I saw him struggle, but he couldn't stifle the loud sneeze that rent the night air. Startled, the dark figure spun quickly in our direction. Her hood fell back. Light blonde hair shone like spun silver in the moonlight. She turned and sprinted away. But not before I saw her face.

It was Kira Chapman.

---

Miguel and I scrambled to our feet. Confused thoughts ricocheted around my brain like kernels of corn in a popper. What was Kira doing here? Where was Rebecca? What the heck just happened?

Miguel was faster than me. He started to chase after her. I grabbed his arm.

"But, *chica*, she's getting away! Don't you want to talk to her?"

"Yes, but we can do that later. She couldn't have seen us—not to know who we are, anyway. I want to keep her off balance while we try to figure out what's going on."

" 'Keep *her* off balance?' What about us? I never thought a high school girl could be a killer!"

"I don't know what to think, just yet." I looked at my watch. It was eleven fifteen.

"I think the show is over for tonight. Let's—" But before I could finish, we heard the sound of an engine. As we looked down the road, the headlights of a Himmel Police Department squad car picked us out like deer on the highway. The car pulled to a stop and Dale Darmody got out.

"Hey, what are you guys doin' here?" He asked, hitching up his pants as he walked toward us.

I signaled to Miguel not to spill exactly why we were there. Instead, I said, "Miguel wanted to see Bunyan in the moonlight."

He gave me an eye roll at the lame explanation, but Darmody was still talking and didn't notice.

"We been havin' some reports of kids smokin' marijuana up here. That's not what you kids are up to, is it?"

He laughed heartily at his own joke and we waited while he wheezed to a close before Miguel said, "*Sí*, I've heard the rumors too."

Darmody began to nod. "Oh, I get it. You're not here to look at the statue. You're checking out a tip, for a story, right? You know, it's not a good idea to come on your own. If there was dealin' goin' on, could be something worse than marijuana. And could be someone on the nasty side doin' it. Himmel isn't like it was when I started out."

"You've got us, Darmody. You can see right through a reporter's ruse," I said. "Well, we probably should get going, let you get on with your patrol. You didn't see anyone on the way in, did you? I mean, you weren't chasing any dealers or anything?"

He laughed again. "I wouldn't be standing here talking to you if I was, would I?"

That was debatable. He went on, "Nah. Well, I did see someone looked a lot like Kira Chapman, Mike and Noelle's girl, that is. She passed me goin' in the opposite direction just a minute ago. Right before I turned into the park. Think I might give Mike a call. It might not've been her, but it's pretty late to be out on a school night. Anything goin' on there, best to nip it in the bud. That's what I say."

"Yes, I'm sure you're right," I said. "Well, our car's in the south lot, so—"

"I remember one time I caught you and Jennifer Pilarski out here one Halloween. You were puttin'—"

"Yes, well, OK. That was a long time ago, Darmody. But we've got to get going. See you later."

With that, I hustled Miguel away before Darmody decided

to trot out all the *Leah Nash, the Teen Years*, stories that he had. Some things are best left in the past.

———

"Why do you think Kira was there? Do you think she killed Holly Mason? What if Kira was a sugar baby, like Sophia?"

I shook my head as I drove my car down Himmel's mean streets, headed toward Miguel's house.

"It would be pretty hard for a high school kid from a small, close family like Kira's to hide something like that. For one thing, when would she be able to hook up with her sugar daddy? What would she tell her parents? 'Mom, Dad, don't be alarmed by the forty-year-old man picking me up for the weekend?' For another, how would she hide the money and gifts sugar daddies give their 'babies'? Yuck, just saying that sounds creepy, doesn't it?"

"*Sí.* But then, why was Kira at the park? Why did your message make her afraid enough to come?"

"I don't know. She must have the phone. She must have been the one who was in contact with Holly, or how would she know to be there tonight?"

"*No se.* What now?"

"Now, we meet with Gabe and tell him what we've been doing. Maybe if the three of us put our heads together, we'll come up with something. I hope so, because right now I'm fresh out of ideas."

## 31

"Just to be clear, there will be no more unilateral decision-making, got it? I'm running this case, not you two. I need to know what you're up to." Gabe, Miguel, and I were sitting around the conference table at his office Friday morning, drinking coffee and eating pumpkin walnut cookies from the Elite. I had just finished catching him up on things, including the happenings of the night before. He was less upset than I'd feared he might be at being left out of the loop.

"I was giving you plausible deniability."

He shook his head. "I'm not saying what you did wasn't smart. It was. But I'm saying you can't keep me in the dark. OK? It might not work out so well next time."

"OK. But actually, it didn't work out so great. I feel like all we did was muddy the waters even more."

"Well, let's see if we can unmuddy them. You two already dismissed the idea that the girl—what's her name? Kira?"

I nodded.

"That Kira was a sugar baby. Let's take it apart again. Let's say, just for a minute, that Kira is—or was—a sugar baby."

"We already went through that."

"Wait, now, wait a minute. We're brainstorming here. Didn't you ever go to a team workshop, Leah? C'mon. No negatives. No idea is stupid." He spoke in the peppy tones of a consultant hired to boost staff morale, but I saw the glint of amusement in his eyes.

"Yes. I've gone to many team-building workshops. That's how I know that lots of ideas are stupid. I think the idea that Kira was a sugar baby is one of them. Miguel and I already ran down that road. How could a teenager living at home hide that from her family? How could she get away to hook up with her sugar daddy? How could she conceal the money and gifts she'd be getting? Plus, she'd have to hide the fact that she was underage from her sugar daddy, too. Otherwise, he wouldn't connect with her—not unless jail is his idea of a good time."

"Feel better now? Got all that negativity out?"

He didn't wait for me to answer. "Good. Moving forward—again—let's say Kira is a sugar baby. She knows Holly well enough to be in phone contact with her. Why?"

"Because Holly was blackmailing her?" Miguel suggested tentatively.

"Outside the box, that's good. What else?"

I didn't want to play the game, but an idea suddenly hit me. It's very hard for me to sulk when I have a thought I want to share. "Because Kira was blackmailing Holly."

"Good one! Two possibilities. Now, how likely is it that Holly would expect to get anything significant out of a teenage girl? Not very," Gabe said, answering his own question.

"Besides, Kira could turn the tables on her," I said. "If Holly threatened to expose her, Kira could threaten to go public with the fact that she was underage and using SweetMeets. The publicity would kill the site, and Holly could be in legal jeopardy, too," I said.

"See how fun it is to play, Leah? Whatever brought Kira to the park, it wasn't because she was being blackmailed by Holly. She wouldn't have had enough money to be useful to Holly as a victim. And even if Holly had approached her, Kira could have turned the situation around and threatened to expose Holly as a blackmailer and as the owner of a predatory website. They both had something to lose in an extortion scheme."

"So, now can we get off the idea that Kira was at the park because she killed Holly?" I asked.

"Hey, I'm processing here. Gimme a minute." He paused to take the last bite of the cookie he held, then reached for another. "I think I'm gonna ask Mrs. Schimelman to marry me. Or at least adopt me."

"Could we concentrate please, Gabe?"

"I concentrate best when I'm fed. Now, I'm fed. All right, before we dismiss Kira as part of the mix, I see one option left. Kira's family has a lot of bills, you said, because of her little brother. Debt can make you desperate. And mom and dad, they're looking at years more of therapy, and maybe surgeries for their son. Mom's providing the daily care, dad's got a full-time job and work on the side, and it's still not enough. They're up against it. Maybe they decide it's OK for Kira to help out with some sugar baby work."

"What? No way!" I said. Besides my gut feeling about Mike Chapman's love for both his kids, Ross's theory about embezzling sprang to mind. Parental love and devotion aside, Mike didn't need to pimp out Kira for cash if he was already diverting it from work. I didn't explain that to Gabe, or Miguel, though. After all, Ross could be wrong, and it didn't have anything to do with this case.

"To have their own daughter make money that way? *Es imposible!*" Miguel said.

"I've seen parents do worse," Gabe said cynically. "Just for the sake of argument, let's say mom and dad are OK with their daughter's side hustle. The three of them are in it together, a nice bit of family bonding. But mom and dad wouldn't be OK with everybody knowing about it. So, when Kira tells them that Holly is threatening to expose them if they don't pay her—"

"One or both of her parents kill Holly? Instead of just telling Holly they'll expose her for running a site for old guys to prey on underage girls? And after they kill her, when they get my threatening text about it, they send their teenage daughter to the meeting? C'mon, Gabe, that theory didn't come from a brainstorm, it came from a brain lapse."

"What happened to no idea is stupid?" he asked in an injured tone.

"That was your rule, not mine."

"Hey, I thought this was a safe space. You should come with a trigger warning. Hand me another cookie."

"You're not as entertaining as you think you are," I said, as I passed him a cookie.

"Really? I find myself very entertaining." He took a bite and then said, "We need to look at things from every angle. But, for now, I'll stipulate that Kira and her family are above reproach. No funny business there. No connection with SweetMeets. So, she's in the park at midnight because?"

"That's where we left it last night. Why would she be there? If she's not involved, and I really don't think she is, how did she get the text message? And why did she respond to it? And then run away?"

"Because she was meeting her *novio*." Miguel had been uncharacteristically quiet for much of the discussion, but clearly, he'd been thinking.

"Her boyfriend?" Gabe asked.

"A boyfriend!" I tapped Miguel lightly on the arm. "Yes, my

super smart partner. Of course, she was meeting a boyfriend. Oralee—that's Miguel's neighbor," I explained for Gabe's benefit. "Oralee told me that she'd seen Gus Fraser sneaking out of his house by the basement window. Ross's daughter Allie told me that Kira and Gus used to be a couple. Maybe they still are, only his parents, or her parents don't like it. So, they meet in secret."

"That would mean Kira didn't have the phone. She didn't have anything to do with it. You two happened into the middle of a secret teen romance, and she got scared and took off," Gabe said.

"That makes more sense than the idea that she's a sugar baby, her parents pimped her out, and they're a family of killers," I said.

"Agreed. So, then, why didn't the owner of the prepaid cell show up?"

"Because he didn't get the message? Or it didn't scare him?" Miguel asked.

"Or he's too tough and too smart to let his hand be forced by an anonymous text," Gabe said.

"She. She's too tough and smart. Come on, can't you see Rebecca is the killer-most-likely? Holly knows all about her old friend. She doesn't have anything against her personally, but she needs money. If Rebecca won't help her, she'll let everyone know the fun they used to have together as escorts. Rebecca realizes that Holly is a threat that won't go away. She can put pressure on her whenever she wants to in the future. Paying up isn't going to solve that. Rebecca isn't about to lose everything she's worked for, lied for even. So, she kills Holly."

"Maybe," Gabe said. "But we're just assuming Rebecca was an escort like Holly, which I agree would be a secret she'd want to keep. We still don't know that for sure."

"I'm working on it. But look at all the things that support the idea that Rebecca killed Holly. Rebecca lied—first she said she didn't talk to Holly, then when that didn't fly, she said she didn't realize who Holly was. Rebecca didn't go with her brand-new husband to a big family event, his grandmother's birthday. She stayed home alone on Saturday night, so that she was free to see —and murder—Holly.

"She took Miguel off the story, and then she proceeded to bury it. She went ballistic when April posted Holly's picture on the website. Harry Turnbull saw a pretty woman with light blonde hair get out of a gray car at Miguel's house late the night Holly was killed. Rebecca's car is silver, but at night, it could have looked gray to Harry. Is that enough for you?"

"It's some pretty good groundwork," Gabe said. "But until we have a motive for Rebecca, and we're sure she doesn't have an alibi, it's not an alternate theory of the crime. We need to know what Rebecca's secret is, and whether it's worth killing for."

"I'm hoping Merlin Duffy knows—or at least that he can point me in the direction of someone who does. I'll put another call into him today, see if maybe he got back from his trip early."

Gabe nodded. "OK, meanwhile, keep it low key, both of you. We want the real killer—whether it's Rebecca or someone else —to feel confident that they're getting away with it. That we haven't got a clue. So, they don't have any time to build a better alibi or cover their tracks better."

Gabe turned to Miguel. "How do you feel about working with Rebecca at the same time you're trying to prove she's a killer? Can you do that?"

"If it helps Uncle Craig, I can."

"Good man, Miguel," Gabe said.

"OK, but can you party with her? Tomorrow's your big soiree," I said.

"*No problema.* Am I not always the perfect host?"

"You are."

"Gabe, you're coming to my Halloween party, aren't you?"

"I don't know, Miguel. I'm not much for dressing up."

"You don't have to," Miguel said quickly. "Some will, some won't. But everybody has a good time at my parties, right?" He looked at me.

"It depends on how you define good time," I said, then smiled so he knew I was kidding. "Gabe, you should go. You could dress as someone from *Law&Order*. Jack McCoy, maybe. Just wear a suit and have a slightly crazed expression in your eyes. Or maybe Adam Schiff would be better. You do have kind of a crabby vibe about you."

"So, you're going?"

"Wouldn't miss it. Not even in the middle of a murder investigation. You haven't lived until you've been to one of Miguel's parties. Something always happens."

"Like what?"

"Oh, no. You have to go to find out for yourself. Besides, you'll meet a lot of people. Miguel knows more people in Himmel than I do. I think Miller is going, and my mother is. And April, who you met at McClain's, and Sherry, the waitress there. And Courtnee. You have to meet Courtnee. And then my, uh, that is my ..."

I stumbled through here, trying to define Nick. Suddenly, I didn't want to say my ex-husband. Even though I'd already described him that way to Gabe. Somehow it seemed disloyal now, as though I were relegating Nick to the past. Which was ridiculous. I settled on saying, "My friend Nick will be there. I've told him all about you."

"Really? All about me?" He cocked an eyebrow and there was a half-smile on his lips.

For some reason, an inconvenient flush suffused my cheeks.

I ignored it and tried to breeze through the moment. "Yes, sure. I think you'll really like him."

"Somehow I doubt that. But, I'll be there. It sounds like it could be fun."

Miguel had watched my discomfort with amusement.

"Oh, it will be," he said confidently.

## 32

When I left Gabe's office, I decided to make a stop at Bob's Donut House, a popular spot with kids and cops on the west side of town. It was out of my way, but at ten in the morning, there was a chance I'd find Darmody there. I wanted to know if he'd ever seen Kira meeting a boyfriend out at the park at night. If he had, that would support our idea that we'd just run into the middle of a teen romance.

"Buy you another one?" I asked, sliding onto a stool next to him at the counter.

"Leah, hi! I shouldn't." He leaned away from the counter a bit to give his stomach a pat. "The wife says one a day is my limit."

"OK. I don't want Angela mad at me. Billy," I said to the man behind the counter, "I'll have a sour cream glazed donut. And a glass of water. You want another coffee, then, Darmody?"

"Well, I only had a cruller. Not a regular donut. So, I don't think it really counts. Make that two sour cream glazed, Billy." He shot me a guilty grin.

"Fine with me, but don't be narking on me to Angela."

He laughed. "She likes you, Leah. I'm the one she'll take

down if she finds out."

"So, I'm kind of surprised to see you this early after being on the job so late last night."

"I hadda drive Angela to her volunteer shift at the hospital this morning. Her car's in the garage. I figured I might as well stop in and say hi to Billy."

"So, anything new at the cop shop?"

"Not really."

"How's Detective Harper doing?"

"Real good. She got some big kudos for getting that murder cleared up so fast."

"Do you really think Craig Kowalski killed Holly Mason?"

He shifted uncomfortably on the tiny stool which held his considerable bulk. "Well, I wasn't part of the team, ya know. And I guess the evidence is pretty strong."

"Yeah, I know. But come on, Craig Kowalski, and murder?" I shook my head.

"Nah, I really shouldn't talk about it. Detective Harper is real big on discipline. And I know you're workin' on Craig's defense. Hey," he said, and then paused.

If thought bubbles were real, one would rest right above his head and it would read, *I think she's tryin' to get information from me. Is that why she bought me a donut?*

Before he gave voice to the suspicion, I tried to allay it. "OK, sure. It's a murder investigation. You have to keep things tight. We're friends, but we each have to be loyal to the home team, right? I get it. Subject closed."

He looked relieved at not having to try to sidestep any trick questions from me. But I had just laid the groundwork for what I really wanted to hear about, Kira in the park. Having upheld the directive not to talk about the murder outside the department, he relaxed when I switched to something he thought was unimportant.

"So, Miguel and I were disappointed about the bum tip we had last night. We didn't see any kids doing anything they shouldn't. But, you know, I got thinking about what you said about seeing Kira Chapman on the road. She's a nice girl. I don't think she was looking for trouble. I bet she was going to meet a boy. You know, maybe someone her parents don't like, don't want her to see."

"Yeah, it could be. When me and Angie were dating, her mom didn't like me at all. We used to meet each other at the cemetery, when she told her folks she was stayin' at a girlfriend's."

"Wow. The cemetery. You've always been a crazy romantic, haven't you, Darmody?"

"Well, she married me, didn't she?" He laughed so hard his belly shook like the proverbial bowl full of jelly. It doesn't take much to set Darmody off. I waited, and eventually he continued.

"But if Kira and a boyfriend are usin' the park for secret meetings, it musta just started. I never saw her out there before. Seen her dad, though, come to think of it. Maybe he was lookin' for her. Not the story he gave me, though."

"You saw Mike at Founders Park at night? That seems weird."

"It was, kinda. It was awhile back, late. I saw this guy just standin' on the end of the pier. The water drops off big time out there. You know, they had that suicide off the bridge over to Omico. Woman was standin' there, lookin' over the water, and all the sudden, she just jumped. So, when I saw a man out there, I moved in fast.

"When I got closer, I saw it was Mike. I hollered, and he come right over. I told him he scared me. He laughed, said he had some thinkin' to do where he could be by himself. I asked him how his boy was doin'. He said real good. He seemed OK. I thought, well, he's just kind of an odd duck. Likes bein' alone.

But maybe he was lookin' for his daughter. Just wanted to keep family business to himself."

My mind had leaped to Ross's theory that Mike was cooking the books at city hall. Had he been destroying records? Throwing them in the water? No, that was stupid. He'd just shred anything he wanted to get rid of, no need to dump them in the water where they might still be recovered.

What if Darmody's first instinct was right? What if Mike had been thinking about jumping into the water and just letting go? Maybe after he figured out that Duane Stanton was on to him, he'd thought about ending everything. If he didn't want to face the disgrace, couldn't pay back the money, would he think killing himself was the answer? But he wouldn't do that to his family. Would he?

"Leah?" Darmody waved his hand in front of my face. "Hey, I been talkin' to you and you're just like, in outer space. I gotta go. Thanks for the donut. I won't tell Angie if you don't."

———

When I got home after talking to Darmody, I got out my notes from my conversation with Merlin Duffy's receptionist Donna Lynn and found her home number.

"Hi, Leah," she said, as though we were old friends. "Did you want to talk about my book club? I've been thinking and maybe you could do like a reading from your book? Or, each of us could read our favorite parts?"

"Sure, Donna Lynn, whatever works for you. But that's not really why I called. Last time we talked, you said Dr. Duffy wouldn't be back in the office until late next week. But I'd like to try him on his cell, in case he gets back a little early. Could you give me his number? Maybe I can get the information I need, and I won't have to bother him at the office."

"Oh. Yeah, sure, I guess. Does that mean you won't Skype my book club?"

"No, no, of course not. I like book clubs."

"Oh, good," she said, sounding relieved. "I've been telling everyone that you're going to be there—on Skype—I mean. It would be sort of embarrassing if you backed out. I've been trying to think of good questions, but it's kind of hard. I mean you probably don't want to hear us just say, 'Oh, we loved your book.' "

"Well, that's something that every author likes to hear, but it maybe doesn't make for a very interesting discussion. But, anyway, if you have that number?"

As soon as I said a grateful goodbye to Donna Lynn, I called Merlin Duffy. My heart beat a little faster. I might be about to discover the Rebecca Hartfield origin story.

"Hello, Merlin Duffy here." The voice was light, pleasant, friendly.

"Dr. Duffy, this—"

"I can't take your call right now, but—" Rats. Merlin Duffy was one of those people who sucker you in with a greeting that sounds so natural and real, you start talking. Only to realize you're talking to a recording.

"Dr. Duffy, this is Leah Nash. I'm a writer from Himmel, Wisconsin. I'm working on a project involving Kinmont College alumni. I'm hoping you can help me locate Natalie Dunckel. If you have any information about her, that would be great. Please call me as soon as you can. I'm working against a deadline. Thank you."

I hoped my mention of a deadline would make him decide to call me back sooner rather than later. But I didn't count on it. Unless the deadline is theirs, most people aren't that concerned about it.

## 33

I was behind, as I always seemed to be, on my IRL work, so I buckled down and spent the rest of the day and most of Saturday working on the draft of my second book. I made a few calls to check some things, reread the latest chapters, then threw one out. That was painful. It's the hardest thing about writing—accepting that some parts you slaved over, that maybe you really love, just don't work. I started in again and stuck with it. Before Nick arrived for the party, I'd pounded out a sizable number of new pages.

He had planned to come down in the morning, but something came up at work. Though I had pretended to be, I wasn't at all disappointed, because it gave me more time to write.

He was already in costume when he got to my place. He wore a tux, and for a prop he carried a martini glass. He really did look like James Bond. He smiled, kissed me, then said, "Are you shaken, or stirred?"

"A little bit of both. You look great. I feel pretty under-dressed next to you," I said. I had dressed like Detective Olivia Benson. It's not that she's my favorite character on my all-time favorite television franchise, but she seemed the easiest to emulate. A blazer, a long-sleeved, somewhat low-cut T-shirt, a serviceable pair of pants, and with zero effort, I was in costume.

"No, you look beautiful," he said. And meant it, I think. He really was the whole package—sexy, bright, handsome, and attracted to me.

"I wondered if Miguel might cancel the party. Given that somebody died in his living room not that long ago. People could be squeamish about attending."

"Are you kidding? That's what will attract some of them. Besides, I think the party is his version of an exorcism. Lots of people, lots of laughing, lots of fun will banish any lingering bad or sad spirits. And, really, could any unhappy spirits stay that way long around Miguel?"

He laughed. "Any news on the Craig front?"

"Not a lot. A couple of ideas Miguel and I are looking into." I didn't want to get into everything right before the party, and there were some things I shouldn't be sharing at this point. He didn't seem to mind, and instead launched into a recounting of his week as we walked down to his car and drove to Miguel's.

I was listening. I truly was, but my mind did wander a little as I girded myself for a social evening with Rebecca that required me to play it cool. I'd asked how Miguel would handle her, but secretly I knew that I was the weak link in this chain.

"I really think the dean is impressed with the research I've been doing."

"That's great, Nick. I'm proud of you." As he continued to speak, I was thinking about Merlin Duffy and wondering if I would alarm him by leaving another message in the morning. If I pushed too hard, I might spook him and he'd try to avoid me altogether. It was hard to play a waiting game, when I was sure he had critical information about Rebecca.

"You can come, right?"

"Uhhh, let me see." I hadn't heard a word Nick had said since the dean was impressed with him. He obviously knew it.

"You haven't been listening at all, have you?"

"No, that's not true. You were talking about the dean loving your research, and—"

He shook his head, and I could hear the effort he made to keep the irritation out of his voice.

"We're invited to a dinner party at his house on Thursday night. Why don't you stay over, and we can make a long weekend of it? The dean's wife is a fan of your book. That won't hurt my standing in the department." He smiled, and I tried to smile back as we pulled into a parking spot a few doors down from Miguel's. Quite a few cars were already there.

"I'd love to, Nick."

"Great."

"But."

He sighed. "What is it this time? You've got a deadline to meet? You have to tail somebody for your second job as a private eye? April needs you to babysit her cat?"

"No, no. Come on, don't be mad. I was just going to say that things are starting to heat up on Craig's case. And we don't have all that much time. I'm just not sure where things will stand at the end of next week. If there's any way I can, I'll be there for dinner and for the weekend."

He didn't say anything for a second, then he nodded. "All right. I'm sorry. I know what you're doing is important. I just feel like we don't spend much time together anymore."

"Well, we're together tonight and I feel like I've got the hottest date in the room. Except maybe for Miguel." He laughed at that, and we walked up to the front door hand in hand.

When we rang the bell, a few bars from the shower scene in *Psycho* played.

"Carol has obviously been working with Miguel," Nick said.

"No doubt."

The door opened, and a masked man dressed all in black with silver accents—boots, tight-fitting pants, shirt, cape, hat, and mask—stood in front of us. He bowed with a flourish and brandished his sword, before his teeth flashed white with a wide smile.

*"Fabuloso, no?"*

"Fabulous, yes. You look like Antonio Banderas, Miguel. Be careful, my mother has a serious crush on him."

*"Gracias."* He turned to Nick. "You're my favorite spy."

"Thanks, Miguel. But I couldn't carry off your costume."

Miguel nodded, accepting the compliment as his due. He ushered us inside, and then leaned down to whisper in my ear while Nick took our coats to the bedroom.

*"Chica*, you look pretty, like always. But you couldn't glam up just a little?"

"Hey, I'm wearing eye makeup. I even went for the extreme lashes mascara. Not everyone is as surface as you. Some people like me just the way I am."

"Oh, I know that. Gabe is here, by the way."

I ignored that as Nick approached, but I gave him a look that said knock it off, and don't make teasing remarks in front of Nick. I can pack a lot into a look when I need to.

"Come on into the kitchen and get a drink. Or fill a plate, there's plenty," Miguel said, leading the way.

---

The house was filled with candles, jack-o-lanterns, and strings of pumpkin lights that hung from the ceilings and across the arched doorways. A small fire burned in the fireplace, and as we passed it, I studiously avoided thinking about the body that had lain in front of it only weeks ago.

In the kitchen, guests had brought more food than a small army would eat in a month. A long table in the kitchen was laden with cheese curds, cheese soup, and an assortment of favorite hotdishes, also known outside of the Badger State as casseroles. My contribution was a cheeseball—hard to mess up, even with only rudimentary cooking skills. On the counter were desserts—pumpkin pie tarts, cranberry apple crisp, peanut butter fudge pie, frosted cookies in the shape of witches and pumpkins. A small table held a stack of cups and a bowl of something fizzy and orange.

"Quite a spread, Miguel. But orange soda for the punch? I don't know ... "

"Not orange soda, it's Hocus Pocus Fizz. Pineapple juice, rum, sparking white wine and food color to make it Halloween color. *Es delicioso*. But be careful, *chica,* it packs a punch."

I smiled at his pun, but before I could say anything, Coop and Rebecca walked in. She looked scary and beautiful at the same time, wearing a pin-stripe jacket over a black dress, chunky silver jewelry, and the trademark side-swept hair of Meryl Streep in *The Devil Wears Prada.*

"I love the look, Rebecca," Miguel said, "Miranda Priestly is my favorite *fashionista.*"

"Who's Miranda Priestly?" Coop whispered to me. "It's a costume then, right? I couldn't tell for sure, but I didn't want to say anything. She's been a little touchy lately. I guess it's the pregnancy. She looks beautiful though, doesn't she?"

I so wanted to say it wasn't the pregnancy, it was Rebecca's natural state of being, probably exacerbated by the weight of lies and possible guilt over killing someone. But if Miguel could fake it, so could I.

"She looks great. Miranda Priestly is a character in a movie."

"How do you like my costume?" He wore a gray striped tie, gray shirt with the collar loosened, sleeves rolled up.

"Um, step back a pace and let me see you better."

"What? You don't recognize me, Liv?"

I was oddly pleased that he pegged my costume correctly, and of course I knew exactly who he was. He'd watched his share of cop shows with me—though I did it for pleasure and he spent more time critiquing.

"What kind of a detective would I be, if I didn't recognize my old partner, Eliot Stabler? Though I have to say, you look pretty much like you do most days."

"It's the only costume Rebecca could get me to wear. You didn't exactly push the boundaries, either."

"Hey, I'm wearing a shoulder holster. Ross got it for me." I pushed my blazer aside.

"What are you two talking about?" Clearly, Rebecca had spotted us having fun and come over to ruin it.

"Just complimenting each other on our costume choices. You look great," I said. And sadly, it was true. She did.

She eyed me suspiciously. Maybe it was better to be at least a little snarky. But with Rebecca, it's hard for me to stop at a little. So, I smiled, turned to Nick, who had been chatting with a pirate I didn't know, and said, "Let's circulate and see who else is here."

An eclectic playlist of vaguely Halloween-like tunes that included the themes from the *Twilight Zone, Scooby Doo,* and the *X-Files* came from the speakers as we wandered through the house. The usual Miguel mix of people populated his living room, dining room, hallways, and kitchen.

We stopped to chat with insurance agent Marty Angstrom, wearing a Batman costume, and he introduced us to his new neighbor, a thin woman in a Cruella de Ville get-up. Sherry Young, who had come as a sexy witch—no surprise there— came up to talk to us, and after a few minutes we drifted away. I scanned the room and saw Claudia Fillhart, my favorite librarian, dressed as her favorite literary character, Jane Eyre. She was chatting earnestly with Courtnee who was in a Supergirl costume. Airhead Courtnee and erudite Miss Fillhart—that had to be the oddest pairing of the evening.

I saw people I'd known all my life and acquaintances I'd made during my time at the newspaper, but there were many guests I didn't know at all. In Himmel-sized towns, you're more likely to know *about* people, than to actually know all the people themselves. For instance, I don't know Mary Beth Delaney's brother Ken Wheatley. He lives in Himmel, but our paths have never crossed. Yet, I know all about him, because I know his sister Mary Beth: he was student council president in Benanski, North Dakota, he just missed being a contestant on *Jeopardy,* and his wife left him for the guy who installed the carpet in his living room.

With fifteen thousand people in the town, and another fifty-thousand spread out over the county of Grantland, most of us find a social group that suits us, and we rarely breach the boundaries. Unless we are like Miguel, and few of us are. His parties always represent a collection of the many overlapping circles in which he moves. His Halloween bash was no exception.

I spotted Will Fraser in earnest conversation with Rebecca in a corner of the room. Their heads were apparently too close together to suit Will's wife, Gretchen. As I watched, she strode toward them, and she didn't look happy. Rebecca must have noticed her, too. She treated Will to one of her faux smiles and then glided off in Coop's direction. Her mission was accomplished. She knew Gretchen had a fairly strong possessive streak, and I was sure she'd chatted up Will just to irritate her. It had worked. Even from a distance it was clear that Gretchen was coming down hard on Will.

"Typical Rebecca," I said to Nick. "Sowing discord wherever she goes. Do you think we should try and rescue him? It is a party, after all." I started in their direction without waiting for Nick's answer.

"Hi, Frasers. I was just gawking at your costumes. You guys look good."

"All Gretchen's doing," Will said. He was dressed as Robin Hood, and Gretchen had come as Maid Marian.

She put on her party face and turned to me with a smile.

"Thank you, Leah. I've always loved to sew. I used to wish we had a little girl that I could make pretty dresses for." The wistful expression on her face softened her, and she looked quite pretty.

"Are you doing any of the costumes for the Hospital Follies?" I asked. And immediately wished I hadn't, because I knew what her follow-up question would be.

"No, we're renting them. The timeline is too short. But, that reminds me, Leah, have you had a chance to draft any of the publicity material for the Follies?"

Oh, boy. I sure hadn't.

"Working on it, Gretchen, working on it. I'll get something to you in a few days. See you soon," I said, stepping away and heading toward April, who I'd spotted standing in the corner a few feet away.

"April's probably overwhelmed," I whispered, as I steered Nick toward her. "Let's talk to her for a minute. You can show her that you're a lot nicer the second time around."

"You're the person that I hope thinks that I'm nicer the second time around," he said. "You go ahead, I want to ask Miguel something." Before I could say it wouldn't hurt to at least say hello to April, he was on his way back to the kitchen.

"Hi, April. Your outfit is fantastic." She looked soft and cuddly, like the fluffy black cat her costume emulated. It suited her. "Really? Rebecca told me that 'Cat costumes are for cute kids or sexy women. Think about it, April. Do you fit either category?' " Her voice was nothing like Rebecca's, but she got the mean girl tone just right.

Used to Rebecca's insults as I was, the casual cruelty of one aimed at someone as vulnerable as April made my blood boil. "To borrow Courtnee's favorite word, Rebecca is a biatch. Don't pay any attention to her."

"I kind of have to. She's my boss."

"About work stuff, yeah, but she's not the boss of how you

feel or what you do outside of work. She lives to make people feel bad. It's what nourishes her shriveled up soul. Don't feed the beast. Listen to Aunt Leah, she'll never steer you wrong. Now, did you make that costume? Because it's seriously amazing."

"My sister June made it. She's the creative one. I just did the cat-face make up."

"I'd say you're right up there with your sister on the creativity scale. It looks like professional theater makeup."

"I used to help out at community theater where I lived before I came back here. Just behind the scenes," she added hastily. "That's where I learned."

"Better keep that to yourself, or my mother will—"

"Your mother will what?" I turned, and there was my mother, resplendent as Elphaba, the witch from the musical *Wicked,* green face and all.

"April, this scary creature is my mother, Carol Nash. Mom, this black cat with the cute face is my friend, April Nelson. I was telling her that if you knew she'd done her own make up for tonight, you'd try to recruit her for the community theater."

"For once, Leah is absolutely right, April. Your makeup is wonderful, and we really need some new blood at the theater, especially behind-the-scenes."

"Well, I—"

"Sorry, April, I tried to warn you. She doesn't take no, easily."

"Pay no attention to her. Leah, don't let us take up all your time. Go. Spread your light around the room."

I made a face at her, shrugged at April, and left the two of them talking. Well, my mother was talking, and April was listening with a dazed expression on her little cat face. A full court press by Carol Nash has that effect on people. As I walked away, I saw my mother's beau, Paul, dressed as the Wizard of Oz, heading in their direction. He loves community theater as much as my mother does. April didn't stand a chance.

I said hi to Mike and Noelle Chapman. She was a very pretty Princess Leia, and he was a not very convincing Han Solo. The room was getting hotter as it got more crowded. I started toward the kitchen to get another glass of Miguel's refreshing special punch. He and Nick weren't there, but Gabe was.

"Hey, you," he said. "I see you went all out on your costume."

"It's my homage to Olivia Benson. I see you went with the Jack McCoy look."

He wore what he usually had on whenever I saw him, a dress shirt, collar and tie loosened, and sleeves rolled up. "When I hear good advice, I take it. How about advising me on what to drink? I'm pretty much past the age where orange soda sounds good to me."

"It's OK," I said. "It's not really soda, it just looks like it." I rattled off the ingredients I could remember, but his expression only grew more pained.

"Pineapple juice? Sparkling white wine? Any chance of a beer?"

"Every chance," I said. I pulled open the refrigerator, but was surprised to see none there.

"Not to worry. Come with me." I grabbed his arm. "Miguel has a fridge in the garage. I'm sure he's got some beer stashed there."

"You can just go in his garage and steal his beer?"

"Yep. We have an understanding. What's mine is mine, and what's his is mine, and it works great for me. No, seriously, I'm sure that's where he stashed the party reserves. Besides, for the lawyer that's going to get his uncle out of a murder charge? I'm sure it's OK if you drink all his beer."

"Yeah, about that." The cool evening air felt good after the stuffiness of the house as we walked the few yards to the garage.

I opened the side door and as we stepped in, I said, "What? Did something happen?"

"No, no," he said quickly. "No new evidence. No surprise witnesses—not yet anyway. But I started thinking today. You know we said that Rebecca might be the owner of the phone—"

"Might be? Are you kidding? C'mon, Gabe, she *is*. I'm telling you. I—"

"Hold on. Could you just listen for half a minute? I told you and Miguel to keep it low key so that if it is Rebecca, she won't know that we're on to her. But the more I think about it, the more worried I'm getting. No matter who killed Holly Mason, if they're connected to the phone, and they were at the park that night, they already know you're getting closer. And that could make whoever it is dangerous. To both of you."

---

I didn't say anything for a minute while I took that in.

"So, you think—"

"I think you should watch your back."

"Aren't you being a little melodramatic?"

"For a smart woman, you're being kind of dumb. Why wouldn't whoever killed Holly try to kill you, if they think you're getting too close?"

"I know what you're saying. But I don't feel like we're close enough to worry Rebecca—or whoever. We've got mostly guesses, so far. Not that they're not good guesses."

"It doesn't matter what *you* feel. It's what the killer feels that counts."

"You're not saying we should back off, are you?"

"Somehow I don't think that would do any good. No, just be careful. Like, don't go out in the dark alone with a stranger, for instance."

"You're strange. You're not a stranger."

I reached into the refrigerator and pulled out a beer from Miguel's stash.

"Here you go. And one for the road," I said, as I handed him another. "Don't worry, I'm not going to take any chances. This isn't my first rodeo."

"I hate that expression."

"Noted."

As we started to leave, he put his hand on my arm and turned me back to face him. "I mean it. Be careful." He was close enough that I caught the scent of his after-shave and saw the faint shadow of stubble on his cheeks. His eyes were dark and serious, and they looked straight into mine for a second before I looked away and said lightly, "I will. Promise."

He let go of my arm. The tension vanished. "Good. I don't have that many friends. I'd hate to lose one and have to start over again."

## 35

Nick was in the kitchen when we walked back inside.

"I was looking for you," he said, without acknowledging Gabe. "Where'd you go?"

"We were on a beer run. Well, more like a beer walk. Miguel's fridge was empty, so, we went to the garage and found some Spotted Cow. There's more there, if you want some."

"No, thanks. Miguel's idea of a martini is pretty lethal. I think I've had enough, at least until there's something to drink to later. And I think there will be."

It annoyed me slightly that Nick hadn't even looked Gabe's way.

"Nick, this Gabe Hoffman, Craig's attorney. Gabe, this is Nick Gallagher."

Nick turned then, as though he'd just noticed Gabe, but I knew that wasn't true. It's a trick he uses sometimes to establish dominance. He was taller and broader than Gabe, and in his suave 007 costume, he definitely cut a more dashing figure. But I fully expected Gabe to hold his own. I watched with amusement as Nick subtly shifted his shoulders and leaned slightly toward

Gabe, not too much, not menacing. Just definitely setting himself up as the alpha male.

Gabe moved quickly, before Nick could. He reached out and shook Nick's hand with a quick, hard grasp. "I've heard some good things about you."

Nick smiled graciously, but the smile curdled as Gabe went on. "It takes a pretty confident man to come as Peewee Herman."

I almost did a spit take with my Hocus Pocus Punch. It wasn't fair—Nick looks nothing like the nerdy bowtie wearing comic—but it was funny.

"Who is that guy? I like him," my mother, who had come in at just that moment, whispered in my ear. I ignored her.

I felt a little bad for Nick. He hates to lose his dignity. Which he doesn't very often. I stepped up and slipped my arm through his. "I think he looks like Jude Law."

Gabe took a step back and looked at Nick as though assessing the accuracy of my comparison. "Mmm, yeah. I can see that. The later years," he added.

"Just kidding with the Peewee Herman thing, Nick. Though personally, I find him very attractive." I didn't dare look at Gabe, because I didn't want to encourage him. He was having way too much fun. I felt Nick's arm tense beneath my hand, but before he could say anything, my mother jumped into the conversation.

"So, you're Gabe Hoffman. Leah's mentioned you a few times. I'm her mother, Carol Nash."

As Gabe shook her hand, he said, "I can tell by looking at you."

"What gave it away? The green skin?"

"Nope. The great smile. I like your costume, too. I saw *Wicked* with the original cast when I lived in New York."

"You did? I love musicals. Do you sing? Or dance? We're always looking for people in the community theater."

"A little. My mother was very disappointed I didn't turn out to be Mandy Patinkin. Or at least Jerry Ohrbach."

"Careful, Gabe. She's gonna drag you over to the piano and start singing with you."

"Never you mind what we're going to do," my mother said with a grin. "I've got big plans for this man." With that she hooked her arm in his and headed for the living room.

"That guy's a little full of himself," Nick said when they were gone.

"He's not so bad. Just a little cocky, maybe."

"Your mother looks like she wants to eat him up—which is very different from the way she always looks at me—like she wants to eat me alive. She hates me."

"No, she doesn't, Nick. She just, well, she doesn't forgive easily. Give her time."

He nodded. Then he said, "Wait here a sec, I have to find Miguel."

That was the second time that night that he'd left me in favor of Miguel. Which made me wonder what the two of them were up to. I poured another glass of punch, did some casual party chit-chat with a couple of people. Then I decided to hunt down Nick and Miguel.

The living room, which had been pleasantly party-time dim when I left it, was now almost dark except for the glow from the fireplace and from one recessed light in the ceiling. I looked around, surprised. The other guests were inexplicably clustered around the exterior of the room, and they had grown quiet.

Suddenly, Nick was beside me, and the music had switched from *Season of the Witch* to Al Green singing a classic soul song in the background. Nick turned to face me and placed his hand on my lower back, and took my hand in his other. Oh, no. Please, please no. But yes. Nick, who is a very good dancer, was going to lead me, who is a very bad dancer, around Miguel's living room in some romantic movie gesture that he thought I would love.

I didn't love. But it was too late. He whirled me around as Al's mellow voice crooned, *Let's Stay Together,* and everyone either swayed with the music or sang along as they watched us. This was a nightmare. We made one tour of the room. I managed to tangle my feet with Nick's and nearly bring us both down. Mercifully, he stopped. I stepped away and looked up at him, trying to be a good girlfriend even though he had just given me two of the worst minutes of my life. "That was sweet, Nick—"

Unbelievably, things got worse. Abruptly, he wasn't standing. He was kneeling on one knee, and he was holding the scariest thing I'd ever seen in my life. A little velvet box. My mouth went dry, and I couldn't think of a way to save this train wreck.

"Leah, these last months with you have been the happiest of my life. You challenge me, you support me, you encourage me, you make me want to be a better man. I know I *can* be with you. I love you, Leah. Will you marry me, again?"

You know that wide-eyed with delirious happiness expression that you see on a woman in a restaurant, or on a Jumbotron screen, when her boyfriend has just proposed? Well, that wasn't how I looked.

Instead, imagine if you will, the horrified look of a woman walking down a lonely path at night, when a crazed killer jumps out of the bushes and starts running toward her with a knife. Her eyes are wide and shocked, her mouth is open but nothing comes out. Do you have that picture in your mind?

OK, then. You've got a pretty good idea of me at that moment. I swallowed and tried to speak. I blinked rapidly. Nick, radiating love and confidence, waited for my answer. Still, nothing came out. A puzzled look came across his face, he started to sway a little bit, balanced as he was on one knee, holding out that damn little box.

I clutched at it, grabbing his hand at the same time to pull him to his feet.

"Oh, Nick! I don't know what to say."

Light, slightly relieved laughter came from the guests and a little swell of applause began. All was well, Prince Charming had won his princess. Nick was smiling and beaming down at me, obviously believing that I was overcome with emotion and unable to express my equally devoted love. Oh, God, what terrible thing had I done to make this my punishment?

I had to stop this before it got any worse. "Nick, no, please. Let's go outside." I turned and gave a tamping down gesture to the crowd. "Would you all excuse us?" I held Nick's hand, and tugged him toward the front door. As we stepped through and I pulled it closed, I could hear the buzz of dozens of little conversations puzzling over what had just happened.

---

Neither of us said anything until we moved a few yards away from the front door.

"Leah, what the hell?"

"I'm sorry, I had no idea you were going to do that. Why did you do that?"

"Why? Because when two people are in love, it's a pretty common thing for them to get married. I seem to remember you thought it was a good idea, once."

"Oh, Nick." I was shaking my head. How could I explain my response, when I wasn't sure I understood it myself? Nick had read me all wrong, so I must have been giving him the wrong signals. I'd consistently turned away any talk of even living together, let alone getting *married*. But clearly, he'd heard yes, or at least maybe. I answered as gently as I could.

"That's because back then I thought *we* were a good idea. It didn't turn out that way."

"Are you going to throw that in my face again? What is it with you, Leah? I was wrong, I'm sorry. How many times, in how many different ways, do I have to show you? What do I have to do? Just tell me, and I'll do it."

"I can't marry you, Nick. But it's not because I can't forgive you or let the past go. I know you've changed. But I have, too. I don't want what I did then."

"What do you want, do you even know?"

"My life is where I want it to be right now. I'm happy in my work, happy with my friends, happy with where I live. And I've been happy with the way things are between us."

"I guess that's the problem. I haven't been. We're in our thirties. It's time to move to the next phase. I'm ready to settle down, start a family, grow my career. I want to be married. You need that, too. I know you do."

"You've changed in some ways, Nick, it's true. But you're making the same old mistake. You think that your wants are the same thing as my needs. You don't really care about what I want. You only care about what you want me to have."

"That's not true. I've been patient. I've been understanding. You're always so busy with work, or your mother, or your friends, or you 'need a little space.' Well, I need things, too. And I've met plenty of women who've made it clear they're available. But I've never taken anyone up on it. Not once." His voice was angry, and hurt—and self-congratulatory.

And it was the latter that made me switch from gentle letdown to full frontal assault. It was the single biggest indication that what I'd felt instinctively, but wouldn't allow myself to admit, was true. Nick was self-absorbed, and though he could be charming, and witty, and thoughtful, it was all always in service to himself.

"Oh, no. Oh, hell to the max, no. You don't get extra credit for something as bottom-line basic as being faithful in an exclusive relationship. Because you know what? Any time you wanted to leave it, you just had to say so. And then you'd be free to see whoever threw herself at your fabulous feet. Patient? You've been patient with me? It takes patience to let another fully functioning human being have a life outside of you? To have friends, and work, and thoughts and needs that don't revolve around you? I don't know what world you're coming from, buddy, but it sure isn't mine."

"No, and I'm glad. Because in your world, you're always going to be right. You're always going to be strong. You're always going to be perfect. But even that's not enough, because you're going to demand that everyone else be perfect, too. There's no bending, no compromising and no understanding coming from you. Just judgment and sentencing. Well, I'm done throwing myself on the mercy of the court. It wasn't my affair that ruined our marriage, Leah. It was you and your impossible standards. No man could live up to your expectations. At least no man I'd ever want to be."

And then he did the worst thing he could have done to me. The unforgivable sin in my book. He turned and walked away without giving me a chance to respond.

## 36

I resisted the impulse to run after Nick, grab him in a choke-hold, and force him to listen to my rebuttal of his unfair, mean-spirited, and—I was afraid—maybe just a little bit right take-down of me.

A noise to the left made me turn. Coop, looking miserable, and Rebecca, looking triumphant, were standing beside the corner of the house. Great. They must have heard the whole thing. I just stared at them. What was there to say?

"Leah. I'm sorry. We came outside, Rebecca needed some air—"

"We stepped out the kitchen door just as Nick went down on one knee. I felt nauseous."

*I'll bet*, I thought. Though it may have made her sick to think that I was going to be happy with someone. She went on.

"Whoever called it morning sickness had it wrong, isn't that right, David?" She squeezed Coop's arm.

"We were in the backyard. We didn't know you and Nick were out here. But Rebecca didn't feel any better, so we decided to go home. We rounded the corner of the house just a second ago." Coop was struggling to help me through the awkwardness, but Rebecca was enjoying it.

"David, Leah's among friends. We can be honest with her. We didn't listen intentionally. But we heard everything. It was brutal, wasn't it? Especially at the last." The absence of any compassion in her voice must have struck even her, because she added, with a complete lack of conviction, "You must feel terrible. I'm so sorry."

Coop walked over then and gave me a hug. "Let's get together for coffee tomorrow, OK? I'll call you."

I nodded. As they left, Rebecca said something to Coop, and he went ahead to the car. She turned back and said, "Don't despair, Leah. At one point, it looked like David and I would never be together. But what's meant to be, will be." When she smiled, I hated her more than I'd ever hated anyone. For what she'd done and was doing to Coop, for the casual way she hurt people, for her lies and her manipulation and the way she always seemed to get away with things. She was letting Craig pay for the murder of Holly, I knew it in my bones. I wanted her to know right then, right there, she wasn't going to get away with it.

"Thanks, I appreciate it, Natalie."

I may have felt murderous rage toward Rebecca, but it paled beside the cold fury that swept across her face as she took in what I'd said.

"What did you call me?"

"I'm sorry?"

"You called me Natalie."

"Oh, that. Yeah, I don't know where that came from. Sorry. Rebecca."

"You don't know what sorry is. But you're going to find out. Trust me."

Standing alone in the dark, watching the tail lights of Coop's car pull away, the full import of what I'd done hit me. After I'd warned Miguel to be careful around Rebecca. After I'd promised Gabe I could play it cool. After we'd all agreed we needed to keep a lid on things until we had more information. I had blown it.

I should talk to Gabe. I should warn Miguel. I should get a drink. I was shivering uncontrollably, partly because my blazer wasn't much protection against the cool fall night. Mostly, though, it was because of the adrenalin coursing through my body after my confrontation with Rebecca and my break up with Nick. I needed to get somewhere warm.

I didn't feel like parading myself through the party and enduring the stares and whispers, or the outright questions from the bolder party-goers. I walked around the house and slipped in the kitchen door. Al Green had been replaced as the music choice. Unless I was mistaken, that was my mother singing *Defying Gravity,* accompanied by someone at the piano. That was good. She's a really good singer, and everyone would be paying attention to her for a while. I'd have the kitchen to myself.

I went to the cupboard where Miguel keeps a bottle of Jameson for me. Hocus Pocus Punch wasn't going to cut it. I pulled it out, got a glass, and took it to the refrigerator for some ice. When I turned, Gabe was standing by the counter, holding the Jameson I'd set there. Wordlessly, I handed him the tumbler full of ice. He poured me a generous shot.

"Rough night."

"You don't know the half of it," I said, after taking the first swallow of my drink.

"I think I know enough. You said goodbye to the ex out there, right?"

I nodded as I took another drink and enjoyed the burn.

"I'm not gonna say anything just now. Except it gets better. And, I don't think Peewee's the one you should give the rose to."

"Stop it."

"Too soon?"

"No, it's not that. Stop trying to make me smile, or feel better. I don't deserve to be cheered up. I really screwed up tonight."

He looked surprised, but then said, "Sorry if I read things wrong. It looked to me like you were dumping the guy. And when you came back in without him … but if that's not what happened. Look, sorry, it's none of my business."

I kept drinking while he was talking, trying to get the nerve to tell him what I'd actually done.

"It's not about Nick. He's gone. I'm more mad than sad about that. But there's something else."

He picked up on the angst in my voice and his tone changed. "What's going on?"

I took a deep breath, expelled it, and then hurriedly raced through the highlights of the breakup and my conversation with Coop and Rebecca afterwards.

"I was upset. Then, when she came back to get one more dig in, I just lost it. I called her Natalie."

He frowned and he shook his head. "Tell me that didn't happen. And if you can't tell me that, tell me she confessed to you on the spot, and she's turning herself in to the police right now. We talked about this. You promised you could keep it under wraps. You said—"

I looked at him miserably. "I know what I said. I know what I did. I'm sorry. I'm so, so, sorry."

"Sorry doesn't help. Let me think a minute." He closed his eyes and rubbed his temples.

I waited in silence and abject misery, cursing my quick temper and my reckless words. Finally, Gabe spoke.

"All right. Let's take a step back. It's not good. But it's not a disaster. Rebecca knows now that you've been digging into her past. And she's smart enough to know it's because of her connection to Holly. She's got to realize that you didn't buy her phony story about not knowing who Holly was. But she doesn't know just how much you know, or how you found out."

A little ray of hope pierced my gloomy conscience. "So, maybe it wasn't that bad, that I called her Natalie?"

"Oh, no. It's that bad. If Rebecca really is the owner of the cell phone, and she really was waiting in the dark in the park the other night, then she already knows you're looking for someone who owns the phone. But she might have felt confident enough that she'd covered her tracks so well, you wouldn't get close enough to her to be a problem. Only now—"

"Now, because I called her Natalie, she knows I've gone deeper into her past than she expected, and closer to finding out why she'd want Holly dead."

"Exactly. If she's the killer and she wants to protect herself, now she knows that she's got to make sure the DA keeps his focus on Craig as the only suspect. So, what's her next step?"

"Well, she'll want to find out how much I know. She's evil but she's smart. She'll figure out that I must have found the Kinmont College stuff online. She may think that's all I know, but she'll check with anyone she thinks could help her out from those days. Like Merlin Duffy."

"Maybe she'll try to reach him. But, remember, you're just guessing that he knows something more about Rebecca. Right now, he's a hope, not a promise. There could be other, better sources from her college days."

"But there were over a thousand students there when Rebecca was. Merlin seemed like a decent place to start."

"He is. I'm not criticizing your hunch. Right now, it's a good thing that he's the only guy you've tried to contact. We can't reach him at the moment, but neither can she. If there are others who could hurt her, she'll try to contact them. If she does, she'll find out no one has heard from you. That may ease her mind for the time being. Tell me again exactly what she said after you called her Natalie."

" 'You don't know what sorry is. But you're going to find out. Trust me.' "

"That could just mean she's gonna make trouble for you with your buddy Coop. Or, it could mean she's going to kill you. But we have to keep reminding ourselves, we're theorizing. Someone else could own that cell phone and someone else may have killed Holly. Rebecca may be a nasty person, but she may not have had anything to do with Holly's death—"

"She did." He ignored the interruption.

"But even if she did, she's not going to lose her head over nothing more than a snide, show-off remark like you made. Still—"

"I know. Her alibi. Coop wasn't in town the night Holly was killed. But now that she knows I've been checking up on her, she knows she may need an alibi. And tonight, I gave her the heads-up to manufacture one. We lost the element of surprise, because I'm an idiot. And if her alibi is strong enough, our theory won't convince anyone."

"Yeah. Well, I'd never say you're an idiot. But letting her get under your skin was pretty idiotic."

He was right. Everything he'd said to me in the last ten minutes had been right. I felt miserable and guilty. And my guilt was turning into anger at myself. The unfortunate thing was that instead of internalizing it, I projected that anger onto the nearest external object, as is my wont. In this case, it happened to be Gabe.

"All right! I get it. I screwed up. Don't you think this night has been bad enough already? I don't need you to pile on. And I'm tired of trying to convince you that I know what I'm doing. I made a mistake. But I know who really killed Holly and I'll prove it, without messing up your precious case." My voice had gotten louder and louder. I knew it, but I couldn't stop it.

Gabe stared at me like I was a crazy person. Which at the moment, I probably was.

"Leah, could you step closer to the window? Everyone in the house heard you, but I'm not sure the neighbors did."

I recognized that voice. I turned around. "Mom! You heard that?"

She nodded.

The cool water of rational thought washed over my fevered brain. Too late. I tried to remember exactly what I'd just said— or shouted.

"I mean, how long was everyone able to make out what I was saying?"

"For the first few seconds, all of us were just aware of a tantalizing rumbling. But the volume increased, so that by the time you got to knowing who killed Holly and proving it, we could pretty much all hear you. Even Roger Delaney, who isn't wearing his hearing aid tonight."

I saw then that Miguel was hovering behind my mother, a sympathetic look on his face. Which was comforting, but it was the only sympathy I was likely to get that night.

"I'm sorry, Miguel." I turned to Gabe. "I'm sorry, Gabe."

To no one in particular I said, "It's time for me to go home."

## 37

On Sunday morning, I sat in my window seat nursing an icy cold ginger ale. I didn't have a hangover, exactly, but I'd had enough between the Hocus Pocus Punch and the shot of Jameson to leave me with a headachy feeling when I woke up.

A pad of paper sat on my lap, on which I'd been sporadically making a list of people I needed to talk to, and things I needed to say. Miguel was at the top of the list, for making a spectacle of myself at his party. Gabe was right up there, too, for lashing out at him when it was myself I should have been beating up. Nick?

No. I crossed that out. He was the one who'd said some really nasty things to me. I was willing to forgive him, given the embarrassment and humiliation he'd no doubt felt, but I wasn't going to apologize for anything I'd said. In fact, he hadn't even let me get off what would probably have been my best shots before he walked away.

The buzzer rang, and when I pressed the button, Coop's voice came over the intercom.

"Leah, can I come up?"

For about the first time ever, I wanted to tell Coop no, I didn't want to talk to him. Had he heard about the blow up after he left the party? I sighed, and said yes, then went to the door to let him in.

"Come on in. Can I get you something to drink? Water? Tea? Coffee? Ginger ale?"

He shook his head and followed me to the sofa. I sat down in one corner, one leg tucked underneath me. He dropped down on the other end, half turned so he could look at me. He began without any preamble.

"I had a long talk with Rebecca last night, after the party."

Oh-oh. She must have already started her disinformation campaign against me.

"Oh?" I looked directly at him, trying to gauge how the conversation was going to unfold. He didn't look angry, just serious.

"Leah, I don't know how else to say this, so I'm going to just say it straight out. It's not a good idea for you to be the baby's godmother. I was wrong."

I was surprised for a second at the sharp pang of disappointment I felt. I didn't see myself raising a child of my own, but I could have had so much fun as godmother to Coop's.

"But, Coop, I—"

"No. Let me finish. This tension between you and Rebecca, it's gotten out of control. I thought, you know, you two might put that aside with the baby coming. But after what she told me last night, I know that's just not gonna work. You can't—or you won't—give up doubting Rebecca. You think that she's not good for me, or that she wants to come between us. She really doesn't.

"I know Rebecca was rough on you in the past. But she's really tried to make up for that. But no matter what she does, you reject it. She was really upset after the party last night. That's not good for her, and it's not good for the baby. I can't keep walking a tightrope between the two of you. She really doesn't want you as the baby's godmother. I have to make a choice, and I choose her." He looked down at his hands, which were folded in his lap, as he said the last few words.

I couldn't let that go. It was time he knew the truth about Rebecca, before she pushed me out of his life completely.

"That's not fair, Coop. You're acting as though this is a one-way street. You think that I'm some horrible person who can't stop trying to undermine your girlfriend—I mean your wife. It's not like that. Coop, you don't know her at all. She's been—"

"I do know, Leah. Rebecca told me everything after we got home."

"Told you what? That she's been lying to you? To everyone? That her name isn't even Rebecca Hartfield? That—" He held up his hand then, and his gray eyes had darkened. But when he spoke, his voice was still calm and measured. Which was way worse than if he'd started yelling at me.

"She told me everything. And I convinced her that we can trust you enough to tell you. We both hope that once you know the truth, you'll stop tormenting her."

I didn't bother to say that I hadn't tormented her. If anything, it had been the other way around. Instead, I said, "What truth? What story has she told you?"

"Rebecca's real name is Natalie Dunckel. You know that already. What you don't know is that she changed it because she was a victim of violent domestic abuse. Her abuser went to prison, but he swore she'd never be out of his reach. That he'd never stop hunting for her."

My mouth dropped open in surprise. "I don't understand. When—"

He cut me off and continued.

"Maybe you'd understand more, Leah, if you'd listen. Rebecca never knew her dad. Her mother left her with her grandmother when she was ten, and just didn't come back. She and her grandmother didn't get along. Her grandmother turned her over to social services. Rebecca went into foster care. She knew she had to turn things around if she wanted a shot at a decent life. She worked hard in school. When she graduated, she got a scholarship to Kinmont College."

I started to speak, but he raised his hand for me to wait.

"She met a guy. He was in medical school at UCLA. He was everything she wanted—rich, nice-looking, good family, good to her. They moved in together. That's when he started abusing her. At first it was just verbal. Afterward, he'd say he was sorry, he didn't mean it, he was under stress, he'd grown up in an abusive house, he was going to counseling, he'd change. He'd beg her not to leave him. He did a number on her, like abusers do.

"She was only nineteen. She didn't come from a normal family, she didn't know what a normal relationship was like. See, nobody ever wanted her. Not her mother, not her grand-mother, not her foster parents. When this guy told her she wasn't any good, she was trash, she didn't have a hard time believing it. But then when she tried to leave, he'd cry and say he couldn't live without her. And he'd be really good to her for a while. Then, she found out she was pregnant. She wanted her baby to have a different life. She thought if she tried harder, didn't 'make' him lose his temper, it would be all right. He said he wanted the baby. It would make all the difference.

"But then one day, she was late coming back from class. He accused her of cheating on him. He hit her so hard, she fell down the stairs. She lost the baby she was carrying. That's part of the reason our baby means so much to her."

I was stunned. Could this possibly be true? "Coop, that's horrifying. I—"

"It is. But it gets worse. She filed a complaint. His rich father got him a good lawyer. And his father came to see Rebecca. Said if she would recant, say that she'd been lying, he could promise his son would stay away from her. More than that, he would pay all her expenses until she graduated. She didn't have any money. She didn't have any family. She was alone. So, she agreed.

"Things were all right for a while. But then her ex showed up. He didn't approach her. He'd wait for her after her classes and watch her walk home. He'd sit in his car outside her apartment for hours. He'd be at the grocery store when she was, in line at the coffee shop when she stopped by. She'd get anonymous bouquets of flowers delivered that she knew came from him just to unnerve her.

"She went to the police, but they couldn't do anything. He hadn't threatened her. He hadn't even talked to her. And, of course, she'd recanted on the complaint she'd filed the year before. They weren't inclined to take her very seriously. All she could do was try to make sure that she didn't go out alone. But then one night, after a friend dropped her off at her apartment, when she went inside, her ex was there."

A thousand thoughts raced through my mind. If Rebecca's life had been as nightmarish as Coop laid out, no wonder she had such a stone-cold heart. But was it true? Rebecca was an accomplished liar. I couldn't let go of that fact.

"What happened to her?"

"He started beating her. He was shouting he'd kill her so loud that when her roommate—Holly Mason—walked up to the door, she heard him. She ran to a neighbor's house and called the police. Then she went back to the apartment. He was so out-of-control that when he saw Holly, he went after her, and knocked her unconscious. Rebecca managed to hit him with a lamp, but that only made him worse. He started on her again. By the time the police got there, he'd broken her arm and one of her ribs. He didn't get away with it this time. He went to prison."

"If that's true, that's beyond awful. But why did she change her name?"

"I told you. He sent her letters, said he'd find her no matter where she was. Said anytime he wanted he could send someone to kill her. She tried to convince herself it was just his way of intimidating her, keeping her under his control. But then she got a visit from an ex-con who wanted to warn her. He said her ex had offered to pay him to kill her. She knew then she'd never feel safe again."

"So, she took a new name, and left California?"

He nodded. "Usually a name change is public record. But in California, they have a program for domestic violence victims that lets women keep it private. She changed her social security number too, and blocked electronic access. She didn't have any ties to California, no family. She stopped thinking of herself as Natalie. She was Rebecca. She is Rebecca."

"But she didn't tell you this?"

"Not until last night. She never told anybody. Her roommate was the only one who knew she'd changed her identity. Even she didn't know what it was, or where Rebecca had gone. It was safer that way. Rebecca was shocked when Holly walked into the paper that afternoon. That's why she pretended to you that she didn't know her. That's why she tried to downplay the murder story. She was afraid that if it got a lot of play in the papers, her ex might see a picture of Holly. He might recognize her. And that might open the door for him to find her."

"It sounds like the script from a movie," I said. I hadn't meant it to come out as though I didn't believe it. I was just trying to absorb it. But Coop didn't take it that way.

"She's not lying, Leah. Who would make up something like that? You've covered domestic violence stories, you know how far some men will go to keep a woman under their control. You know she has reason to be afraid."

"Coop, I don't know what to say."

"I'm leaving later today for a conference in Chicago. I'd like to be able to tell Rebecca that she can stop worrying. That you're not going to say anything. You can understand that, can't you? Please, can I count on you, Leah?"

"You can always count on me." I said. But I couldn't bring myself to literally promise that I wouldn't keep looking into Rebecca's past. Coop was too far gone for his normal cop instincts to kick in. But I wasn't. I just had a gut feeling that something wasn't right.

Fortunately, Coop heard what he wanted to hear and assumed my pledge of loyalty to him meant I'd do what he had asked. But in my book, loyalty doesn't mean blind obedience. It means being faithful to the best interest of someone you care about, no matter what the cost. And I knew with certainty that pursuing the truth about Rebecca was in Coop's best interest.

"Thank you. Maybe after the baby is here, she'll feel differently. I just have to do everything I can to make things easy for her." He looked pretty miserable, for which I was glad. I'd hate to think he could drop the hammer on his best friend without feeling at least a little bad about it.

"It's all right. I get it. I just want you to know, I've never had a better friend than you, and I never will. No matter what happens, remember that."

He nodded, but didn't say anything. When he stood to go, he gave me a hug. I hugged him back hard, but I didn't say anything, either.

———

After Coop left, I thought about going round to Miguel's and helping with after party clean-up, but I knew he'd have a crew of friends there, and I just didn't feel like talking to a lot of people. I texted him, confirmed he didn't need help, then told him I was going dark for the rest of the day to work on my book. I needed something to take me out of the tangled-up threads of Holly Mason's life and death. Sometimes, it works best to just step away, focus on something else, and let my unconscious do its work. I made a sandwich for lunch and was just getting ready to get serious about writing when my mother called.

I assured her that I was fine, and that yes, I could've handled things better with Gabe, and that I owed a few apologies.

"You know, Mom, I lived for a lot of years without you over my shoulder making sure I behave. I do know how to clean up after myself."

"There'd be less need for clean-up, if you actually did know how to behave," she said tartly. "I'm with you a hundred percent on Nick. What a showboat that man is. Making a major production out of a proposal you didn't even want—thank God. You had me a little worried, but then I saw your face when he started dancing you around the room. I knew how that was going to end. I'm just saying that yelling at Gabe at the top of your lungs, at Miguel's party was—"

"I got it. I got it. I'm going to apologize to both of them. Just not right this minute. It's cold and rainy outside. I'm going to spend the rest of the day working. When I'm done with that, I'll call Clinton and let him know what a good girl am I. Maybe I can get a little love from my agent, if not from my mother."

"You get plenty of love from me, and you know it. I was thinking about making some apple bread tonight and dropping it off at your place tomorrow. But if you don't feel the love— well, maybe I should just give it to Paul."

"Wait, no. I take it back. You are love, Mom. You're Marmee March to Jo. You're Lily Potter to Harry. You're Mildred Pierce to Veda. You're—"

"OK, cut it out. I know you think that I'm more like Sofia to your Dorothy. But I do love you lots. I want you to be happy. I know you can take care of yourself, and make your own decisions. I just wish you'd pay more attention to my helpful input."

I laughed then, and as usually happens after a conversation with my mother, I felt better when I hung up. I made a peanut butter and honey sandwich, brewed a cup of tea, and sat down at my computer. Before I started writing, the phone rang again. April. I really didn't feel like talking, but I picked up anyway.

"Hi, Leah. It's April."

"Hi, April. What's up?"

"I just wanted to say that I think you did the right thing last night, breaking up with Nick. I never thought he was right for you, and I hope you're not feeling really bad about things. But in case you are, I thought maybe you'd like to go to a movie with me tonight? Or if you don't, well, you probably don't, right? I mean you have a lot of friends to do things with. That was a dumb idea. Never mind. But I did want to tell you, too, that Miss Oprah really loves her catnip mice, and if I can ever do anything for you, I'd really like to. That's all. Sorry to bother you."

She finished so quickly, I was afraid she'd hang up before I could thank her for the call. "Hey, wait, hold on. It's not a dumb idea at all, it's a really thoughtful one. But I'm fine. I'm just going to hunker down here and work on my book all day, and probably into the night. In fact, I'm going dark as soon as we hang up. No calls in or out, and no doorbells answered. I've really got to get serious. But I'd like to do a movie with you sometime. We'll see what's coming up and make a plan, OK?"

"Really? OK, yes, sure. Sorry to interrupt. I'll see you tomorrow, then. And Leah, this sounds weird, I know, but thanks for being my friend. It means a lot."

"No thanks needed, April. It's my pleasure. See you later."

Sometime, when this was all over, I was going to have to find out who or what had hurt April so badly that the smallest kind-

ness loomed so large in her life. In the meantime though, my
short-term priority was my manuscript.

I chose a favorite super-long playlist that inspires me while I
write. It was overcast enough outside that I needed a lamp on,
but I pulled the curtain shut so no one would see the glow and
think I was at home. All was in readiness. I went into full-on
work mode.

Outside of a couple of short breaks, I worked at a steady
pace for the next six hours. I knew that words pumped out at
that speed and volume would require some serious editing
before moving on, but it felt pretty good to get so far into the
book. I closed down and called Clinton to ease his mind and
have him tell me I was doing a good job. It would be really nice
to have *someone* say that. Unfortunately, it went straight to voicemail. I didn't bother to leave a message.

Instead, I took a long, hot shower and sang my head off
while I did so. Afterward, I put on my favorite pjs and checked
the time. It was quarter-to-nine. But bed sounded pretty good to
me. Maybe I could sleep away the frustrations and dissatisfac-
tions of the last couple of days, and wake up to a brand-new
morning where all my questions would be answered and all my
problems solved.

## 38

I'd gone to bed so early that, even though it was still dark out and my covers were warm and cozy, I was ready to wake up when my phone started buzzing the next morning. I pulled it toward me. April. I looked at the time, and then I sat straight up. In my experience, a six a.m. phone call is rarely good news.

"Hello? April, what is it?"

Only the sound of sobbing came through the phone.

"April, are you all right? Where are you? Talk to me, please!"

"I-I-I. Leah, I'm here. Please come, please come right away."

"All right, all right. I'm on my way," I said, throwing aside the covers. "Just tell me where. I'll be right there."

I jammed my feet into a pair of shoes and reached for a jacket to throw over my pajamas. April started crying again with a high-pitched wail that sent shivers down my back.

"April! Take a breath. Just tell me where you are. It's going to be all right."

"I'm downstairs. At the door. At the back door."

"OK, I'm on my way down." What April was doing at the office this early, and why she sounded like the sole survivor of an attack by aliens, I couldn't imagine. All sorts of things ran through my mind as I ran down the backstairs. Was she hurt? Had her cat died? Was her sister all right? What was her sister's name again, May? No, that wasn't it. June?

But nothing that I imagined came close to the reality I found when I reached the ground floor and burst through the door. The security light overhead was burned out. The only illumination came from the parking lot lights. April was kneeling on the ground, her back to me. She rocked back and forth, sobbing. I ran over and touched her shoulder. As I did, she looked up, and I saw her cheek was streaked with something dark. Her hand was, too, as she pointed at something a few feet away.

A body wearing a bright yellow slicker lay on the ground, face down. The hood was pulled partially away, revealing white blonde hair soaked with rain and blood. It was Rebecca. And she was very, very dead.

---

"April!" She stopped crying, but her eyes were huge and frightened. I pulled her to her feet as a wave of nausea rose from deep inside me. I clamped my mouth shut and held my breath to ward it off as I pushed and prodded April away from the scene.

"Did you call 911?"

As she nodded, I could hear the wail of sirens headed our way. "What happened? What are you doing here so early? Did you see anything? Did you see who did that to Rebecca?"

"No, no. I came in early because I forgot to set the coffee timer. She was really mad on Friday, because there wasn't any coffee when she came in at seven. Last night, I remembered I forgot to turn the timer on when I left for the weekend. So, I set my alarm and got up early today. I wanted to be sure the coffee was ready when she got here. But when I—when I—when I—" She started breathing faster and couldn't get her words out.

"Take it easy," I said, and patted her on the arm. She managed to finish her sentence this time.

"When I got here she was dead!" The last part came out on a wail.

"April, when did you get here?"

"Just before I called you. I parked in the back, and I ran up to the door, and then I saw her. I saw the yellow slicker. Oh, Leah, I thought it was you! I saw the slicker, and it was like the one you have, and I thought it was you! I ran over, and I reached out, and the hood fell back, and I saw her hair. There was blood on her hair, and on her hood, and on the ground. And she was cold. She was so cold. I've never felt anything that cold."

She moved her hands toward her face, but stopped when she saw the blood, seemingly for the first time. She stared for a second, and then she started to cry and to shiver, as the first police car pulled into the parking lot. I wrapped my arms around her and pulled her in for a hug as she sobbed into my shoulder.

The glare of the headlights picked us out and illuminated the body lying a few feet away. A door slammed. A voice shouted, "Raise your hands, and step away from the body."

Detective Erin Harper stood in front of us, her gun drawn as she motioned for us to move toward her. I raised my hands in the air and nudged April to do the same.

A female cop I didn't recognize moved forward as Erin Harper cocked her head toward us. She did a quick pat-down, nodded to her boss, and said, "All clear."

"Was that necessary?" I asked.

"Just a precaution. Standard procedure when two people are hovering by a body in the dark." My anger faded as I acknowledged that she was right. The other officer moved away. "Which one of you called it in?"

"I did," April said, her voice quavering slightly.

"Your name is?"

"April. April Nelson. I'm a receptionist here."

"A receptionist? You're in awfully early, aren't you? What time does the office open?"

"Eight o'clock, but I came in because I forgot to put the timer on the coffee machine on. Rebecca gets in at seven, and she likes to have her coffee first thing. But when I got here—" her voice wobbled uncontrollably, and she had to start over. "But when I got here, she was. I saw. She was, she was dead!" She began to cry quietly again. Detective Harper pulled a tissue from somewhere and handed it to April, but otherwise ignored her tears.

"Rebecca? Is that Rebecca Hartfield, the publisher? She's the victim?"

"Yes, that's her," I said. "Detective Harper, is it possible for you to question April inside? She's soaked to the skin. My apartment is on the third floor. If we go around to the front and use that door, we won't disturb the crime scene."

"Not any more than you already have," she said a little sharply. I knew that having two civilians in close proximity to the body—one of them even having touched it, increased the chance of contamination of the crime scene. But it wasn't as though we had any choice.

"I'm sure nobody is sorrier than April that she discovered the body. I'm not that crazy that I had to be here, too. But we didn't cavort around messing up your crime scene if that's what you're implying. We touched as little as possible, but it was a pretty traumatic experience for April. I'd like to get her someplace warm before she goes into shock."

She stared at me, and I thought she was going to say no, and make us wait there in the pouring rain as punishment for my attitude. I readied myself for an argument, but it didn't come.

"Hang on a sec," she said abruptly. Three more cars had

pulled up, and cops had started piling out. The ambulance was there, too, though Rebecca was long past needing it now. She yelled over her shoulder, "Davis!" The female cop who had patted us down jogged our way.

"Yes, ma'am?"

"Ms. Nash has an apartment upstairs," she told her, pointing at me. "Take the two of them up through the front door. No phone calls and don't leave them alone together. I'll be up to question them once I get the crime scene organized."

## 39

April was too stunned, and I was too shocked to say anything, so the three of us walked in silence through the parking lot and then around to the front of the building. Rebecca was dead. I could hardly grasp it. Coop was going to be devastated. A worse thought hit me. The baby. There wasn't going to be any baby. He had been so excited. Right now, at this very minute, he was waking up in his Chicago hotel, happy with his job, in love with his wife, excited about the future. He had no idea that everything was different now—and would be different, for the rest of his life.

I felt heartsick for him, but other thoughts began to crowd that feeling out. My chief suspect for Holly's murder was dead. The person I'd been counting on to throw reasonable doubt on the case against Craig Kowalski was now a murder victim herself. Somebody had killed Rebecca. Why? And who? How could Rebecca not be Holly's killer? Everything had lined up so beautifully.

*Except what Coop told you, and you refused to believe. That Rebecca's secret wasn't something terrible she'd done. It was something terrible that was done to her.*

"Shut up," I muttered to that annoying little voice in my head.

"Did you say something?" the police officer asked.

"No, nothing. This is my door," I said, as we stood in front of the *Times* building. I unlocked it with the key that purely by chance was in the pocket of my jacket, instead of on the hook by the door where I was supposed to keep it. If I ever started putting things where they belonged, I'd really be in trouble. We walked up the stairs and to my office door, where again, thanks to my careless ways, we were able to get in. I led the way to the living room.

"April, why don't you get in the shower? There's a clean towel on the shelf, and shampoo, and all that stuff in the bathroom. It's right off my bedroom, remember?" I said.

She looked at me blankly. Before I could repeat my suggestion, Officer Davis addressed April. "Looks like you've got a little blood on your cheek. On your right hand, too. Did you cut yourself? Are you hurt? Any blood anywhere else?"

Small town police departments aren't equipped with all the resources of big city cop shops, but they're not all Mayberry, either. Himmel uses the Wisconsin State Crime lab, but most HPD officers are trained in evidence collection and crime scene protocol. Officer Davis clearly was.

April stared at her hand in a dazed way. "I don't know. I don't think so." She held out her arms. There was a small dark spot on the cuff of her jacket, but nothing else that I could see.

"She touched the body," I said. "She thought it was me. Rebecca and I have the same color rain coat. April reached up and moved the hood. The back of Rebecca's head is covered in blood. It must be hers. Look, is it OK if she hops in the shower? She's shivering, and I think she'll be able to answer questions better if she's warm and dry."

Officer Davis nodded. "Sure. Just let me get a quick photo of your hand and that spot on your cheek? Is that OK with you, April?"

I wasn't sure that was a good idea. April, as implausible as the idea was, could be a suspect. The person who finds a body often is. I didn't object, but it wouldn't have mattered if I had. The efficient Officer Davis had already taken several pictures with the camera on her phone. She was a quick one. Smart, too. I was a little surprised I didn't recognize her. African-American cops aren't all that common in Himmel. As in, there aren't any. Except, it seemed, for her.

I moved over to April and put an arm around her shoulder. "You're going to feel a lot better after you get a hot shower and some warm clothes. Really. There's a sweatshirt and a pair of sweatpants hanging on a hook in my closet. Help yourself."

"But I can't wear any of your clothes. They'd be way too small."

"Oh, come on. We're not that far apart in size." If I had to guess, I'd say April was a couple of sizes larger than me. She was built differently, more on the pear-shaped side, but nothing one of my roomier sweat suits couldn't handle. I hated that even in the midst of trauma her reflexive reaction was that she was too fat. Her self-esteem hovered right around minus ten.

"Go. Get in the shower. Cry your head off there if you need to."

As she left the room, I wished I was by myself. I wanted to think through what Rebecca's death meant, and what I needed to do next, and how I could best help Coop. But that wasn't going to happen until Erin Harper was through with us.

"You want some coffee?" I asked Officer Davis.

"Yes, thanks, Ms. Nash. I could really use some."

I nodded and started the coffee. While we waited, I tried to get her to warm up to me a little. I like to have as many friends in the local police department as possible.

"My name is Leah. You don't have to call me Miss Nash."

"All right," she said, but didn't offer up her own name.

"How are you liking Himmel?"

"It's fine."

"Where are you from?"

"Milwaukee," she said. Maybe her big town background disinclined her to small town friendly chit-chat. I was about to try again when there was a quick rap on the door. It had to be Erin Harper.

"Come in, it's open," I said.

She spoke to Officer Davis briskly as soon as she stepped inside.

"I've paired you with Simmons. He's got your orders."

"Yes, ma'am." She jumped to her feet, and the two of them stood together conferring in low tones for a few minutes. When Officer Davis started to leave, I called to her. I had seen the longing look she cast toward the coffee-maker when her boss had arrived.

"Wait a minute. I'll get you a to-go cup." I dug around in the cupboard, found a commuter mug with a lid and filled it. "Keep the cup, and come back for a refill if you need one."

"I might do that, Leah," she said. Then she added, "My name is Gertrude."

I didn't see that coming. Stereotyper that it seemed I was, I'd been expecting her to have some lush and lovely sounding name like Sharessa or Delania. She saw my surprise and grinned as she took the cup. "My friends call me Rudy."

## 40

As Officer Davis left, Detective Harper turned to me. "Where's Ms. Nelson?"

"She's still in the shower." But even as I spoke, the sound of rushing water stopped. "She should be out in a minute."

"All right. We can go over your version of events."

I motioned her over to the sofa, and we both sat down. She pulled out a small notebook and a pen, but I noticed she also hit the record button on her phone.

"I don't know much about the 'events,' " I said. "I was sleeping. April woke me with a phone call around six. She was pretty hysterical. I threw on a jacket, ran down the backstairs, and found her next to Rebecca's body."

She then walked me through seeing April kneeling and crying, and confirmed that other than checking to make sure Rebecca was dead, neither of us had touched the body or removed anything from the scene or done anything that might interfere with the investigation.

"Did you go out yesterday?"

"I didn't go anywhere. I was home all day."

"Alone?"

"Mostly. Coop, Lieutenant Cooper, came by around eleven. He stayed about an hour. I had some lunch, I talked to my mother on the phone around one, and then I worked for about six hours on a book I'm writing. After I knocked off, I took a shower. And I went to bed around nine."

"That's pretty early isn't it?"

"I was pretty tired."

"And you didn't go out at all?"

"No, I told you."

"Did you hear anything last evening, or last night? A car driving up? Voices? Anyone coming or going out of the building?"

I shook my head. "Sorry, no. I'm on the third floor. The building's been completely remodeled. The windows are new, the walls are insulated. I doubt I would've heard a semi pull up last night. And I sure wouldn't have been able to hear anyone at the back entrance. What time do you think Rebecca was killed?"

"Don't know. Rigor's set in, so probably at least eight hours. Medical examiner can't say yet."

"With the cold weather last night, it could be pretty hard to get a decent window for time of death," I said. "It's going to be tough to find witnesses. There isn't a more deserted time in downtown Himmel than Sunday night."

"Tell me about it. That's why the department cut out night patrols here to save money. There's never anything going on."

"Except when there's a murder."

She didn't respond. Instead, she sighed and seemed a little more human to me as she tucked back a stray hair that had dared to spring itself from her tight French braid. She was stressed, and with good reason. Coop wouldn't be able to come near this investigation because of his personal involvement, and he was the best investigator in the department. Plus, while any murder is treated as a priority, there would be tremendous pressure to find the killer of a cop's wife.

"I understand Ms. Nelson thought the body might be yours, at first. Any reason why she'd think that?"

"You'll have to ask her, but I assume it's because Rebecca and I had the same kind of raincoat, and her face was hidden."

"Can you think of any reason someone might want to kill you?"

"What? No."

"I heard that at a party on Saturday night, you said you knew who really killed Holly Mason. You don't think that maybe you upset somebody who thought you were getting too close?"

I was taken aback. How had she heard that? Then again, my mother had said the entire guest list could hear most of what I said. Detective Harper hadn't been there, but a lot of other people had.

"Wait a minute. You arrested Craig Kowalski for Holly's murder. Are you saying you think someone else did it?"

"I'm saying, I know you've been asking a lot of questions. And that you said you knew who killed Holly Mason where a lot of people could hear you. I still think Craig Kowalski is good for the murder. But now I've got another one, and I have to try and figure out why. I have to consider the possibility that you upset somebody, for whatever reason. And maybe you were the intended victim, not Ms. Hartfield."

"Well, if I was, it wasn't because I was so close to unmasking the killer."

She changed topics abruptly.

"Ms. Hartfield used to be your boss, didn't she? How did you two get along?"

That was a loaded question.

"I didn't like Rebecca, but I'm not in the habit of killing people I don't like."

"Know anyone else who didn't like her?"

"I can't speak for anyone else."

"So, you didn't leave the house yesterday. You didn't see or hear anything last night. You don't know of anyone who might have wanted Ms. Hartfield dead. Or you."

"That about covers it," I said.

"I'm not your enemy, you know."

"I didn't say you were."

"You've made it clear that you think I screwed up by arresting Craig Kowalski."

"Yeah, I do."

"And you don't like that I told you to stay clear of the case. It wasn't personal. It's because you're an amateur, and amateurs let their feelings get in the way. They aren't objective."

"In this case, I think your objectivity is a handicap. You don't know Craig, so you don't understand that he isn't a liar. If Craig had been so angry that he lost control, if he'd beaten Holly in a blind fury, as soon as that fury passed, he'd accept his punishment. He wouldn't lie. He wouldn't run. He wouldn't put his family through a trial. I'm not saying Craig couldn't kill—in the right circumstances, maybe any of us can. But Craig would never lie to escape punishment."

Unexpectedly she said, "I checked out that lead Lieutenant Cooper gave me. The old guy at the bar, the one who said he saw a woman running away from the murder scene. Don't look so surprised. I don't ignore leads. But there wasn't anything there. He was just a confused old man with the DTs."

"I disagree. I think there's something to his story."

"Yeah? What else have you got?"

I was a little impressed that she'd followed up on Harry Turnbull. And Coop thought she was a good cop. I wavered for a second, but pulled back from the edge. Before I told her any of what I knew about Rebecca's past or anything else, I wanted to talk to Gabe. Maybe Erin Harper wasn't the enemy, but she wasn't Craig's ally either.

At that point, April shuffled into the room, her skin rosy from the shower, her hair damp and clinging to her head, and her eyes puffy from crying. But at least she didn't look shell-shocked anymore.

---

"Ms. Nelson—may I call you April?"

She nodded.

"Are you feeling better?" Detective Harper asked, as she opened her notebook and set her phone up to record the interview.

April nodded again. I handed her a cup of coffee with two sugars, and pointed her to the seat on the sofa where I'd been sitting. I sat down on the rocking chair.

"Thank you. I'm sorry I was so emotional before," she said, to both me and the detective. "It was just—I've never seen a dead body before. And I never expected—" As she spoke her lip started to quiver. Detective Harper interrupted to refocus her.

"Yes. You had a big shock, April. I just have a few questions to ask. Maybe Ms. Nash would like to take a shower or whatever. You and I can just talk over what happened this morning." Her voice was friendly enough, but April was suddenly teary-eyed again.

"Oh, but can't you stay, Leah?" April begged.

"Absolutely."

Erin Harper didn't look happy, but she didn't object. She walked April through what her job was at the paper, and how long she'd worked there and asked her again why she was there early.

"Now, Sunday night is a pretty unusual time to be at the

office. Do you know any reason why Ms. Hartfield would have come in to work last night?"

"No. I know she worked nights sometimes. Once she called me at home, and asked me where a file was, and I had to come in to find it for her. I didn't mind. But she didn't say she was coming in last night."

"Wait a minute," I said.

Detective Harper flashed an annoyed look at me, but I plowed on. "Rebecca could have set up a meeting with a source here last night."

"Do you know something? You need to tell me, if you do. This is a murder investigation."

I wanted to nudge her into digging deeper into Rebecca's past, but I didn't want to be the one to give her the story that Coop had told me in confidence. I'd much rather she found out for herself. Then, she could be the one to disillusion Coop when Rebecca's sad tale of domestic violence turned out to be phony. And I was beginning to have an idea about what was lurking in Rebecca's phone records.

"No, I'm just raising the possibility. It wouldn't be unusual to have an off-hours meeting with a source. Her phone records would show if she'd called someone, or who might have called her to set something up, right? You could see who she was in contact with the past few weeks."

"Thanks for the tip on conducting an investigation. I think I know what records to review and how to handle them."

"Right. Sorry," I said, just narrowly avoiding adding "not sorry" to my insincere apology, but I think she knew it was implied.

"Now, April," she said, returning to her questioning, "let's just go over one more time what happened when you got here this morning. What did you see?"

"Nothing. I mean, the parking lot was empty, except for

Rebecca's car. I parked at the far end of the lot—I'm trying to get in more steps. It's so hard for me to count calories, but I thought maybe if I could get more exercise, I might lose some weight that way." I knew that April was babbling about her diet because she didn't want to get to the part about finding Rebecca with her head bashed in. Detective Harper was surprisingly patient with her.

"OK," she said and nodded, then brought April gently back. "You must have had to run toward the door, with rain coming down as hard as it was this morning."

"Yes. That's why I didn't really see anything until I got right up there. I had my head down while I ran toward the back door. It was kind of dark there—one of the lights is out. I had to push back my hood so I could see. And then I caught a glimpse of something yellow out of the corner of my eye. I turned and, and—"

I thought she was going to lose it again, but she pulled herself together.

"I saw someone lying there. I thought it was Leah. She has a yellow slicker. But when I ran over and pulled the hood back, I saw the hair. Blonde hair. I knew it was Rebecca. And I knew she was dead. There was blood and she was so cold. I couldn't do anything. I couldn't help her." She gulped hard before continuing.

"I called 911, and I called Leah. I couldn't have done anything, could I, Detective?" she asked with tears in her eyes.

"No, there wasn't anything you could have done for Ms. Hartfield. I think that's enough for now." She flipped her notebook shut and turned off her voice recorder.

"Is it OK if I call my sister now? It's just that she'll be worried."

"Yes, April. Go ahead and call." She stood up then, and I did, too. I walked her to the door while April phoned her sister.

"You think of anything—or you decide to tell me what you're withholding—give me a call. I'm a good cop. I'm just doing my job. It would be easier if you cooperated. I'll be in touch."

I nodded. As I shut the door, I reminded myself not to underestimate Erin Harper.

## 41

"Damn it, Leah. I told you to be careful."

"Me? I'm fine. Rebecca's the one who's dead."

I'd called Gabe as soon as April and her sister left. We were sitting on stools pulled up to the kitchen island, untouched cups of coffee growing cold in front of us. I'd just finished updating him.

"When April found the body, she thought it was you. And when you got in my face at the party, you were yelling that you knew who killed Holly. You think maybe that's what gave her killer the idea to come after you?" A little vein on the side of his forehead was kind of sticking out, and his warm brown eyes looked pretty stormy at the moment. He was angry at me. I was surprised how much I didn't like that.

"Gabe, I'm really sorry I yelled at you like that at Miguel's. I was mad at myself, not at you. I'm sorry that I acted like such a jerk."

"Are you listening to me at all? I don't care about that. I'm saying that I heard you loud and clear say that you knew who murdered Holly. A lot of other people at the party heard you, too. Maybe Holly Mason's killer."

"Yes, I'm listening to you. And right after Rebecca's body was found, I thought she couldn't be the killer. But now that I've had a chance to think again, I'm still pretty sure she was."

The look he gave me was a cross between bewildered and exasperated. He closed his eyes for a minute and took a deep breath.

"Not two minutes ago, you said that Coop told you why Rebecca changed her name, how Holly knew her, and what her secret was. That she was hiding from an abusive ex, not hiding that she was an escort."

"I know, I know. And if that was her secret, I agree, she wouldn't have killed Holly because of it."

"Exactly."

"But I still don't think I'm wrong."

I thought he might have muttered, "Do you ever?" under his breath, but I chose to ignore it.

"I don't buy for a second the story Rebecca told Coop. That she lied about her identity because she was afraid of a stalking ex. But a lie is always better if there's some truth in it. So, let's say that it's true that Holly was her roommate. It's true that she and Holly found each other by chance. What's not true is that she was worried Holly might tip off her violent ex-husband and lead him to her. She was worried that Holly would tell her real secret —that Rebecca was a high-priced escort once, just like Holly."

"Again with the escort. We have no hard evidence that Rebecca was actually a high class working girl, do we?"

"Well, no, not yet. But I'll be talking to Merlin Duffy soon, the guy from Kinmont College. And he should know the truth about Rebecca's domestic violence story."

"OK. Let's say for a minute that you get that evidence. There are still a couple of big holes in your theory."

"Like what?"

"Like Holly 'just happened' to come to Himmel where her

long-lost college roommate she hadn't seen in almost twenty years lived?"

"What? You've never bumped into an old friend from high school in some city far away? Or sat next to someone on a plane who turns out to be your college roommate's cousin? Weird stuff happens all the time."

"OK. All right. I'll stipulate that weird stuff happens. 'Of all the gin joints, in all the towns, in all the world, she walks into mine.' "

"Yes," I said, pleased by his ability to quote an iconic line from *Casablanca*, in a reasonably good Humphrey Bogart voice. "What's the second hole?"

"If Rebecca killed Holly, who killed Rebecca?"

"Prepaid cell phone man."

"Who?"

"Holly's blackmail victim. There were always two theories that worked for Rebecca killing Holly. One was that Holly came to town specifically to see Rebecca, that she'd kept in touch with her, knew exactly where she was, and was going to tap her for financial help. The second possibility was that Holly came to Himmel because she was trying to solve her financial problems by blackmailing a client, and she found Rebecca by chance. Where I went wrong was deciding that she came specifically for Rebecca.

"If we go with the other idea—that she came after a blackmail victim and happened on Rebecca, then it works that Rebecca killed her and that someone else, Holly's prepaid cell phone man, killed Rebecca."

"Why would Holly's blackmail victim kill Rebecca?"

"Because Holly told Rebecca who the guy was, and what she was blackmailing him with."

"And you think that because?"

"They were escorts together, and Holly is the only person

who knows Rebecca's real story. She doesn't have to fake it with her. Holly tells her that now she has the upper hand with the kind of guys she and Rebecca had to fawn over in the old days. She asks Rebecca if she knows this local guy. They talk, they laugh, and now Rebecca has the information."

"So, if they're so happy together, why does Rebecca kill her?"

"Because Rebecca realizes that now that Holly knows her name and where she is, she'll always be a threat. Holly is here to blackmail a client, because she's backed into a corner. Why should Rebecca believe that Holly won't come after her someday, if she needs to? No. It's too dangerous for Holly to know all about her. So, she kills her.

"Then, she takes Holly's laptop, cell phone and purse. She checks through them to see if there's anything useful. And she checks to make sure there's nothing remotely connecting her to Holly. Like, for example, that Holly wasn't writing her memoirs detailing their happy Kinmont College days as high-priced hookers. Or, wait, how about this? Holly doesn't tell her about who she's blackmailing, but Rebecca finds the information on her phone or her laptop. That would work, too."

"I might be able to use something along those lines to argue for reasonable doubt for Craig—it could show that someone else had reason to want Holly dead. But then why would Holly's blackmail victim kill Rebecca? It seems like she did him a favor."

"Not really. Because with Holly dead, he becomes Rebecca's blackmail victim."

He shook his head. "That doesn't make sense. Why would Rebecca want to blackmail him? What was she trying to gain?"

"You don't know Rebecca like I did. She has—had—to have the power. It wasn't about money for her. It was about leverage and the ability to make people do what she wanted them to. It's how she got rid of the last sheriff."

"So, you think that Rebecca found out either directly from Holly, or from Holly's laptop or phone, a secret about someone from Himmel. Then, she contacted him and arranged to meet him here, last night."

"Yes. But she went too far. Holly's victim just got out from under her thumb, and before he even has time to enjoy feeling that his secret is safe, Rebecca threatens him. He may have paid Holly off, but he's not going to go there again with Rebecca. He agrees to meet her. He arrives early, waits for her, and kills her. I'd be pretty surprised if Rebecca's phone and laptop aren't missing, and for the same reasons that Holly's were."

Silence.

"You don't agree? Come on, it explains who killed two people, and puts Craig in the clear."

"I don't *dis*agree, and I'll use it, if it comes to that. But Craig isn't in the clear yet."

"But you said it's all about reasonable doubt."

"It is, but it would help if we knew who Holly's blackmail victim was. Right now, it's just a straw man the prosecution could knock down pretty easily. And the district attorney may decide that Craig is a possible suspect for Rebecca's murder, too."

"Why would they suspect Craig?"

"Cops like to keep things simple. They've got one murder on their hands, Holly Mason. They've got a suspect under arrest. Craig. But he's out of jail. Now there's a second murder, Rebecca Hartfield. And she's killed in basically the same way."

"But Craig and Rebecca aren't connected."

"Look, we're sitting here coming up with a theory that says Rebecca killed Holly, and then Holly's blackmail victim killed Rebecca. Over at the cop shop, they're going to be doing their own theorizing. Rebecca covered Holly's murder. They might figure that she found out something that proved beyond a doubt that Craig killed Holly. Craig found out about it, and killed her to keep her quiet."

"That's ridiculous."

"Is it? I could make the case. We need to get that SweetMeets client list. If there's some local names on it, there's a good chance we can find Holly's blackmail victim. If he exists."

"Yes. And if Detective Harper checks out Rebecca's phone records, I'll bet she'll find the same prepaid cell phone number there that we found in Holly's phone records. And that's the link that shows prepaid cell phone man was Holly's victim, and probably Rebecca's killer. But the SweetMeets list is kind of on you, isn't it? What's happening with that subpoena? Can't you shake some justice loose for us?"

Before Gabe could answer, there was a prolonged buzz from my back-entrance bell, followed by repeated short bursts. I pushed on the intercom, and Coop's voice, almost unrecognizable, came roaring in.

"Leah! I'm coming up. I need to see you!"

Gabe stood immediately and slipped on his jacket. "I should go. He's going to want to see you alone. I'll call you later. We can finish talking then."

"Yeah, all right. Thanks, Gabe."

I walked him to the door and opened it. Coop stood on the other side. His eyes were red and his expression bleak.

"Coop, I'm so sorry, man. If there's anything I can do ... " Gabe's voice trailed off. He clapped his hand on Coop's shoulder for a second, then said goodbye. Coop just nodded.

I reached out to hug him, but he kept his arms down at his sides.

"Come on in. I've got coffee, or—"

"Rebecca's dead." His voice was dull and flat. His eyes were, too.

"I know. I'm so sorry." I reached out and touched his hand.

"Are you?"

"What? Of course I am."

"You hated her."

I started to deny it, but decided to just let him talk without attempting to justify or defend my feelings about Rebecca.

"I love you. You loved Rebecca. I could never, ever feel anything but sorry for the pain you're in right now."

"Leah, my baby is gone, too. My child and my wife. They're both gone." He buried his face in his hands then, and his breathing came in strangled gasps as he struggled to control his emotions. It was the most heart-wrenching sound I'd ever heard.

I put my arm across his shoulders and felt them heave beneath it.

"Coop, I don't know what to say. If I could do anything, I would."

He looked up then, and sat up straight, moving away so that my arm fell away from him.

"Haven't you done enough?" The sudden hostility in his voice took me by surprise.

"I don't understand."

"Why did you do it, Leah? Why do you always do it? Why did you have to keep poking and prying and trying to find out about Rebecca's past? Why can't you ever just leave things alone? Rebecca's life was her life, it was her business, and mine, not yours. If you hadn't been digging around, if you had just left her alone, she'd still be alive. My wife and my baby would still be alive."

"I know you're hurting, but, Coop, I didn't have anything to do with Rebecca's death. I—"

"Didn't you? I told you that Rebecca was afraid. I told you that she had an ex-boyfriend who threatened to kill her, to never stop looking for her. Don't you get it? He must have found her, because of you. He found her, and he killed her."

"Coop, no. I did some checking on Rebecca, yes, but everything I did was online. I didn't even talk to anyone who knew her before. No one could have found her because of me, because I didn't ask anybody any questions. You're upset. You're not thinking straight." My words tumbled out as I tried to reassure him that I hadn't led a killer to his wife. But even as I spoke, a tiny spark of doubt flared up. What if Rebecca hadn't been lying to Coop?

It wasn't strictly true that I hadn't talked to anyone. I didn't see how it could hurt that I'd told Merlin Duffy's receptionist that I was researching Kinmont College, or that I'd left a couple of messages for Duffy directly. But what if it had? What if Duffy heard Natalie's name in the message I left, and mentioned it to someone else—someone who then passed it on to another someone and another, until word reached Rebecca's ex that the woman he'd been obsessing over for years was now reachable?

I didn't want to admit the possibility. I pushed it away. Her story of domestic violence was just another of Rebecca's lies. And Coop was so wracked with grief he was lashing out to feel the pain less.

"Coop, you can say whatever you need to, you can think whatever makes you feel better, but, please, know that I would never want to hurt you like this."

He looked up then, his eyes filled with a sadness that was hard to witness.

"I know you wouldn't want to, Leah. But that doesn't mean you didn't."

## 42

Coop was too wounded to think clearly. Once a little time had passed, he'd realize that it wasn't anything I'd done that had caused Rebecca's death. I worked hard at convincing myself after he left. If I could get proof that Rebecca was lying about her domestic violence past, then he'd have to see her death wasn't my fault. And the quickest way to find answers might be Merlin Duffy. Forget about waiting for a call back. I'd keep ringing his phone every hour for the next week if that's what it took to get him to pick up.

"Hello, Merlin Duffy here."

I waited half a beat to make sure I wasn't talking to a recording.

"Hello?" he repeated.

"Hi, Dr. Duffy. This is Leah Nash. I left a couple of messages for you."

"Oh, sure. You're on my list of things to do. But I've had so many things to take care of since I got back. Can I call you later this week? I—"

"Wait, no, please. I'm sure you're busy, but this is really important. And it can't wait. Please, I just need a few minutes."

"Well, I—what's this about exactly? Your message said you're looking for Natalie Dunckel?"

"My message was a little vague, because I didn't want to scare you off. I'm investigating a murder I believe she was involved with—another classmate of yours. Holly Mason."

"Holly is dead?"

"Yes, but Natalie is as well. She was killed last night. But people here knew her by the name Rebecca Hartfield. Did you ever hear that name?"

"Wait. Both Holly and Natalie are dead? I haven't seen either of them for almost twenty years. I don't understand why you're calling me. Are you with the police?" He sounded on the verge of hanging up.

"No, let me explain. Holly Mason—did you know she ran an online dating site called SweetMeets?"

"Yes, I've read about it. But you say that she's dead?"

"Yes. I'm calling you from Himmel, Wisconsin. It's where Natalie Dunckel lived for the past couple of years. And it's where Holly Mason died a few weeks ago. I'm working with the defense team for the man accused of killing Holly. I was checking into Holly's past and found the connection to Natalie. I reached out to you because you were at Kinmont at the same time, and, frankly, because your name is unique enough that you weren't hard to trace."

"I still don't understand what you want from me. I didn't know Holly at all, just by sight. I knew Natalie a little better, but we weren't close. I don't think she was close to anyone."

"I'm just trying to get a handle on their time at Kinmont. Did you ever hear anything about Holly and Natalie working for an escort agency, while they were at college?"

"Not while I was at Kinmont. I read an interview Holly did after her website started to take off, and she mentioned it. I can't say I was surprised. She was, well, I think the best way to say it is that she was very comfortable with her sexuality. And she didn't care what people thought. But I'd be very surprised if Natalie had done anything like that. She was beautiful, but—reserved is the word that comes to mind. She wasn't like Holly. Natalie cared what everyone thought, and she wanted them all to think she was perfect."

That wasn't what I wanted him to say.

"But isn't it possible that even if you didn't hear any rumors, some of your other classmates might have?"

"I think we all knew pretty much everything there was to know about Natalie after all of that with her ex."

All hope that Rebecca's story to Coop was a lie wasn't lost, but pretty close. I took a breath and asked the next logical question.

"All of what with her ex?"

He proceeded to tell me the story Coop had relayed about Rebecca and her abusive boyfriend, and the final confrontation that left her with a broken arm, Holly with a concussion, and him with a prison sentence.

"The story was that he'd beaten her up before, and his father got him off, and paid Natalie's way through school, so she wouldn't prosecute. But she had to the second time."

"And everyone knew about this?"

"Maybe not everyone. But it was a pretty big scandal on a pretty small campus. I think that was probably almost as bad for Natalie as the actual beating was. She hated that everyone knew her life wasn't perfect, that she wasn't perfect. I assumed that's why she dropped out of sight after graduation."

So, Rebecca had been telling the truth. This wasn't good. It wasn't good at all.

"Do you know the name of the man who assaulted Natalie?"

"I wouldn't, except that I called a friend from Kinmont after I got your message, to see what she remembered about Natalie.

She hadn't heard from her either, but she remembered all the details about the assault and the arrest. Neither of us could come up with the guy's name, though. But Selena never lets anything go. She called around after we talked, and then she texted me his name. It was Peter. Peter Hines."

And with those last few sentences, Merlin Duffy sent me to my own particular circle of hell. The thing I didn't want to face, the blame I didn't want to accept might actually belong to me. I had called him to dig into a past Rebecca had a right to keep private. And as a result, I may have opened the door for her abusive ex to find her. On top of that, the carefully constructed theory that I had argued so persuasively to Gabe wasn't true. Rebecca didn't have a shameful secret she was hiding that Holly had held over her head. She didn't have a motive for killing Holly.

I thanked Dr. Duffy, then got off the phone as quickly as I could.

I made a call to Jess Patterson, a private investigator friend of mine. I had to know if Peter Hines could possibly have been in Himmel, Wisconsin the night before, and if he had finally caught up with Rebecca, because of me.

---

"And so, Father, Coop is devastated, and he's really angry with me. Rebecca wasn't lying. She was a victim of domestic violence. And if I did lead her killer to her, it's about the most awful thing I've ever done. Except for maybe one other thing."

I sat in a chair in Father Lindstrom's office at the St. Stephen's parish center, holding a mug of tea I wasn't drinking. I'd given him the shortest version I could of all the things that had happened since Holly Mason died.

He didn't ask me what that one other thing was. He just

paused to take out a clean white handkerchief. He used it to wipe the steam that had risen from his Star Wars tea mug and settled on his glasses. When he was done, he replaced it and his glasses, and continued waiting for me to speak.

I sighed heavily. He might as well know the worst.

"See, I'm feeling really bad about dismissing Rebecca's story about her past as a lie. But then I've been having this thought that even if the worst thing happens to be true, and her ex-boyfriend found her and killed her, it doesn't have to mean that she didn't kill Holly. Sure, Merlin Duffy never heard that Rebecca was an escort, but that doesn't mean she wasn't. Maybe that's what she was doing when her abusive boyfriend met her, and that's why she put up with him so long, because being with him meant she didn't have to do escort work. You think I'm a bad person for even going there, right?"

"You're not a bad person, Leah. You're a very good person, with a very good heart. But you're also a person who doesn't give up easily. Sometimes that's a positive quality. In this case, it isn't. And once you have made your mind up about a person, it's very hard for you to change it. Rebecca may have made some very bad choices in her life, and she may have done some very destructive things. But you need to let go of the idea that Rebecca killed Holly."

"But why? Just because someone did something terrible to her, it doesn't mean she didn't do something terrible to someone else. She still could have a motive and she still doesn't have an alibi—Coop was out of town the night Holly died." I sounded a little unhinged even to myself. It was as though if I could prove that Rebecca had done something as heinous as murder, my unintentional betrayal of her wouldn't loom so large.

"You're wrong, Leah. Rebecca does have an alibi. She was with me."

His words hit me like a 2x4 to the head.

"I don't understand."

"Normally, I wouldn't reveal this, but these are extraordinary circumstances. Rebecca came to see me on the Saturday Holly Mason died. I was very surprised. I knew her only slightly, she was not a member of St. Stephen's, and it was rather late in the evening, about ten."

"What did she want?"

"She told me that while she wasn't Catholic, she had no friend to turn to, no one that she trusted. She was suffering under a great burden of guilt, and she asked if I could advise her and keep her confidence. I agreed. That's why I won't tell you the substance of her conversation, only that she was here with me."

Rebecca, unburdening herself to Father Lindstrom? I could hardly believe it, but I knew he would never lie to me.

"Father," I leaned forward in my chair, willing him to see the point I was trying to make. "Whatever she said, she was manipulating you. I know her. You said she stopped by at ten. What time did she leave?"

"That's my point, Leah. She didn't."

"What?"

"She didn't leave. We talked for a long time. I grew quite tired. I went to the kitchen to make tea, to help myself stay alert. When I came back in, she had fallen asleep. It had been a very emotionally draining conversation for her. I hesitated to wake her up. Instead, I covered her with an afghan and went to bed myself."

"Well there, you see? You don't know when she woke up and left. She could have gone out right after you fell asleep. That would give her plenty of time to kill Holly." I had been so sure for so long that it was Rebecca that I couldn't let go even as the final few strands that held my theory together were unraveling before my eyes.

"I'm afraid that at my age, I often get up during the night. I looked in on her at about one a.m. She was still there on the couch. As she was when I awoke again at three, and as she remained when I arose at six a.m."

One last try at proving that Rebecca was guilty. "But she could have left during the night while you were sleeping, and then snuck back in. That would be the perfect alibi for her."

He shook his head sadly. "Leah, even had she managed to match her return to the exact time when I looked in on her, each time I checked I noticed the same thing. She had slipped off her shoes while we talked. They were sitting at the same odd angle—one perched on top of the other—that they had been when I went to bed. I think that with everything else, that's a detail she couldn't have managed."

I slumped back in my chair, defeated. Not only had Rebecca been telling the truth to Coop, but there was no way she had killed Holly. I had no theory of the crime. I had no theory at all. The only thing I had was an irrational, biased, stubborn refusal that had blinded me to the truth, and cost us weeks of effort with nothing to show for it at the end.

## 43

Miguel was seated at the kitchen bar with me. He'd come upstairs on a brief break from a frantic day at the paper, trying to figure out how to manage things with Rebecca no longer there. He'd found me staring into a glass of Jameson, which I had poured an hour earlier, when I'd returned from Father Lindstrom's, but hadn't even touched.

He'd barely asked me what was wrong before I launched into a monologue of all that had happened since the early morning hours when I'd texted him about Rebecca's death. Now, I was at the self-pitying part, where I unloaded all my guilt and fears on him.

"So that's where we are. Rebecca is dead. And maybe it's my fault. And she isn't the one who killed Holly. She wasn't an escort, and even if she had been and wanted to hide it, it wouldn't matter. She's got a rock-solid alibi. Craig's trial is coming up fast, and I don't have anything for Gabe to work with except a few phone records from a cell phone we can't trace and a lot of speculation. And I've just outlined for you how bad I am at speculating. I'm so sorry, Miguel. I've let you down, I've let Craig down, and I even managed to let Coop down."

He shook his head and wagged a finger at me.

"No. No. No. You didn't let me and *Tío* Craig down. It's not over. We'll find the man with the phone. And Coop? I don't believe it. I mean, I believe Rebecca had a *chico malo* for a boyfriend, when she was young. But I don't believe that he tracked her down and killed her last night. Coop is feeling so bad. He is so *herido*. He doesn't mean it. It's not your fault Rebecca is dead."

"You think?" I felt the first slight shift in my burden of guilt.

"*Yo se*. It's not possible. Well, only a little possible. Merlin Duffy calls his friend on Thursday, *sí*? How could there be time for Peter Hines to track Rebecca down by Sunday night? He didn't even know then that her name was Rebecca. You're not thinking straight. No! Snap out of it, *chica*."

"Maybe. It's just that after Coop was so sure and upset, and then I started thinking about how often a random remark has led me to a witness or a source I need. Then, when Merlin said he'd told someone who told some other people about Natalie ... well, it just started to feel like I'd really screwed up."

"You didn't. I know it. You were wrong about how Rebecca fits. It doesn't mean you're wrong about everything. Your theory, it's like an optical illusion."

"Right. It's not real. That doesn't make me feel any better."

"No, listen. Someone shows you a picture and you say it's an ugly witch. They say no, look again, it's a beautiful *señorita*. You look again, and it's true. Nothing has changed but the way you look at it. You need to look at your theory in a different way. Then, you'll work it out."

I loved that he wanted so much to make me feel better. He patted my hand, and I couldn't stop myself. I reached over and ruffled his perfect hair.

"You know, you're about the best little brother I never had."

"*Gracias*. You're the best *hermana mandona*," he grinned then.

"What does that mean? No, don't tell me, I might not like it." With an effort, I smiled, and forced myself at least for the moment to ignore my own woes and focus on Miguel's situation.

"Tell me what's going on with the *Times*. I'm sure A-H Media expects the paper to publish as usual this week, even without a publisher."

"I'm supposed to keep things going for now. Someone from corporate is coming later this week to talk to us."

"About how to manage without Rebecca?"

"I don't know. Maybe to tell us we're closing." He shrugged his shoulders, but I knew he was worried. Privately, I was afraid he might be right. I didn't want to consider what life in Himmel would be like without Miguel.

"Don't think like that. You've got a chance to show what the *Himmel Times* can do. Don't let the dailies put you in the corner. You have the inside track on two major stories. Take April off the reception desk, she can handle more than that. She knows Rebecca's administrative routine, let her pick up the slack there. Call Marie Chalke, see if she wants to work as a stringer. She was a pretty good reporter before she quit. Talk to my mom. She's only part-time at St. Stephen's, maybe she can help you out at the reception desk."

"Thanks, *chica*. But now you remind me I have to go. No rest for the wicked. I didn't know Rebecca worked so hard. I'm not worried about Uncle Craig. I know you'll think of something."

At the moment I felt as though his confidence was sadly misplaced.

---

After Miguel left, I tried to take his advice to heart. I'd stop beating myself up. I'd take all the pieces of information I had and look at them from a different perspective. And all the while I did that, I'd be hoping against hope to get a call from Jess telling me that Rebecca's ex couldn't have been her killer, because he was in prison, or he was living in Antarctica, or he'd succumbed to some horrible disease. I didn't care what the reason was, as long as it kept Coop from ever looking at me again the way that he had today.

Miguel was right. I wasn't wrong about everything. My resentment and dislike of Rebecca had misled me into making Holly's death too complicated. It was really pretty simple: Holly tried to blackmail someone. Her victim killed her instead. If we could get the list of SweetMeets clients from the area, there was a really, really good chance that Holly's killer would be on it.

We could compare any local names on the list with people who were at Miguel's Halloween party. If we came up with a match, there was a chance that Gabe's instinct had been right. And maybe the killer tried to kill me—not knowing how in-the-dark I was when I bellowed out my claim that I knew who killed Holly. And, he had killed Rebecca instead.

I hoped that wasn't true, and not just because I didn't want a killer after me. It wouldn't help things much with Coop if I hadn't led Rebecca's ex to her, but instead she had been killed because of what I'd shouted out at the party. Either way, it would come down to my big mouth causing his wife's death.

On the other hand, if I could help find Rebecca's killer, maybe Coop would forgive me. Gabe had to get that list. Or maybe I should throw myself on the mercy of Holly's sister, Suzanne. But I shouldn't try that without checking with Gabe. Gabe. Right. I should call and fill him in on my epic fail today. When he left, we were still merrily detailing how Rebecca's murder of Holly had led to her own.

I was so smart, so compelling in my argument I had won him over—to the losing side. He was going to wish Craig and

Lydia had never asked for my help. No, I couldn't face talking to him right now. Tomorrow would be soon enough for him to find out what an overconfident idiot I'd been.

I paced my apartment for a while. Through the tall windows in my loft, I could see the sky darkening with gray storm clouds. It was growing colder inside and out. I turned on the fireplace and sat on the window seat with pillows at my back, and a legal pad on my lap. Making a list of ideas and issues, cross-referencing them, and conducting a thorough Q&A with myself is usually a reliable way for me to organize things in my mind. But this time, I couldn't focus. Instead, I stared out the window for long periods of time, but my pen wasn't lifted and my pad of paper stayed blank. The dismal atmosphere outside matched how I felt inside. Later, the darkness in the street below was pierced by the light of street lamps winking on, but there was no relief for the gloom in my mind.

My phone dinged with a text. My mother. I'd only had the briefest of conversations with her in the morning and had promised to call later. Then things had spun out of my control. Now, I couldn't deal with it. But if she didn't hear from me soon, she'd be on my doorstep. I responded to her text by saying I needed to be alone, but promised to stop by St. Stephen's the next morning during her shift there. She wasn't satisfied, but after pinning me down to a definite time, she agreed.

I left the window seat and sat on the sofa, staring at the fire.

**44**

I jumped when the phone rang. For a second I couldn't orient myself. The only light in the room came from the fireplace. My phone kept ringing insistently. I felt around for it. Not finding it, I stumbled to my feet and followed the sound to its location on the window seat.

"Hello?"

"Leah, it's Jess."

"Jess? What time is it?"

"Oh, sorry, I forgot about the time difference. It's ten-thirty here, so it's twelve-thirty in Wisconsin. Were you sleeping?"

"Yeah, never mind, it's all right." I was fully awake and my brain had begun to function. "Did you find out something about Peter Hines?"

"I did. I checked the California Department of Corrections website—there's an inmate locator online. He wasn't listed—"

"Oh, no." I'd been hoping to learn that Rebecca's ex had been locked away for years. That way I could be sure that he hadn't had the opportunity to hunt her down and kill her. Jess could hear the heavy disappointment in my voice.

"Hold on," he said. "The data in the online site isn't always up-to-date. I reached out to a buddy of mine who works in the California DOC, and he checked for me. Peter Hines isn't in the system. Hasn't been for fifteen years."

"If he's not in prison, then that means he could be anywhere. He could have been right here, killing Rebecca last night." I felt sick to my stomach.

"Nope. Whoever killed your old boss, it wasn't him. Peter Hines has been dead for three years himself. Stepson killed him for attacking his mother. Kid got off with self-defense. And that was justice, if you ask me."

A wave of relief flooded through me. It wasn't my fault. I wasn't the reason Rebecca was dead. I had a chance to fix things with Coop. I felt a sudden surge of optimism. I'd dig up prepaid cell phone man even if I had to go and rip the SweetMeets client list out of Suzanne Mason's hands myself.

---

I'd gone back to sleep after Jess called, this time in my bed. The immense relief I'd felt at his news had drained my body. I fell into a deep and restful sleep. So restful that I didn't wake up until almost nine-thirty. I hopped in the shower and tried to hurry, but the hot water felt so good, I just couldn't. I made up for the time I lost by throwing on jeans and a sweatshirt and giving the quickest of blow dries to my hair. It looked pretty bad, but I made the happy discovery that it was finally long enough to pull back with a hair clip.

Then I made a quick dash to the Elite to pick up coffee and some *apfelkuchen,* and pulled into the St. Stephen's parish hall only a few minutes after the scheduled ten-thirty coffee date with my mother.

"My heart is just breaking for Coop," she said. "I was no fan of Rebecca, but he loved her. And the way he talked about that baby. Don't take what he said to you too hard, Leah. He's just trying to make sense of something there's no sense in."

"I know. Sort of. I feel a lot better after talking to Jess. Knowing for sure that Rebecca couldn't have been killed by her ex at least absolves me of that guilt. But Coop was right in a way. I disliked Rebecca so much that I couldn't cut her any slack at all. I wanted her to be pure viciousness, and, I guess, as it turns out, she wasn't. She was pure human instead. She did some really bad things, but she had some pretty bad things happen to her. I'll never think she was a good person, but I can't think she was an evil person, either."

"Well, that's quite a speech, and quite an insight. It's tough to take an honest look at ourselves and our motives. I'm proud of you, sweetheart."

Praise from my mother can still cause a little swell of pride in me.

"Thanks, Mom."

"You're welcome. Fortunately, I, myself, have achieved a level of perfection that makes self-inventory unnecessary."

"I see our tender moment has passed. Well, on that note, I believe I'll fight you for the last piece of apple cake." I reached over to snatch it out from under her hovering hand. She made an effort to slap my hand away. The quick movement dislodged a stack of papers on the desk and sent them cascading to the floor.

We both dived down to retrieve them. When they were back in a tidy stack, I saw that one errant piece had floated under my chair. I reached down and grabbed it. As I started to add it to the pile, I noticed the writing on the front.

It was a check in the amount of four hundred dollars, made out to Kibre Web Development. My voice was barely above a whisper as I asked, "Mom, who's Kibre Web Development?"

She was busy reorganizing the papers that had fallen and didn't answer.

"Mom!"

She looked up, surprised at the urgent note in my voice. "Who owns Kibre Web Development?"

"Why, that's Mike Chapman's business. He named it after his kids—Kira and Brendan—Kibre. I think that's cute, don't you? Oh, you couldn't do me a favor and drop this off for him, could you? Father Lindstrom was supposed to put it in the mail yesterday, but he forgot, and Mike's so nice about doing all the changes to the parish website. And he hasn't charged nearly enough, as you can see. I'd like to at least pay his bill on time."

"No, I can't drop it off. I have to go. I'll talk to you later. Bye."

I left her staring at me, still holding the check in her hand as I ran to my car, pulling my phone out to call Ross. Mike Chapman was Kibre Web. He developed the SweetMeets site. Mike was Holly's "old friend."

"Ross, where are you?"

"Nice to talk to you, too, Nash. I'm on my way back from Omico. I got some breaking news for you on my investigation."

"Oh, I think I'm gonna beat you in the breaking news category. Get to my place as fast as you can, will you?"

"What's got your hair on fire?"

"You'll see when you get here. Just hurry up, please."

"All right. I'll see you in twenty minutes or so."

## 45

The name Kibre Web Development acted like a pinball caroming its way across the disconnected thoughts in my mind. First, it hit a string of random statements, then a succession of unrecognized clues, on to a series of undervalued observations until it reached its final target, and ding, ding, ding, the game made sense.

The phone calls and the texts between Holly's cell and the mysterious prepaid phone were messages back and forth between her and Mike, her one-time personal or professional "old friend" and quasi-business partner. When he refused to help her save her business, she threatened to destroy his family, and she brought the proof to show she could do it. She had photos, or texts, or sexting messages—or all three.

Mike came to see her at Miguel's that Saturday night. She showed him what she was willing to give to his wife if he didn't help her. Mike lost it. How he hooked up with Holly originally, who knew? But he'd chosen to be with his family, and he wasn't going to lose them because of her. He was furious at her threat. He couldn't see any other way out. So, he killed her. When she was dead, he took everything that might connect him to her—

her laptop, her phone, and her purse. He destroyed the equipment, then drove out to the park. He threw the damaged technology off the end of the pier and into the muck below, just before Darmody saw him that night.

I was on a roll. I jumped up and scrolled through my phone contacts. I called Darmody to check if the night he'd seen Mike on the pier was the Saturday night when Holly was killed. He was in the mood to chat, but I got off as soon as he confirmed it.

When Oralee looked out the window that night, she thought she saw Craig's car in the driveway. But it wasn't his, it was Mike's. Both Mike and Craig had gray cars. But more importantly, Mike's car had a Himmel Band Parents bumper sticker, just like Craig's. And it was that detail that had made Oralee sure that the car she saw was Craig's.

I was getting really excited—was I getting carried away? Normally, I don't worry about that much, but I was feeling a little gun-shy about putting out yet another theory. I didn't want to strike out again. I needed a pragmatic thinker to keep me on track here.

My mind went to what Ross had said on the phone. I'd been so busy working on Craig's case that I hadn't paid much attention to what Ross was doing. When he told me Duane had been tracking down embezzlement at city hall, it made sense. When he said Mike Chapman was the embezzler, it made sad sense. But if now he had something new about Mike, and I had something new about Mike—was it possible they were the same thing?

Where the heck was he? It shouldn't take this long to get here. I had picked up my phone to call him back, when my doorbell rang.

I stood at the door waiting for Ross as he huffed up the stairs.

"I thought they hadda put elevators in these historic buildings when they remodel 'em."

"You can lodge a complaint with the landlord," I said, pulling him inside and pushing him over to a seat on the sofa.

"Ross, I need you to help me think."

"That's a first."

"Don't let it go to your head. You're the only one available. I really need to get this right this time."

"OK, shoot."

I gave him a condensed version of my theories about Holly and Rebecca's murders, hitting the highlights only of the work Miguel and I had been doing.

"I managed to put all the facts together like a toddler going to town on a Lego set. Everything was upside down and sideways. It all fell apart. I tried again and it seemed to work, but I didn't know I was missing a crucial piece. But, Ross, I just got some information that changes everything. Now, I can see how things really fit."

"Spit it out, Nash. I'm gettin' old waitin'. "

I started walking around the living room as I talked.

"Holly Mason had an old 'friend' who helped her get Sweet-Meets started by developing the website about three years ago. He did it for nothing up front and a cut of the profits after they started coming in. He, Holly, and Holly's sister Suzanne made good money out of it, and then he moved on about a year ago.

"Then a little while ago, the business went into free fall. One of the sugar babies blackmailed her sugar daddy and got arrested. Word got out and clients started to bail. Then an enterprising sugar baby signed a tell-all book deal, guaranteed to name names, and the bottom dropped out of SweetMeets.

"Holly was in serious financial trouble. She had an idea for a fresh start, but she needed capital. When she couldn't get investors, she tried to fall back on her original formula for success. She contacted her web developer friend and asked him to do the work for a share of the profits. He said no."

"Where are you going with this, Nash?"

"Where I'm going is that the web developer is the reason Holly came to Himmel. She was blackmailing someone, all right. But it wasn't a client, it was the web developer who refused to help her save her business. I think she had souvenirs from their friendlier days—explicit texts, photos, that kind of thing, and threatened to show them to his wife."

"That sounds about right. We had a revenge porn case last year. It wasn't kids either. Two people in their fifties, shoulda known better. The guy posts some pretty racy photos, and I'm thinkin', lady, why would you let him take those pictures? I—"

"Exactly, you get it then. Someone as savvy as Holly would've had plenty of insurance for future use, should she need it. This morning I found out who owns Kibre Web Development, the company that did the SweetMeets web design. Ross, Holly's old friend—it's Mike Chapman. Also, Mike's car was at Miguel's house the night Holly died. The neighbor who saw it thought it was Craig's, because it had a Himmel Band Parents bumper sticker. But Mike has the exact same sticker on his car. Craig wasn't there, it was Mike."

"You got Mike Chapman figured for Holly Mason's killer?"

"I do. And there's more. Holly had been texting and phoning back and forth with the same number for a couple of weeks. She texted that number the night she got here. But it's a burner phone we couldn't trace. So, I tried to smoke out the owner after Holly was killed. I sent a text to the number. It said *Be at Founders Park 11 tonight. Paul Bunyan statue. You know why.*"

"Now that was all kinds of crazy. I wouldn't expect even you to set up a date with a killer."

"Give me some credit. I didn't. Miguel and I went and hid in a stand of trees behind the statue. All I wanted to do was see who showed up. I wasn't going to confront anyone."

"And Mike showed up?"

"No, but his daughter did."

"Kira? She's just a kid. What's she got to do with anything?"

"She's not exactly a kid. She's a seventeen-year-old who thinks her dad's having an affair—that's what she told Allie. I don't know if she overheard him talking to Holly, or she stumbled across his second phone and read a text that Holly sent and misinterpreted it, or whatever. But if she kept monitoring the phone—and that's what I'd do—she might've intercepted my text and shown up to confront the woman she thought her dad was cheating with. It's obvious the burner phone belongs to Mike. It's another link to Holly's murder."

He sat there just shaking his head for so long I began to get worried.

"Ross, if you think this is all garbage, go ahead and tell me. I'd rather hear it from you, now, than from Gabe or Coop later. Coop has washed his hands of me. Gabe isn't going to think much of me either, when I tell him how I led him down the wrong road on this yesterday—again. So, go ahead, show me what I'm too stupid to see."

"It's not that, Nash. I don't think you're wrong. I need you to fill in more of the detail work before I decide that. I'm shakin' my head because a few weeks ago, you didn't want to believe me when I said Mike was embezzling from city hall. Now, you got a murder pinned on him. You better sit down for what I'm gonna tell you," he said, gesturing for me to join him on the sofa. "It's really gonna blow your mind."

## 46

"I think Duane Stanton was murdered, and Mike Chapman did it."

"But Duane's death was an accident," I said, unable to immediately take in what he was saying.

"Seemed like it, didn't it? But I been thinkin' a lot. See, everything makes sense about Mike embezzling from city hall to pay for his kid's medical expenses. And destroying the records to cover his tracks, that makes sense, too. But what was bothering me was the luck."

"The luck?"

"Yeah. Mike knows that Duane is on the fraud trail from seein' the Open Information Act requests in the system. But Duane doesn't know who's responsible, yet. Mike can get rid of the requests. He can get rid of Duane's files. But if he doesn't get rid of Duane, he knows he's goin' down. I don't believe he waited around hoping luck would get him out of this mess. I think he made his own luck. I think he pushed Duane off that bird watcher's platform."

"Have you got any evidence?"

"I got hold of the file from the investigation of Duane's acci-

dent—I still got a few friends in the department. I read everything, looked at things real close. Nothing suspicious at the
scene. It looked like Duane musta leaned over too far in the
corner there, tryin' to see some special bird—crazy hobby, if you
ask me. It's over a hundred-fifty-foot drop there, and it's rocks
down below.

"But then I checked the report for what they found with the
body: wallet, cell phone, loose change, keys, watch. Nothing
else. Next, I moved on to what was in his car: flashlight, rain
poncho, first aid kit, binoculars, registration, pen, county map.
And there it was."

He paused and looked at me expectantly, like a supportive
teacher encouraging a student to come up with the right
answer.

I drew a blank.

"It's like that thing, Nash. You know, it's not what's there. It's
what isn't. Like in Sherlock Holmes. 'The curious incident of the
dog in the night-time.' "

My face must have revealed my surprise both at his literary
allusion and his very unique take on a British accent.

"My grandma and me used to read a story every night from
*The Boys Sherlock Holmes*. She loved that guy."

I was momentarily diverted by this glimpse into Ross's
personal history. I determined to follow-up on *The Adventures of
Ross and His Grandma* at the earliest opportunity. But Ross's
impatience brought me back to the present.

"The binoculars, Nash. The binoculars were in the car. In
the CAR, Nash. Not with the body."

"Ohhh." I finally got it. "Duane was a bird-watcher. If he was
out there that morning to watch birds, he'd have his binoculars
with him. He wouldn't have left them in the car."

"No. He wouldn't. Not an uptight tidy little guy like him.

He'd have those binoculars right round his neck on their little leather strap. But he didn't."

"So, you think Mike got Duane out there on some pretext, pushed him off the platform, went to his house and got rid of his files, and deleted everything from the database at work?"

"I sure do."

"Wow."

"What?" I hesitated to criticize Ross's reasoning, given all my own false steps. On the other hand, who had more experience with faulty reasoning than me?

"Do we really think that Mike Chapman, mild-mannered, family guy Mike, committed murder twice? Duane one week, Holly a few weeks later?"

"I don't see that as a problem. A guy kills once to get outta trouble, it's not so hard to kill again to fix another mess. Killing Duane took care of one problem. Killing Holly Mason took care of another. And you know what? Now that I'm thinkin' about it, maybe your old boss got killed because Mike was trying to take care of another problem: you. Maybe he heard your big announcement at Miguel's party. I wasn't even there, and I heard about it. Did you ever think of that?"

"It's been mentioned. But, Ross, something just doesn't feel right."

I got up and started pacing. "It makes sense that Mike would kill Holly to keep his sordid past secret and his family intact. It makes sense that he'd kill Duane to cover up a major embezzlement. But here's the thing: why would Mike even *need* to embezzle money, if he was making big bucks from his share of the SweetMeets profits? He could've used that cash to cover Brendan's expenses."

"Maybe he worked for SweetMeets before his kid got hurt, and that money was already gone. So, he had to embezzle to take care of the medical expenses?"

I shook my head. "I don't think so. SweetMeets started up around the same time Brendan was hurt. So, it fits that he did the web work for Holly and made enough money to get out of medical debt. But when and why did he embezzle money from the city?"

"I don't know. Coulda been a long time ago and Duane just tumbled to it now. It's gonna take a forensic accountant to dig through and find all that stuff."

"You were going to talk to Will Fraser about getting one. Did you?"

"Yeah. I told him this morning that I was following up on an idea Duane Stanton had, and it was looking like someone was embezzling at city hall. I said he might want to bring in someone to look at the books."

"How did he react?"

"He didn't get too excited, but that's Will. I told him it would be a good idea to keep it on the QT, until he knew what was going on. I didn't want Mike to get wind of it."

I nodded. "I think it's time for us to bring in the professionals."

"*You* want to bring in the professionals? Never thought I'd hear you say that."

"I don't have anything against the police. Some of my best friends are cops," I said.

He gave me a sardonic smile.

"I think we've done a pretty good job connecting the dots, Ross. But I think we've taken it as far as we can go without help. We've got to get an answer to why Mike would need both to embezzle from the city and work for SweetMeets, when either should've brought him plenty of money.

"We need a special agent from Wisconsin DOJ to look at the city books and do a deep dive into Mike's finances. We need someone to do an actual into-the-water dive, too, to recover the equipment Mike dumped in the impoundment. We need an expert in smartphone forensics to retrieve deleted texts from Mike's second phone. And those things are just the beginning. The police have the resources, but I want to be sure we present what we've found as persuasively as we can. I have a feeling Detective Harper is going to take a lot of convincing."

"You got no argument from me, except on the 'we' part. I got my disciplinary hearing next week. I don't want lame-ass Lamey to add impersonating a police officer to the charges. Technically, I'm not supposed to be doing police work while I'm on suspension."

"But you weren't. You were just asking questions as a concerned citizen. Citizens have a right to ask questions."

"Yeah, OK, you're the first one I'll call if I need to have a first amendment defense. Meanwhile, I gotta take a step back. You'll have to talk to Harper alone."

"She's the lead on Rebecca's case, too. It's going to be tricky. She's made it clear that she's not crazy about my 'interference.' "

"Who is?"

"Thanks."

"Hey, she might get mad. You got that effect on people. But if she thinks about it, she's gotta look at what you got. She can't risk not bein' part of fixin' a problem she was part of creatin' by arresting Craig. And cops really don't like to arrest the wrong guy, you know. If she hears you out, she'll know she's better off checking things out than having Craig's lawyer rub her nose in it in court. Or havin' you feature her in your next book. I could tell her something about that."

"Well, I'm not going anywhere with anything until I talk to Gabe. It's really his call what we do next. He's the one directing Craig's defense. And after all, that's the main thing here. You can at least meet with me and Gabe, can't you? I'd like him to hear your take on Duane directly from you."

"Yeah, I can do that. But don't wait too long to get moving on this. If we're even half right about this, Mike's a dangerous guy. If the police get involved and bring him in for questioning, at least he'll know it's too late to take another run at you—if that's what he was doing when Rebecca got killed."

Ross's phone rang before I could answer.

"Yeah? I'm kinda busy here, Al. Uh-huh."

I was only privy to Ross's side of the conversation, but I could hear muffled tears and pleading as he shifted the phone on his ear. His daughter was obviously upset.

"OK, OK. I can't understand what you're saying, Allie. Slow down. No. You what?" His voice was gruff and angry-sounding. "No, no. I'm not mad. Well, yeah, I am, but not at you. She said what? I'm goin' over there. No, I'm not gonna make it worse. Stop cryin' now, OK? It'll be all right." He hung up.

"Problems?"

"Allie's pretty shook up. She just told me she was at the Frasers', eatin' lunch with Gus. The high school had a half day today. Gretchen came in and saw 'em and laid into Allie. Turns out Gus has been sneakin' out to see Allie at night."

"Sneaking?" I flashed on Oralee's mention of seeing Gus leaving and coming back via the basement window.

"Allie wasn't sneakin'. I knew she was seein' Gus. But I guess his parents didn't. Gretchen really got mad."

"At Allie? Seems like Gus is the one she'd be angry with."

"Well, she took Allie up one side and down the other. Sent her home cryin'. If they don't want Gus dating, that's for them to work out with him. But she's got no right to take it out on Allie. They're not gonna make my girl cry her heart out. I gotta go."

"You're a good dad, Ross."

His face reddened and he said gruffly, "You can check in with Craig's lawyer. Maybe the three of us can meet up later. I'll call you."

Shortly after Ross left, I headed for Gabe's office. I had too much to tell him to do it with a phone call. Besides, I needed to look him in the eye when I told him that my Rebecca obsession had led me to the wrong conclusion about who killed Holly.

"I'm sorry, Leah, Gabe is in court." Patty was at her desk in the reception area, controlling access to both Miller and Gabe's offices.

"Do you know when he'll be back?"

She looked at her watch. "Well, the hearing started about an hour ago. It shouldn't be too much longer. Unless something unexpected happens."

"Is he coming right back here? It's just that I really need to talk to him as soon as possible."

"I would think he'd be here shortly. Certainly by four-thirty. Do you want to leave a message?" she asked, holding out a small notepad and a pen to me.

"Yes, thanks," I said, and leaned over to begin writing. Immediately, I realized there wasn't enough paper in the whole pad to write down what I needed to say.

"Never mind, Patty. Could you just tell him to call me as soon as he gets in?"

"Well, he has quite a few messages to answer. But I'm sure he'll get to yours first."

---

I didn't feel like going back home. I'd spent most of the past couple of days cooped up in my apartment. I wasn't ready to see my mother and answer all of her questions yet. I couldn't call Coop. I'd already taken advantage of Father Lindstrom's listening ear. Miguel had already put in his time with me for the day.

So, I pulled into JT's party store and poured the strongest, hottest brew available at the coffee station into my insulated travel mug. I needed a major dose of caffeine. But when I went to take a sip in the car, I discovered I'd outsmarted myself. The coffee was so hot I couldn't drink it, and my insulated mug was guaranteed to keep it that way. I put it in the holder next to me and drove the short distance to Riverview Park.

The park is kind of the poor man's version of Founder's Park, on the opposite side of town. When we were really young, my mom used to walk me and my sister Annie there, to play on the swings. Later, after Annie was gone and my youngest sister Lacey was growing up, I took her there to play. Coop and I spent a lot of time there as kids, too. As an adult, I'm drawn there still, to watch a new generation of kids playing in the park. It's a world that I can't go back to, though sometimes I would like to.

I tried my coffee again, but it wasn't going to be drinkable until I took it home and put an ice cube or two in it. I put it down, and closed my eyes for a minute. I couldn't get the image of Mike's son Brendan, with his big brown eyes, his determined, halting steps and speech, out of my mind. What would his life be like when Mike's secrets were revealed and his punishments meted out? And what about Kira and Noelle? It was difficult to think of Mike as someone who would betray his family like that. And Mike as a killer was as hard to imagine as Craig. Harder, even.

I'd never worked on an investigation before where I felt less certain. Ross was right. Mike fit the profile of an embezzler almost to a T. And the absence of binoculars when Duane's body was found was very suspicious. Mike's ownership of Kibre Web Development was indisputable—as was the fact that Suzanne had identified the web developer as a former client of Holly's. Why was I having such a hard time accepting that Mike had done the things it so clearly seemed that he had? He had the access to commit embezzlement. He had the need. And he had the strong urge to protect his family when things started to fall apart. It just felt off, somehow. As though we were over-looking something.

Despite the turmoil in my mind, the warmth of the late afternoon sun did its work and I began to drowse. I drifted into a dream. In it, Mike Chapman drove up to Miguel's house with Rebecca beside him. But when the car door opened, Harry Turnbull stepped out. Davina Markham appeared on the driveway stroking Gretchen's black cat. Then Kira Chapman came up to me and said, "It's impossible," and handed me a ringing phone.

It took a second for me to shake myself back to consciousness and realize that it was my real-life phone ringing, not the one in bizarro dream world. I looked at the caller ID. Gabe.

"Hi, hey I really need to talk to you. Can you meet me at—" I said, but he cut me off.

"No. I need to talk to you. We got the SweetMeets client list."

"What? That's great. Have you—"

"Oh yeah, I've looked through it. Guess who's on it? No, don't bother. The city manager. William Augustus Fraser, address 6235 Pinkley Avenue, Himmel, Wisconsin. And our Will was an early adopter. He signed up with SweetMeets three years ago, right after it started up."

"What did you say?"

"Will. I said Will Fraser, the city manager, is a SweetMeets client. That means—"

I stopped listening, because I knew what it meant.

"Gabe, I have to go. Meet me at seven-thirty at McClain's. I'll have Charlie Ross with me."

"Wait—"

"No, seriously. Be there. All will be revealed. Bye."

As soon as I hung up, I called Ross's cell phone. When he didn't answer, I tried him at home.

Allie picked up on the first ring.

"Allie, this is Leah. Is your dad there?"

"No. He went to the Frasers' house."

"I know. I was there when you called. Have you heard from him?"

"No. He's not answering. I'm afraid he's making it worse. You know how he is. And now Gus is here—"

"Gus is at your house?"

"Yeah, he blew up at his mom after I left, and he came to our house. She's gonna blame me for that, too. She hates me. My dad won't mean to, but you know him, Leah. He's gonna make things worse. I wish I never told him about it."

"Listen, I'm not very far from the Frasers', and I want to talk to your dad. I'll zip over and extract him before he does any serious damage, OK? But I need him for a little while. He's got to help me work something out. So, don't worry if he's not back for an hour or so."

Thank God Gabe had called with the news that Will was a sugar daddy, before Ross and I met to tell him we had Mike down for at least two murders. Because now the picture I was seeing showed me something I liked a lot better. Will made way more sense as the embezzler, and the murderer, too.

As I drove the few blocks to the Frasers', I ran over things in my mind. Will had the same access Mike did—even better, really, to embezzle city funds. And sugar babies aren't cheap. Gretchen would definitely notice that kind of money going out of the family coffers. So, Will had a motive to steal. Stealing from the city wasn't a great long-term plan, because sooner or later the fraud would surface, but Will struck me as an in-the-moment kind of guy. The kind who does whatever works in the present, and doesn't worry about the consequences until he can't escape them.

Will as the embezzler solved the problem Ross and I had been wrestling with: why Mike would run the risk of stealing, when he had access to money through his web work for Sweet-Meets. The answer was, he wouldn't. But for Will it was different. He didn't have another way to get the money he needed to support the sugar baby he wanted.

But then Duane's relentless quest for the big fish in government waste led him to the embezzling. Isolated facts were dropping into place with lighting speed in my mind. Duane had met with Will the week he died, according to his calendar. Had he proudly told Will what he was on the trail of, wanting to be a little important again, wanting to end the jokes about his small time finds? Will asked Duane to keep it quiet while he got an official investigation launched—so they didn't alert the embezzler. That bought him a few days to find a way out of the mess— or to run away from it. But he had to face the fact that the only way out was to get rid of Duane and get rid of his files. So, he did. And he was home free, until Holly Mason arrived in town to blackmail him.

But wait a minute. Holly was here to see Mike to pressure him to work on her new websites, not to blackmail Will. Wasn't she?

I realized suddenly that I was at the Frasers'. Ross's car was in the driveway. I didn't relish seeing Gretchen at the moment. She might be an overprotective mother who had been out of line with Allie, but karma was going to bite her in the butt pretty shortly. And it was going to hurt, a lot. But I had to pull Ross out of there before Will got home. We needed to reorder our thinking before we talked to Gabe, and definitely before Gabe and I went to Erin Harper.

As I walked up the driveway to the front door, I could hear raised voices. That probably wasn't good. It was easy to make out Gretchen's voice, high-pitched and full of anger. Standing at the front door, I heard her shout.

"I'm done talking! I am not putting up with this! Do you understand?"

Oh, boy. That was definitely not a scene I wanted to crash. Instead of ringing the bell, I took a couple of paces to the left and peered through the bushes in front of the living room window. I hoped Ross would be getting ready to leave, and I could just wait for him to walk out. He wasn't.

When I looked inside, I saw that Will was there, too. They were both seated in chairs, and they didn't look like they were going anywhere. Gretchen was standing in front of them. She was holding a gun.

## 48

Holy shit! I let out an involuntary gasp. A thrill of fear ran through me. Had Gretchen heard me? No. She was on a screaming rant directed at Will. Her gun was aimed directly at his crotch.

"You ruined our family because you couldn't keep it in your pants. You ruined everything I worked for. Everything I did was for you. For our son. For this family. I could kill you! I will kill you!"

Will sat slumped in his chair, his eyes wide with terror. Next to him, Ross leaned forward slightly and spoke to Gretchen.

"Gretchen, take it easy, now. You got a right to be upset. But think about your son. Think about Gus."

She whirled on him.

"What do you know about my son? My son is all that matters to me. He's not going to be like his father. You keep your daughter away from him!"

I couldn't wait any longer. I turned and ran to my car, punching numbers on my phone as I did.

"911. What's your emergency?"

"A woman with a gun. She's unstable. She has two hostages. 6235 Pinkley Avenue."

She started to ask follow-up questions. I didn't have time to wait, and neither did Ross. I tossed the phone down on the car seat. I grabbed the hot coffee from the cup holder. Back at the front door, I craned my head to catch a glimpse through the window. Gretchen was still standing there.

I turned the knob and let myself in. I pulled the lid off the scalding coffee. I crept the short distance down the hall. Gretchen was still ranting. I took a deep breath, then charged into the room shouting, "Hey, Gretchen! I've got the Follies poster for you to see."

She turned at the sound of my voice. I flung the burning hot coffee toward her. It splashed on her face and neck. She cried out. She flung the gun aside, writhing in pain. It skittered toward Will. Ross leapt from his chair, but Will got there first.

"That's the last time you're going to scream at me, you bitch!"

Ross grabbed Will's hand. They struggled. The gun went off. Ross crumpled to the floor on his side.

"Ross!"

Will pivoted toward me as though seeing me for the first time.

Gretchen screamed at him, still holding her hand to her face.

"What are you going to do now, you stupid little man?"

He turned back to her. "Shut up, Gretchen. Shut up or I swear to God I'll kill you!"

I ran over to Ross and knelt beside him. Blood was seeping through the hand he held on his belly. More blood was soaking through the back of his shirt. His face was ashen. His eyelids fluttered. I heard the wail of sirens. I pulled off my hoodie and wrapped it around him, pressing to stanch the flow of blood.

Allie's face was in my mind as I began to murmur something between a hope and a prayer. *Stay with me. Stay with me, Charlie. Stay with me.* Gretchen was yelling again, but I didn't look up.

"Like I killed Duane Stanton for you? Like I killed Holly Mason because of you? You're not man enough! No matter what your little sugar baby slut tells you."

"I said shut up!" Will roared. Two shots fired in rapid succession rang out.

Police with guns drawn burst into the room, too late.

---

I nudged Allie as soon as I saw Dr. Aadhira Patel come through the doors of the surgical unit waiting room at Himmel Hospital. We both jumped up.

"She's smiling, Allie, don't look so scared," I whispered.

"Your father is doing fine," Dr. Patel said. "The bullet went through his lower left abdomen, a little higher than his belly button. It missed all the major organs, and didn't hit any bones on the way out. He's a lucky man."

Allie burst into tears, and I felt like it, but didn't. "Thank you, Dr. Patel. How soon can Allie see her dad?"

"He's in recovery now, it will be awhile. A nurse will come and get you."

"How long will Ross—that is, Detective Ross, have to be in the hospital?"

"I can't predict exactly, but barring complications, he should be released in a few days. He will have to take it easy for a while, though."

"Oh, he will," Allie said, "I'll make sure of it. Thank you, so much. Thank you. Thank you, Dr. Patel," Allie repeated. She probably would have continued endlessly, if the surgeon hadn't patted her on the hand and said, "You're very welcome, have a good night," and then left as quickly as she had come.

The others who had been waiting with us surged forward with relieved smiles, and hugs or pats on the shoulder for Allie. Miguel had heard the news on the scanner. A couple of deputies from the sheriff's department had shown up, and a buddy of Ross's I hadn't met before. I looked at my phone and saw how late it was. I was supposed to meet Gabe at McClain's over an hour ago. I'd turned it off while we waited to hear about Ross, and now it was blowing up with texts, mostly from Gabe.

"Miguel, can you stop by McClain's and tell Gabe what's happening? I want to wait here with Allie and then take her back to my place."

"*Absolutamente.* I'll be working late tonight. Stop by when you get home." He gave Allie a quick hug and took off.

I turned to tell my mother she could go, too. She had insisted when I called her that she needed to see me in the flesh to make sure I was all right. Then, she'd stayed to wait with me and Allie until Ross got out of surgery. Before I could say anything to her, I saw Erin Harper out of the corner of my eye, headed our way.

She spoke to Allie first.

"I'm Detective Harper with the Himmel Police Department. I take it you're Detective Ross's daughter. Allie, is it?"

Still snuffling and mopping up tears, Allie said, "Yes. Do you need to talk to me?"

"No, It's Ms. Nash I need to speak to. I just wanted to tell you I'm sorry about your dad, but I'm sure he'll be fine. He's a brave man. You should be proud of him."

Allie smiled shakily, and I liked Erin much better for having said that. She gave Allie a return smile, and said, "Do you have someone to be with you tonight?"

My mother stepped forward. "Yes, she does. I'm Carol Nash, Leah's mother. Allie's coming home with me."

Allie looked a little surprised, but not unwilling, which was a good thing, because with my mother in maternal mode, resistance is futile.

"You can sleep in Leah's old room. We'll go down to the cafeteria and get you something to eat while we wait for your dad to wake up enough for you to see him."

"I'm not hungry, really. I just want to wait here."

My mother is pretty good at emotional reads, and she could tell Allie needed to be near her dad more than she needed food. "OK. After you see him, we'll run by your house and pick up anything you want for the next couple of days, until he's ready to go home. When we get to my house, I've got some homemade chicken and dumplings that will hit the spot. And cranberry cake for dessert."

"Thank you," Allie said.

"I want to go with you," I said.

"Sorry, the detective needs you. If you don't end up in jail, stop by later and you can have a piece of cake." My mother can be a very cold-hearted woman sometimes.

## 49

I wasn't sure what to expect as I followed Erin Harper into an interview room at the Himmel Police Department. She surprised me by tossing her notepad aside and not turning on a tape recorder. She offered me a bottle of water, which I accepted, and then cracked open her own.

I saw then that her brown eyes looked tired and there was a faint vertical line between her eyebrows. Random strands of wavy hair were pulling loose from her tight braid as though she'd been poking at it with her fingers.

"Look, I've just spent three hours interviewing Will Fraser. I've got his version of what happened this afternoon. It looks like Craig Kowalski didn't kill Holly Mason."

"That's what I've been telling you," I said.

"Yeah? Well, if you'd told me everything, instead of cherry-picking what you felt like sharing, maybe we would have found that out a lot sooner."

"Oh, no. Come on, you ordered me to stay out of your way. Would you really have listened to anything I said?"

"Maybe not," she admitted, then sighed heavily. She didn't look very know-it-all now. She didn't sound it, either.

"I screwed up. I admit it. Everything fit with Craig Kowalski. I wanted to prove myself so badly, show I could solve a case in forty-eight hours. I might just have blown any chance to prove I'm not filling some quota. That I can actually do the job."

This humble Harper was new. But to my surprise I wasn't enjoying seeing her brought down low.

"I'm sure it's not that bad, Erin." I ventured the use of her first name, given that most of the stiffness had gone out of her manner. She didn't correct me.

"Yeah, it really is. I've got a meeting with the police chief and the DA first thing tomorrow, and it's not going to be pretty. I was wrong about who killed Holly Mason. Now, they're going to question whether I can get anything right, and I've got two more homicides on my plate—Duane Stanton and Rebecca Hartfield. Of course, I've got Gretchen's confession to Duane's death—assuming you and Detective Ross corroborate what Will Fraser told me his wife said."

"Yeah, we both heard it. But I had Will down for it, not his wife. So, don't feel so bad that you missed a couple of steps. Craig ticked all the boxes. If I didn't know him, I'd think that was a slam dunk, too."

She looked at me suspiciously to see if I was being sarcastic. I wasn't.

"Someday I'll tell you all the wrong turns I made trying to prove someone besides Craig could have killed Holly. The only thing I can see that you missed was pursuing the SweetMeets database."

"Well, that was a biggie," she said with a half-smile, but it was resigned, not amused. "But once we got Sophia Kowalski's name from Suzanne Mason, everything fell into place. I should have known better. Nothing ever comes together as easy as that."

"Hey, you're talking to the queen of 'I should have known better.' Don't beat yourself up."

"Thanks. I wonder ... "

"Yeah?"

"Well, I've got Will Fraser's story, and I'll be taking an official statement from you tomorrow—if I still have my job, that is. I know you don't owe it to me. And I'll swear this conversation never took place if anyone asks, but I'm asking for some help. I'd like to hear not just what you found out, but how you put it together, too."

I could get in some jabs here, some payback for the way she'd patronized me and the snide remarks about amateurs. But I didn't.

"I'll show you mine, if you show me yours."

"Unofficially, and not for publication?" she asked.

"Yes."

"All right, let's do it. What I got from Fraser is that basically it's all on his wife. He admits to embezzling and why, but he says Gretchen did everything else on her own—Duane Stanton, Holly Mason, and Rebecca Hartfield."

"Rebecca? He said Gretchen killed Rebecca? Why did she do it?"

"No, you first. You tell me how you got to who killed Duane Stanton and Holly Mason. Then I'll give you Rebecca." I didn't argue. As long as Erin was in a giving mood, there was no sense irritating her.

I didn't bother going over all my miscalculations and false starts, I just jumped in with what Ross and I had worked out.

"Duane went to Will to tell him that someone was embezzling city funds. He had no idea it was Will. Will said he'd get right on it, but not to tell anyone else, so that the embezzler wouldn't be alerted. Will had no idea how to fix things, so he went to Gretchen."

She nodded. "That's Fraser's story."

"I'm guessing, though, that Will didn't tell Gretchen why he was embezzling."

"Right, again. He told her that he borrowed city funds to invest in a new business that promised big dividends. He planned to use the profits to pay back the money and put the rest into their son's college fund. But the business went bust, he couldn't pay back the money, and Duane was about to expose him."

"That was fairly smart of Will. Gretchen would be really angry at how stupid he'd been, but she'd like that he did it for the family. Still, she'd know she had some fixing to do. This wasn't just a garden variety Will screw-up, of which I'll bet there had been many." I was thinking of what my mother had said about Will and Gretchen's relationship—that it wasn't easy to live with a full-time charmer.

"You didn't know Duane, Erin," I said. "But, trust me, there was no way he would ever let go of that embezzlement investigation, no matter how Will might have tried to deflect him. Gretchen would have recognized that. Will would go to prison. They'd lose their house, their savings, Gus's college fund, everything. Not to mention the humiliation. Gretchen saw killing Duane as the best solution for her. So, that's what she did. Very efficiently, too."

"Looks that way. Fraser says that he didn't know that Duane was murdered. He thought it was an accident until Gretchen told him today."

"Maybe he didn't. It's possible that Gretchen wouldn't trust him with that information."

"I hate that that guy might be able to wriggle his way out of murder charges. But with his wife dead, at this point it's pretty much he said/he said. No "she said" in the picture. Fraser also says that he had nothing to do with Holly Mason. Never met her, was shocked today when Gretchen admitted she's the one who killed her. You buy it?"

I shrugged. "Part of it, maybe. I don't think he knew Holly Mason. I mean, he probably knew who she was, but he was one of thousands of SweetMeets clients. I doubt he had any contact with her. But I don't think he's stupid enough not to have known what Gretchen did."

"I agree. He admitted that the night Holly was killed was the night he told her the truth—that he had a sugar baby. And she was the real reason he had embezzled," Erin said.

"And that there was a better than good chance he was going to be featured in a book she was writing?" I asked.

"How did you know?"

"Suzanne Mason told me that a sugar baby was writing a tell-all. It was pretty much the death knell for SweetMeets."

"Yeah. Fraser read about it somewhere. He said he had to tell his wife, so she could think of a way out. For an unfaithful son-of-a-bitch, he had a lot of faith in his wife's ability as a crisis manager."

"But this time Gretchen didn't go into fix-it mode, right?"

"He had to get himself half-drunk before he got the courage to tell her, and then he dumped it on her right after she got home from a twelve-hour shift at the hospital. She lost it. Kinda like she did this afternoon."

"It sounds weird, because she just tried to kill him, but I think she really loved him. I imagine it really hurt, when he told her about his sugar baby, and how he'd endangered their family for some young girl who was just using him. He betrayed Gretchen, after she'd given everything she had to him. It had to cut her to the core. I'll bet she went ballistic. Cried. Raged. Every apology, every word of remorse he offered just fueled her fire."

Erin looked at me quizzically. "Sounds like you might know something about that feeling."

"That's a topic for another day. So, how was it that Will didn't notice when Gretchen stopped raging and took a quick trip to Miguel's to kill Holly?"

"She screamed at him to get out of her sight, or she'd kill him. He believed her. She poured a drink and went to the back patio. He took his bottle and went upstairs to bed. He didn't see Gretchen again until morning. What he says he doesn't know, and what I can't figure out, is how Gretchen knew Holly Mason was almost literally in her backyard that night."

"I can help you there. Gretchen stopped by the kitty boutique downtown on Saturday. Davina, the owner, told her that Holly Mason had been in and was renting Miguel's house for the weekend. She was quite excited at her D-list celebrity sighting, but Gretchen wasn't impressed."

"Now, how do you know that?"

"I was just chatting with Davina and she told me. You should try it. Just chatting, I mean. Small towns run on chat. You can learn a lot."

"It's starting to look that way. So, her husband told her about his SweetMeets affair, and she realized that the woman who had created the site that was going to ruin her life—"

"Was right in her backyard," I finished. "I bet she sat there, drinking and looking over at the lights in Miguel's house. Thinking that if it weren't for Holly Mason, Will wouldn't have embezzled, and she wouldn't have had to kill Duane. Her marriage, her whole life wouldn't be about to be exposed as the empty shell it was. But Gretchen was a fighter. I think she marched over to Miguel's to confront Holly. I don't know that she intended to kill her—in fact, she probably didn't. Too messy, and if she were in planning mode, Gretchen wouldn't have left so much to chance.

"I think she was just running on rage, and she had to see Holly, face-to-face. But we know from the way that Holly responded to Craig that she probably laughed Gretchen off, and said something nasty about not keeping her husband's interest. Something, anyway, that unleashed the fury inside Gretchen, so that she picked up the poker and killed Holly. Then she ran back home, and that's when Miguel's neighbor Oralee Smith saw her."

"Wait a minute. Oralee, the neighbor who told us Kowalski's car was in the driveway? She started us after Kowalski, a guy who wasn't there, but she didn't tell us about the murderer who was?"

"That was earlier in the evening. The motion sensor in her backyard went off around eleven thirty. She got up to see if the deer were eating out of her bird feeder again. They weren't. But she saw Gretchen instead."

"Why didn't she say anything about it?"

"Don't be too hard on Oralee. She didn't think it was important. She assumed Gretchen was chasing her cat, something she did quite often. Oralee thought you were looking for unusual things—like Craig Kowalski's car in Miguel's driveway a second time. Oh, and here's something I didn't think was important at the time that might have helped."

"Do tell."

"The day after Holly's body was discovered, I was in the Elite Cafe with Ross. Gretchen and Will stopped by to—that's right—chat. And, of course, we talked about the murder. Gretchen said that it must have been horrible for Miguel to find Holly lying in his living room. But I never said where Holly's body was found. And Gretchen had already claimed that she and Will hadn't heard anything about the killing until Ross and I told them that very minute. So, how did she know that Holly was lying in the living room, as opposed to any other room in the house?"

Erin shook her head. "I'm going to need a serious drink when this is all over," she said. "Now, tell me this, even if Gretchen acted out exactly like we think that night, and killed Holly in a fit of rage, what was she going to do about the sugar baby book? She couldn't kill everyone connected to that."

"Well, she had a little time. The embezzlement danger was behind them. Obviously, she couldn't murder everyone associated with the book, but maybe a libel lawyer could help them keep Will's name out of things. Or maybe she and Will could move away and ride out the storm where no one knew them. Or she could have had a Scarlett O'Hara moment and decided to think about it tomorrow. When you guys arrested Craig Kowalski, that was a piece of luck that probably made her feel pretty optimistic."

"Don't rub it in."

"I guess the question is, do you believe Will's story? Do you think he knows more than he's admitting?"

"I wouldn't trust that guy as far as I could throw him. He just oozes little boy charm. Makes me feel sticky just being in the same room with him. What's bothering me is that the person who could tell us everything, who could contradict Fraser's story, is dead—and Fraser killed her. Pretty convenient, isn't it? He's putting it all on his wife for killing Duane Stanton and Holly Mason. He's saying that he had to kill Gretchen to save himself and Charlie Ross and you. He's trying to make out he's some kind of hero for killing his wife."

"What about Rebecca? You said Will blamed Gretchen for her murder."

"Fraser said that Rebecca had threatened him at the party on Saturday night. She said she knew what Duane Stanton was on to, and that she was on to it, too. She told him that it would be in his best interest to meet her Sunday night at her office to discuss it."

A picture crossed my mind. Will and Rebecca talking at the party. The smile she gave him as she walked away. Gretchen and Will in heated conversation after.

"Hey, Leah! Still here. Still waiting. What are you holding out on me now? Come on. I'm running a special on amateur theories tonight."

"I'm not holding out. I just thought of it." I recounted the scene I'd witnessed with Rebecca and Will, then the intense conversation between Will and his wife.

"What Will told you makes sense. Duane might have said he'd keep his findings to himself until Will could look into them, but he didn't. He couldn't help himself. After all the ribbing he'd taken about his paper clip fraud and missing pen mysteries, he'd want to show off a little. I'd guess that he hinted pretty heavily to Rebecca when they met. After he died and nothing happened, Rebecca decided to poke around a little. It wouldn't be hard to find that out. Millie Gertzman would know. She's the clerk Rebecca would have gone to first, if she wanted to check up on Duane's research."

"You're just full of investigating tips, aren't you?" But this time she smiled after she said it.

"Sorry. I know you know what you're doing,"

"Thanks for that. Not sure I deserve it. According to Fraser, when he told Gretchen Rebecca wanted to meet with him, she was furious. She told him not to go. That she'd think of something to save his ass, again."

"And then Will doesn't keep the appointment, Gretchen does? And she bashes Rebecca in the head, so that the embezzlement story finally goes away?"

"That's what Will says must have happened. But he was pretty quick to repeat that he didn't know, he didn't have anything to do with it. I'm wondering if Gretchen was so fed up with being Will's fixer that she told him to take care of it himself. She'd already killed two people. Maybe she wanted to spread the guilt around. I'd really like for it to be that weasel Fraser."

"You really think Will has it in him to kill two people so violently—his wife and Rebecca? If Gretchen hadn't confessed, I'd be more likely to pin Duane's murder on him. Just a quick push, no mess."

"Yeah, but he did shoot his wife without a second thought. Look, I don't know the guy, but I know the type. When it comes to self-survival, they've got an amazing ability to come through for themselves, no matter how much they let everyone else down. It would be pretty sweet if I could wrap up three murders with one dysfunctional couple. And not let Will Fraser squirm away."

"Well, here's to simple solutions," I said, lifting my bottle of water toward her.

"I'm not sure simple is possible here. And there are still some loose ends."

"Oh?" I asked, trying to sound innocent. It's not that I was going to hide Mike Chapman's involvement, but I wanted to get to him first and give him a chance to come forward on his own. That would look a lot better for him.

"Whose car was in your friend Miguel's driveway the night Holly was killed, if it wasn't Craig Kowalski's? And where are Holly's laptop and phone and purse? And why was Holly here? A weekend getaway just doesn't fly, anymore. It's beautiful here in the fall, I grant you, but Himmel isn't exactly a tourist spot."

"What? How can you say that? Himmel is a little bit of heaven on earth. Just ask the Chamber of Commerce."

But Erin wasn't going to let it drop.

"You know something," she said shrewdly. "We've come this far. Come clean."

I bought some time before answering by polishing off my water.

"OK, I do know something. But I want to give the person a chance to come forward. I just need to have a short conversation with the person." I used the awkward phrasing to avoid proving her even with the gender clue.

She was shaking her head before I even finished. "Uh-uh. This is a two-way street. That was the deal."

"I know, I know. I'm not reneging on it. But I just need to talk to one person who knows something relevant. I promise that if the person does not come to you later tonight, I will tell you what I know first thing in the morning. You can come to my house and pound on my door at five a.m."

She didn't answer.

"But wait, there's more," I said, imitating the breathless urgency of a television commercial. She didn't seem to find that funny. I dialed it back. "I can save you a lot of time. Don't make it hard for me to talk to this person I need to see, and I will give you so much background on Rebecca Hartfield that the police chief will think you're the best detective since Sherlock Holmes."

I watched as she weighed whether she'd be better off accepting my offer, or trying to strong arm me into giving up my "person." Either I had won her trust, or she was just too dead tired to put forth the effort to beat the information out of me, because suddenly she capitulated.

"All right. But if 'this person' isn't in my office within the next two hours, I will hunt you down. And I will make sure this is the last time I ever give you the benefit of the doubt. Or anything else. Understood?"

"Understood. There's just one more thing, Erin."

"Yeah? What?"

"What I want to know is what made Gretchen lose it so

badly today? After all the risks she'd taken, everything she'd done to protect her imaginary perfect family, why did she completely turn on Will?"

"I think we'll have to interview Detective Ross to find that out. Thanks to you, he'll be around to tell the story."

I shook my head. "Ross saved himself, and probably Will and me both. But yeah, I'm anxious to have a little chat with him tomorrow, too."

## 50

Mike had been hiding a secret for a very long time. He had gone to great lengths to protect his family and keep them from ever knowing. As I rang the Chapman's doorbell I searched for the words that would convince him it was time to let it go—before the police forced him to.

"Mike, I know," I said when he opened the door. It wasn't what I'd planned to say, the words just came out of my mouth. But they were enough.

He didn't make any false protestations, didn't ask what I was talking about. He gestured me in and pointed me toward the living room. Noelle was sitting on the couch, her arm around Kira. Mike sat down next to his daughter and held her hand in his. I took the chair opposite. Noelle looked resolute, Kira upset, and Mike resigned, but together they were a portrait of family solidarity, and I knew there were no secrets between them anymore.

"I think it's time you come clean about what happened the night Holly Mason died. What do you think, Mike?" He looked at Noelle for reassurance. She nodded her assent, and he began.

"I met Holly years ago. I was in a bad place. Noelle and I

weren't getting along. I was alone at a conference in Chicago. She was at the hotel bar, I was having a drink. Anyway, I'm not going into the details. It was stupid, so stupid, and I will never stop being sorry."

I glanced at Noelle. She didn't look angry, just sad. This story wasn't new to her.

"It only lasted a few months. It wasn't a romance, it was just —I don't know what it was. When Noelle got pregnant with Brendan, I ended it. There wasn't any drama. We just went our separate ways. I realized my life was with my family. And I've never forgotten it since."

"That's how you knew Holly, but how did she get back in your life?"

"She wasn't in my life, she was the way I saved our son's life —my family's life. Brendan needed so much—surgeries, hospital stays, special equipment, physical therapy, speech therapy, medication, regular check-ups. We didn't have Noelle's paycheck anymore. The bills were so high. I took out a second mortgage on the house, but that wasn't nearly enough. Noelle had sacrificed everything. I couldn't let her know how bad our finances were. I didn't know what I was going to do. Brendan needed really expensive, specialized help in order to get well again. He'd never have a chance at a normal life without it. Then Holly called."

"She asked you to develop the SweetMeets site."

"Yes. I'd been doing work on the side for a while, but I didn't have the reputation or the contacts to get a really big contract. She didn't have the money to get a really big firm to do the work. She trusted that I could do it, and I trusted that she was right on how fast the payback would be. I didn't really have another choice. I managed to keep us one step away from collection agencies until the profits came in from SweetMeets, and they came in fast."

"But you quit. Why?"

"I paid everything back. Even managed to put something aside for future expenses for Brendan. But I never felt good about working on the website; I just couldn't see another way out. When things steadied out, I told Holly I was done."

"But SweetMeets started losing money after some pretty bad PR recently, and Holly was scrambling to save her business. So, she reached out to you."

He nodded. "She wouldn't take no for an answer. She kept calling, and finally she came to Himmel. She texted me and said she was in town, and to meet her the next night. I was afraid if I didn't, she'd come here."

"What happened when you got there?"

"She wasn't asking any more. She was threatening me. She told me that she had texts and some photos." His head was lowered as he said the last part, so it was hard to hear his words, but the shame came through clear as a bell. Saying that in front of his teenage daughter had to be one of the worst experiences of his life.

"She said she'd go to Noelle if I didn't help her. I was angry and panicked and my mind was racing. I told her I had to think about it. She told me not to take too long. If she didn't hear from me by morning, the next Chapman she talked to would be my wife."

"What did you do then?"

"I left, and I drove around for a while. I was so angry, at Holly, at myself, I couldn't think straight. I didn't want Noelle to find out about Holly, but I didn't want to work on the Sweet-Meets site any more. I didn't know what was worse—telling Noelle the truth, or going back to work for Holly. Finally, I drove to the office, and I plotted out a decision tree—it's how I problem solve. I put in all the possible actions, and the outcomes. What if I helped Holly? What if I told Noelle? What if I did nothing?

"What if Noelle didn't forgive me? What if the kids hated me? What if I went back to doing something I didn't believe in? How would I feel if Kira were involved on a site like Sweet-Meets? It took a long time, but when I was done, I knew what I had to do. I couldn't bear to hurt Noelle. I was afraid she wouldn't forgive me. That I'd lose my family. But I realized our family wasn't real if I had to lie to keep it. I had to tell Noelle the truth about everything, and then I'd have to live with what she decided. I went back to tell Holly. And when I got there—" He started to cry then and had trouble finishing his words.

Kira had been growing visibly agitated while Mike spoke. Now she put a hand on his and said, "No, Dad, don't. I'm so sorry, I didn't mean—" She stopped mid-sentence and looked in my direction.

"You were at Miguel's that night, weren't you?" I asked.

She nodded, miserably. "I found Dad's second phone. I was in his office looking for a charger, and I heard it go off. I pulled open the drawer and took it out, and that's when I saw the text. It said to be at an address on Schuyler Street. I'd overheard Dad talking to somebody a couple of times. He'd sounded upset, but when I asked him about it, he got mad and made like it was such a big, secret thing. He said it wasn't anybody and to mind my own business.

"I started to think maybe he was having an affair. And then when I read that text, I knew. Dad had told me that he had to work really late that night. That he was rebooting the system or something and had do it at night when no one was there. Mom and Brendan were at Mayo. I knew he was really meeting his girlfriend. It made me so mad that he would do that to Mom. To our family. I thought they'd get a divorce, and what would happen to Brendan? And to me? Because he chose some slutty woman instead of us.

"That night, I drove over to the address and parked down the block so I could see the house, but I wasn't right across from it. And I waited. I was praying that Dad wouldn't show up. That he'd realize how wrong it was, that he'd realize he loved us after all. But then I saw his car. I watched him park in the driveway and walk up to the door. A woman with red hair came out, and she took him by the hand and pulled him inside. I waited for a while, but he didn't come out and I was crying so hard I just drove home."

"Oh, sweetheart," Noelle said, and stroked her hair, but she let her daughter continue. Mike had moved slightly away, as though he didn't deserve to be part of the family tableau.

"But you went back, didn't you, Kira?" I asked.

She nodded. "I just couldn't stop thinking about him with that woman. I was getting madder and madder. Finally, I couldn't stand it anymore. It was after midnight. I got in my car, and I drove right back. I was going to confront them both, tell them what horrible, lying, cheating people they were. I pulled into the driveway. I was so upset, I didn't even notice that Dad's car wasn't there. I ran up to the door and pounded hard, but it wasn't shut tight and it pushed open.

"I went right in, thinking I'd find them there together, ready to rip into both of them. But when I walked into the living room, Dad wasn't there. The woman was lying in front of the fireplace, and she was so still, and there was blood on the floor. I checked to see if she was breathing. She wasn't. She was dead. And I thought—" she paused for a minute then spoke in a rush.

"I thought, I'm glad she's dead. But then I thought that Dad had killed her! I turned around, and ran out as fast as I could. I got in the car and peeled out of the driveway. I couldn't breathe. I couldn't think. I drove home and ran up to my room." Now she was crying, but Mike had pulled himself together and put his arm around her as she turned her face into his chest and sobbed.

"Mike, what happened when you went back to tell Holly to go to hell?" I asked.

"The door was ajar. I called through it, but she didn't answer. I went inside and I saw her, like Kira said, lying face down. When I went over to her, something silver on the floor near the body caught my eye. I recognized it right away. It was a charm. A little silver saxophone charm that we had given Kira on a necklace for her birthday. At first, I couldn't think how it got there. And then I remembered how Kira had questioned me when she caught me talking on the phone to Holly, and how I thought I'd put my phone in my drawer, but it was sitting on my desk that morning. And it hit me in a rush. Kira thought I was having an affair."

"You thought Kira had followed you, that she waited until you left, and then she confronted Holly and killed her?"

"It sounds crazy, now. But Kira has always had a quick temper. And Holly had a way of saying things that could set people off. I know, now, it was my own guilt that made me wild with worry. I wasn't thinking clearly. I knew it was my fault. And I knew I had to protect her. I picked up the poker and I wiped it clean. I wiped off the door handles, and then I took Holly's laptop and her phone and her purse. I had to get rid of them in case there was anything to connect me to Holly, and possibly from me to Kira. I thought maybe it would look like a break-in gone wrong."

"You went to Founders Park, didn't you?"

"Yes. I drove over the laptop and the phone to destroy them, then I dumped them and the purse in the muck off the pier. Officer Darmody saw me, but I told him I was just driving around because I couldn't sleep, and I wound up at the park. He seemed to believe me. When I got home, Kira was in her room and the light was off. I decided if she didn't say anything to me about what she'd done, I wouldn't confront her. I would protect her and Noelle and Brendan."

"Kira, why didn't you say anything to your Dad?"

She had stopped crying and was wiping her eyes with her sleeve. "I didn't want him to go to jail. I wasn't sorry that woman was dead. She tried to ruin our family. My mom has been through so much, I couldn't stand for her to know about Dad and be hurt like that. I was so angry at Dad for what he'd done to our family, but I still wanted a family. I loved him no matter what."

"That's why you got so angry at Allie that day in your drive-way. She said Sophia must feel terrible knowing her dad was a murderer, but you were afraid it was your dad who had killed Holly."

She nodded.

"Did you go to Founders Park because you thought someone knew that your dad had killed Holly, and you wanted to find out who it was?"

Again she nodded, and asked, "Did you send that text?"

"Yes. I thought whoever showed up might be Holly's killer."

"Dad still kept the phone in his desk. I knew his code was my birthday month and Brendan's—1011. Dad uses that for everything. I kept checking his phone, and that day I saw the text. I don't know why, I just wanted to see, that is I—" she fumbled her words.

"To see if I was lying about anything else? I don't blame you." Mike said.

She didn't reply, but the obvious answer was yes.

"So, you went to the park to find out who knew about your dad and Holly. That was a little dangerous, don't you think?"

"Some kids go there to buy weed. I know some of the kids

who sell. I was going to pretend I was looking to buy some, if anybody asked me. But I didn't think whoever texted would be looking for a kid, so I'd be all right. I was kind of nervous, though, and when I heard a noise in the trees, I got spooked and ran. There weren't any texts after that. I was worried, but there wasn't anything else I could do."

"Kira, honey," Noelle said. "You shouldn't have had to do anything. You should have felt you could come to me, if not your dad, no matter what. You were walking around with a burden way too big for you to carry. We should have seen it. Your dad and I both let you down."

"Mike, I have to ask, were you going to let Craig go to prison for something you thought your daughter had done?"

"No. I was hoping that his lawyer would be able to get him off. Then I wouldn't have to expose all the things I'd done. If he was found guilty, I'd speak up then. At least, that's what I told myself. But then yesterday, I ran into Craig's wife and daughter, and it really hit me what I was putting them through. I couldn't look them in the eye. That's when I knew I had to tell Noelle everything."

"But I heard them," Kira said. "I was upstairs and I heard them talking. When Dad told Mom that he thought I had killed Holly Mason, I couldn't believe it. I knew then that he couldn't have done it, not if he thought I had! I just burst into their room and I told them what really happened."

I couldn't understand how Noelle could have learned all that she had in the past twenty-four hours, and yet managed to retain the aura of calm that she projected. She must have read the question in my eyes. She sat up a little straighter and folded her hands together. She spoke directly to me, her gaze level and steady.

"It was a terrible shock—all of it. I'm holding it together now, because I have to. But it isn't easy. I'm hurt and angry and resentful and confused. But I know one thing. I love Mike, and I love our kids, and I know that my family is worth fighting for. I don't know if that's enough, but I hope it is."

She reached over and gave Mike's hand a squeeze. He looked ashamed and embarrassed, and like he thought he was the luckiest man alive. I was pretty sure I wouldn't have had Noelle's forgiving response. But then, I didn't have two kids and a twenty-year marriage to consider.

"We spent most of last night and this morning crying," she said. "This afternoon, we decided there was no choice. Mike and Kira had to go to the police, first thing tomorrow. Then I got a call from a friend who volunteers at the hospital. She told me that Gretchen Fraser was dead, and that she had confessed to killing Holly Mason. For half a second, we considered just staying quiet, because Craig would be free now. But there have been too many secrets in this family."

"You need to talk to Detective Erin Harper. Call now. Trust me, the sooner you talk to her, the better it's going to go for you."

---

I'm not sure if I was more tired that night than I've ever been, but it was darn close. It was after eleven by the time I got home. I saw Miguel's car in the parking lot, and the lights were on in the *Himmel Times* offices, but I just didn't have the energy to stop in.

I called my mother to check on Allie when I got upstairs. She'd been able to see her dad for a few minutes, and she was good after that. Then I finally got around to calling Gabe.

"Leah, what the hell? Do you know how many times I've called you?"

"Let me check. Yes. Five. Oh, and you texted me six times."

"And you think it's funny that you ignored them all? I get a message to meet you and Charlie Ross at McClain's at seven thirty. You don't show up, but the place is buzzing. Gretchen Fraser is dead. She killed Holly Mason. Then Miguel shows up and says you went off with Detective Harper. You didn't think it might be nice to give me a call and let me know what's going on?"

"I sent you Miguel. I filled him in on everything I knew. Didn't he tell you?"

"Well, yes."

"And did you talk to Craig?"

"Yes, after I talked to the district attorney. That's one unhappy man. I think he's ready to do whatever he can to limit the fallout. That includes getting the charges against Craig dropped as fast as a judge can rule."

"OK, then. So, it's all good. You know what I know—mostly," I amended, remembering that when Miguel talked to Gabe, he didn't have the information from Erin or what I'd finally put together from Mike.

"What do you mean 'mostly'?"

"You know what, Gabe? I want to talk to you, too. But more than that, I want to go to sleep. And I'm about to, standing right here with the phone pressed to my ear. So, if you don't want to listen to my delicate snores, as I drift off into dreamland, you'll hang up and call me in the morning. In the after nine o'clock morning. In fact, I'll meet you for breakfast at the Elite."

## 51

"Nash, you gotta get me outta here."

The urgency in Ross's voice was genuine. He was propped up in a hospital bed, surveying the breakfast that a dietary aide had placed on his tray.

"Sorry, Ross. You already used up your weekly rescue quota yesterday," I said. "That doesn't look so bad, what is it? Cream of rice?"

He shuddered. "Can't you get me a fried egg? Hash browns? Some sausage?"

"Again, sorry. You'll have to ask your doctor about that. But I can give you an update on what's been happening since you checked out at the Frasers' yesterday."

"Yeah, I don't remember much after you threw the hot coffee at Gretchen. Nice move, by the way."

"Thank you." I launched into what I'd found out and answered his questions until he was satisfied.

"I like it. It hangs together. But I think Erin Harper has the wrong end of the stick if she thinks Will killed Rebecca. Gretchen was twice the man Will ever was. He hasn't got it in him to kill anybody. Take it from me, Gretchen killed Rebecca."

"Well, you're forgetting, Will did kill Gretchen. So, pushed hard enough, anyone can do anything. At least I'm beginning to think so. But what I want to know is, what made Gretchen lose it so badly yesterday? She was cool as they come after killing Duane and Holly. And probably Rebecca—although I hope Erin is badass enough to get Will to confess to that. What made Gretchen go so crazy?"

"It was me."

"Yeah, I can see how you'd have that effect."

"Hey, you want to hear, or you want to be a smartass?"

"Can't I do both? OK, OK, I'm sorry. I'm listening."

"Remember, I told Will yesterday that he needed to get a forensics investigator in?"

"Ohhh. Of course. With everything else, I forgot that little piece. He went home and told Gretchen, and it was the last straw, right?"

"Yeah. Will musta got there just before I did, and told her that I picked up where Duane left off on the embezzlement. I heard her yellin' at him when I knocked on the door. Nobody came, but I was pretty hot myself after she treated Allie the way she did. I walked in, and they were in the living room. She barely lost a beat and started rippin' on me for Allie. I could see she was really losin' it.

"Will tried to calm her down. She walked out, and I thought she was goin' to take a pill or something. I started talkin' to him about Allie, and then Gretchen walks back in. With a gun. A real nice one, too. A semi-automatic pistol. Kimber Micro 9mm Bel Air. Pretty stylish."

"Geez, Ross, I don't want to hear about how cool the gun that almost killed you was. I want to know why Gretchen flipped out enough to use it."

"I'm tellin' ya. Will finally got the balls to tell her that it was *déjà vu* all over again, that I was takin' up where Duane left off.

Then, right after that, I walk in and she starts goin' off on Allie. Sometime in there, she musta figured, *What the hell?* She might as well shut the whole thing down, startin' with me and Will."

"Do you think she was going to kill herself after she killed you two?" I shuddered, imagining the blood bath I could've walked into, if I'd arrived just a few minutes later.

"I wonder if she felt like she was never going to hit the bottom of Will's capacity for screwing up. She killed Duane, she killed Holly, she killed Rebecca. Even the blood of three people wasn't enough to wash away Will's original sin."

Ross's take on the situation was less fanciful than mine, but he had a fitting allusion of his own.

"I think she musta felt like the dumbass things Will kept doin' were kinda like those brooms in that cartoon. You know, the ones that keep multiplyin' and comin' at Mickey Mouse."

"*The Sorcerer's Apprentice.* Yeah, Ross, kinda like that."

When I walked into the Elite to meet Gabe, he was sitting at a back table and Mrs. Schimelman was plying him with two kinds of rugelach. I stopped at the counter and got myself a coffee.

"Leah, I got some good rugelach here. Two kinds, chocolate and strawberry. I give your new boyfriend a free sample. He's getting Craig free."

"He's not my boyfriend, Mrs. Schimelman," I said, hastily. "I'm working with Gabe."

"Oh, *ja?*" she asked, her tone conveying that she didn't believe a word of that. "I hear you canceled Nick at the party. Bye, Felicia!" She pulled the towel off her shoulder and waved it to emphasize her words. "He's not right for you. Too many teeth."

I wasn't sure where that particular criticism came from, but I didn't pursue it.

"Yeah, OK. Well, good seeing you, I bet you want to get back up front. Looks like it's getting busy at the counter."

"Oh, I get it. OK, I go. But I see you again," she said to Gabe.

"Mrs. Schimelman, these rugelachs are so good, I might move in with you."

She gave a light swat at him with the towel she still held in her hands, then walked away, ample hips swaying and her shoulders shaking with laughter.

"Did you get the charges against Craig dropped?"

"Leah, it's nine-fifteen in the morning. We don't see the judge until one. But, unless you give me some unwelcome new information, it should happen this afternoon. Do you have any unwelcome information? In fact, exactly what information do you have? I'm pretty interested in finding out how we got to Gretchen as the killer, Will as the embezzler, and Mike Chapman as—I'm not sure what to call him."

When I finally finished answering all his questions, he said, "Miller was right."

"Oh?"

"He said, 'Leah never stops swinging.' "

"I'm not sure how to take that."

"As a compliment. From both of us. You didn't have much to go on but your faith in Craig, and you had a lot going against you—a mountain of evidence that pointed to Craig, a police detective who wanted you to butt out, not enough time, you didn't even have Coop to bounce things off. And then your boyfriend scared the bejesus out of you by proposing. That's how it looked to me, anyway. But you kept on swinging. You can bat for my team anytime. By the way, what's up with double X?"

"Double X?"

"Ex-husband, ex-boyfriend. Doesn't get much more ex than that, does it?"

"No." I agreed. "It doesn't. He texted me this morning."

"Oh? You going to give him another try? You know my advice on do-overs. They usually turn into don't-overs." His words were casual, but I wasn't unhappy to hear the disappointment in his voice.

"No. I think I'll take my lawyer's advice on this one. How much do I owe you for the consultation?"

"It's pro bono. But I wouldn't say no to dinner at your place one night."

"I think that can be arranged. How do you feel about Honey Nut Cheerios?"

"I'm more of a plain Cheerios guy, but I can be flexible."

"No need. A Leah Nash dinner party is all about choice. I'll see you Saturday at seven."

"If not before."

---

When my phone rang on Wednesday afternoon and I saw that it was Coop, I was relieved. I hadn't called him yet. I'd been a little afraid to, because we had parted so badly the last time. I wanted him to hear from Erin Harper that Rebecca hadn't been killed by her crazy ex, which meant I hadn't been a factor in her death. I knew he'd call me when he was ready, and now he had.

"Come on in," I said, after I'd buzzed him up. He still looked pretty terrible. His face, usually smooth and clean shaven, was covered with several days beard growth. His gray eyes were bloodshot, as though he hadn't slept in a while.

"How about some coffee? Or a beer? I've got some Leinie's in the fridge." Leinenkugel is a favorite of Coop's, and it seemed like he could use one.

"No. I'm not staying long. I just needed to talk to you."

"OK, sure. Let's go in the living room."

He followed me, and I took the rocking chair. He sat on the sofa, but sort of perched on the edge as though he couldn't relax enough to sit back. He had taken his HPD cap off and was turning it around in his hands.

I waited, not wanting to say the wrong thing, and totally lost as to what the right thing might be. Finally, he started talking.

"I'm sorry for what I said to you. About it being your fault that Rebecca was killed."

"That's OK. You were in shock. I'm sorry that I didn't believe you when you told me about her past—about the domestic abuse." It didn't seem necessary to tell him that even worse, I'd thought his wife had been a high-class hooker. Sometimes I do know when to keep my mouth shut.

"I can see why you didn't. Because I don't know which of the things Rebecca told me were true and which were lies. I don't know anything anymore."

"What do you mean?"

"I got the autopsy report today. Rebecca didn't lose the baby."

What was he saying? Was he in denial? Did he think that—I didn't know what he could be thinking. "What do you mean?"

"I mean there wasn't any baby. Rebecca wasn't pregnant. She had never been pregnant. Ever in her life. So that part of the story she told me, about how her ex-boyfriend beat her so badly she lost the baby she was carrying, that wasn't true."

"Why would she make that up?"

"I don't know. What else did she lie about? And how could I have been so blind? To lie about a baby—she knew how much I wanted to have a child. She let me buy toys and paint a nursery and start building a cradle and—" He stopped abruptly. "I'm a damn poor excuse for a detective. But I don't understand. She showed me the pregnancy test. She had it all wrapped up in that little box. How could it not be real?"

"Oh, Coop, I'm sorry. But it wouldn't have been hard. You can buy joke pregnancy tests that look like the real thing."

"Some joke. So, Rebecca bought one of the fake tests and wrapped it up and presented it to her big, dumb boyfriend." He was shaking his head in disbelief. "I thought she was so vulnerable; she was so scared to tell me. She made me feel like I was the only person she really trusted. That she needed me. That I knew her like no one else did. It was all an act. Every bit of it. Everything about her was an act. If I could be so wrong, how can I ever trust my own instincts? How can I be a cop if I can't trust my own judgment?"

"Hey-hey-hey. No. Come on. Slow down there. You were emotionally involved. You loved her. You loved the idea of a family. And I don't think Rebecca lied about everything. I think she did love you—at least as much as she could love anyone. Maybe that's why she lied about it. She was desperate to have you." I didn't know if that were true, but I'd never seen Coop so despairing. It scared me.

"You know, she went to see Father Lindstrom the night you went to Bemidji for your grandmother's birthday. He wouldn't tell me what she talked to him about, only that she was suffering from guilt and confused about what to do. Maybe she was struggling with the fact that she was lying to you, deceiving you, the one person she ever really loved."

I could hardly believe it was me attempting to provide some absolution for Rebecca, but I just wanted that desolate look to leave Coop's eyes. If it took pretending that the woman he'd loved had loved him back, then I was OK with that. It didn't work, though.

"I'm leaving," he said abruptly.

"Leaving? Town? For how long? Where are you going?"

"I took a leave of absence from work. I'm going to stay at a buddy's cabin in Minnesota near the Canadian border, outside of Baudette."

"But, Coop, are you sure? Don't you think you should be around your friends now, your family?"

"No. I need to be alone. Don't look so worried. I'll be fine. There's good hunting up there. The cabin's got wood heat, no hot water. I'll be busy chopping wood and making fires. It'll be good for me."

"I *am* worried. You might not have cell reception up there. What if you get sick? What if there's a blizzard and you're stranded? Do you even know anyone there?"

"No. That's the point. The town is only five miles away, and there's a snowmobile at the cabin. I can get help if I need it, Mom."

He said the last word with a trace of a smile and a hint of his usual teasing voice. But I knew he was trying to hide how much he was hurting. I felt like my heart was going to break, thinking of him alone, grieving, uncertain, lonely, and so far away. But I had to respect that it was what he needed to do.

"How long will you be gone?"

"As long as it takes."

"As long as what takes?"

"For me to get my head on straight. To figure out if I can be a good cop again—or if I never was."

"Stop it. You were, you are, you'll always be a good cop. It's what you were born to do. Don't let Rebecca take that away from you, Coop. Don't take it away from yourself."

He put his cap back on then and looked away. When he looked back, I saw that his eyes were wet. I reached out and hugged him hard, and he hugged me back.

"I gotta go."

"Sure, all right. But let me know when you get there, OK?"

## 52

"So, *chica,* I don't suppose you want to give up writing books to start a real detective agency. Santos and Nash? No? Nash and Santos?" Miguel had come up to my place following a meeting with A-H Media on Friday morning.

"It didn't go well, did it?" I asked, even though his face told me the answer.

"No. They want to close it down. They're going to send someone from HR to talk to us about unemployment benefits, and resume writing, and COBRA insurance next week. We'll print next week, but Thursday's edition will be the last one."

"Oh, Miguel," I said, coming around the island to the side he was standing on. "I'm so sorry. For you and selfishly for myself. I'm trying to get used to Himmel without Coop, and now there might be Himmel without you? What are you going to do?"

"Send out resumes, I guess. Or maybe I'll see if *Tía* Lydia needs a shampoo boy at her salon. I do have the magic fingers," he flexed his hands and tried to smile, but it was easy to see how upset he was.

"There's no chance Ass Hat Media will sell the paper, and someone will buy it and keep you guys on?"

"The VP who came down said that the market wasn't good, and they were throwing good money after bad by holding on to it looking for a buyer. If they shut it down, they can make more money from tax losses than they could by selling it. I said we would take a pay cut, we could make it work, but no."

"If only there were somebody who … " My voice trailed off.

"Who what, *chica*? Somebody who what?"

"Can you let yourself out, Miguel? I've got to go." I grabbed my jacket and ran out the front door, down the stairs, and then down the block, leaving Miguel thinking I had lost my mind. But actually, I'd just found it.

---

"You're really sure you want to do this, Leah?"

I was in Miller Caldwell's office three weeks after the conversation with Miguel that had sent me flying down the street to see him, busting past a protesting Patty to present my fabulous idea to him.

"You're not backing out on me now, are you?" I felt a small flutter of nervousness in my stomach. I didn't know if I could pull this off even with Miller. Without him, there was no chance.

"No, I just want to be sure you understand the risk you're taking. When we sign those papers today, it's final."

"Well, you're taking the same risk. More, really, because you're putting up more of the money."

"Yes, but I'm a little better situated financially than you."

"That's an understatement. But if my new book sells well, and I get a good advance for the next one, I'll be fine. Besides, I can always move back in with my mom if things go south. Wait, I never said that. Don't you believe in the dream anymore?"

"I do. I've just been involved in business and corporate law long enough to know that even the best dreams can turn into nightmares."

"That's not going to happen. This community needs a newspaper. Full of fact-checked, well-sourced, nonpartisan news. *What's happening in the schools? Why were three cop cars out on River Road last night? How much is the new bridge going to cost? Who was top scorer at the Himmel basketball game? When is the vote for the new millage?* It's why the *Times* started a hundred years ago. It's still important today. Social media is great, but it's not journalism. I know it will be hard, but we've got smart, talented, enthusiastic people who want to make it work."

"All right. You had me at fact-checked." He smiled then, and I felt a surge of gratitude for this man who had given so much to the community, and who was willing to take a chance both with me and on me.

"OK, then. Let's go buy us a newspaper."

## DANGEROUS FLAWS: Leah Nash #5

### A chilling murder shocks a small Wisconsin town.

True crime writer Leah Nash is stunned when police investigating the murder of a beautiful young college professor focus on her ex-husband Nick. Leah has no illusions about her ex, but despite his flaws, she just can't see him as a killer. Reluctantly, she agrees to help Nick's attorney prove that he isn't.

But Nick's lies make it hard to find the truth, and then a damning piece of evidence surfaces and plunges Leah into doubt. Is she defending an innocent man or helping a murderer escape? She pushes on to find out, uncovering hidden motives and getting hit by twists she never saw coming. Leah's own flaws impede her search for the truth. When she finds it, will it be too late to prevent a devastating confrontation?

*Dangerous Flaws* is the fifth standalone book in the Leah Nash series of complex, fast-paced murder mysteries featuring quick-witted dialogue, daring female characters, and plots with lots of twists and turns.

### Get your copy today at SusanHunterAuthor.com

# LOVE READING MYSTERIES & THRILLERS?

Never miss a new release! Sign up to receive exclusive updates from author Susan Hunter.

**Join today at SusanHunterAuthor.com**

As a thank you for signing up, you'll receive a free copy of *Dangerous Dreams: A Leah Nash Novella*.

## YOU MIGHT ALSO ENJOY...

**Leah Nash Mysteries**

Dangerous Habits

Dangerous Mistakes

Dangerous Places

Dangerous Secrets

Dangerous Flaws

Dangerous Ground

Never miss a new release! Sign up to receive exclusive updates from author Susan Hunter.

**SusanHunterAuthor.com/Newsletter**

As a thank you for signing up, you'll receive a free copy of

*Dangerous Dreams: A Leah Nash Novella.*

# ACKNOWLEDGMENTS

Thanks are due to my beta readers, who caught mistakes, provided suggestions, and listened patiently as I wrestled with alternate endings. Thanks also to the readers who emailed me with questions, comments, and kind words.

Most of all, thanks to my husband Gary Rayburn, whose energy, enthusiasm, and belief sustain me every day—but especially on writing days.

# ABOUT THE AUTHOR

Susan Hunter is a charter member of Introverts International (which meets the 12th of Never at an undisclosed location). She has worked as a reporter and managing editor, during which time she received a first place UPI award for investigative reporting and a Michigan Press Association first place award for enterprise/feature reporting.

Susan has also taught composition at the college level, written advertising copy, newsletters, press releases, speeches, web copy, academic papers and memos. Lots and lots of memos. She lives in rural Michigan with her husband Gary, who is a man of action, not words.

During certain times of the day, she can also be found wandering the mean streets of small-town Himmel, Wisconsin, looking for clues, stopping for a meal at the Elite Cafe, dropping off a story lead at the *Himmel Times Weekly*, or meeting friends for a drink at McClain's Bar and Grill.

*For more information*
www.SusanHunterAuthor.com
Susan@SusanHunterAuthor.com

## DISCUSSION QUESTIONS

1. How did you experience the book—did it take you a while to get into, or were you engaged from the start? Or did it never engage you at all?

2. Are there situations and/or characters you can identify with? If yes, how?

3. What did you like, or dislike, about the writer's style?

4. What passages or scenes from the book stood out for you?

5. Would you like to live in Himmel, Wisconsin? Why, or why not?

6. Leah calls to mind the quote "Often wrong, but never in doubt." How much of her success—and her failure—is due to her willingness to charge ahead regardless of what others think?

7. Leah has an eclectic group of friends: Miguel, Coop, Father Lindstrom, April, Charlie Ross, arguably even Courtnee. How does each add balance to and enrich her life?

8. At what point in the book did you know "whodunnit"?

9. If you could change something about the book, what would it be and why?